*Here Will I Remain*
The New Hope Series, Book I

Also by Gretchen Craig

## NOVELS
*Always & Forever*
(The Plantation Series, Book I)
*Ever My Love: A Saga of Slavery and Deliverance*
(The Plantation Series, Book II)
*Evermore: A Saga of Slavery and Deliverance*
(The Plantation Series, Book III)
*Elysium: A Saga of Slavery and Deliverance*
(The Plantation Series, Book IV)

*Tansy*
*Crimson Sky*
*Theena's Landing*
*The Lion's Teeth*
*Livy: A Love Story*

## SHORT STORY COLLECTIONS
*The Color of the Rose*
*Bayou Stories: Tales of Troubled Souls*
*Lookin' for Luv: Five Short Stories*

# Here Will I Remain

*The New Hope Series, Book I*

## Gretchen Craig

Copyright © 2016 by Gretchen Craig
*www.GretchenCraig.com*

*All rights reserved.*

*Kindle e-book edition available from Amazon.com.*

**ISBN-13: 978-1540484147**
**ISBN-10: 1540484149**

# Here Will I Remain
*The New Hope Series, Book I*

# Historical Note

Imagine an old map of the U. S. divided into three territories, British in the east, Spanish in the west, and French in a huge swath in the middle. By 1682, New France stretched from the Great Lakes to the Gulf of Mexico and from the Appalachians to the Rockies. Because Louis XIV was on the throne, the French named this territory *la Louisiane française*: Louisiana.

*Here Will I Remain* is the story of French settlers in the lower reaches of Louisiana, on what is now the Mississippi Gulf Coast. Biloxi Indians already inhabited the area and had an intricate civilization established long before the French arrived, but to the newcomers, Louisiana was a wilderness to be tamed and exploited. These hardy souls braved an unfamiliar climate, exotic beasts, and thick jungle in order to clear the land and make their fortunes.

The way to make these fortunes was to plant indigo. Indigo made the best blue dye, and even though it had been used since ancient times, it was expensive and the supply did not meet the demands of aristocratic Europeans.

French colonists took up the challenge, but they were lonely. The Church at times disapproved of liaisons with native women, at other times allowed it, but at last the French court decided what the French settlers needed was French women.

Over a few decades in the early 1700s, a number of French ships delivered wives-to-be to the colony. These women are best-known as casket-girls after the small chests each carried to her new life. Many of today's Louisiana families proudly trace their ancestry back to a casket girl sent over from France.

The casket girls were from convents and orphanages, respectable women of good moral character. There were, however, other groups of women taken from prisons and asylums and sent to Louisiana. These are the interesting women in *Here Will I Remain*.

# Chapter One

*Catherine de Villeroy
Aboard the New Hope, 1720*

"She's waking up."

Catherine opened her eyes to see three ragged women hovering over her.

"Take some water," one of them said.

Catherine shoved the cup aside, afraid she'd be sick.

The floor rocked and the air smelled of the sea. With sudden understanding, she clambered to her feet, staggering, and fought the panic threatening to overwhelm her.

He'd put her aboard a ship.

She held off the women trying to steady her and groped her way to the stairs leading up toward a patch of bright blue sky. Fighting her wide skirts, she pushed her way on deck.

A brisk wind tore at her dress, chilled her face, and puffed the sails, propelling them through white-capped waves, and all around, nothing but blue water. Nausea threatened to overwhelm her. *Hugo had put her on a ship!*

Rough, dirty hands reached for her. "Here now, mademoiselle. You get below decks where you belong."

Catherine jerked her elbow from the sailor's grip and reeled to the side of the ship, hung her head over the side, and heaved.

"She don't belong up here."

"I likes the look of her." A sailor put his arm around her waist and stuck his fingers down her neckline. "Give us a feel, *chérie.*"

She whirled around and slapped his leering face. "You touch me again and I'll have your hands cut off."

"Leave her be," a grizzled sailor said.

The other sailors laughed and hooted. "Out of the way, Jacques, you old fart. I'll have me a go at her, see if I don't."

"You men, get back to work!" A young officer in blue and white, his brass buttons shining in the sunlight, flicked his rope end. "You, Antoine, get a move on."

"Sir," Catherine demanded, "turn this ship around immediately."

The officer raised his eyebrows. "Turn the ship around?" He laughed at her and gave her a push toward the hatchway. "Below decks with you."

"You will take me to the captain," she said in her most imperious voice.

"The captain has better things to do than talk to a fancy trollop."

Catherine spied the man on the poop deck, his hands behind his back, looking down on them as if he were God himself. He had to be the captain. She grabbed handfuls of skirt and marched toward the stairway.

The young officer took hold of her again. "I've never struck a woman, but if I have to . . . "

Catherine raked her nails across the man's cheek and ran for the stairs to the upper deck. Sailors barred the way, grinning and laughing at her.

"Get her legs, Jones." The officer grabbed her arms and she was lifted off her feet. She twisted and bucked, but they had her. At the hatchway, they stuffed her panniered skirts through the opening and tumbled her onto the floor below decks.

"You try that again, mademoiselle, you'll find yourself in chains."

She scrambled to her feet and clawed her way up the stairs. "I must see the captain. At once!"

The hatch closed over her head, plunging her into dusky light.

"Look what you done, you damned whore. Could have had a breath of fresh air blowing down here except you had to act up."

"Who you think you are? You nothing but a fancy tart."

A gentle hand helped her down. The woman was big as a man, a head taller than Catherine. "Come sit down before you fall."

Catherine jerked away and landed on her butt. Crab-like, she scurried to put her back against a huge cask. She was surrounded by women, all of them staring at her in the dim light. They were dressed no better than tavern wenches, their hair held back in simple braids.

"Is this a prison ship?" Catherine whispered, her throat tight with fear.

~~~

Catherine felt encircled by silence. From below decks, the thrum of the wind in the rigging seemed far away, and the women's voices were merely a murmur. Perhaps they thought she couldn't hear them.

"Never seen shoes like that," a woman said. "Embroidered, I mean."

"They wouldn't last long if she had to walk on cobblestones."

Catherine pulled her feet under her broad skirts.

"I'd like to feel that satin under my fingers," a young woman said. "I worked in a dress shop, before."

Before what, Catherine wondered.

"Her hair must have towered a foot over her head before it drooped over. You think all that powder makes her scalp itch?"

"I always wanted me a little lace." That woman reached her hand out to touch the lace dripping from Catherine's wrists. Catherine recoiled.

"Leave her alone, you lot," the big woman said.

"You going to make her your pet, are you, Marie Claude?"

"Bridget, you ever stop being mean?" Marie Claude answered.

Catherine shivered. The brazier in the built-up hearth cast a little light and very little heat. When a cold gust fluttered the little flames, one of the women climbed over a keg to close the side hatch against the wind, making it even dimmer.

Catherine's head ached, her stomach roiled. She thought she'd be sick again. The space smelled of unwashed bodies, stale sweat, dirty feet, and worse. She guessed much of the reek came from an open bucket in the corner. She shuddered. She would have to use that bucket herself before long.

"You haven't had a thing to drink all day," a woman with greasy brown ringlets said as she offered Catherine a cup.

Catherine accepted the cup and sipped at the water. It tasted of the wood barrel it had come from.

As the little light coming in through the seams around the hatches waned, the upper hatch opened and three sailors came down the steps. "You ladies hungry?" a beak-nosed fellow asked.

"Always," the one called Marie Claude said.

They had with them a basket of bowls and spoons and a big pot of something that smelled like mutton. Catherine put the back of her hand to her nose.

A woman with a scar across her cheek passed Catherine a bowl and a spoon. "No," Catherine said, shaking her head.

"It ain't *foi gras,* but it's what we got."

Catherine pushed it away.

"You got to eat."

"Leave her be, Gabrielle. She'll eat tomorrow."

Catherine was sickened at the way the women slurped down the noxious smelling stew, all except the mean one Marie Claude called Bridget. She didn't have a bowl at all, but she looked pleased nonetheless.

The men sat on the floor and chatted with some of the women, teasing and winking. Catherine stared at the sailors' bare feet. The other women seemed to think nothing of their filthy thick soles or their long yellowed toe nails.

Every bowl scraped clean, the sailors collected them and the spoons. "All right then, Bridget, *ma chère,* come along."

The mean one got up, straightened her faded red dress and patted her hair. She followed Jacques up the stairs to the main deck.

"Wonder what the captain will feed her tonight? Good ale, white bread?"

"She'll have a bit of himself in her mouth before that, don't doubt it."

"No need to be vulgar in front of the princess," someone snickered.

The woman meant her, a princess. Catherine didn't care what they thought. She lay on her side, her back to the women. In the morning, she would demand to see the captain. He would turn the ship around and take her home.

Then Catherine would see that Hugo paid for what he'd done. She remembered it all now that her head had cleared. They'd been at le comte d'Orléans' for a musical evening. The scented candles, the perfumes and colognes had given Catherine a headache and she had wandered out to the terrace for a breath of air. Cousin Hugo, smiling, had walked right up to her and pressed a cloth over her mouth and nose. The next moment of awareness had been right here, in this foul hold.

On a start, she felt of her throat. Her necklace, her earrings, her ring. Hugo had her brilliant sapphires. She felt sick, imagining her cousin forcing her beautiful ring on to his fat pinky. Oh, he would pay.

She would tell Grandfather what Hugo had done. Not only would Hugo not get his hands on Catherine's own fortune, Grandfather would cut Hugo from his will. Hugo would be destitute.

Imagining Hugo in rags, his hair unpowdered and tangled, his stockings snagged and filthy did not satisfy her. She entertained herself devising more painful fates for her traitorous cousin before she fell asleep.

In the morning, she awoke stiff and sore. All the cots and hammocks were taken and she had slept on the hard plank deck. The sailors brought down some kind of mush for breakfast, but again, Catherine could not stomach it.

"You have to eat," a woman said to her. Catherine didn't know who she was and didn't care. Every cell of her body boiling with rage, she bent over her knees and hid her face. If she looked directly at these women, they would be seared by the heat of the hate inside her. If Hugo were here, she would burn him to cinders just by gazing at him.

After breakfast, the women filed up the steps onto the main deck for their exercise. Catherine struggled to push her wide skirts through the opening again, and someone behind her said, "You might as well pull those pannier things out from under your skirts. Ain't nobody here impressed with how wide your dress is."

"Without the panniers, her skirts will drag and she'll be tripping the live-long day."

Whether they talked to her or about her made no difference to Catherine.

The women promenaded briskly around the deck in the cold wind, the sailors encouraging them with lascivious wit. No one had a decent cloak, though the other women all had shawls pulled tightly around themselves. Catherine hugged herself, but the shivering wouldn't stop.

At the stairs to the poop deck, Catherine let the other women walk around her. With a quick glance around, she scrambled up.

The captain turned his gaze from the horizon to look at her with cold eyes. "Mademoiselle, you trespass."

Catherine looked him right in the eye, her chin up. "I am Catherine de Villeroy, granddaughter of le comte de Villeroy. No doubt my cousin paid you to transport me, but I will pay you far more to return me to my home. My grandfather will make you a rich man, Captain."

The captain snorted a laugh. "Your comte de Villeroy doesn't want a murderer in his household, woman. Better you should disappear than disgrace such a family. And so you shall disappear."

Catherine fisted her hands. "That's what he told you? I am no murderer. You will turn this ship around at once."

The captain caught the lieutenant's eye. The young man, scabs crusting his cheek where she had clawed at him the day before, wrenched her arms behind her, and with another sailor aiding him, hustled Catherine down to the main deck, through the parading, tittering women, and shoved her back into the stinking hold.

Catherine scrambled back up those same steps to be met with the officer's hand on her head, holding her down as the sailor closed the hatch on her. She beat her fists against the rough boards, but no one opened the doorway.

Trembling with fury, she paced across the lower deck. Her wide skirt caught on the bucket the women squatted over and sloshed the contents onto her silk satin. Abruptly, Catherine lost her stomach and vomited on the floor. She reeled to the other side of the space, as far from the mess as she could get, and fell to her knees. A high keening whine escaped her lips, and then she bent over her lap and sobbed.

Catherine's collapse didn't last long. Was she not the granddaughter of le comte de Villeroy? She wiped her face, drew a shuddering breath, and straightened her back. Cousin Hugo would not defeat her so easily. And she would not be satisfied with his destitution. No, Hugo would pay a steeper price than poverty when she made her way back to Paris.

By the time the women returned below decks, Catherine was calm but determined. Wherever this ship was bound, she would find the authorities and be returned to Paris. Cousin Hugo could expect a much shorter life than he had imagined.

~~~

The second time Catherine's ridiculous skirts caught on the protruding nails of a crate, she yanked the voluminous panniers out from under her dress.

"You'll trip, now your skirts are dragging the floor," the big woman said. "Take the dress off and I'll cut you a new hem."

"You got one of the baskets with a pair of shears?" the one called Gabrielle said.

Each of the girls had been given a basket with a draw-string top, a gift directly from the king. He wanted Frenchmen to colonize the new Louisiana territory and those Frenchmen needed French women. Naturally, women were reluctant to leave their homes, their families -- to leave civilization -- in order to colonize a wilderness. Therefore, the king's agent had swept through the prisons and asylums, choosing women with no options but who seemed healthy enough and young enough to survive the journey. In return for their leaving the fetid confines of the Salpêtrière to undertake the king's business, Louis generously provided everything a woman needed to start a life in the wilderness: one spare dress, a shawl, a needle and thread, and a comb.

"How many of us got scissors?" Gabrielle called. Renée and Annette raised their arms. "So we got twenty-two women and three pairs of scissors. Guess they think we'll all live on top of each other, borrowing back and forth."

"What you give me to borrow my scissors?" Renée said.

A snaggle-toothed girl laughed. "She might pull you bald-headed if you don't share."

Marie Claude ignored the foolishness and cut a straight line around the hem of Catherine's dress. With the remnants, she stitched a shawl for her.

"You're very kind, Marie Claude," Catherine said. "Thank you."

The big blonde smiled, only a little shy. "I like to sew."

After a few days, Catherine knew nearly every one of the twenty-two women's names. Gabrielle sported a scar across her cheek. Agnes seldom seemed to realize where she was. Bridget amused herself with spiteful remarks and enjoyed dining with the captain every evening. Marie Claude had little to say, but it was she who quietly put a stop to the inevitable disputes and flares of temper.

All of these women had led hard lives, she learned. Prostitution, vagrancy, thievery, even violence had landed them in the infamous prison, the Salpêtrière. From there, they'd boarded the *New Hope,* taking them to the Louisiana colony for a second chance at life, a chance to be respectable wives and mothers.

In the evenings, Marguerite sang to them and prodded them to join in the old folk songs they all knew. She was heavily pregnant, and radiant with joy. No, she didn't know who the father was, Catherine heard her explain, but it didn't matter. A child was God's gift to her, and she had had few enough gifts in her life.

"What about you, Catherine? You looking forward to being a mother and having children to love and take care of?" Marguerite asked.

"Certainly not," Catherine said. The very idea. It would be bad enough even if she had nurses and nannies, and by all means a wet nurse, to take care of it.

Catherine didn't sing with the others, or pass the long boring days in desultory conversation, which was not at all like her. She was sociable, she was sunny, but these women hardly spoke French, their accents and dialects nearly incomprehensible. They knew nothing of music or literature. They could not read. They had never heard of le comte de Villeroy. No, Catherine's preoccupation was not survival or hope for a better life. Her veins ran hot imagining the vengeance she would wreak on Cousin Hugo.

She had known Hugo was in debt. He routinely appealed to Grandfather for a larger allowance. He'd even tried to convince Grandfather to let him marry Catherine so that he could gamble away her fortune as well as his own. But Grandfather told him no and no, and so Hugo had resorted to abduction. She would never have guessed he could be so ruthless, him with his soft middle and softer hands. The man even affected a lisp. But he'd had the spine to kidnap her. He could establish her death with some ruse and become Grandfather's sole heir. Presto, no more debt for Hugo, and endless misery for Catherine.

It was the hate that kept her from curling up and dying. She forced down the awful gruel, drank the tainted water. Another woman, Pauline, lay on her side, weeping, and refused to eat, refused even to go above decks when they had their hour of sunshine and exercise.

"You like the Salpêtrière better?" Marie Claude said, nudging Pauline and shoving a bowl of foul mush into her hands. "Eat. Or die. Your choice." In the end, Pauline died, and the sailors tipped her body into the ocean for the fish and the sharks. And so Catherine ate, she walked the deck, and she plotted Hugo's demise.

A storm kicked up. Ice coated the rigging and the deck. Waves rocked the ship side to side and heaved the bow up and down. The timbers moaned and leaked, and the howling of the wind filled every ear.

Below decks, nausea and cold and terror tormented the women. Wind shrieked through the rigging, the mast creaked. Surely the lashing wind and waves would tear the ship apart. The women doubled up in their cots and hammocks to keep warm and to comfort each other, everyone but Catherine who lay alone in her corner, shivering, her hands tucked between her legs for warmth. She would surely die in the night, her blood freezing in her veins. Then at least she would not feel the rats sniffing at her feet or know the horror of the black icy sea closing over her when the ship sank.

Marie Claude stood above her, balanced with her feet spread apart. "Don't be stupid," she shouted over the howling storm. "Get up."

The big woman hauled her to her feet and tugged her to her own cot, lay down, and pulled Catherine down next to her. "Go to sleep."

Eventually the shivering stopped and Catherine believed she would live through the night. Because of this woman's kindness.

For two days, the hatch didn't open. No one brought them food or water. The deck was slippery with icy water and vomit and urine. If the ship didn't sink, Catherine would die from nausea and despair.

The third morning, the hatch opened and let in brilliant sunshine. Sailors clambered down the steps with buckets and mops and cheery smiles.

Jacques teased and cajoled till they were all up and helping the sailors make the place habitable. Catherine stood aside as the men and women mopped the deck, exclaimed at how fierce the storm had been, and laughed as they all denied they had been frightened, no, not me, not at all.

Rachel poked at her. "Not a one of us chose to be poor, princess. Not a one of us grew up thinking, oh I hope I can be a whore some day. You're here. You're one of us." Rachel thrust a mop into her hands and pointed to a corner where a latrine had spilled.

Catherine had never mopped a floor in her life. Had never cleaned anything, not even her own hair. The granddaughter of a comte had an army of other people to do those things for her.

Across the room, Marie Claude nodded at her. She had saved Catherine's life, getting her up off the icy floor, sharing her body heat. All right. Catherine gagged, but she shoved the mop through the filth on the floor.

When the floors were clean and everyone was fed, the women set about putting themselves to rights. The sailors had captured barrels of rain water and they were allowed a whole bucket just for face washing. After that, they paired up to comb out their hair, and Rachel claimed Catherine. "I want to see what kept that tower of hair up. You got sticks in there?"

Catherine's scalp was sore from the scaffolding that still nestled in her fallen hairdo and as she looked around at the women squeezing tiny insects between their fingers, she realized she was as infested with lice as the rest of them. She swallowed back the horror and just managed not to cry.

The others watched as Rachel untangled the mess, showed off the scaffold hidden in Catherine's hair, and combed out the powdered tangles. With brisk efficiency, Rachel then braided the long locks to keep them out of the way.

"Now you do me," Rachel said and handed her the comb.

Catherine, the proud lady who had never deigned to comb her own hair, unplaited Rachel's dirty hair, gritted her teeth to pinch out the lice she found, and tried to make a neat braid.

"No, like this," Marie Claude said, and showed her how to braid. Catherine realized every other woman on board had learned to braid hair when they were small children. Yet no one sneered at her. For the first time in her life, a glimmer of humility lit her mind.

The days wore on, cold but bearable. Catherine forgot her rage for hours at a time in the monotony of ship life.

The fourth week out, somewhere in the middle of the Atlantic Ocean, fever struck. By then the ship's biscuits were full of weevils, the meat was spoiled, the fresh water fouled. No wonder the fever found them, living close together and as weakened as they were.

As fever rolled through the women, the able took care of the sick. Catherine was one of the first to succumb, but she recovered and turned herself into a woman who could clean another woman's foul body, ladle cold soup into a mouth full of bad teeth, and think about her patient's pain and not her own distaste.

Rachel was the worst patient of all. She moaned when fever wracked her, which Catherine could not fault her for. But when she began to recover, she complained about the food, about the cold, about the smell. When Marie Claude handed her a bowl of the stew they all had to stomach, Rachel had cried and shoved it away.

"Your choice, Rachel," Marie Claude said. "Eat it, or die." The same thing she had told poor Pauline.

Rachel ate it.

Sweet Marguerite's skin radiated heat, her pregnant body too dry even to sweat off the fever. Catherine bathed her face and spooned water into her mouth no matter how many times Marguerite coughed it back up.

"Try, Marguerite. Swallow a little," Catherine urged.

Marguerite groaned and grabbed her big belly.

"You only need water in your stomach, and the cramps will go away."

Marguerite turned wild eyes on her. "The baby," she whispered.

Catherine put her hands on the taut mound and felt the ripple of hard muscle.

"Oh God," Catherine whispered, and tried not to show Marguerite how scared she was. She stroked Marguerite's belly. "It'll be all right. We'll take care of both of you. Take a little water now."

"It's not time, it's not time," Marguerite wailed.

"Marie Claude!" Catherine called. When she stumbled across the shifting deck, Marie Claude knelt by the cot.

"You know how to deliver a baby?" Catherine whispered.

Marie Claude shrugged. "I saw a calf born once when I was a girl."

"Good, good. What should we do?"

Marie Claude gave her a look.

"You know more than I do," Catherine hissed.

On a big exhale, Marie Claude said, "Do what you're doing. Keep her face cool, keep her company."

Muttering in her fever, Marguerite whipped her head back and forth. With a new contraction, she screamed and groped for Catherine's hand. Catherine crooned reassurances in her ear, but she didn't think Marguerite could hear her.

Time dragged on. Catherine's hand ached from gripping Marguerite's, and her heart contracted with every shriek. How long could Marguerite go on like this? In spite of the wet cloths on her forehead, her skin was unbelievably hot and her open eyes looked blank.

Marie Claude pressed two fingers to Marguerite's neck and looked at Catherine. "Feel that."

Catherine found the pulse in Marguerite's throat. The heartbeat was so very fast, hardly any steadiness or rhythm to it.

"She can't last much longer like this," Marie Claude said.

"What should we do?"

"Nothing we can do. It's up to God, you know that."

Soon the contractions strengthened and came one right after the other. Marguerite wasn't even screaming by now.

Suddenly, as if the baby meant to escape the fever, he came out in a gush of hemorrhage. Marie Claude caught the tiny slippery body while Catherine gripped Marguerite's hand.

"Look, Marguerite. You have a son," Catherine told her, but Marguerite was already gone, and her baby boy never drew his first breath.

It was Agnes, who seemed hardly to know where she was much of the time, who told Catherine and Marie Claude to rest. She washed the bodies, the tiny wells of the baby's ear, the bloody fluids of his birth. *When the wind whistles through the willows,* she sang softly, one of Marguerite's favorites.

Jacques came down and sewed mother and child in a rough canvas shroud. Above decks, Catherine squinted in the sunlight, the sky bright blue with puffy white clouds scudding overhead. The captain said a perfunctory prayer, Catherine crossed herself, and then watched as the bodies slid into the sea.

Back on their own shadowy deck, no one spoke for hours. Finally Gabrielle brought Marguerite's small basket to Catherine.

"You're the only one without one," Gabrielle said. "You'll be needing the shawl, the needle, the comb, all of it."

"Thank you," Catherine said. She pulled the basket into her lap and cradled it if as if it would comfort poor Marguerite.

~~~

Those first weeks of the voyage, Catherine had seethed with hate and anger. During the endless, monotonous days, she plotted her revenge and imagined stripping Hugo of the finery he was so fond of. No more lace or velvet, no more silk hosiery or red heeled slippers -- she would see him in rags and parade him through the Tuileries, everyone he had been so eager to impress jeering and snickering as he passed by. Or perhaps she would strip him of any clothes at all so as to display his flabby body as she marched him past all the maids he harassed, all the footmen he berated, all the laborers he disdained. The humiliation would nearly kill him, but not quite. To finish him off, she would have him staked naked in the woods while snow and sleet came down. He'd hear wolves howling in the hills. He'd be terrified. Sometimes she imagined he died from sheer dread that the wolves were coming, sometimes that the wolves actually did come.

And of course confining him in a dark dank dungeon with spiders and rats for all of eternity was always an option.

By the time the ship approached the Atlantic coast of the Americas, however, misery had burned away Catherine's anger. There had been the terror of another storm, and then another. Fever had run through the ship again. Everyone suffered from the flux. Food and water grew more foul with every day, and she couldn't forget Marguerite's cold gray face or the tiny baby who never drew breath.

Catherine fell into a bleak despondency. She didn't think of Hugo or Grandfather, didn't think of Paris or the comforts of home. She simply endured.

At last, a sailor atop the highest mast called out, "Land ho!" Catherine wanted to weep. Land. Soil. Grass. Trees. All within reach.

As the *New Hope* entered Charleston harbor to take on water and stores, the young officer announced no one would be going ashore except the provisioners. Catherine joined the other women in outraged protest, but the officer shrugged and said, "Captain's orders," as if that god-like being could not be contradicted.

Catherine stood at the rail with the others and yearned to walk on the green hills, grass beneath her feet. At least a gentle wind carried the smells of lush growth to them across the bay.

*If only*, she thought. If only she could get off this ship, if only she could bathe, if only she never had to go below decks again. That other life of fine wines, glittering jewels, and enchanting balls seemed to belong to some other woman. She was just like the girls taken from the Salpêtrière now: filthy, smelly, and skinny.

Jacques and the other sailors who had acted as their stewards said good bye. They were disembarking to take another ship back to France, their contracts with the *New Hope* at an end.

Jacques hesitated as he told them goodbye. "I don't know these new men coming aboard. Here," he said, and handed Gabrielle his knife. At a nod from Jacques, his two friends handed theirs over, too.

The captain took on half a dozen sailors to replace them and had no interest in how they handled the women. The worst of the new caretakers was Juan Peron, a Spaniard, who believed the twenty women below decks were a harem for himself and his cronies.

Juan Peron, Romero, and Benoit dragged Annette and Helene down to the lower deck and imposed themselves on them. The girls returned limping and crying. Catherine had not realized even whores could be hurt by -- that -- that they could be raped. But they were hurt, physically and emotionally.

"We have to stop them," Catherine said to Marie Claude.

Marie Claude nodded. "We will."

The next time the three men brought down their meal, the women ate in silence. Once they'd all finished, they passed their dirty bowls and spoons to Juan Peron. As the sailors prepared to take them above, they encountered Marie Claude, Catherine, and Gabrielle at the bottom of the stairs. Each of them held a knife.

The other women crowded around behind the men, trapping them. Even if the men had dared pull their own knives, the women left them not an inch of elbow room to reach their blades.

"You touch one of us again, you will lose your balls." Marie Claude's tone was mild, but the light in her eyes made Juan Peron's gaze dart back and forth, gauging the threat and finding it credible.

Catherine had done little more with a knife than to cut a pear, but the stink of Jean Peron's fear made her feel powerful. She twisted the blade in his face so he could see the play of light on its edge.

"Now ladies," he said, bravado being his only defense. "You know -- "

"Yes. We know. And now you know what will happen to you." Marie Claude nodded to the other women and they let the three sailors ascend the stairs, their haste almost comical.

"All you accomplished was to make them mad," Bridget said. "They probably won't bring our breakfast or fresh water or anything else now."

"Bridget, maybe you like being a whore. The rest of us had enough of that life back in France."

Bridget smirked. "What about you, princess? You wish you'd had a turn with Romero, sweetie?"

Catherine blanched. Never in her life had anyone insulted her like that. She hardly knew how to respond.

"You must have been born to whore, Bridget," Rachel said. "Long may you enjoy it, at least until your nose falls off from the pox."

No one spoke to Bridget for days, but she had the captain's table and his bed to console her.

They sailed south from Charleston, then rounded Spanish Florida and crossed the great gulf. The closer they came to their destination, the more eager Catherine was to be off this ship. The smells, the rats, the constant motion of the sea, the interminable boredom -- she could hardly bear it any more.

At last. The captain anchored the *New Hope* off shore, the bay too shallow for a ship of this size. The sun lit a white beach. The wind smelled of mud and sea.

Catherine was cold exposed to the wind on the deck, but this cold was nothing compared to the icy crossing of the Atlantic.

After so many weeks together aboard a ship beset by storms, fever, rats and rancid food, the sailors treated them gently as they handed each woman over the side.

Catherine -- all of them -- weakly clung to the rope ladder and, once in the boat, to each other, half sick, and dirty beyond belief. Their clothes reeked of vomit and sweat and fear.

As soon as her feet touched the shore, Gabrielle fell to her knees and dug her hands into the sand. Rachel threw herself face down and stretched out full length on the first solid ground she'd known in more than two months.

Catherine pulled off her shoes and plowed into the surf. She didn't care how cold the water was, she wanted to feel clean again. She used sand from the sea bottom to scrub at her face and her hands. She dunked her head under the water and held her breath, over and over, hoping the salty water would kill and slosh away all the vermin. The waves washed her silk dress, her undergarments, and the rashes that covered her skin.

Overhead, the bright blue sky and gulls wheeling and cawing. All around her the sound of the surf and the smell of the salt-laden wind. And underfoot, blessed sand.

Shivering, she stayed in the chilling water until a new man dressed in faded finery hollered at Catherine and several other women who had followed her into the water. "Ladies, this is most unseemly. Come out at once."

Shivering, Catherine finally waded back onto the sandy beach and wiped the salty water from her face. She didn't care if salt dried on her skin, marked her dress, crusted in her hair. She smelled of the sea instead of sickness and despair.

# Chapter Two

*French Louisiana*
*The Choosing*

Monsieur Bonnard gathered the women on the shore and introduced himself. "As your agent here in Louisiana, I am now responsible for you ladies. I realize the crossing was difficult and therefore will allow you three full days to put yourselves to rights."

Catherine shivered in the breeze, her dress and hair still wet, her shoes in her hand. She raised her face to the sun, so very glad to feel the sand between her toes. She was not sure where they were, somewhere on the southern coast of King Louis's great American territory. A green land, trees and bushes and vines growing in great profusion. She recognized oaks and pines, but other trees were entirely strange.

They were on a barrier island, it seemed, water on either side of a finger-like isle. A small, rude fort was made of vertically arranged logs with a few wooden buildings set outside the barricade. Soldiers stood about in their blue and buff uniforms, their arms crossed, gazing at the women with close attention.

Bonnard paced, his hands behind his back. "You know why you're here. The king wants this land colonized, and the colonists need wives. Otherwise," he paused to smile at them, "men are not at their best."

"I know what an agent is," Rachel said, blunt as always. "You're selling us, that's what you mean."

"Indeed not, madame. I am the king's agent, paid by the king to facilitate the marriages you all desire. Whatever small fees I am given are merely compensation for seeing to your needs."

"What if I don't want a husband?" one of the women in back asked.

Bonnard smiled, but Catherine didn't see any warmth in his eyes. "Of course you want a husband, my dear. It is why you are here."

"Not like we were given a choice," Rachel muttered.

"Better than the Salpêtrière," Marie Claude whispered.

"The soldiers will set up tents and cots for you to rest in. Meanwhile, drink your fill of this fine spring water and shortly your dinner will be served to you."

Bonnard dismissed them with a wave of his hand, but Catherine did not let that deter her. The long passage across the sea was over, and the tamped down rage at Hugo's injustice seethed anew. She gathered herself together, as regal as she could be in ragged wet clothing, and called to the agent. "Monsieur Bonnard."

He turned and examined her from head to bare toes.

"I will speak to you, sir."

He sighed, much put upon. "What is it, madame?"

She raised her chin and looked him in the eye. "I am Catherine de Villeroy, granddaughter of le comte de Villeroy. I was kidnapped in Paris and perfidiously put aboard the *New Hope*. You will please to arrange my return passage at once."

"An aristo, eh?" Bonnard's smile was poisonous. "Not a princess? Not the long lost daughter of King Louis himself?"

Catherine controlled her temper. "I can speak French, English, and German. I can sing six Handel arias. I can recite my lineage back twelve generations. I am Catherine de Villeroy."

"A governess, were you? Dressed in a stolen gown? I understand, women are not always to blame when they fall on hard times. A master molested you? You ran away? I have heard all the stories, madame." His smile was genuine this time. "Although you are the first granddaughter of a comte I have met." He dipped his head and sketched a bow. "Good day to you, madame."

"Wait!"

He turned back to her, his face hard and cold.

"My grandfather will reward you for my safe return."

A mocking smile lit Bonnard's face. "Of course he will. He'll make me a rich man, will he?" He made no effort to hide his contempt. "Sup with the king will I?" He waved his hand in dismissal. "As I've said, I've heard it all before."

Her fingers twisted in her skirt. "There has to be someone else I can talk to."

"There is not. I am the king's agent in Louisiana. Even the commander of the fort must yield to my authority over you. Now get back with the others and leave me alone."

Catherine stilled, every sense numb as Bonnard walked away from her. For the first time, it seemed possible she would not reclaim her life. Who was she if she could not be Catherine de Villeroy, grandaughter to the great comte de Villeroy?

Little Agnes, of all people, came to her and took her hand. Agnes didn't speak, she just lent the warmth of her own hand.

Bridget sashayed up to Bonnard. "Bonjour, Monsieur Bonnard." Catherine didn't care what Bridget said to the man. She stared at the ground until, gradually, her lungs pulled in a harsh breath.

Agnes squeezed her hand and let go. "The tents are up. Come out of the wind in those wet clothes."

For their supper, soldiers roasted turtles over a fire right on the beach. Catherine had thought she could not eat, but as the first whiff of fresh meat reached her nose, she attacked her tin plate of grilled turtle with her bare hands. She felt like an animal, gulping down the first fresh food the women had had in all those weeks. She ended up sick from it, and the sounds and smells of the others throwing up their dinner were all around her.

That night, she lay awake in a tent, unnerved by the stillness of the cot she lay on. No sound of water rushing past the hull of the ship, no creaking of timbers and rigging, no wind whistling down the hatchways. Crickets, instead, and the murmur of the soldiers' voices gathered around the campfire.

She wasn't going home. The truth of that fact burned in her chest like a live coal. She didn't cry. Instead, she imagined a steel sphere to encompass the hot coal of her fury. She would not let that fire die out, but she would keep it contained until she could use it. For someday, maybe not until she was gray and toothless, Catherine would find a way to go home, and then Cousin Hugo would suffer every hell she could devise.

The next morning, though a cold wind blew off the Gulf, the sun warmed them. Catherine and the others spent the day glorying in fresh food and fresh water. The first day ashore, they'd all walked like drunken sailors, but this second day, they regained their land-legs.

Bonnard called them all together. "Now then," he said. "I will explain your situation more thoroughly and answer your questions. First of all, understand that this is where you will live out your days." Bonnard looked at Catherine. She only thinned her lips and stared at him.

"You have not led exemplary lives or you would not be here. Whoring, certainly, but that is hardly enough to put you in the infamous Salpêtrière prison, is it? Thieves, many of you, and I have learned that one of you is a murderer."

He meant her. Cousin Hugo's malice hadn't been satisfied just to drug Catherine and have her hauled aboard the *New Hope*. Oh, no, he'd had to poison any chance of fair treatment with this tale of murder. She could just imagine Hugo looking doleful, insisting that it was better for everyone if she simply vanished rather than disgrace a noble family.

And the captain had told Bridget, the hateful viper. Now Bridget had informed Bonnard. What favors did Bridget earn in return for that little piece of slander?

"The men here are hard-working and ambitious," Bonnard said, "and they offer you a better life than what you have known." He gave Catherine a sneering smile. "Except of course for our princess." Bridget and one or two others snickered.

"You will work hard, please your husband, bear his children, and your past will not be held against you."

Catherine's pulse roared in her ears. Marriage? Before a priest? No. This couldn't be happening. She was supposed to marry Charles. She was supposed to be a countess.

She pressed her fingers against her mouth and shut her eyes. She could not marry a commoner. Grandfather would take care of it. Once she was home, he would talk to the archbishop and the marriage would be annulled. But until then . . .

"Who believes this bilge?" Rachel muttered.

The third day, the day of reckoning, Bonnard gave them one final talk to convince the women they were very fortunate to be here. Many of the women nodded, Marie Claude among them. How bad had their lives been, Catherine wondered, that being sent half way around the world to be married off to strangers was better than what they'd had?

Bridget seemed entirely confident she would have the best man available. Agnes spent much of her time simply absent, her body seated next to Marie Claude or Gabrielle, but her eyes vacant. Marie Claude didn't seem to have a worry in the world.

"Aren't you worried about who you'll be living with from now on?" Catherine asked.

Marie Claude shrugged. "I can get along with most anybody, and I'd rather be here than be a whore. Why? Are you scared?"

"I'm terrified," Catherine admitted. She tightened her arms around herself. "What if he's dirty? Or hateful? What if he -- ?" What if he touched her, she wanted to say.

Bonnard gave the women their last instructions. "You go up on that platform and you smile. No man likes a wife who can't smile. Make eye contact, maybe do a little posing. You know what I mean. You have what men want. Show it off. Otherwise -- "

"Otherwise what?" Rachel said. Rachel poked at Bonnard every chance she got simply for the fun of it. Sometimes, when she was particularly clever, she could make the agent bluster and turn red.

"What use are you to anyone if you don't find a husband?" he sputtered. "You don't think I'm going to feed you, do you?"

"You'll have to take us back to France if no one wants us," Gabrielle said.

Bonnard laughed. "You'll never see France again, *ma chère*. If nobody here wants you -- " He rubbed his chin, thinking. He looked Gabrielle up and down. "I have considered setting up a brothel. All these soldiers, sailors, settlers who don't have wives, maybe even some of the Indians. You could be my first whore. Maybe you're even good at it."

After Bonnard's ugly laugh, nobody had any more questions.

Throughout the morning, settlers pulled into the landing in their heavy wooden dugout canoes. They greeted one another and then moseyed over to have a look at the women standing in a row. The men ambled down the line, eyes crawling over their bodies, and discussed among themselves this one's bosom or that one's hips. Catherine's skin crawled as roving eyes undressed her, as if she were a common -- as if she were not the granddaughter of le comte de Villeroy. What pride she had left after all these weeks of torment shriveled in her breast.

She had tried to ignore Bonnard and what he told them their fate was to be. But now she believed it. One of these men would claim her, she would belong to him, she would no longer be Catherine de Villeroy.

Bonnard rang a bell to call all the settlers to the afternoon's main event. As the men gathered, Bonnard hissed at the women: "Smile, or it's the soldiers and the sailors for you."

Catherine hung back, Agnes and Marie Claude keeping her company. "Nothing to be afraid of," Marie Claude told her, and seemed to believe it.

The women lined up and climbed the steps onto the platform four at a time. Annette, the prettiest among them, was the first one chosen. "A good price," Gabrielle murmured. Catherine didn't care about that. Her heart pounded and her hands sweated.

Next to be chosen was Helene, tall and big-boned, built for field work, but sweet-faced. One by one the colonists picked a French bride who at least spoke their language and remembered the songs and stories from home.

Only half a dozen men remained when it was time for Catherine to mount the platform. She locked her knees and chanted under her breath, *I will not faint, I will not faint.*

The sun glaring into her eyes, Catherine focused on the dark hats of the men below her. They bent their heads to murmur together, shifting from one foot to the other so that their folded-brim hats undulated like the rolling swells of the sea. Blood rushed through Catherine's ears like the sound of surf in a storm. So newly ashore after weeks aboard ship, she swallowed down a surge of nausea and told herself not to be afraid. They were only men, and only one man would have her, not a horde. They were individuals, were they not? See, there was one who merely stared without the leering grin of the two on his right.

Next to Catherine, Marie Claude stood as though planted on the platform. On Catherine's other side, tiny Agnes might have been made of wood. No doubt she'd gone away again, escaped to some safe place inside her head. Catherine wished she knew how to do that.

The men chatted with each other while they stared at the three women, no doubt thinking that if they waited, the broker would have to lower the price on the last girls. Catherine scanned their faces looking for a pair of kind eyes -- young, old, fat, skinny, she didn't care, if only he were kind.

Such a fool she was to let hope creep in. She would not find a kind man here today. She might not find a man at all. Catherine shuddered, hiding her trembling hands in her skirt, and imagined her fate if no one claimed her. Soldiers, sailors, Indians, Bonnard had said. Any one of these colonists had to be better than whoring in a brothel.

"I'll take the little one," a tall man called. He absently pulled at the slender moustache over his lip, his eyes intent on Agnes.

"A splendid choice, monsieur," Bonnard said. "Step over here and we'll complete our business."

Catherine tugged at Agnes's skirt and hissed, "Agnes. Wake up. Agnes, look at me."

Agnes turned her brown eyes on her and it was if Catherine looked into the blank face of a doll. "Agnes, you're to be married. You're saved, *mon amie*."

Catherine took the girl into her arms and whispered into her ear. "No more going away, Agnes. You hear me? Live, Agnes."

With a shuddering breath, Agnes nodded. She was back in her body again.

"Come on down, *mon petite ange*." Monsieur Bonnard took Agnes firmly by the arm.

Catherine looked at the man who would soon be Agnes's husband. Better dressed than any other man in the yard, he had a patrician nose and the bearing of one who thought well of himself. Catherine couldn't see his eyes in the shadow of his hat, whether they were dark or light, kind or cruel.

As the man guided Agnes away with his hand on her back, Bonnard climbed back up onto their little platform to revive the auction, for that's what it was, whatever Bonnard said.

"I remind you gentlemen these ladies are available to you at a price only to reimburse me for the cost of their long transport across the ocean, around the Florida peninsula, through the great Gulf. An expensive endeavor, but I am not a savage, selling these unfortunate women. I ask only that you see their intrinsic value to you, as helpmates as you build your plantations, as partners in a cold bed. Look at this sturdy one here. She could bear you a son and plow your fields the same day."

Catherine hated the snickers of the men who scorned Marie Claude for her size. And she despised Bonnard for making light of a desperate situation, desperate for her and Marie Claude, at least. She eyed the velvet coat Bonnard wore. It was fine once, but he was shabby now, the coat threadbare and stained. He could not afford to take any of them back to France. His profit lay in pairing them off, not in feeding and transporting them.

"Two of the lovely ladies left to choose between," Bonnard said. "It is true, these girls are not at their best after more than two months aboard ship. You all remember what the crossing was like -- you probably all lost a tooth or two yourselves. They'll clean up good, they'll do fine with some fresh food and clean water. Don't be shy, now. How many white women have you seen these last years, eh?"

"Which one is the murderer?" someone called.

*Oh, Bridget, you had to tell that lie even here.* Catherine closed her eyes.

"That would be the blonde," Bonnard said. "Likely the man had it coming, wouldn't you say? Pretty thing, eh? You plan on murdering anyone else this lifetime, *ma petite*?" Such a grating laugh the man had.

"You mark the price down, monsieur, I'll take the big ugly one." The man's eyes were small and close together, his nose a fleshy knob in the middle of his face.

Marie Claude sucked in a breath, and Catherine squeezed her hand.

"Excellent, monsieur." The broker delivered Marie Claude to the man who would be her husband in the next ten minutes. That was the edict from King Louis. Deliver the girls, but don't release them until the priest had bound the men to them under God's watchful eye.

"All right, one lovely lady left, gentlemen. If you stood as close as I, you would see the girl has eyes the color of the sea, skin white as milk. You fear the little murderer? She needs only a firm hand and she'll be meek as a lamb."

Catherine's knees shook, but she would not collapse, she would not. She stared over the men's heads as Bonnard snatched Catherine's hand, held it high, and forced her to turn so the gentlemen might see her form. "A fine figure, as you can see, if you have only the imagination to see beneath the poor girl's dress. A man could enjoy removing such a rag, eh? What am I bid?"

No bids. No offers. Catherine swept her gaze over the men. Not one of them looked her in the face.

Then the worst would happen. She closed her eyes and tilted her head back, condemned to whatever Bonnard chose to do with her. She could expect no kindnesses from him.

"I'll take her."

Her eyes darted to the man who'd spoken. He had not been there a moment before, she was sure of it. A filthier human being she had never seen, mud on his clothes, on his hands and face, even in his hair. As he approached the platform, the smell of pig washed ahead of him.

The man held up a single coin. The broker snorted in disgust. "One livre? Sir, you take me for a fool."

The man of mud didn't even look at her. "Take it or leave it."

Bonnard chose to leave it. "Gentlemen," he appealed to the remaining men, "you see a woman in perishing condition. Only treat her kindly, bathe her, feed her -- and she will give you years of service. What am I bid?"

Someone spoke to the man with a single coin in his hand. "She's a murderer, they say."

The filthy one shrugged, tossed the coin in his hand, pocketed it, and turned away.

The gathering remained silent. No takers. Catherine swallowed hard, her pulse thundering, her mind swirling, not with thoughts, but with images of a red mouth with broken teeth leering over her, of filthy hands tearing the clothes from her body, groping her. Or she could go with this mud-covered man with a single livre in his hand.

"Monsieur!" she called. "Wait!"

"Here now," the broker said. "You have no say in the matter, woman."

She elbowed past Bonnard in his worn velvet and clattered down the steps. The man covered in muck had turned at her call and watched her as she strode up to him. She saw no welcome in his eyes. Swallowing hard, Catherine drew upon her last shred of courage. "I will go with you, monsieur."

Giving her only a cursory glance, he tossed the coin to Bonnard and strode to the dilapidated chapel inside the fort where the priest waited. The ceremony took no more than five minutes and Catherine was now Madame Jean Paul Dupre.

Carrying the small basket containing all the worldly goods the king had provided poor Marguerite, Catherine followed her husband on rubbery legs, the man not bothering to see if she kept up. As they approached the bay, a big black dog leapt out of a dugout canoe and bounded toward Dupre. Its paws on his chest, its tail wagging madly, the hound licked his dirty face. The man gave him a quick scratch behind the ears. "In the boat," he said to the dog. To Catherine, he said nothing, but she clambered into the dugout on her own and settled at one end, the dog between the two of them.

Catherine gripped her hands together to keep them from trembling. She'd come close to panic back on the platform when this Monsieur Dupre had turned away, leaving her to her fate as a rejected woman, so poisonous not even these women-deprived settlers would have her.

Her head ached and the sun glinting on the water pierced her sore eyes. She clamped her jaw shut to keep her teeth from chattering. She was not cold in truth. The sun was shining. She just had to calm down. This was not like her, to be so overwhelmed by fear.

She'd seen what happened to the girls on the *New Hope* who gave in to fear and self-pity. Pauline, huddled in on herself, weeping, starving herself -- she had died, and the sailors had tipped her body into the ocean for the fish and the sharks. *I'm stronger than that*, Catherine vowed.

"What is your dog's name?" she said, breaking the silence.

He looked at her as if he'd forgotten she was there. "Débile."

"Débile?" How long had it been since she'd laughed? "Is he such a moron, then?"

Dupre looked at his hound napping in the bottom of the boat. "It suits him." He looked off up the bayou and said no more.

If he were a quiet man, Catherine didn't mind as long as he was a peaceable man. He surely couldn't be bad or mean, not when his dog had rushed to greet him and lick his face as Débile had. A dog, even if he were a moron, wouldn't love a cruel man.

Very well, if he was going to ignore her, then she could study him as she liked, her husband, her savior. He didn't look like a knight who'd ever worn shining armor, covered in mud as he was. He didn't even look interested in the woman he'd bid for. A paltry bid, and now she had time to think of it, a humiliating one, but no one else had offered a single sou.

Evidently monsieur was a poor man who slopped his own hogs. He seemed to have fallen into the sty just before he came to the auction. He wore coarse canvas britches held up with suspenders that might once have been red. He wore no coat, only a voluminous linen shirt, the sleeves pushed up to his elbows. He'd tied his dark hair into a queue hanging half way down his back. His beard might be three or four days old. Medium height and lean, the muscles of his forearms worked as he paddled them upstream. As for his face, she'd have to wait until he washed to make out his features. Surely he washed now and then.

At least she needn't be embarrassed at her own sorry state. Salt had bedulled the lustrous satin of her gown, red blotches covered her skin, and her beautifully fitted gown hung on her.

And now, she was a pig farmer's wife. How her dear friends, those cats Antoinette and Celine, sipping coffee in the salons at Versailles, would laugh to see her like this. But hadn't she been just as bad as they, sneering at a lady whose hem was too short or too long, whose plumes were a bit bedraggled from the wind, whose rouge was too red?

The day before it all happened, Catherine had snapped at the maid because her chocolate was not hot enough. No more maids. No more chocolate. No more walks down the long gallery at Versailles, admiring and being admired.

Ragged and weary now, she rode in a crude dugout canoe with a stranger, and was surprised that all she felt was simple relief.

Lulled by the rhythmic sweep of the oar through the water, by bird song and warm sun, Catherine examined this new world fate had thrust her into. Dupre paddled them up a sluggish stream where trees stretched their limbs over the water. Nowhere in France was there such lush greenery, even in summer, and it was the end of February as far as she could tell. Sunshine bathed her skin and she breathed deep, slow breaths. That hard lump in her chest dissolved into nothing.

Catherine looked at Monsieur Dupre and felt a rush of gratitude. Whatever life this man took her to, it would be better than the *New Hope*.

She swallowed hard so as not to gag when the wind shifted and blew her husband's stench into her face. She couldn't be the delicate lady here, and, really, she had nothing against pigs. Catherine smiled to herself. This morning she had not expected to find amusement ever again, and yet, here she was, from one of the grandest families in France, and she was grateful for a pig farmer covered in muck. It cheered her that she still had it in her to be amused by a bit of irony.

"Do you live alone?" she asked.

"A dog. Three pigs."

"Company, then," she said and tried a smile on him. He did not respond.

No matter. It was beautiful here, green leaves still on the trees in winter time. No snow, no sleet, no gray skies. A paradise, this colony of Louisiana.

Catherine startled at sight of an enormous, horrid creature sunning itself on the bank. Its tail alone had to be longer than a man, its hide was like cobblestones, and long fangs protruded from its closed mouth. Her heart racing, she drew her hands from the sides of the boat and clutched them to her breast.

"What is that?" she whispered.

Dupre glanced at the monster. "Alligator. We don't play with them." She detected a slight smile beneath the grime. So the man had a sense of humor. She stared again at the creature napping on the bank and shuddered. Well, even Eden had its serpent.

By the time they'd crossed the sound and Dupre had paddled them up the bayou, the shadows were long. He stopped at a cleared bank and dragged the dugout up the slope as Débile splashed his way out of the water, shook himself, then ran ahead of them up the path. With dark coming on, the temperature had dropped and Catherine shivered in her thin shawl. She had no cloak, no hat. Crossing the Atlantic, in January, she and the other women had wakened to frost in their eyebrows from the damp below decks. She had survived that, she would survive this.

Following Dupre up a narrow path through tall grass, Catherine's first sight of her new home was the pig wallow, the first scent the sickly sweet smell of pig waste. Automatically she reached for the scented pomander in her hidden pocket before she realized there was no pomander, no defense against the reeking wallow.

Dupre leant over to scratch the sow's ears. "I'm back, old girl." Two shoats wiggled up to him and thrust their noses into his hand. "All right, all right," he said gently, pulling at their ears.

"Ought we to be introduced?" she said from behind her hand.

He gave her a piercing look from beneath his dark brows before he returned his attention to the pigs. "Madame Dupre, meet Mama Suzette, Beauregard, and Brigitte."

"*Bonjour*," Catherine said and executed a deep curtsy. Her husband showed no appreciation for her fine porcine manners.

Fifty yards beyond the wallow, upwind she hoped, was the house. The cabin. The hovel, if she were to be precise. Dupre unfastened the leather drape over the door and gestured for her to enter.

Catherine glanced around the cabin. There were two windows, open to the air, a fireplace, a neatly made bed, a chair, and a small table under which Débile sprawled. Her determined good spirits faltered. This rude cabin -- Grandfather's hounds lived better than this.

"Get a fire going. I'll check the traps."

"Of course," she murmured. She never had, but how hard could it be? She had seen the maids light fires every day of her life.

He marched out of the cabin leaving her to it.

Catherine found flint and steel on the mantle next to a leather-bound book. Not a printed book, a blank book to write in. She opened a page at random and scanned a poem written in a spidery bold hand. Not an idyll, no tranquil, happy scenes in these verses. Was her husband the poet? She heard Débile outside and hastily put the book back on the shelf next to the quill and ink pot.

She turned her mind to building a fire and struck the flint with the steel. Nothing happened. Finally, she got a spark, but the log in the fireplace ignored it. She tried again and again, feeling more stupid with each strike.

Dupre came back and laid a skinned rabbit on the hearth. He crossed his arms and watched her a moment.

"There's kindling in a box to your right."

Kindling. Of course. She propped some wood slivers against the log and tried again, and again. And this man standing there watching her. Humiliation made her hands even clumsier.

He nudged her aside with his knee. "Watch." With a handful of moss and wood slivers, he built a sort of pyramid under the log. One strike of the flint, the moss caught the spark, and *voilà,* fire. He tended it carefully, blowing gently, until the log caught the flame.

Dupre walked out with the bucket. "Watch Débile doesn't get our supper."

While Dupre was gone, Catherine hugged her arms to herself and took a deep breath. She knew how to play the harpsichord. She sang like a nightingale, her many suitors had proclaimed, she wrote poetry, mediocre as it was, and painted flowers, again with mediocre talent, yet she was acclaimed an accomplished woman in the grandest court in the world.

Now she realized she knew nothing.

Her husband had not ridiculed her, however. He had not been particularly kind, but neither had he been unkind. Breathing deeply, she reminded herself that she had a roof over her head. She was to be fed fresh meat. And the bed would not rock and sway like the hammocks on the *New Hope*.

The bed, made of sapling trunks with the bark still on them, was high enough to shove a sizable chest underneath. Rather narrow, however. They would share that bed. Elbow to elbow. She had never lain with a man. Would he expect that of her tonight?

She bit her lip. Her time at Versailles listening to the gossips and dodging men with groping hands had given her a fair notion of what happened between men and women. It didn't sound very pleasant. She pressed her fingers to her lips and blinked back tears. What if he came to bed smelling like pig?

Débile thumped his tail and looked at her with mournful eyes. With a pang of longing for her three little white poodles, Catherine knelt and smoothed her hand over his big head. "Hey, there, boy," she crooned. "Aren't you the big fine dog?"

A tremble of fear made her hand shake as she stroked the velvety ears. She was in this man's power. He was bigger, stronger. She was helpless, again. She hated it, how frightened she was.

But she was not Agnes who chose to escape inside her head instead of facing life. She gathered herself and breathed deeply. This was better than the brothel Bonnard had threatened them with.

Besides, the man must need her or he wouldn't have paddled all the way down to the auction. He'd got her on the cheap, no doubt about that, but perhaps that was all the money he had.

She'd hardly heard more than a dozen words from his mouth, but he seemed well-spoken, and he was literate. He was certainly a self-contained man. She hoped -- no -- she was not to hope. She'd told herself all the weeks sailing across an endless ocean that hope only led to heartache.

It was dusk when Dupre returned. Water dripped from his hair, his shirt, his pants. He must have bathed in his clothes in the bayou. He caught her studying his lean face with the deep lower lip and the dimpled chin and glared at her as if she'd said something disparaging. She lowered her eyes and stepped back so he could empty the water bucket into the big iron pot on its hook over the fire. He tossed the carcass in the pot and she supposed that would be supper, eventually.

He pulled his chest from under the bed and rummaged in it for dry clothes. With his back to her, he stripped and dressed.

After a quick glance at taut flanks, Catherine turned away to find something to stir the pot with.

As he pulled on dry stockings, Catherine sat on the stump he used for a chair. "My name is Catherine."

He nodded. She supposed he knew that from the ceremony.

"I want to tell you -- " She cleared her throat. "I'm grateful to be here. Thank you."

He gave her a strange look. "You realize this is all there is to this place. This cabin."

"Yes, I realize."

He snorted a kind of laugh. "Tell me tomorrow after a full day's work if you're still grateful."

"I will be."

~~~

Jean Paul stared at her, this woman he'd just bound himself to for life. Her lips were pale and peeling, her face sun-burned, her hair dull and dirty. He reminded himself that no one looked good after two months aboard ship with bad food and water, nausea, the runs.

It wasn't just her bedraggled state, though. She'd looked scared to death standing on that platform. The last woman. What would have become of her if no one had claimed her? Nothing good. He smirked. He, Jean Paul Dupre, a hero who rescued damsels from a dreadful fate. The gods loved their irony, did they not?

Where had she come from that she should be grateful for this particular corner of hell?

He pulled on a boot and ignored her. He didn't want to know. All that mattered was that she had a strong back and a willingness to work.

He plodded out the door and headed to the garden. When he returned with a pocketful of guavas, a handful of sweet potatoes, an onion, and a tattered head of cabbage, the woman said, "Let me."

She washed them in the water remaining in the bucket and tossed the potatoes, the onion, and the cabbage, the whole thing, in the pot. When she reached for the guavas to toss into the boiling water, he stayed her hand. "Not those."

Maybe she'd never seen a guava, but who didn't know to peel the papery skin off an onion?

God, he hadn't eaten since yesterday. He'd have to remember what it was like not to tear into a piece of meat and devour most of it himself, tossing the remainder to Débile. He'd had manners once, he supposed he could remember how to eat like a gentleman.

"Are there candles? A lantern?"

"No."

"Plates, knives, spoons?"

He rummaged behind the kindling box and produced the plank he sometimes used as a platter. From the mantle he took a spoon. "Madame," he said with a small bow and presented it to her.

From his belt he took his knife, a razor sharp blade he'd used for everything from defending himself against the king's enemies to carving up rabbits. Did she realize what danger she could have placed herself in, following him to this isolated place? Did she realize what a stranger could do to her out here in the wilderness with no one to know? She was lucky it was he she'd finally come with.

He handed her his knife, and she smiled at him, foolish woman.

"Thank you. Cups?"

He would be content to drink from one of the gourds and his guest could have the tin cup. But she was not a guest, was she? His throat tightened at what he had done, brought this woman here. As his wife. Forever.

She had washed the potatoes in the bucket. No doubt she'd expect clean water in her cup.

He took the bucket and walked through the gloaming to the stream that flowed into the bayou. He lingered, watching the night descend and the bats come to life overhead.

He didn't know how to be with people anymore. Didn't know how to have a conversation. Suzette and Débile were company, but they didn't have much to say.

It had been madness, dashing down to Fort Louis to bring home a stranger, one who apparently had a past as dark as his own. He didn't want her here. But he couldn't take her back. No one else wanted her either.

He shouldn't have done it. He knew as soon as he opened his mouth to bid for her and saw how that poor woman, drawn and strained, had looked at him like her savior. How desperate did a woman have to be to look like that at a man covered in pig shit? So he'd offered a mere livre to get himself out of the bidding, but it hadn't mattered. She was his, such as she was.

Her dress was ridiculous, a silk satin that would have been appropriate for an afternoon with the king. Yet she had been eager enough to come with him. A sure indication of desperation.

Maybe she read, maybe she was intelligent. He hoped so. He shook his head. If she did or she didn't have a wit between her ears, she'd help clear more land, and later, help plant a crop.

As he approached the cabin, he remembered what the man at the auction had shouted out. "Is that the murderer?"

# Chapter Three

## *Agnes*
## *Awakening*

As her new husband paddled them up the bayou, Agnes unclenched her fingers and looked at her hands. The trembling had stopped. *Everything's fine Everything's fine.* She wasn't hungry, she wasn't chained to the wall, she hadn't been beaten in all these weeks. *Everything was fine.*

She glanced at the tall man, her husband, to find him staring at her. She ducked her head. She was too small, not strong enough to be much help to him in the fields, so it must be the other he wanted her for. She closed her eyes tight. She would disappear into herself again, how else could she bear it.

But Catherine had said live every moment, no matter what. Else she was as good as dead, no? That is what Catherine meant. She would try.

Oh good Lord, she didn't know his name. The priest must have said it, but all she'd heard was the blood rushing through her ears. Married. To a stranger.

Agnes swallowed and straightened her spine. She wouldn't go away. Look at the trees, she told herself. Green, in winter. The water, no ice anywhere. A remarkable place. She drew in a deep breath of soft, warm air.

At last, he pulled the dugout onto a cleared bank with wooden steps laid into the mud. Once he'd tied the dugout to a tree, he took her basket out of the boat and held his hand out for her. "Come," he said. "We're here."

His hand was warm, callused, and gentle. Perhaps he would be kind. She could hope for that, anyway.

The silvery glint of water indicated a pond lay on the other side of the cleared ground. In the yard around the cabin chickens scratched in the dirt. Beautiful chickens, red feathers catching the sunlight. She'd raised chickens in the back yard behind the bookstore. Sometimes, when Papa was sleeping off another drunk, she'd gone to the coop and talked to her hens. They would coo and cluck at her, and she would not feel so alone.

Her husband smiled at her oddly. Perhaps he felt as uneasy with her as she did with him. He wasn't used to company, after all. They hadn't seen another soul since they left the fort.

"Come, my dear. Let me show you your new home."

The cabin seemed sturdy enough, made of rough-hewn logs. There was a small deck before the door to wipe one's feet on before entering.

The inside was bright from pale sunshine streaming in the western window. How she had missed windows when she'd been confined at the Salpêtrière. She stepped to the opposite window where tomorrow she could watch the sun rise. Outside she could see a garden and beyond that, thick forest.

He set her basket down at the foot of the bed, but Agnes wasn't ready yet to look at the bed. She examined the fireplace, the table and chairs, the crockery laid out on the table. On the mantel were a dozen small carved wooden animals. No books, she noticed with some disappointment, but she breathed in the scent of wood and smoke and let out a long breath. The waiting and wondering were over. This cabin, this man, these were her destiny.

Flushing hot, Agnes said, "The privy?"

"Behind the cabin. See to your needs, my dear, and I'll get the fire started. It'll be cold when the sun goes down."

When she stepped back into the cabin, a bright cheery fire burned in the clay fireplace. An animal of some kind, a rabbit perhaps, was spitted over the fire. It smelled old, maybe even rancid, but it would be safe enough to eat if he cooked it well.

Her husband clapped his hands and then rubbed them together. "Well, then. You will please to disrobe, my dear."

She stood there stupidly, her hands at her sides.

A trace of impatience crossed over his face. "You aren't a virgin, are you? I was led to understand all you girls had come from the Salpêtrière?"

She nodded.

"Well, then. You no doubt have done this since you were ten years old. Disrobe, if you please."

He was staring at her bodice, so she began to undo her buttons. Not looking at him, she said, "I was not always a prostitute, monsieur."

"Of course," he said with evident disinterest in her history. When the dress fell at her feet, he said, "The chemise as well, and any other garments you have about your person."

"I would like to know your name, sir."

His head jerked back. "My name? Of course." With a flourish and an abbreviated bow, he said, "I am Valery Villiers. And you, my dear, are Madame Villiers."

"Yes. Thank you."

When she stood fully exposed before him, he raised his arm and made a twirling motion. She turned for him, displaying herself.

"You needn't blush, madame. I am your husband." He began to open his britches, his eyes roving over her body. "You are rather scrawny for my taste, but no doubt you will fatten now that you are ashore. I know full well how distressing life aboard ship can be. Lie down now, and spread your legs."

She did as she was told. He had not raised his voice to her, had not hit her. He was kind. Or kind enough.

He came down on her, his long length pressing her into the thin mattress. When he was done, he let out a sigh and rested his weight on her slight form. "Good girl," he said as he rolled off her. "We'll do well enough together. You may put your clothes back on until later when I will have you again."

She had not gone away while he was rutting her. And she was fine. She smiled, for herself, proud she'd found the courage to live through the ordeal without disappearing. She wasn't hurt at all. Everything would be fine.

"Can you cook, my dear? I will teach you, and you will prepare all our meals. Take that fork and pierce the rabbit. See how the juice is still red with blood? It will cook longer before we eat. You may take the bucket to the pond and bring back water, if you please."

At the water's edge, something splashed and some other creature rustled the brush alongside the bayou. She had never feared four legged creatures.

Her bucket filled, she paused, wondering if -- yes -- there before her was magic. Not one, but three will-o'-the-wisps glowed over the pond. There were fairies here, too? Oh yes, she knew they were merely a natural phenomenon, something about gases rising from the bottom of a pond. That didn't make them any less wonderful. All it took to have magic in the world was to believe, and she chose to believe in these lovely luminous orbs. She breathed in quietly so as not to frighten them. There had been fairies at the pond on her grandfather's dairy farm, too. She and Maman had made up stories about them, naming them Queen Madeleine and King Charles.

She set the bucket down and whispered their names. The glowing balls seemed to drift toward her and she held her breath. When they slowly floated away, she whispered after them, "Oh please come again. Please."

Feeling she was not so alone in this desolate place, she hauled the heavy bucket back to the cabin. Firelight glowed in the windows. A half-moon had risen over the roof line. A cozy sight, but how was she to live without books, and music? She bit her lip. There was no choice. This life -- it was all she had.

Over their supper of root vegetables and roasted rabbit, Monsieur Villiers told her about himself. Second son of a second son, and so he had to make his own fortune in this world. Indigo, Blue Gold they called it, would make him rich. He would clear more land and more land, he would hire laborers, even if they must be Indians, and plant more indigo than anyone else on this bayou.

He had always been quick and able, Valery told her. The best swordsman in Burgundy, the sharpest wit, the most adored lover of women all over the province.

He did not mind that Agnes was a whore from the infamous prison. When he was rich again, he would take care of her, she needn't fear. Perhaps she would have his child, even two, and would not that be a glorious thing.

He was a child himself, Agnes thought, boasting of his prowess in every endeavor. She smiled at him to show she appreciated how fine a man she had married. Behind that smile she hid a trace of amusement. So very proud he was, sitting in a simple cabin in the middle of nowhere.

She would be safe in this man's impenetrable self-regard. He didn't see her, didn't want to know her. He was polite, but Agnes did not confuse nice manners with regard. She would live in Valery's courtesy as distant from him as the stars.

He began reciting his pedigree, a rather distinguished one if not of the first water. So her husband was one of the Burgundian Villiers. She had heard the name, of course. "And what of you," he said, licking his fingers. "Agnes, is it? You have a family name, perhaps? You had a father to acknowledge you?"

"No, monsieur," she lied.

"Well, Agnes. I shall have a smoke while you clean away our dinner. Then you may disrobe again and go to bed."

She lay on her back under the scratchy wool blanket, drowsy from the warmth and a full belly. The fire crackled as it burnt down, cicadas sang loudly in the woods and occasionally a bull frog bellowed to its mate. Familiar sounds from *grand-père's* dairy in the country.

She woke when her husband pulled the blanket from her to gaze on her nude body. He was nude himself this time. He lay down beside her and pulled her on top of him. "Straddle me, my dear. There's the girl." And so she, who thought she knew all about what men wanted of women, learned something new.

# Chapter Four

## *Catherine and Jean Paul*
## *Adjustments*

Jean Paul eyed the hickory tree, judging where it would fall if he made the first cut just there. It wouldn't do for the massive thing to fall in his garden nor in the patch designated for his indigo seeds. Satisfied it would fall where he wanted it to, he swung his axe into the trunk and felt the impact shudder through his arms and shoulders. The hardest tree in these woods, and this was a big one.

He welcomed the burn in his arms and back, the sting of sweat in his eyes. He could live in that intense awareness of the physical present and forget regret, anger, and hurt. In this mindless state, all his pain transferred directly from his heart to his arms to the axe and into the unfeeling tree.

Time meant nothing to him when he gave himself to the labor. He returned to himself only at the final thwack of the last stroke when the hickory swayed and teetered, then crashed to the ground precisely where he'd meant it to. A moment of pure elation, fleeting as it was, rewarded him. His limbs felt light, and he smiled in a surge of satisfaction.

This had been his life for months, felling tree after tree to clear enough land to make a farmstead, these moments of pleasure punctuating the long days of boredom, loneliness, and punishing memory. Tomorrow he would choose another tree, maybe that oak with the moss dripping from its limbs, and swing his axe until the memories dissipated themselves into his muscles and out his pores.

He put his axe aside and drank deeply from the gourd of water. Twenty yards away his new wife hacked at the ground with her hoe. She had no idea how to handle it. Her back and shoulders must ache like three hells every evening. Willing as she was, obviously she was unaccustomed to hard labor. The blue silk dress she wore had been expensive once, but now the seams behind her arms were ripped open. The hem line had been unevenly hacked off, he assumed because it had dragged the ground without the panniers and crinolines it required to make a fashionable, wide tent of the skirts. A dress worn only by the highest class in French society. He supposed it was fortunate that it was silk; bedraggled or not, the fabric would last forever.

The neckline too was far lower than a working class woman would ever have worn, and now the pale skin of Catherine's chest was red from sunburn. He could make her a paste from bear grease and slippery elm. Maybe that would ease the sting.

No, not from the working class, his wife. What's more, her hands were soft, her speech was refined, and she had the bearing of a woman who expected life to award her every wish she conceived.

He almost felt sorry for her, watching her flail around with as much efficiency as a three year old. Her old life had certainly not prepared her for this one.

Well, she would learn to wield that hoe, to light a fire, to cook a meal. Maybe she could adapt her hopes and dreams and let her past life go. He wished her more luck with that than he'd yet found.

~~~

Catherine had never done anything more strenuous than dance the minuet, yet here in the wilds of Louisiana, a place notably different from Paris, as she had observed any number of times, she spent another day shaping the earth into furrows with blistered hands.

The gratitude she'd felt the first days had been sincere, but it was wearing thin. Visions of her soft thick mattress covered in sweet-smelling linen sheets, a rose-colored satin counterpane, feather pillows -- how she ached to curl into her bed and sleep. Surely fate had intended her to wear satins and velvet, to sip chocolate before rising to a fire already built by a silent, invisible maid.

And the food -- surely she, Catherine de Villeroy, had not been meant to eat rabbit or possum, yams, onions, and cabbage over and over. What she wouldn't give for a ham steak with roasted potatoes, fresh asparagus, strawberry jam. And coffee! How she missed coffee. And fresh cream.

If Cousin Hugo could see her now, how he'd gloat. He would be bathed, perfumed, and powdered before donning his coat of midnight blue, the one with the silver embroidery -- while she wore the same ruined silk even in the field. He would breakfast on flaky croissants and coffee, strong and fragrant, while she ate corn meal mush. She breathed in, sure she could smell that rich coffee all the way across the ocean.

How easy it had been for him to take her from le comte d'Orleans' soiree and sneak her aboard a west-bound ship while she was drugged and helpless. With no body, no inconvenient blood stains, it would be easy to explain her disappearance. He need only say, *My dear Cousin. She was always a passionate, wayward child. Ran off with a penniless Italian, you know, and their carriage overturned as they crossed the Alps. Treacherous, those mountain roads.*

And now dear Cousin Hugo could claim not only her fortune and her jewels, but also assert he was Grand-père's only heir.

No doubt Hugo assumed she would die on the crossing or perish in this wilderness. Well, she would not. She would help this dour, silent Dupre with his little farm. She owed him that. And someday there would be money enough to pay passage back to France. Hugo would suffer for what he'd done.

Meanwhile, she had this earth to hoe, and at suppertime, yet another rabbit to dine on.

As soon as it was dark, she crawled onto the thin moss-stuffed mattress and immediately fell into the sweet oblivion of sleep.

Later in the night the ache in her back, her legs, her hands woke her. She couldn't get comfortable in the narrow space between Jean Paul and the rough wall. He slept like the logs behind her, his breathing deep and even. If he'd just move over a little she could lie on her back with her arms at her side. He didn't like it if she touched him, but she couldn't bear to lie here another hour staring at the dark, feeling trapped between his bulk and the wall.

"Monsieur?" She tried a little louder. "Monsieur?" He might as well be dead for all the response. She gently put her hand on his shoulder. He was warm, his bare skin smooth, firm, sculpted. He snuffled in his sleep and shifted so she had a little more room. At least this time he didn't jerk awake, alarmed and surly.

Still she couldn't sleep. She longed for home and the life she'd expected to lead. Blanc mange. Roast goose. Lace. Mirrors. Maids. Hot baths. Music and dancing. And conversation! The list of what she missed went on and on. And there was Grand-père, who had not saved her, but whom she yearned for just the same.

After an uncomfortable, restless night, she rose to breakfast on a cold sweet potato. She stunk. Her hands were sore, the blisters painful and often bloody. But she bound her hands, followed her husband outdoors, picked up her hoe, and began the endless chore of tilling the earth.

She didn't know what was the matter with her today. The hoe seemed heavier with every passing hour. Surely they didn't need a garden as big as this? Surely this plot she hoed was big enough to feed a hundred people, two hundred. Late in the morning, exhaustion, pain, and sleeplessness defeated her. She fell to her knees in the black dirt, hunched over and wept.

If only she could have a hot bath. A pot of coffee. If only she could sleep in a soft, clean bed.

She wished her husband would come to her, would take her into his arms and carry her into the cabin. *Sleep*, he'd say with a gentle touch to her forehead.

Of course he did not, the rhythm of his axe striking the tree trunk never faltering. She picked herself up, wiped a dirty arm across her face, and carried on. How she hated this hoe.

In another hour, Dupre felled yet another great tree. Yes, he was a hard-working man -- they would never lack for firewood -- yet she wanted to rail at him, to beat him with her fists. He never talked! "Build the fire." "I'll check the traps." That's what her husband thought conversation was. She resented him fiercely. He was never tired, never sore, never lonely. Why had he bid for her at all if he was going to ignore her the live-long day?

She realized she had dropped the hoe again and was staring off at nothing. Not that her husband would complain. Oh no. That would mean speaking to her.

He didn't want to talk to her and he didn't want to touch her, even lying elbow to elbow in that bed. She knew she was ragged and dirty, but men had pursued her since she was fourteen years old. Surely she had not turned into such a crow in the months since she'd been carried aboard the *New Hope*. Maybe she had. She hadn't seen herself in a glass since the night Hugo's men dragged her away.

But if he didn't notice her, she noticed him. Every day he wielded the axe, clearing more land, his shirt off, his muscles working. Catherine had never seen a man's naked chest before, had never guessed at the power in his arms and shoulders. Every man she had known strove to maintain a sleek, refined profile in his layers of linens, silks, and velvets. Muscles would only spoil the line of their coats.

With his dark hair and eyes, Monsieur Dupre must be from the south of France where the men sometimes looked more Italian than French. Provence, if she placed his accent correctly. Likely every soul in this colony had expected a different life than this. Disappointment, trouble, misery must have propelled them all -- why else would anyone come to this humid jungle?

Maybe her husband had fled France ahead of debt collectors, or angry gendarmes, or maybe he had expected an adventure, a chance to make a fortune in the new colony. The pamphlets had promised that -- come to the new world where the opportunities are limitless. A very tempting proposition for third and fourth sons facing impoverishment.

Or maybe he was a criminal, given the chance to leave France forever in exchange for his life. That would explain why her Monsieur Dupre had not balked at taking home an avowed murderer. He could be a murderer himself! She scoffed. Nobody as grumpy as he would bother with murder -- there might be some satisfaction in murdering someone, and he was averse to any kind of satisfaction.

At any rate, she would not ask him why he was here. Why would she expect the truth if he had committed a crime? They would remain strangers then, wary of one another, for she would not volunteer the details of her past either.

But they must find a way to live together. It might be many years before she could return to France. She admitted to herself her restitution might never come, and even if she did make it home, she would still be Madame Jean Paul Dupre. And who was Madame Dupre? She didn't know yet, but she knew her life as a social darling, beloved and cossetted and admired, was over.

Yet the blood of French heroes ran through her veins. She would not despair. She raised her face to the sun, closed her eyes, and prayed that she would remember to be grateful Hugo had not killed her, that this stranger had given her a home, such as it was, and that calluses on her hands were replacing the blisters. Amen.

Catherine picked up her hoe and glanced at the clouds moving in. When the rain came, she'd have a hard time moving the earth into these very necessary rows. They still had a patch of cabbage, which she had once despised but now ate with a fair degree of tolerance. She didn't know what else Dupre intended to plant, but he was insistent the furrows be laid straight and even beforehand.

When the rain came late in the afternoon, the warmth she'd built up in her body by honest labor dissipated under cold raindrops blown by an even colder wind. Her husband worked on as if the sun still shone, so Catherine persevered, her skirt so heavy with mud she moved like an old woman through the field.

Stepping through the sucking mud, her shoes fell apart. She couldn't say she was any more uncomfortable for it. She wore only her dress and a chemise and was as wet as if she'd dunked herself in the bayou. And now she was barefoot. She thought of her old suitor Monsieur Moncrief and laughed to herself. He who was never seen without his red high heeled slippers and his beauty patch placed just so near his mouth -- if he could see her now.

Dupre disappeared into the forest and soon reappeared carrying a snared rabbit by the hind legs. "That's enough," he told her as he passed by on the way to the cabin.

She came in dripping and bedraggled to find he was building the fire and Débile was already in his place under the table, filling the cabin with the aroma of wet dog. The shivering Catherine had endured for the last hour turned into teeth chattering and knee knocking.

He glanced at her. "Get out of those wet clothes."

She was too tired and too cold to care whether he saw her nude, but he seemed intent on building the fire anyway. She stripped and struggled into her night gown, then wished she had thought to bring in a bucket of water. With trembling fingers, she unbuttoned her gown to put the wet dress back on to go to the creek with the bucket.

"What are you doing?" he said.

"We need water."

"I'll get it."

He reentered the weather and returned with the rabbit skinned and the bucket filled. Catherine held her hand out for the rabbit and plopped it in the pot. Giddy with fatigue, she nearly laughed out loud. See? She could cook as well as he.

She looked at him expectantly and he fished the usual sweet potatoes and an onion out of his pocket. Careful not to touch her, he handed them over and she cleaned them, and peeled the onion, before dropping them in the stew pot.

"Where are your shoes?" he said.

"Oh, I forgot them. They're on the edge of the field. The soles have come off."

He uttered a foul oath and marched back into the rain to retrieve them. When he came back, he tossed them on the floor near the fire and turned his back to her to strip off his clothes.

She no longer felt shy when he disrobed. He had a beautiful body -- why shouldn't she look at it when he had his back to her? He was her husband, was he not, even if only in name?

She wrinkled her nose, smelling her own stale sweat. She'd gotten past the need to change into fresh clothes five times a day, but the thought of putting that same filthy blue dress on tomorrow depressed her spirits. Her husband's pants and shirt reeked as much as her dress. She was going to have to figure out how to wash clothes.

"Do you have any laundry soap?" she asked as he pulled on his dry shirt.

"No."

No candles, no forks, no plates. An image of her fine china coffee cups came to her, the porcelain so thin she could see her fingers through it. Ah, well.

He dragged the chest out from under the bed and fished around in it to pull out a pair of well-polished leather boots, the kind the king's musketeers wore.

"I don't suppose -- were you a member of the king's royal guard?" she asked.

"Yes."

He unfolded the deep cuff at the top of the boots, laid her detached shoe sole on the leather for a pattern, and cut into the soft cuff with his hunting knife.

"Oh," she said. "You're ruining your good boots."

He drew in a deep breath. "I'm not a musketeer anymore."

He might not talk to her, or touch her, but she supposed he did take care of her. After the first day's blisters, he'd handed her a jar of grease and told her to rub it into her sore hands. It seemed to help -- the blisters now had blisters, but underneath, calluses were building.

Once he'd made a sole, he cut the upper part of her ruined shoes apart and made a template of them to cut more leather from the top of his boots.

"You're very skilled," she said, but of course he didn't answer her.

She watched him work, keeping quiet as he seemed to prefer. When the stew was ready she dished the potatoes and the meat onto the plank. "May I have the knife?"

He handed it over, handle first, and she cut the meat into pieces, dipped the cup and a gourd into the broth, and called him to supper.

They ate in silence, as always. Catherine had thought she'd be satisfied with a quiet man, but she'd changed her mind. Surely she could get more than five words at a time out of him.

"It's kind of you to make me new shoes."

"Not kindness. You cut your foot out there in the mud, you'll likely die of infection."

"And you would not have got your livre's worth out of me?" she said with a laugh.

Ah, she won a little smile out of him. "Something like that."

Catherine went to bed first but lay there watching the firelight play over his features as he bent over the leather. Did his body ache from working all day like hers did? Perhaps not. His shoulders and back were hard with muscle.

Her husband was an attractive man with his dark brows and eyes and his perfectly made body. It stung her that he didn't find her attractive in return. When had she ever known a man who didn't smile at her, flirt with her, eye her with appreciation? Her husband had no admiration in his glance, no desire for her person. Under the weight of his indifference, she felt drab and dull.

Remembering the hazards of self-pity, Catherine reached for a more positive thought. The attentive gentlemen at court had flattered, lied, and hidden their thoughts behind painted smiles. Jean Paul did none of that. If he said a thing, she could believe it. There was at least a measure of security in that.

He put aside the leather, stood up and stretched. "I'll go to Fort Louis in the morning for brads. Without a wooden outer-sole, these shoes won't last the week."

She sat up in the bed. "I'll go with you."

He gazed at her with his unreadable eyes. "Why?"

Because there will be people there to talk to. Because I don't want to be left here alone. "Why not?"

He shrugged "Suit yourself."

~~~

The next morning, Dupre pulled the dugout ashore at Fort Louis and helped his wife out of the boat. Débile loped off to discover whether any other dogs had left their scent to tantalize him.

Most people came into Fort Louis on Sunday. This was Thursday, as far as Dupre knew, and there were only a few Indians and the soldiers going about their business. If Catherine had hoped to find some of her friends from the *New Hope* in town, she'd be disappointed. Was she lonesome on the bayou with only him, Débile, and the pigs to talk to?

He knew what would happen once she got in the general store, his barefoot beauty. She'd finger the pretty ribbons, the bolts of calico, and gaze longingly at some frippery she had no use for, and then she'd turn those green eyes on him, begging him to buy them for her. Well, he wasn't going to. She'd chosen him that day, hadn't she, so she'd chosen to be a poor man's wife.

He counted out the exact number of brads he'd need to attach wooden soles to her shoes. He glanced at Catherine standing in the middle of the floor, her hands clasped behind her back, gazing at everything on the shelves. Things they didn't need, like shoe black and hairpins, even garters. Who the hell needed satin garters out here?

But she was still exhausted at the end of the day, and far too skinny. He added a ten-pound bag of corn meal to his order.

His wife -- God, what a thought -- his wife seemed focused on the stack of candles in the corner. She had not said a word, and had not turned her big eyes on him beseeching some luxury like hair ribbons or pomade.

He supposed candles were not much to ask for. He plucked three tapers off the display and added them to the nails and corn meal.

The smile she turned on him dazzled him down to his core. He turned away. He didn't want to be dazzled. He paid the merchant and walked back toward the dugout.

The weather had turned cold and it was clouding up again. He wore his old wool uniform coat, but she had only that worn shawl over her dress. She'd be shivering and shaking before they got back to the cabin.

She'd worked hard, had a third of the garden turned over, ready for planting. All that without whining even once about her blisters or the scant, monotonous diet, or having to sleep next to him in the narrow bed.

That first day, he'd expected the worst. When she had sat down on the stump he used for a chair, it was as if she perched on a satin sofa with gilded legs. She conducted herself like a damn queen, as elegant a woman as he'd ever seen. And when she'd fallen to her knees and cried, out in the field, he'd thought she was finished, that she would curl into a ball and stay that way until he carried her to bed.

But Catherine had pulled herself up, without even looking his way for sympathy or help, picked up her hoe, and got back to work. For a woman who arrived with soft white hands and a ragged gown that must once have cost a small fortune, she had grit. How could he not admire that?

She got into the dugout and held her hands out for the packages.

"Wait here," he said and marched back to the general store. When he returned, he handed her a cloth bundle, got in and paddled.

"What is it?" she asked.

"Open it out," he said.

She carefully untied the string and put it in the basket with the candles. If her speech was any measure, she had not grown up having to save string. She was learning.

A line appeared between her brows as she frowned, trying to make out what it was. She shook out the fabric and turned it so that the black embroidery on the dark green wool made her understand it was a woman's garment.

Catherine grabbed the cape to her breast and beamed at him with watery eyes.

"Thank you, Jean Paul."

He nodded and put his attention back on the stream.

That was the first time she'd used his Christian name. She was Catherine. He supposed he would learn to call her that, eventually.

He hadn't planned to go to the auction, didn't need a woman in his life. But it had been in the back of his mind ever since they'd posted the notice at the general store -- women were coming, not good girls certainly, but white women who would remember ale and fresh bread, songs, jokes, women who would be from *home*.

The morning he'd taken her had started out as any other day. His sow Suzette greeted him as usual, Débile nosed his big forehead into his hand. Then a deep and lonely quiet had descended on him like damp heavy air. He'd closed his eyes, shaken at how despair had crept in with no warning.

Week in and week out, he'd kept himself on the farmstead. How long had it been since he'd spoken to another human being?

With stunning urgency, a fire suddenly blazed in his chest. He had to get to Fort Louis before it was too late.

He strode toward the dugout when here came the piglets, running to him for a scratch and a pet. Beauregard plowed right into him and knocked him on his face in the mucky wallow.

What possessed him to not plunge into the stream to wash the muck off him he didn't know. He'd only known he had to get to the auction, had to find someone, anyone, to bring back to this lonely place. He'd almost been too late, and once he'd arrived, seeing that last bedraggled woman on the platform, he'd had second thoughts. Women wanted things. They wanted things done for them. He had nothing to offer a woman, did he? And yet, the words had come from somewhere -- *I'll take her*.

At the other end of the dugout, Catherine rubbed a hand over the closely woven wool, a small smile on her face. How had a beauty like her ever dared to come with a man as filthy as he'd been?

He looked away, wondering what she had done in her life that made her desperate enough to follow a man covered with pig muck. Murder, they'd said. He would have thought he would recognize another murderer, but she seemed peaceable, even cheerful.

The sky was about to open up when they reached home. "Make the fire," he told her and went to check his traps for rabbit or possum or whatever had been caught in the noose.

Suzette and her piglets must still be in the wood foraging for acorns, but they'd be back later. The wallow was their home, and . .

. well, wasn't he being fanciful? He was about to say the pigs kept close because he was their friend. Good thing he had another human being on the place or he was going to turn into a pig himself.

Thunder and lightning made for a cozy evening in the little cabin with the fire built high. He worked on Catherine's boots while she sat and watched the rain through the door, the cape wrapped tightly around her. It was nice, the two of them and Débile in silent comradeship, the rain on the thatch a comforting sound.

That panicky, trembling feeling that sometimes took him in the great quiet had not recurred since he'd brought her home. Well, he scoffed to himself. *Home.*

As dark fell, she tied the drape over the door and climbed into bed. He banked the fire, shucked off his clothes, and climbed in beside her.

She faced the wall. He lay with his back to her. His heart pounded and his loins ached with need.

Heat built up behind his eyes. Why not touch her? He'd married her. He couldn't believe Joubert or Villiers or any of the other men who had taken a woman lay beside her like a flaming log without touching her.

But they had not been burned and broken by Belinda Chevette. She had ruined him so that he could never trust another woman. Never.

He tucked his hands under his arms, clamped his jaw shut, and pretended to sleep.

# Chapter Five

*Marie Claude
The Old Life and the New*

Marie Claude had stitched the straightest, finest seam in all the village at home. That skill had not been enough to find her a husband, big and homely as she was. When the cow died and Papa got sick, there were too many of them to feed, so Marie Claude bravely set off for Paris hoping to become a seamstress.

At the first modiste she applied to, the mistress eyed her great hulking body and said, "Hold out your hands."

Marie Claude's fingers were blunt, her hands large and callused. The mistress had laughed. "La, I'd as soon ask an ox to hem a handkerchief." All the girls who bent over their needles, their soft hands working with delicate silk and lace, tittered. Flushing, Marie Claude exited feeling like a great lump, but she didn't give up. She tried again, and again, with no better reception at any of the other modistes.

Well. She'd known her hands and wrists were big and rough. They'd had to be to pull turnips from the soil or drag a stubborn donkey in from the fields. But what was she to do now? There was no place for her at home anymore. She'd spent her last coin. She would have to sleep under the bridge again tonight, hungry and cold.

The next day, she approached an ale house and asked for work. No, the proprietor said. He didn't need anyone. Try at the Swan and Goose. No, they didn't want her either. And so it went, another day without eating, so many days that she felt her belly was going to eat her from within if she didn't find food soon.

Under the bridge that night, one of the girls who hung about the street gave her a sliver of bread. "You could do what I do, you want to eat. You don't have to be pretty or nothing. Just willing."

Marie Claude did without food another day, light-headed and weak. She was going to die if she didn't do something. That night, she followed Chantal into the shadows where at last a man took her against a wall and gave her a coin. By the end of the evening, she'd made enough for a bowl of mutton stew and a mug of ale.

"You'll do better when you learn how to present yourself," Chantal assured her. "It's not so bad. You get used to them after a while, might even get some regulars who'll treat you pretty good." Chantal eyed her shrewdly. "You're lucky, you know. Being so big. The men aren't going to mess with you, knock you about, when you're as big as they are."

And so Marie Claude began her new life in the great city. As Chantal said, it wasn't so bad, most of the time. She didn't make as much money as the pretty girls, but there were men who liked it that she was so big and homely. One of her regulars, a man several inches shorter than she, enjoyed whispering insults as he pumped away at her, scorning her for her broad shoulders, for her potato nose. She charged him extra for the privilege, as Chantal had advised, and he paid it.

Not many of the girls were more than twenty-four or five, so Marie Claude figured she could hold out another year or two, until disease took her like it did most of the whores.

But that wasn't what happened. A big man, bigger than she was, took her down the alley, but he couldn't grow hard no matter what she did for him. He twisted his fist in her hair, pulling and yanking as his frustration grew. Suddenly he pushed her away. "You're so damned ugly nobody could get it up for you," he said and slapped her hard. Again and again he slapped her. She held her arms up to block him, but he kept coming at her. Hardly knowing she was going to do it, she pulled back her meaty arm and threw a punch into his jaw. Enraged, he came after her with his fists, pounding her face and then her gut so pain shot through her whole body.

He was going to kill her. She ducked under his arms and grabbed hold of his lapels, swung him around and bashed his head against the brick wall. He slumped to the ground, silent and still.

"Hey!" The one who'd been doing Chantal called out and ran over. "He's dead, you bloody whore."

Chantal gaped, her eyes wide. "What have you done?"

From the end of the shadowed alley, a man who'd been with La Belle Iris rushed up. "They'll hang you for this."

The man on the ground groaned and stirred. She bit her fist -- thank the Lord he was alive. Marie Claude turned on her heel and ran, but she didn't escape the two men.

The gendarmes took her away. Because her face and neck and chest were badly bruised, the judge declined to hang her. Instead, she was taken to the Salpêtrière and chained to the wall.

Then this was where she would die. She was glad her mama and papa would never know. They would imagine she worked in a milliner's shop sewing fine straight seams for a living.

It was early winter. The great stone hall of the prison was unheated, the walls damp, the straw dirty. It wouldn't take long, she hoped, before they took her out in a shroud.

Instead, she was taken blinking and squinting into the sunlight. She'd been chosen, she was told. King Louis needed her to apply her special skills for his loyal subjects in the new colony. She was so stupid, she thought at first she was to sew for them. But of course not. The Frenchmen toiling in Louisiana needed women.

And now here she was, in Louisiana, in Leopold Joubert's bed.

He said nothing about her looks, maybe because he was even uglier than she was. Not a very nice man, her husband. If she lay abed a moment longer than he did, he cursed at her and shoved her with his foot to get her moving. Another time, not ten minutes after he'd smelled up the whole cabin with his farts, he complained that she stank. And in the bed, after he'd done with her, he took his three fourths of the mattress right in the middle. Yes, he was a mean man.

But he hadn't beaten her yet. She wondered if she'd let him. He was her husband. Maybe she was supposed to let him. Well, if it wasn't too bad, she'd let him.

Or maybe she should show him the first time he tried it that he might end up with a broken nose. She'd wait and see.

She was confused about the poverty they lived in. Even on her papa's little plot they'd had a milk cow, so many chickens they sold the eggs, half a dozen pigs, and most years enough grain, pumpkins, turnips and such to last them the winter. Here they had provisions from the store, whatever monsieur hunted, some sweet potatoes and a row of green things left in the winter garden. Yet the man owned four slaves and his clothing was the most splendid she had ever seen. And there were more clothes in a big chest in a corner of the cabin. Linen shirts with lace at the cuffs, brocade waistcoats, silk stockings, shoes, one pair with painted red heels.

For all the fine clothes in the chest, however, Joubert wore rough clothing every day as he labored pulling out stumps or cutting logs for a new shed. He slept in the same bed as she, ate the same poor food, shat in the same privy. So much for fine clothing.

Monsieur was not a practical man. He worked hard, but he didn't work smart. He hewed logs and split them to build the shed only to find some pieces were too long and some were too short. She did not tell him how foolish he was -- perhaps the man had never measured anything in his life.

Worse, he had no idea how to use his slaves. The first time she saw them, her jaw fell open so far she could have caught flies. Four young men, their skin nearly black, with even blacker tattoos on their faces. They watched her like she might eye a strange dog, not sure if it would bite or wag its tail. And she watched them, too. They likely were not even Catholic. Who knew what they were capable of?

In the next days, they seemed harmless enough. They worked most of the morning with axes and chisels, hollowing out great chunks of a giant tree. In the afternoon, however, they were likely to lay about in a sunny spot even though Marie Claude and Joubert worked from breakfast till dark. No one in her village except the very old or the very ill just sat around and expected food to appear on their plates.

Marie Claude gave it some thought. She would not like to be a slave herself. She would not have these men mistreated. But Joubert allowed them to help themselves to the corn meal, dried peas, and salt pork. Maybe that was the problem.

Early the next morning she walked across the cleared field to the shack where the four men slept. The lazy things were still abed. She knocked on the wall with her big fist and called them to get up.

They came out, hitching up their pants, yawning and rubbing the sleep out of their eyes. Pierre bent over coughing. They all seemed to have a cough, maybe got it from each other over the winter. She would look along the bayou and in the woods to see if she recognized any of the herbs her mother had used to soothe coughs. Maybe ginger grew here, or licorice root.

She waited for Pierre to catch his breath, and then she told them how it would be from now on.

"I'll give you your rations every night. If you work hard all day, you'll be hungry and I'll give you the full ration. If you linger in bed or lie about, you won't need as much food and I won't give you as much."

They looked at each other with their dark eyes and then looked at her. She couldn't read those strange faces with the black skin and the tattoos. Maybe they were thinking they could knock her down and take what they wanted. Well, two of them were bigger than she was, but the other two were not. She'd make them sorry if they tried it.

"You understand?" Maybe they didn't even speak French.

"*Oui*, madame."

And that was that. She hoped these poor souls did not resent her taking control of something Joubert had been loose about. As for whether her husband resented it, well, she didn't live for smiles from him. This was her farmstead too, now, and she would see it prosper.

# Chapter Six

## *Agnes*
## *Remembering*

Agnes "went away," as Catherine called it, whenever life was more than she could bear. Safe inside her own head, she didn't have to feel anything, not rage or fear or hate or grief. Where she went, there was only safety, like being wrapped in a soft gray woolen blanket, no light piercing the fiber, no despair penetrating it.

Now that she was trying very hard to stay present in her own life, all those emotions she had suppressed crept back into her mind and bubbled to the surface. Perhaps here in this small cabin in the wilderness, only one personable gentleman to please, a man who had actually married her, Agnes felt safe enough to waken from her long stupor. And once wakened, all the feelings she had suppressed came roaring out of her consciousness.

Rage was the first emotion to overtake her. She woke in the night, her hands fisted, her teeth clamped shut. The trembling of her body finally woke her husband. Valery sleepily placed his hand on her belly to soothe her, muttering some incomprehensible words of comfort before slipping back into sleep.

The next day Agnes exhausted herself carrying around such anger she could barely speak, nor could she relax her body for him that night when he wanted her.

"What has happened, *ma petite*? Your body is hard and stiff. Have I hurt you?"

She heard the genuine puzzlement in his voice and touched his cheek in the dark. "You have not hurt me, husband." He resumed his exertions and she willed her body to loosen.

The first night her husband had taken her, he had been cool and perfunctory with her body. Gradually, he had come to treat her less like a convenient vessel for his needs and more like another human being. She had not expected, had never experienced, a considerate lover, but the last night, she had actually felt a stirring in her lower belly. Perhaps, one day, she might even experience this famous pleasure some of the whores talked about.

Now, however, the anger she had so long trapped deep down in her heart had hold of her, and the memories flooded back.

That day when Gaspar had come to collect her from her father's bookstore, she'd looked at him and said, "What?"

"You are mine, *chérie*. Didn't your father tell you?"

"What?" she'd said again, her wits completely flown.

She turned to Papa and saw the truth on his face.

"Monsieur Gaspar is fond of you. Surely you noticed, Agnes?"

She turned back to Gaspar, who eyed her with a smug grin on his face. *Fond*, Papa called it? The man had ogled her ever since he first came into the store three weeks before. His gaze had followed her as she shelved a stack of books, making goosebumps rise on her arms.

He had been well-dressed, his wig freshly powdered, his cane topped with a silver knob. Father had hastened to wait on such an important looking man.

"A book of Far Eastern poses," he had requested.

"Poses?" her father had said.

Gaspar had leaned forward and said in a whisper Agnes was clearly meant to hear. "Poses of Pleasure, sir."

Papa retrieved a book from beneath the counter where he kept the volumes Agnes was not supposed to see. She'd known what they were about, of course. She had looked when she was sixteen and Papa was out of the store.

However, Gaspar had not been satisfied merely with the book. He returned again and again to purchase some trifle so that he could ogle Agnes, eye her breasts, undress her with his eyes. He repulsed her with his big belly, his fat neck and fleshy red lips.

She hated the man, and she was meant to go with him?

"Papa, no. What can you mean?"

Gaspar had taken her arm and squeezed it. "Your papa means that he has foolishly gambled away all his assets, including this very fine store. You, however, are a very good exchange, *ma chérie*. I am more than happy to forgive your father's debts."

Terrified, Agnes had struggled against his bruising grip. "Please, Papa!" But Papa had taken his sad face into the back room so that he would not see his only child dragged out the door and into Gaspar's waiting carriage.

That night, Gaspar opened his book of amorous poses. She turned her face away, but he grabbed her by the chin and forced her to look. "This one," he said. "We will begin with this one."

Gaspar was a big man, she was a small woman. She didn't even try to fight him. She had no spirit left anyway -- her own father, selling her as if she were no more than a pig or a donkey.

He coaxed her to assume the pose in the book. "Here, *ma chère*, lie just so. No, your legs are like this, see?"

Agnes ignored him. She went away instead, the first time in her life she did so. When she wouldn't cooperate, he took hold of her legs and arms and twisted her body to match the pose of pleasure he desired.

When he was sated, he instructed her that she would remain in the bedroom the following day. A footman would bring her a tray each mealtime, and she would spend her time studying the exotic poses. "We will work our way through the book, mademoiselle. You will overcome this virginal shyness, and then what a great pleasure we will have together, *n'cest pas*?"

The next night he entered her chamber clad in a canary yellow dressing gown and reeking of musky cologne. "Here, mademoiselle, see I have brought you something pretty to wear." Red satin garters, black stockings, a corset in red and black. "Put them on, my dear," he said. He meant to watch her, it seemed. Agnes did not refuse outright; she simply did not respond. When he grew impatient with her, he dressed her himself and made her walk back and forth across the bedchamber while he watched her with fervid eyes. Then he made her look at the second illustration in his favorite book. "Assume the pose, my dear. If you are very good, I will order a pot of chocolate for you."

For two weeks, Agnes remained unresponsive physically and mentally, and Monsieur Gaspar discovered bedding a woman who was limp as a rag doll did not feed his fantasies. He might have beaten her for his disappointment, but he did not. Instead, since the poor pleasure she offered did not justify the great sum of money he had paid for her, Gaspar recouped some of his loss by selling her to Madame De Bree's brothel.

Madame installed her in a small but elegant bed chamber decorated in red and gold. Agnes by then was merely an empty receptacle of cold flesh, feeling nothing. She hardly noticed the men who came to her bed, hardly noticed what they did with her. She proved so unpopular with the clientele that Madame finally tossed her out. Thus, at the age of seventeen, Agnes found herself on the street where she wandered, starving, hardly present, until the gendarmes picked her up and sent her to the Salpêtrière.

Now that Agnes was wakened and present on this little farm in the great territory of Louisiana, it was difficult to control all those unruly storms raging inside her. She calmly, placidly cut up a head of cabbage when, as if from nowhere, searing anger at her father's betrayal suddenly boiled up from her core. She slashed at the skirts of her dress, a keening like a wounded animal echoing in the empty cabin. Blood soaked the fabric and the salty scent permeated the air before she realized she had scored her thighs with the blade.

The knife dropped from her hand and she folded onto her knees. Gasping sobs ripped through her, shaking her whole body.

Gradually, she calmed. The steady rhythm of her husband's chopping firewood outside soothed her. There was no betrayal here.

She fingered the slashes in her dress and laughed, and her body trembled all over again. She only had two dresses. She would have to mend this one. And how would she disguise the wounds on her thighs when her husband asked her to disrobe tonight? Shaken and emptied, she got to her feet and pulled up her skirts to examine the cuts on her legs. They were not deep, nor so very many. She would claim she was too cold to lay open to his gaze until they healed. He seemed an accommodating man. He would not insist.

She cleaned her legs with water from the bucket and changed her dress.

Over the next days, her terrible rage evolved into a tearing grief for what she'd lost, the life she'd loved in the bookstore, the future she had expected as the wife of some pleasant, scholarly man. Most of all she grieved the loss of the father who had shared quiet evenings with her, the two of them interrupting one another's reading to share a thought or a clever phrase.

If only she could grieve in the simplicity of a natural loss, a father who died and over whose grave she could pray. But her own father had robbed her of the chance to love him in life and beyond. He had chosen to forfeit his daughter rather than face penury and disgrace. If only she'd known he was gambling again -- but what use was *if only*?

Carrying the heavy weight of grief on her back and the heat of anger in her chest nearly pushed her back into her safe haven of gray mist, but she resisted it.

*Listen*, she told herself. *Birds are singing. Look. Trees are blooming.* She picked a branch of spring blossoms and examined them minutely. What a wonder, each tiny bloom pink with a streak of red near the stamen. She held them to her nose and breathed in.

*This* was life. This flower, birdsong, white clouds, sun glinting on water -- these were reason enough to keep breathing. Reason enough to let feeling come, wash through her, pain her -- and yet stay in the world anyway.

Throughout March, in fits and starts, some days more successfully than others, Agnes grew strong enough to experience anger, fear, grief, disappointment, and yet survive them all. She had two years of living to make up for, and she didn't fault herself for sudden flashes of anger that stiffened her body or flashes of grief that resulted in sudden spates of sobs.

Her husband Monsieur Villiers, who talked excessively of himself, was unaware of the storms lashing her.

The day he found her crying behind the privy, she'd thought her belly would tear open with retching sobs. That Papa could have given her to Gaspar, could condemn her to a life of shame, wracked her whole body with grief and fury.

Vaguely, carelessly kind, her husband took her in his arms and patted her back. "Poor dear. It will pass," he said without enquiring what *it* was. "Why don't you go down to the pond and wash your face? That's a good girl."

If her husband had no curiosity about her at all, that meant she didn't have to relive the shame of telling him what her father had done, what she had become in the brothel. That meant that every day she found it a little easier to stay present.

~~~

All day Agnes tended the chickens, hoed the garden, and smiled at her husband without allowing herself to lapse into that stupor that had been her refuge for so long, yet she yearned for something, a touch of magic, to soothe her troubled heart.

In the evening, Agnes visited the small pond near the house to look for her friends the will-o-the-wisps. Most often, the mysterious glowing balls failed to appear, but this night the hazy green lights hovered above the marshy pond as if they'd been waiting for her. If only they could hear her, she would tell them how she longed to disappear into the night with them. Where the swamp fairies lived, there would be no burning rage, no grief, no loneliness.

The delicate balls of gas rose slowly and then floated down again. Agnes reached a hand out, hoping they would come to her, hoping they had come *for* her. Instead, they drifted silently away. "Take me with you," she whispered, but her fairy friends dissipated into the night air, leaving Agnes behind. Her heart too heavy for her legs to support, she slipped to her knees and put her hands over her face.

"Agnes?"

*Oh not now, don't ask me to smile at you now.*

Valery touched her shoulder. "You are unwell?"

"No, monsieur. I am well." She began to rise, but Valery pressed her shoulder down and sat beside her.

"I think you are unhappy, madame."

She smiled bitterly into the dark. "It's nothing."

Agnes's husband's shoulder brushed against hers. "It is a hard thing, to leave France, eh? You miss someone you left behind?"

*Ah no please, not kindness.* She didn't know how she could keep rein on her emotions if he were kind to her.

"You are not alone here, Agnes. I am perhaps not the best of husbands, but I will try to be good to you."

When he pulled her close so that her head rested against his shoulder, a great sob erupted. Her whole body shook with the force of her grief, and Valery held her, murmuring soothing words and stroking her hair.

"Come," he said when the storm had passed. "Let's to bed. I will hold you until you sleep and tomorrow will be better. You'll see."

When Agnes woke in the morning, she was still in her husband's arms. He had not taken her last night as he usually did. Perhaps he was a more sensitive man than she had realized. She stared at his sleeping profile, the dark lashes curled against his high cheeks, his strong, straight nose, and the sharply defined lips.

She had recognized that he was a handsome man, but what was now clear was that her husband, who had seemed insensitive and totally absorbed in himself, was after all capable of sympathy and kindness.

She cupped his cheek with her hand, raised on to her elbow, and kissed him softly.

His eyes opened, dark and deep. He returned her gaze, and for the first time, she felt he truly saw her, not just a whore, not just a woman to whom he'd carelessly given his name. Her. Agnes.

She kissed him again. Murmuring her name, his arms came around her, and in the sunshine coming through their window, they made love on their narrow cot.

Something had changed. Valery stroked and touched her in new ways. He nuzzled her neck and kissed her behind her ear. When he finally entered her, gently, slowly, she drew a deep shuddering breath. *Oh.* She had never experienced this filling of her body as pleasure. He began to rock into her, giving her time to match his rhythm.

He waited for her, coaxing her, while her body began to simmer, then to smolder and to burn. She ached for the conflagration, reached for it, and in a sudden burst of sparks, she cried out and lost herself in brilliant explosive pleasure.

With rapid, frantic thrusts, Valery plunged into her for his own completion, and for the first time Agnes gloried in the heat and power in a man's body. Valery rolled off and held her in his arms while they both drifted back into sleep.

# Chapter Seven

*Catherine and Jean Paul*
*Nearly Love*

The warm spring weather held, a harbinger of the summer heat. Jean Paul judged it wouldn't last long and then the tail end of winter would charge back for one more cold spell, but today, Jean Paul worked bare chested, sweat rolling down his back.

The sounds of children laughing and hollering broke the usual stillness of the place.

Catherine held her hoe upright and called to him, "Who's that?"

"Indian kids. They play in the spring sometimes."

"Do we know them? Their families?"

"Not really. I've traded with them for corn now and then. For a deer hide, once."

"What do you give them in return?"

Jean Paul heaved a breath. "A little labor. They don't have an axe."

"So you do know some of them."

"I guess."

"Could we -- "

"No." She was going to want to invite the neighbors for tea, was she? Offer them little cakes and did they take one lump or two? They were Indians for heaven's sake.

He walked off leaving her with her mouth open. Even now he could surprise her with how rude he could be? She should know by now that this was a solitary life here on the bayou. Everyone worked from sunup to sundown, there was no time for a social life, nor an inclination for one, either. At least, not on his part.

After half a morning chopping away at an oak tree, must be three feet across, he set his axe aside and picked up his gourd for a long cool drink. The mindlessness of physical labor had deserted him in the last days and even as he swung his axe, memories crowded in. He had given Belinda his whole heart, had believed that they would marry, maybe buy a small farm in Provence near home. Fill a cottage with children. That's what he'd believed. Had she plotted against him from the beginning?

The bitterness in his soul fouled the taste of the water. What a fool he was, to let the past rule him, but he had not been able to break Belinda's perverse hold on him.

He'd rest. Then he would cut another tree. That's all he knew to do.

He wiped his hand across his mouth and watched Catherine wielding her hoe. He'd sharpened it last night sitting by the fire, so at least it had a good edge. She had improved, most of the effort now in her arms and shoulders. If he'd been inclined to laugh at her, it would have been those first days when she'd chopped the dirt by bending at the waist, up and down, like a woodpecker after bugs in a tree.

With her back to him, she bent into the business of preparing the earth for the spring garden. Her backside was shaped like an upside down heart, the faded silk clinging to her hips. There wasn't another man on the continent who wouldn't have bedded her by now.

He thought about it. Too much of the time. All of the time.

But he could not put aside the feel of Belinda in his arms, the taste of her lips, the soft whispers in his ear. He'd think of turning over in the bed to Catherine, and Belinda's face would hover in his mind's eye.

Catherine still wore the bedraggled blue dress he'd first seen her in. He knew she had a cotton dress in the basket she'd brought with her. Why didn't she wear it? He would not ask. They shared a plot of land, a hearth, a bed. That was all there would be between them.

Jean Paul wiped a sleeve over his sweaty face. He wasn't much of a husband was he? What were the vows? To love her and honor her all the days of his life? Was it honoring his wife to keep another woman between them? He knew it was not. But he at least meant to take care of her.

He watched her laboring like a peasant. She was unprepared for this life. What would happen to her if he fell ill, got snake bit or carried off by a big puma?

He should at least show her how to find help even if the dugout were washed away or burned or -- well, whatever catastrophe descended on them.

"Catherine," he called.

When she looked up, he tipped his head toward the forest.

"Leave your hoe," he said. "Débile, come."

She followed him in amongst the trees. "You're going to cut a particular tree out here?"

"No."

"Then why do you carry your axe?"

"Wolves, boars, snakes, pumas."

That hushed her up. He wondered if she had ever seen any of those animals, certainly not a puma. He wasn't surprised when she started in again.

"What do you call that tree with the white buds?"

He sighed. He didn't know these trees any better than she did. "White bud tree."

"And the one with the red buds?"

"Red bud tree."

He heard her snort behind him and smiled in spite of himself.

It was dark in here even on a bright day, the tree canopy thick and overhanging with patches of open sunlight. He remembered the enchantment of the forest last spring when the blooms opened and turned the woods into a garden of white and pink and green.

"Where are we going?"

The woman couldn't be quiet.

"Jean Paul, where are we going?"

He'd heard her ask the first time. He had once been courteous, he'd once been nice. "The Biloxi village is up this way."

"I didn't even know there was a path back here," Catherine said.

He blew a breath out, trying to be patient. Really, she at least deserved a husband who didn't snap at her. "I discovered it one day when I was tracking a deer, hoping for a clear shot. I lost the deer, but I found the Indian village."

"And they're friendly?"

"This village is. They've been good to the settlers, acting as guides, showing men deer trails, nut trees."

Overhead, gray and white birds sang lustily. Behind him, Catherine whistled a fair imitation of the bird song. Jean Paul turned around and stared at her. She was very good, better even than he was.

She bristled at his look. "You never whistle?"

He turned back and continued up the trail, but he heard her mutter, "Of course you don't." He almost laughed. Maybe, someday, he'd whistle for her and make her smile, or blush. It would be a fine thing to see a blush on Catherine's face.

When they reached a path branching off from the main trail, Jean Paul stopped. "The village is that way."

"Aren't we going visiting?"

"No. Débile," he called, bringing him back. "I just want you to know where it is."

"Oh." She looked like a child denied her Sunday treat.

"Maybe later on, in the summer, I'll take you."

"So. We just turn around and go back now?"

"That's right."

Jean Paul could feel sullen waves radiating from her where she walked behind him. Did she think the Indian women were dressed in their best skins and calicos, awaiting morning callers, the tea pot at the ready?

He turned around and stopped. "Catherine, I don't want you on this path by yourself."

"It looks easy enough to follow."

"I'm not worried about your getting lost. I'm worried a puma will carry you off."

Behind him, Catherine recited, "Wolves, boars, snakes, pumas. What is a puma?"

"Have you ever seen a tabby cat stalk a bird and pounce on it? Pretty soon, there's nothing left but the feathers?"

"So a puma is a cat?"

"A big cat. Big as Débile. With proportional teeth and claws."

"As big as Débile? Then you're quite right. I do not wish to be carried off by a puma."

They ate a cold lunch. While Catherine cleaned the table, Jean Paul stepped back into the sunshine. God, he needed a bath.

"Want a swim, boy?" he said to Débile.

With a single bright bark, Débile signaled that he knew that word and pranced joyfully toward the bayou.

On the way, Jean Paul stopped at the wallow to speak to Suzette and the piglets where they dozed in the shade. He squatted on his heels and discussed the cost of bread with his sow, rubbing her ears, listening to her soft grunts of appreciation while Débile nosed the drowsy piglets.

"Jean Paul?"

He straightened up.

"You're going into the river?"

He nodded, noticing how red her face was. She needed a hat.

"Do you mind? If I come in with you? It's just that . . . I'm afraid to go in by myself."

"You can't swim?"

"No, it's the gators. I mean, I can't swim, but it's not so deep right here, is it?"

He had meant to take his clothes off before he waded into the water. Did she intend to take her dress off? Out here in the light of day?

He'd seen her nearly naked, of course, when she changed into her night dress, but that had been only quick glimpses. Stolen glimpses. In a dim cabin with only the fire for light.

His mouth was dry but he managed to swallow. "Come on, then."

Débile ran ahead to splash into the water, sending little waves all the way across the bayou. One of the piglets decided to play rather than sleep and followed Débile into the water. Dog and pig climbed out on the other bank and snuffled at all the interesting scents creatures had left in the night.

At water's edge, Jean Paul pulled off his boots, then stripped off the rest of his clothes. He waded in, shivering as his heated body met the cold water. He took a few strokes into the stream and turned to see if Catherine followed him.

She had her back to him, tugging the dress over her head. Underneath she wore a silk sheathe and nothing else. She turned to the bayou without looking at him and carefully stepped into the water. "It's cold."

"You'll get used to it."

With her arms wrapped around herself, she eased in, the water closing over her pale flesh. She'd probably never been in water that wasn't heated just to the right temperature, and no doubt scented with rose petals.

She was in up to her waist, then to the top of her bosom. She just stood there a moment before she took a deep breath and moved her arms through the water.

"You should learn how to float," Jean Paul said.

"Float? Why?"

"So you won't drown. You can float even if you can't swim."

"Show me."

Hell. If he lay on his back floating, his private parts would be on full display. At least the water had shrunk the interesting bits. Somewhat.

He lay back, spread his arms, and stared at the sky. Then he folded in on himself and treaded water.

"Try it," he said.

Catherine spread her arms and splashed backwards. She immediately submerged and came up coughing, water streaming out of her hair.

He was going to have to coach her. To touch her.

He swam to her and put his hand on her back. "Try it again."

He helped her lie back and kept her afloat with his fingertips. She was stiff as a corpse.

"Relax. Let the water hold you. It will if you let it."

The wet silk of her shift clung to her breasts, the fabric so shear he could see the rosy color of her aureole, the nub of her nipple. She was staring at him, red-faced, and he looked away.

"Relax," he said again, this time keeping his eyes on the far bank of the bayou. "I've got you."

He could feel her body loosening.

She trusted him. Somewhere inside, maybe it was in his heart, an ache began to throb.

She closed her eyes and let the water carry her. Finger by finger, he let her go. "You've got it," he said softly. "You're floating."

Her eyes still closed, she smiled.

Slowly, so as not to disturb her equilibrium, he backed away, but she heard him anyway and panicked and sank, her hands grasping at air.

He hauled her up and she clung to him, her arms around his neck, the length of her body pressed against his.

If he wrapped his arms around her, he'd never let her go. If he kissed her -- he couldn't. He mustn't.

Gently, but firmly, he set her away from him. "You're all right now." He waded back to shore and put his smelly clothes back on.

Once she was out of the water, he strode back to his axe.

The rest of the day, they worked, they ate a silent supper, and they went to bed not long after dark. He lay awake, aware of her heat behind him, of her breathing as she fell asleep. Finally his weary body pulled him into his own dreams.

In the darkest hours, he woke when Catherine gasped and knocked him in the back.

"What is it?"

She groaned and bumped into him again.

"What?" He rolled over and tried to see her by the little light the embers cast. This was no nightmare. She was panting hard, gripping her leg.

"Cramp?" he said. He shoved her hands aside and kneaded the knot in her calf. Good heavens, it was bigger than a hen's egg.

"Big breaths -- slow it down," he told her.

"Oh God Jean Paul it hurts!"

He dug into the muscle, pressing on the spasm with his thumbs. She couldn't stifle the moans and could not slow her breath down.

"You'll faint if you don't quit breathing so fast."

His fingers eased from deep kneading to firm strokes up and down her lower leg. "Flex your foot, slowly, just a little."

"Ahhh!"

"Too soon. Wait a while."

She still breathed hard, as if she'd run up the grand staircase at Versailles with stays tied too tight. He could just picture her doing that, her gown splendid, her face radiant, on her way to some grand fête for the king.

His fingers gentled, stroking more slowly, warming the muscle. He could feel the spasm ease under his probing as her breathing returned to normal. One hand on her instep, the other on her calf, he gently flexed her foot.

"Better?"

"Oh my stars, I've never felt such pain."

"If we had horse liniment, I'd rub some in to the skin. But we don't have any horse liniment. Or a horse," he added with a smile.

"You'd put horse liniment on me?" She sounded outraged.

He withdrew his hands. "Forgive me. I had forgotten that the limbs of princesses do not respond to remedies the rest of humanity uses."

He rolled off the bed and pulled his shirt and boots on.

"I didn't mean . . ."

He left the cabin. It was cold, too cold for a thin shirt, but he walked down to the bayou to see the moon gleam on the water.

He had over-reacted, taking offense like that. She never mentioned her former life, as evident as it was that she had been born to finer things. She didn't put on airs like she was above him or anyone else. He hadn't been fair.

He didn't know what to do with her, that's all. Another man, any other man would bed her and work her and that would be as complicated as it got. It was more complicated for him though. He'd never been one to take bedding lightly. He had given his heart to only one woman, and look what that had got him.

He heaved in a breath. The sky was clear, the stars were out. He supposed he should apologize. He'd rather pull a bull out of a bog, though.

He walked back to the cabin, shucked off his boots, and lay down. She had her back to him, squeezed up against the wall as she had done the first nights.

"You all right?" he asked.

"Yes. Thank you," she said, her voice small and cold.

What if he took her in his arms? Just to comfort her? Would she let him? He lay on his back, imagining it, her body against his, her head tucked under his chin.

Why did he do this to himself? He knew why. Because the wounds in his heart pained him more than the ache in his body. He turned on his side, his back to her, and pretended to sleep.

# Chapter Eight

*Marie Claude*
*Blue Gold*

As bad as it had been on board the *New Hope*, Marie Claude had not been lonely. The girls had crowded together for comfort and warmth. They'd helped each other through sea-sickness and fever and fear. Now she knew what loneliness felt like. Like the deepest purple silence.

At home Mama used to sing as she milked the cow, and Papa hummed as he worked. Her little sisters Annique and Evangeline giggled away their days, and in the evening the family would tell stories until it was warmer to be in bed than sit by the dying fire.

Monsieur Joubert had little to say to her or she to him. The slaves talked among themselves and sometimes she would hear them laughing or singing. But they were men, foreign and strange, and they were slaves.

She could manage though. Quiet never killed anybody. She liked being outdoors, liked working the soil. There was pleasure in seeing her garden ever closer to being a very fine garden indeed. And this was pretty country, so much green, so many birds, and here was a tiny frog.

She bent to lift it carefully into her palm. No bigger than her fingernail, it still had a nub of a tail from its tadpole days. Gently, she rubbed her finger down its back. At home, the frogs in the pond had sung to them on summer evenings, almost like music, it was.

Joubert paused as he passed by her. "What you wasting time on now?"

She held the little creature out for him to admire, but her husband knocked her hand, spilling the frog on to the ground. With a smirk, Joubert stomped on it, grinding it into the dirt.

He laughed at her gasp and walked on.

Marie Claude pressed her hand against her belly, sickened. She'd never seen a meaner thing done in her life. She'd rather her husband hit her than see such meanness.

Thomas, the oldest of the young slaves, walked over and looked at the ruined frog at her feet. After a quick look at her face, he knelt in the dirt, dug a small hole for the frog's burial, and smoothed the dirt back over it.

Thomas gave her a brief nod and went back to the log he was chiseling. Tears threatened to fill Marie Claude's eyes. The rest of the day, she held that small act of kindness close.

What made Leopold Joubert so mean? Because he was ugly? Well, she was ugly, and so was her brother Michel, and they were not mean.

At mid-day Thomas moved over on the log where he sat and nodded at the space for her to sit down with them. Eat with the slaves? Well, why not? Joubert certainly didn't enjoy eating with her in the middle of the day. He saw enough of her pudding face at night, he said.

The four men spoke French, but they were hard to follow. They talked among themselves in their own kind of French, and Marie Claude was content just to sit there for the company.

This was nice, she thought, and was glad she wasn't alone on this place with the hateful man she'd married. But she did wonder about Joubert. All those fancy clothes in the chest, but none of the fancy manners she expected a finely dressed man to have. But what did she know of finely dressed men?

Well, if she wanted to know something, she would just have to ask. After supper, she said, "Why did you leave France?"

He glared at her. "How is that any of your business?"

She shrugged. "Did you have land?"

"Sure, I had land. Acres of it. I'm no peasant."

"Why did you leave it?"

"Enough with your damn questions."

"You kill somebody?"

"No," he said in a mocking voice. "I didn't kill somebody. Maybe I should have."

"They run you off your land though, didn't they? Why else you leave it?"

"Shut your trap and go to bed."

Already she knew she would never have a friend in Leopold Joubert.

~~~

Spring progressed. It must be nearly April, Marie Claude guessed.

Monsieur Joubert gripped her elbow and marched her toward the sunny patch he'd been clearing for days.

"Right here," he said and pushed a leather bag into her chest. "This is where you'll plant the indigo."

She'd never heard of indigo. She peered into the bag.

"They're worth their weight in gold, these seeds," Joubert told her.

"What are they, some kind of bean?"

He laughed in his nasty way. "Never you mind. Just do it right."

It would be easier to *do it right* if she knew what kind of seeds they were. She guessed her husband didn't know any more than she did about how to please these seeds, so she experimented. She planted a row with just enough soil to cover them, another row just a little deeper, and another deeper yet. She'd know something in a week or two when the seeds sprouted. If they sprouted.

And then it rained. And rained and rained. She was afraid her vegetable garden and the seeds worth their weight in gold were going to be washed away.

"This is unusual, so much rain in just a few days?"

"Rains all the damn time," he said.

So she slogged through the mud to save her garden and the golden seeds. Using a spade, she cut a small trench on each side of the rows for the water to drain into. She had never grown a single crop that thrived in sodden ground.

Gently she replanted the shallowest seeds, pleased at the familiar feel of good black earth under her fingernails. She had not been homesick at all when she was in such trouble, on the streets and then in the prison, but now with a field to hoe, plants to nurture, she thought of her father's little farm. She would never see her family again, and that hurt, but she would not likely have seen them again if she'd become a seamstress in Paris. Well, this was the life she had to live, and so she tucked the memories away to enjoy on a sunnier day.

Washing the mud off her hands and feet, Marie Claude thought about all those women she'd known on the *New Hope*. Most of them were rough city girls who had been cheated or lied to or used by some man until they found themselves on the streets and then in the Salpêtrière. They wouldn't know the first thing about planting a garden. That Bridget, who spoiled herself every chance she got -- likely a life spent on her back had not taught her how to tend chickens.

As for the few well-spoken ones, she had no idea how they came to be in the prison. They didn't ask each other questions like that. Little Agnes, for instance -- what had happened to her to make her go off into her own head like she did? Nothing good.

And Catherine. Marie Claude suspected from the posh way Catherine spoke that she was unaccustomed to outdoor labor of any kind. Now she thought about it, she herself was probably better suited to this new life than any of the other women.

Well, they would learn. They all would, if they meant to survive.

Marie Claude passed by the slaves out working in the rain just like she was. It was only a sprinkling right now, but it wouldn't help Pierre's cough.

The four of them had been chipping away at lengths cut from a huge cypress tree. She could see now they were shaping the logs into rectangular vats.

"What are they for?" she asked Thomas.

"Indigo."

She looked at the row upon row of her seedlings. They seemed to be hardy stock, flourishing in spite of downpours the last few days. And they were to end up in these vats?

Thomas straightened, his chisel in his hand, and wiped the rain out of his eyes. "We chop the indigo when the buds form. Pile the plants in here with water, let them ferment, then drain the water into the next vat, and then to the next, until we have cakes of indigo. Blue dye."

"You know how to do this?"

"It's why your monsieur bought us. We know about indigo."

Marie Claude eyed the vats, the first nearly finished, the second one looking better, the third still a log. "And he will sell this indigo?"

"He will be a rich man, madame."

She didn't miss the flat tone in Thomas's voice. He was looking at her and she wondered what she was supposed to understand from that look. That monsieur would be rich, and Thomas and the others would still be slaves? Yes, she understood that.

She herself couldn't imagine being rich. In fact, she had no real desire for it. She would certainly like another dress, a washtub, a new pair of boots. Some chickens. And while she was wanting, she supposed she should wish for a nicer man for a husband.

"Hm," she said. She frowned when Pierre coughed, harsh and urgent from deep in his chest. All four of them had coughs, most of the time, it seemed like. Especially when it was raining, but Pierre's was the worst.

"I'll make some more of that ginger tea."

Thomas was giving her that strange look again. Well, he could look all he wanted, but she had work to do.

After supper, a lantern lit on the mantel piece, she said to her husband, "So you're going to make dye out of those indigo plants."

"That's right."

"Thomas was telling me how you'll use those vats they're working on. He said you'll be a rich man."

"I'll be the richest man in the colony in a few years. Only one other indigo processor in the whole territory, and all these settlers are going to grow indigo for my vats."

"Hm," she said.

"That's your answer to everything, isn't it? *Hm.*" He made it sound like a pig grunt. "Guess you're thinking about being a rich woman when I'm a rich man. Don't count on it, *wife.*"

Now what did he mean by that? When he got rich, she wouldn't be his wife anymore? Well, that would be all right with her. She could clear a plot of land for herself, grow vegetables, fish in the bayou. She'd be fine without a husband.

# Chapter Nine

*Catherine and Jean Paul
Rejection*

Jean Paul woke when his wife's feet tangled in his legs, feet so cold they chilled his calves. She was curled on her side, her braid fallen into the cleft between her breasts. Carefully so as not to wake her, he curled the free end of her braid around his finger, feeling how silky it was. His knuckles brushed her breast; quickly, he withdrew his hand.

Once he had not considered whether a woman had treachery in her heart when he bedded her. Once he'd thought women were made of sunshine and roses, softness and love. He could never believe that again.

He startled, a drop of water falling on his face. Damnation. It had rained all night and now they had leaks, two of them dripping steadily on the foot of the bed. No wonder her feet were cold.

He got the fire going; she rose and dragged the bedding closer to the hearth to dry out. Naturally, his dog strolled over to lie on the blanket. "No, Débile," she said with a laugh, gently shoving him off the blanket. Here she was in a small cabin with a smelly dog, and a smelly man, if it came to that, and she laughed.

The thin cotton nightgown she wore had no embroidery, no lace, no ruffles, no ribbons. He could see her body quite plainly when she bent over the blanket, laying it out in front of the fire to dry. There was a little meat on her bones now and he thought her breasts were fuller.

He turned away. No point looking at her. He didn't want that in his life.

"It's going to rain all day. You stay inside."

"What are you going to do?"

"Patch up the leaks in the roof."

"I could cut the fronds for you and hand them up."

He stared at her. She'd be muddy, wet, and cold if she came out to help him. If she should take a fever . . . A little shiver of fear coursed through him. Out here, no medicine, no doctor. He didn't think he could bear to lose her, not now he was used to feeling her warmth in the bed behind him, to seeing her working about the garden, to hearing her talk to Suzette and the piglets.

"I have no desire to play nursemaid to a sick woman. Stay inside."

~~~

Catherine had watched Jean Paul shave this morning. She'd never seen a man about his toilette. It had been . . . intimate. He only shaved about once a week, and it was such a private, personal act that, frankly -- since no one could hear the thoughts in her head -- Catherine had found it erotic.

She was sure her husband in his icy indifference would be dismayed to learn she had such thoughts. He made it clear there would be no warmth between them, that he would continue to hold himself aloof.

Catherine sat down with a tortoise shell bowl of nuts. Using the back of Jean Paul's hatchet to crack them, she set about picking out the nutmeats.

In her girlhood, Catherine had imagined marrying a prince. He would be very handsome, they would adore each other, they would be beautiful and happy every day of their lives. Long before Cousin Hugo demonstrated that not all men were princes, she had come to a different understanding of marriage.

She would marry well, of course. She and her husband would be cordial and respectful to one another, perhaps even grow fond of each other, but there were no examples in her acquaintance of husbands and wives who actually loved each other. She had supposed there were compensations enough with parties, dancing, music, flirting.

She would have married Charles, le compte de Toulon. Their families desired the union, and she and Charles had known each other since they were children. Charles had kissed her not long before Hugo spirited her away in the night. It had been pleasant. Odd that she had not thought of Charles at all these last months.

Nevertheless, it would have been a good match. They would have been happy enough.

Happy enough? Was that all she wanted now? If Jean Paul had been an aristocrat, would she have favored him? He was handsome, but he was grim and single minded. He had no charm, no joy in him.

Yet he wrote poetry. And he talked to his pigs. There was more to Jean Paul Dupre than an ill-humored grump with an axe.

She put her thumb in her mouth to suck at the torn cuticle. Nut shells were far sharper than she'd expected.

At any rate, there were no parties, dancing, music, or flirting here to divert her from a lonely marriage.

It might be many years before she could return to France. How depressing to spend those years with this cool distance between them. She did not require that she and Jean Paul Dupre -- sour-faced pig farmer -- fall in love with each other. Yet she yearned for something more between them. If they were not to be lovers, could they not share a joke, a conversation, a touch?

He was a man with a hole in his heart, she thought, but he had shown moments of kindness, even a hint of warmth. There was a person somewhere underneath that gruff exterior. If she deserved a warm, affectionate husband, he deserved the same from a wife.

When she was just entering her womanhood, over tea one gray wintery day, Great Aunt Isabella had told her, "In any relationship, the one who gives the most is the one who *can*." That would be she, Catherine Villeroy Dupre.

It shouldn't be so hard if she were patient. After all, had he not made her a pair of shoes, bought her a wool cloak, rubbed the cramp out of her leg in the middle of the night? And the way he'd looked at her when she lay practically naked in the water, learning to float. Whatever reason Jean Paul had for remaining distant and unapproachable, Catherine didn't think it was because he wasn't interested in her.

She would not give up. She would teach him to how to share a little warmth, a little of himself.

One thing a good wife would do is worry over her husband. Jean Paul was out there in the cold rain working on the roof -- he could catch a chill. She entertained the notion of an ailing Jean Paul lying abed, letting her spoon broth into him and fuss over him. He'd probably grumble the whole time, but he couldn't walk off and turn his back on her if he were stuck in bed.

Done. She'd shelled enough nuts they could munch on them for days.

She got up to stoke the fire and it occurred to her: she had never taken care of anyone in her life. But that didn't mean she couldn't. She could now do many things that she had never expected to do. Wear the same dress day in and day out. Eat the same bland food every meal. Work in the sun, her complexion turning brown, her hands growing calluses.

What must it feel like to be needed, she wondered as she picked up the empty water bucket. She believed it would be sweet for a man like Jean Paul to need her.

During a lull in the rain, she dashed toward the spring to fill the bucket.

And dug her heels in for a skidding stop ten feet from the water.

A gator lay half on the bank, half in the water, its toothy jaws opening. Catherine hurled the bucket at it and ran screaming back the way she'd come, her mind totally shut down, all her being concentrated on how fast her legs could move her.

Jean Paul ran for her, a look of terror on his face. She plowed into him and tried to crawl inside him.

He held on until she could breathe, then he took her by the arms and peered into her face. "What?"

She still gasped, unable to speak.

"Damn it, what happened?"

She shook her head.

"Catherine, look at me."

She pointed, panting. "Gator."

She fell into his arms again only this time she felt all the tension leave his shoulders. "A gator?" he said again as if he wanted to laugh. She didn't care if he laughed as long as he held her.

So there they stood in the rain, soaked to the skin, holding on to each other. Catherine had been wooed by accomplished lotharios at Versailles, had had poems written to her, songs composed for her -- yet she'd never known any moment as tender as this. He held her in the cold rain while she was terrified, and he didn't let go.

Jean Paul didn't want to let her go. He'd thought his heart would burst when he'd heard her screaming, thinking a bear, a gator, a puma had got her. She still trembled. As long as she trembled, he could hold her and inhale the scent of his wet Catherine.

As she calmed, he became aware of her breasts pressed against him, of her thighs through the wet cloth.

He touched her chin. "All right now?"

She smiled at him and that dreamy look came over her face, her eyes soft and unguarded, her lips open. The way Belinda had used to look at him. Pain shot through him as sharp as a knife. Belinda -- there was no truth in a look like that.

He put her away from him. "Go back inside, dry off." He marched back to the notched log he used as a ladder and climbed back onto the roof.

Catherine hugged herself, disappointed and hurt. If she went inside now, she'd weep for loneliness.

But she had vowed she would not give up. Ignoring the rain as it started up again, she headed for the palmettos at the edge of the woods. With an armful of fronds, she climbed the notched log to the roof and handed them over. Jean Paul didn't give her so much as a word or a look, just took the fronds and laid them out to be lashed to the others.

# Chapter Ten

*Catherine and Jean Paul*
*A Kiss*

Another cold dawn, but at least the roof was fixed. Jean Paul dared any drop of rain to make its way through that thatch now.

Those were Catherine's knees poking him in the butt, curled up against the cold. When she was so scared, he'd held her, and she'd clung to him. He ached, in his chest and in his loins, to hold her again.

But what if she got pregnant, what then? He could barely feed the two of them. Better to go on as they were. She didn't complain.

He rolled off the bed and built up the fire for her. "Thank you," she murmured and closed her eyes again.

He liked the way she looked in the mornings, her eyes half open, her hair coming loose from its braid. He smiled to himself. She didn't even know how to fix her hair in a decent braid. Likely she had never done it for herself until -- whatever had happened to her to put her on board the *New Hope*. Murderer? He couldn't see it. But he'd proven he had no understanding of women, hadn't he?

"Come on, Débile," he said and picked up the water bucket with its interesting teeth marks from when Catherine had hurled it at her gator. She was still skittish about going down to the spring. He couldn't blame her.

Outside, he breathed in the crisp morning, gazed up at the pearly dawn, and felt an unexpected moment of pure joy. A line of bright yellow lined the lower edge of the sky, and his limbs felt strong and his mind was clear. Maybe it was true, time heals all wounds. And maybe it was Catherine, who smiled at him even though he kept himself aloof and cold.

Did she guess how much he wanted her? Probably not. She wasn't like Belinda, practiced at love and seduction, and yet he wanted her more than he'd ever wanted anyone. Anyone? Even Belinda? Was it true? Could *she* be pushed out of his heart to make room for another?

Fanciful thoughts. Pointless thoughts. They were partners, that was all.

If they both worked hard and had a little luck, they could be reasonably prosperous in a few years. Even their first small crop should yield enough cash to buy her one or two dresses, some crockery. No doubt Catherine would have ideas of her own about what they needed.

Was she still grateful to be here as she said she would be? He could ask her. They could talk. She'd like that.

She came outside and paused at the doorway, looking up at the sky. "Going to be a pretty day," she said. My God, he admired her spirit. Here she was in the wilderness, tired, sore, putting up with him, and she still smiled.

She walked into the yard and ambled down toward the wallow. He'd caught her talking to the piglets a time or two, which had embarrassed her, but she kept doing it.

As soon as Brigitte and Beauregard saw her coming, they ran for her with little piggy grunts of delight.

"Whoa," she said, laughing. But they barreled into her, knocking her down so hard her legs went straight up in the air.

Jean Paul burst into laughter. He'd never seen anything so funny in his life. Holding his side, he held a hand out to help her up. She gave him a flaming look, which made him laugh all over again.

"You should have seen yourself," he said, trying to stop laughing at her. She was not pleased with him. "Really, Catherine."

Straightening her dress, she said, "You're a cad," and glared at him with wet eyes.

He stepped close to her, smiling. "Don't be mad," he said, his fingers on her cheek. She stilled at his touch, so close he saw tiny streaks of blue mixed in the green of her eyes.

He took her hands in his. When she arrived, her hands had been soft and white. They were roughened now, and red, the nails chipped. He rubbed his thumb over the calluses in her palm.

He meant to simply brush his lips across hers, to simply share this unfamiliar moment of contentment, of friendliness, but she leaned into him, her mouth soft and warm and giving. Without his volition, his hand slid up her back to her neck and held her as he deepened his kiss.

She slipped her hand over his heart. Her lips parted.

Heat surged through him. He pulled her close and took her mouth. His senses filled with her, with Catherine. When her arms went around his neck, he pressed her against his groin.

Oh God, she was pushing him away. "Catherine."

She leaned back from him, her eyes huge, her fingers over her mouth. "I . . . "

He couldn't let go of her. "You what?"

She bit her lower lip, a shy smile hovering. "I've never been kissed like that."

He stared at her, fighting to get his body under control. Trying to remember why he should not kiss her, should not touch her if he didn't have to.

"You haven't?"

She shook her head, beaming at him.

Pregnancy. That was why. He couldn't afford to get her pregnant. Couldn't afford to care for her, or let her get close to him. He didn't know her. She didn't know him. It was better that way.

He dropped his hands from her arms and stepped back.

"Well. That's how musketeers kiss."

With that purely stupid comment, he picked up his bucket and headed for the spring. By the time he got back, she'd have breakfast started. They wouldn't talk about what he'd done. He'd eat, then he'd get to work with his axe. One more tree felled, there'd be ground enough to plant the indigo.

He heard Catherine bustling around in the cabin when he returned. He paused at the door, delaying the moment he had to face her again. She was a virgin, if her kiss was any measure. His own kiss had been hot and demanding. He'd even pressed her against his erection. What would she think a kiss like that meant?

Nothing. That's what he had to show her. It meant nothing.

~~~

Yesterday had passed with a cold distance between Catherine and her husband. This morning, she still felt the chill he chose to radiate. She touched her fingers to her mouth, remembering the press of his lips on hers. But the kiss they'd shared might never have happened. What kind of man kisses a woman as if she were all he wanted in this world, and then walks away from her as if holding her, touching her, tasting her had meant nothing to him. Nothing.

What did he see in her that so repelled him? He did not want her touch. He did not want even her friendship. Had he believed what the agent said, that she was a murderer? Or maybe it was only that she was an aristocrat. Yes, she was spoiled and she knew she was of little use, but she worked hard, she didn't complain, she was learning.

She wished he'd never kissed her. Then she wouldn't have known, wouldn't have yearned for more, wouldn't have discovered how much lonelier she could be.

Not so many weeks ago she thought she had cured herself of wanting. Gratitude, that had been her dominant feeling. But with the crises past, with life having a sameness, an orderly routine, want crept back in. Catherine supposed that was just being human, and she couldn't help wanting more. Of course a couple of china plates would be nice, coffee and croissants, but what she craved was a connection with the man she worked and slept beside.

She had once told herself not to hope, either, yet how did people get up in the mornings, day after day, without a little hope? So, Catherine decided, she would hope. Life was not static -- the last months had proven that. And hadn't she herself changed? Jean Paul could change his attitude toward her, he could. She would believe that.

She surveyed the ground yet covered with weeds. She supposed if it were not cleared, they could not plant a garden, and if they did not plant a garden, they would have to live on rabbits and fish. And didn't Jean Paul also mean to plant indigo? That ground too would have to be broken up.

And so she once again picked up the dratted hoe. Sometimes she thought it was now an extension of her own limbs.

So many times she had swung this hoe into the dirt imagining Cousin Hugo's face under the blade. She realized, in a moment of wry humor, there had amazingly been no blood in these imaginings, but smacking him with the hoe had been satisfying nevertheless.

That was another change in her. If she had a moment to think about Hugo and what he'd done to her, she was white with rage. But, as Great Aunt Isabella always said, *don't waste energy fretting until you can actually do something about it. Patience,* she had advised. Of course at the time, she had been talking about some snub at court that had hurt Catherine's feelings, not an injustice great enough to change her entire life. The advice remained good, though. Catherine should spend her energy on figuring out how to live this new life.

A little brown bird boldly alit not ten feet from Catherine's hoe. It indulged itself in a quick dust bath and then pecked at the dirt, found some tidbit, and flew directly onto a branch not far away. Tiny voices cheeped in excitement as the bird flitted into a nest of moss and twigs.

A bird's nest. Catherine had never seen a bird's nest. Of course she'd seen drawings of them, but with her own eyes? She stood on her tiptoes, trying to see the baby birds cheeping so loudly and lustily. She needed something to stand on. At the woodpile, she chose a log awaiting its fate as kindling and rolled it under the branch.

She got it situated, found her balance on it, and peered into the nest. Four scrawny, big-headed babies fussed at the mama bird for more more more. *Ohhh.* Never in her life had she seen such a wonder.

Their heads were all big open pink mouths. Catherine gripped her hands together. She felt like singing, or crying. Why had she never looked for birds' nests at home? How had she let such a marvel escape her? Were they sparrows?

She could come see them every day. She could watch them grow, and one day she would see them learn to fly. If she had stayed safely in her own world, she would never have seen such a sight. She would have missed this -- what did she feel? Elation? Joy? Yes, joy.

Catherine had read the poets who extolled the beauty of nature, of being one with nature. She'd thought she understood, but she hadn't. Now she did. These little baby birds, somehow, felt as if they belonged to her and she to them.

She looked around at the tilled earth and at all the leafy trees. She heard the birds singing, the wind sighing. She was as much a part of this piece of God's earth as the sparrow or the squirrels or even the earthworms in the ground.

Why had she never known that? What a wonderful, blessed feeling, to be part of this fabric of life. How could a yet another silk ball gown compare to the riches in this little field?

Down by the spring, the Indian children were playing, calling out and laughing, proof a body didn't have to be unhappy living here in this wilderness. She would remember this moment, this lesson in philosophy from a little brown sparrow and little brown children.

She stepped off her log and left it in place so she could peek at the babies again whenever she wanted to.

The children were shouting and shrieking as if there never had been more fun than two boys in a shallow stream. No gator there today, she assumed. She had seen the boys only once when she took the bucket down for fresh water. The leafy green canopy over the burbling stream made an inviting playground. The boys had smiled at her, and then they ran screaming as if she were a bear coming after them. She'd smiled to be made part of the fun.

At the sharp crack of a tree trunk breaking through where Jean Paul had cut it, Catherine paused to watch the great bole slowly tip then crash into the exact spot he had intended it to. If there were a competition to see who was the most accurate tree feller, Jean Paul would win first place.

Catherine clapped her hands in appreciation and was rewarded with a rare grin. The line between his eyes disappeared and at that moment he seemed very young.

He walked over to her, the axe crossed behind his shoulders.

"Look, Jean Paul." She took his arm as if it were an ordinary occurrence, touching him. "Step on the log and you can see the babies."

He watched them for a long time, hardly moving. Finally he looked down at her and grinned. "Ugly little cusses, aren't they?"

"Their mama doesn't think so."

"You going to be their honorary auntie?"

She lifted her chin. "That's right. Honorary auntie."

"It'll be fun watching them, won't it?" he said.

She felt her whole body in the smile she gave him. "We can watch them together."

Jean Paul gave her an odd look. Could the man not even smile about baby birds?

He nodded toward the tree he'd just felled. "That's the last one for now. We can plant the indigo today."

"That would be a lovely change from this everlasting weeding. Where?"

"Over there," he said. "The sunniest patch. You know the burlap bag? If you'll get that, I'll borrow your hoe and get the rows started."

"Oh, no, Jean Paul. A hoe is a delicate instrument. You might damage it, make it dull, put a ding in the blade."

With the merest quirk of his mouth, he said, "If I promise to be very careful with it?"

She handed it over with a smirk.

For one lovely moment, Jean Paul held her gaze and smiled. With that beam of sunshine to sustain her, Catherine went in for the seeds.

Jean Paul built up a row of soil and then found a stick to bore holes just the right depth. Catherine followed along behind him, dropping in the seeds. This was the first time they had actually worked side by side, and even if it was just putting seeds in the ground instead of, say, playing a duet at the piano forte, Catherine felt closer to him, at least for now.

"So this is our cash crop," she said. "How do we get the dye out of the plants?"

"We don't. We'll harvest it in a few weeks, bale it up, and take it to the broker to be processed. It's complicated, I understand, and you have to have know-how and vats and an agent to take the dye back to France."

Both of them lifted their heads and listened. The Indian children's screaming voices had changed timbre. That was a cry of pain. Jean Paul dropped the hoe and the two of them ran for the spring.

An older boy huddled over a younger one, both of them chattering.

Jean Paul knelt down. "He's cut," the oldest boy said in heavily accented French.

There was a huge gash on the bottom of the youngest child's foot and it was bleeding profusely. Jean Paul examined the wound as if it were only a scratch, not a hint of excitement, much less worry.

"Catherine, come hold him right about here and squeeze a little."

Catherine had rarely seen blood at all, and this was a lot of blood. She felt light-headed, but she knelt and wrapped her fingers around the boy's calf.

Jean Paul pulled his knife from its sheath and cut the bottom three inches off his shirt tail. With sure hands, he wrapped the boy's foot quite tightly and then lifted him into his arms.

"Come on," he said. "We need to get this sewn up."

At the door to the cabin, he turned to the older boy. "Find a stick for him to hold in his teeth."

"What should I do?" Catherine said. "Boil water?"

Jean Paul smiled. "That's for having babies. Will you hold him in your lap?"

"Of course."

Jean Paul pulled a sewing kit from his chest and found needle and thread. Next he gathered up a clean shirt and the little bottle of turpentine he kept on the mantle. Good for everything, he'd told her. She'd had a nasty looking sore on her palm where a blister had popped. He had daubed turpentine on it, and it felt as if he'd stuck a hot poker in the wound. She swore she could taste the stuff on her tongue, and it was not a pleasant taste. By morning, however, the puffiness around the blister was gone.

Blood saturated the boy's bandage and dripped onto the floor. Catherine looked away and pressed her mouth to the top of the boy's head, rocking him in her lap. He couldn't be more than four years old. His cries had diminished to whimpers, but he turned his face into her breast when he saw Jean Paul's needle.

The older boy came in with a stick, the bark peeled off it. Catherine had no idea what good a stick would be, but she trusted Jean Paul to know what he was doing. Musketeers must incur minor wounds all the time if only from sword practice.

"This is for your mouth, understand?" Jean Paul put the stick in his mouth to show him how to grip it in his teeth.

The older boy translated and put the stick in the child's mouth.

Jean Paul unwrapped the wounded foot and took another look at it. "This will hurt, but tell him this is the worst part."

When the child gripped Catherine, the oldest's tone grew sharp and scornful. It wasn't hard to guess he was telling the boy in her lap to buck up, be a man.

Jean Paul held the mouth of the turpentine bottle over the gash, looked the wounded boy in the eye and said, "Ready?"

"Go ahead," the oldest boy said. He looked like he might be eight years old, but he spoke as if he were Jean Paul's equal in authority.

The child moaned at the agony of turpentine in the wound, but he kept the stick in his mouth and did not cry out.

"A brave young man," Jean Paul said. Catherine smoothed her hand over his straight black hair and murmured soothing words in his ear.

Seating himself on the floor for the best angle, Jean Paul dipped the threaded needle in the turpentine, then pinched the flesh together and sewed the gash closed. The child trembled, but he bore the stitching without even a whimper.

With a strip of cloth from his clean shirt, Jean Paul wrapped the foot. The little boy couldn't seem to stop trembling. "Shock," Jean Paul said. He grabbed the quilt off the bed and wrapped it around Catherine and the boy.

"We have any sweet potatoes left from last night?"

"Under the cloth," Catherine said.

Jean Paul fed the child a few bites and that seemed to calm him. "What's your name?" he asked the child.

"His name is Ake," the older one said. "I am Hoya."

"Hoya, don't let him walk on that foot for a few days, all right?"

The excitement all over, Jean Paul carried the child and the little procession proceeded to the path back in the woods.

After a twenty minute walk, Hoya ran ahead of them up a side path to the village. Catherine followed Jean Paul, Ake in his arms, and entered a clearing with thatched huts, women, children, dogs, and two men waiting for them.

"*Bonjour*, Akecheta," Jean Paul said to the older man.

"*Bonjour*, Dupre."

The younger man, broad shouldered and handsome, nodded to Jean Paul and greeted him in that abbreviated way men here in the colony used. "Dupre."

"Mato."

At Versailles, these greetings would have been accompanied by bows and flourishes and assurances of everlasting pleasure at encountering one another. Rather silly, now that she thought back on it.

A woman came running from the other side of the village, Hoya at her side. She held her arms out for the child and though Catherine could not understand her, it was evident the mother was scolding Ake at the same time she hugged him close.

"Those are my grandsons you have brought home, Dupre. You have been a friend to them."

"I was glad to do it."

"Come, we will talk."

When Catherine took a step forward, Jean Paul leant down to Catherine's ear. "He doesn't mean you." When she looked at him blankly, he added, "You're a woman."

Catherine quirked an eyebrow at him, but she stayed behind as he joined the men sitting outside a large hut. Half a world away and still the women were excluded from the most interesting conversations.

Two dogs ambled up and eyed her warily. Catherine held her hand out to be sniffed. "You are very fine dogs," she murmured sweetly. "Big, ugly, fine dogs."

They sniffed and seemed satisfied. With their escort, she walked into the village and passed a man scraping a deer hide stretched on a frame. A woman was grinding meal in a wooden trough, another was nursing a baby. Several men stood together, their arms crossed, and watched her as she passed by. Everyone eyed her, their faces neither hostile nor friendly. Only some children who ran screaming by her in a game of chase seemed oblivious to her presence.

Villages were the same the world over, she supposed. Whenever she had passed through the village near Grandfather's estate, the men, women, and children had all stared at her then, too.

Catherine approached a young woman on a blanket with a small child tugging at her hair. He was bare bottomed, and his chin was wet with drool. The mother gently opened his little fist and smiled at Catherine. She was perhaps eighteen or nineteen, her hair a glossy black, her skin smooth and brown.

Catherine took her smile as an invitation and knelt beside her. "*Bonjour.*"

"*Bonjour*," the young woman said with a shy smile.

How extraordinary to find this girl greeting her in French. In Versailles, they all believed France was the center of the world. Perhaps it was true.

"I am Catherine," she said pointing to her chest.

"My white people name is Fleur."

"*Fleur*? Flower. What a wonderful name."

"You are that man's woman?" Fleur nodded toward Jean Paul. With a sly grin, she said, "He is very handsome."

Catherine laughed and looked over at Jean Paul where he sat among the men of the tribe. Sun shone on his dark hair, tied back in a queue. His profile showed a strong jaw, a perfect nose, and heavy dark brows. Yes, he was a handsome man.

Jean Paul turned his head toward her as if he felt her gaze on his skin. Her breath stuttered at the intensity in his eyes. Someone spoke to him and he broke the connection.

Catherine drew a deep breath. Well, my goodness. All those times she'd resented his indifference -- that look in his eyes was not indifference.

"You came on the big ship? The one with all the wives?"

"Yes," Catherine said, composing herself. "A horrible big ship. I am very glad to be on land again."

"Then your home is far away," the young mother said.

Catherine's eyes watered suddenly. Silly. There was only trouble at home, yet she missed her grandfather, and her trio of fluffy little white dogs who had followed her everywhere. But there was no need to speak of them.

Fleur reached behind her for a small basket of nuts and offered them to Catherine. Fleur herself took two nuts in her hand and squeezed, cracking them effortlessly.

"We have a tree of these nuts," Catherine said. "I have been using the back of my husband's hatchet to crack them." She took two nuts and squeezed them, but nothing happened.

Fleur laughed and said, "Let me."

They ate nutmeats, feeding tiny bits to the baby with his half a dozen teeth. "These are nuts fallen to the ground," Fleur said. "Not so good as the new nuts in the fall, but still they are my favorite. I could show you a bee hive close to your home."

"You know where my home is?"

"Of course."

Of course the Biloxi watched the whites. She and Jean Paul, all the colonists, were intruders in these people's land. Humbled, she said, "Your people are very generous to welcome us here."

Fleur shrugged. "Some welcome, some do not."

Catherine wanted to invite Fleur to her own home, to serve her coffee and cakes. She had no coffee and she had no idea how to make a cake, but hospitality surely didn't depend on coffee and cake. "We also have a tree of yellow fruit, guavas my husband calls them. I would be pleased if you came to visit me and gathered nuts and guavas."

Fleur's pretty face shone with a smile that made her brown eyes twinkle.

~~~

Jean Paul sat with the Biloxi men, patiently waiting while the social niceties were observed. They passed around a cup of their home brew made of berries and who knew what else. Jean Paul sipped at the harsh drink, remembering the smooth taste of Bordeaux, served with warm brie and crusty white bread. He mentally gave himself a shake. If he let himself think about all the things he left behind in France, he'd waste his days in pointless regret.

"I have a deer hide," Akecheta said.

Jean Paul nodded, recognizing the beginnings of a negotiation.

"There is a dead tree," Mato said. "If it blows down in a storm, it might fall on someone's hut."

"I have an axe."

And so it was arranged. Jean Paul would chop down the dead tree and Akecheta would gift him with the deer hide. He suspected he had the better part of the deal.

Jean Paul found Catherine sitting with her new friends. He was struck by the sight of her with a sleepy baby in her arms, her face bent to nuzzle his neck. He stared for a moment, not willing to examine the faint emotion the sight produced in him.

"Let's go," he said.

She handed the baby to his mother. "This is Fleur," she said. "My husband, Jean Paul."

"Madame," he said and dipped his head.

Jean Paul led the way toward home. "What lovely people," Catherine said.

He gave her a look, trying to imagine Belinda sitting on the ground and cradling a savage's baby. When his wife smiled like this, she was as pretty as Belinda ever was. He turned away from her and strode on.

# Chapter Eleven

*Agnes*
*A Fair Exchange*

Whether it was time, or a kind husband, or the good wishes of the will-o-the-wisps, whatever the cause, Agnes had begun to smile these last days. This morning, she lay next to her gently snoring husband and realized she even laughed at Valery's foolish jests, enjoying his deliberate attempts to amuse her with nonsense.

Valery now called her *ma petite* or *mon petite chou*. Agnes had been accustomed to much worse. *Chein, vache, saleté, putain.* The last had been quite true, though *whore* was certainly not a profession she had aspired to. She thought it was lovely, his casually calling her his little cabbage.

Lucan, her lusty rooster, announced it was time for her to get up. Lucan had proudly managed to amass more than a dozen hens in his harem, and she hoped to have hatchlings soon.

Agnes stepped into the yard and watched her hens forage for bugs and other tasty bits lying about in the dirt. There was a littering of feathers in the coop and on the ground underneath, mostly red with a few black ones as well. She gathered them into a small bundle to prettify the table. Her husband was a man who would stop whatever he was doing to admire a red bird flitting from tree to tree, and his little animal carvings were whimsical and charming. Valery would appreciate a feather bouquet.

As she went about cooking corn meal mush for Valery's breakfast, she heard a great squawking and rushed outside to see a hawk and Lucan in a flurry of wings, feathers, and yellow beaks. Agnes ran outside, flapping her skirts, and chased the hawk away. She did a quick count and found all her hens were still with her.

"Lucan, you are our hero," she crooned as he strutted around, his feathers still spread on display. "You are such a *coq magnifique*, you should have a harem twice this size. We'll see what we can do, hm?"

Valery leaned out the door with an exaggerated scowl. "Here you are talking to your chickens, woman, and my breakfast burns."

"Oh no." She pushed past him to rescue her pot of mush. The cabin smelled of scorched corn. "Oh, Valery. I'm so sorry."

He wrapped an arm around her waist. "It is not so very tragic, *mon chou*. I must tell you, I have eaten burned mush before."

He kissed the top of her head and went outside to tend to his toilette while Agnes fanned at the smell. With a sigh, she dished up their breakfast.

Valery gallantly cleaned his plate without complaint and pushed his chair back. Agnes held him down with her hand on his shoulder. "Sit still," she commanded. "Your moustache has grown untidy."

"Many pardons, madame. I shall repair it at once."

"That is not my meaning, sir. I shall see to it myself."

He grinned at her. "You will be my barber?"

"Why not? I have trimmed my father's moustache many times."

"Very well. I put myself in your hands."

From his shaving kit, Agnes retrieved the tiny scissors with handles fashioned like peacock feathers. She snipped and combed and pronounced him very handsome. He held up the tiny mirror, the only one they owned, and admired her handiwork.

"Handsome indeed," he said, smiling at her. He drew her to stand between his legs. "I have never had a lady barber before. It is strangely arousing."

Agnes laughed. "Now?"

"*Mais oui*, now."

"But I haven't gathered the eggs -- "

"I cannot speak for your hens, *mon chou*, but I am sure your rooster would agree with me. Certain things come first."

He grabbed her up and carried her to the bed, Agnes laughing at the silly grin on his face.

Her lover's newfound tenderness made her realize she was not the only one who had been lonely. He had lived here by himself, no one to talk to, not even a dog, and when she first came, he had not known how to deal with her except in the most rudimentary way. Now he allowed her to see there was more to him than the boastful, shallow fellow he had presented in their early days together.

When Valery had brought them both to completion, he closed drowsy eyes for a respite. Agnes gave him a quick kiss on the nose and left the bed. There was work to be done.

She first went outside to collect eggs. Villiers was a good provider. Besides the eggs, they had game, meal, dried peas, and nuts from the tree on the edge of the woods.

Agnes would have said that her hard-working husband was decent, charming, and kind, but that afternoon, she discovered that he was blessed with neither foresight nor assertion.

Three Biloxi Indians, a woman and two sons, pulled their dugout onto the landing. Her hair was straight and black, her face broad and brown. She wore a leather tunic, and her two boys wore leather breechcloths, vests, and soft leather shoes. Such a friendly, open face the mama had as she indicated in broken French that they wished to trade for a chicken.

Villiers was jovial and happy to trade. "Choose your hen, madame," he said to the woman. All smiles, she pointed to one and her boys scrambled after it, laughing at all the chickens in the yard running and flapping and squawking. Agnes enjoyed their fun herself though she was sorry they'd chosen Henrietta, one of her favorite layers.

Then Agnes realized her husband's good spirits overwhelmed his good sense. The woman offered him a very small basket of yellow fruits and he nodded and smiled as if she'd offered him a nugget of gold. Foolish man. If she and Papa had run the bookstore like this, they'd have been bankrupt in a month.

The thought struck her like a splash of cold water. Her husband needed her. She had sense. She had foresight. Before her troubles, she had not lacked for assertion. Had she not once confronted the butcher when he sold her a piece of mutton that had gone off?

Agnes pointed to the basket of nuts in the canoe, indicating the guavas were not enough. The woman gave her a shrewd look and smiled, then added three handfuls of nuts to the basket of guavas. At Agnes's raised brow, she added two more handfuls, then raised her own brow. Agnes had been told that was all she would get.

Agnes was giddy as she followed her husband back to the cabin. How long had it been since she had done anything but submit and cower? She, Agnes Villiers, had a home, and a husband who needed her. She was a nothing no more.

"Have a guava, my dear," he said, reaching into the basket. "They are not so tasty as a plum or a pear, but they are quite refreshing."

They strolled companionably in the sun eating guavas. They would be good stewed with some honey. Perhaps there were honey bees in the woods.

"Monsieur," she said.

"You may call me Valery, *ma chère*."

"Valery, I have some experience in selling merchandise."

"Do you indeed? You were not always a whore?"

She forced herself to remain pleasant. "No, Valery, I was not always a whore. I bought and sold books. And more to the point, monsieur, I raised chickens and sold eggs."

He spat out a bit of peel, not particularly interested.

"It will be some time before you may profit from your indigo, is that not so? You would be pleased to make a more immediate profit, yes?"

"Of course." Now she had his attention.

"We will build coops and nesting boxes to encourage the hens to brood. More chickens, more eggs, and I believe the other wives, perhaps even the general store, will buy our eggs."

"Perhaps," he said.

With enthusiasm and a very little flattery, Agnes persuaded her husband that he should build the coops and she would manage the chickens and the marketing.

"Oh! Valery, have you seen bees in the area? We could make hives and then have all the honey we want and even some to sell. Yes?"

Valery sighed like a very weary man. "You know how to raise bees?"

"Not yet."

Valery laughed. "Very well. Chicken coops and bee hives."

Without thinking, Agnes stood on her tiptoes and kissed her husband's cheek. Insatiable man, he grabbed her around the waist and took her into the cabin even though it was the middle of the morning. A very fine day indeed.

~~~

Valery lay with Agnes's head on his shoulder. She invariably fell asleep after he'd made love to her. A good sign she had been well pleased, he believed. As had he.

Valery had married a woman full of surprises. His Agnes had a head for business. He admitted that he did not. He worked hard, and he had goals, but bargaining and buying and selling -- well, he had never needed those skills.

Now it took all he had in him to create a farm out of this wilderness. The labor did not daunt him even though he had never planned this life -- he had enjoyed being a glamorous musketeer, swaggering about Paris in his plumes and cape, and pursuing oh-so-willing women.

But as he had cleared the land, the vision grew. With his own hands, using only the muscles in his back and shoulders, enduring heat and insects, he was carving a home out of the forest. Something uniquely and inarguably his.

Of course he had missed the bustle of Paris the first weeks. The city was never silent, never lonely, never truly dark. What surprised him, however, was how the quiet here on the bayou had seeped into his bones. This was peace. This was -- home.

Agnes had made this her home, too, putting a bouquet of chicken feathers on the table, silly woman. Without rousing her, he kissed the top of her head. He had married a woman with a talent for business, a gift for whimsy, and a sensual appetite to match his own. He could have done much worse the day he'd chosen her.

# Chapter Twelve

*Catherine and Jean Paul
Keeping Secrets*

When Catherine woke, her husband was watching her. What remarkable eyes he had -- quite gray, but with a starburst of yellow around each pupil.

"Good morning," she said.

He gave her a slight nod and rolled out of the bed.

No need to be disappointed, she told herself. His abrupt, silent response to her greeting was typical. It was nice, though, that he had been looking at her, for once. An acknowledgment that she did exist. Some days she wondered if he noticed that.

Catherine got breakfast started -- guavas, sweet potatoes, and corn meal mush. As they ate, she said, "I'd like to go to mass tomorrow morning."

He gave a little shake of his head.

"We haven't been even once. Do you never attend mass?"

"No."

"Why not?"

He gave her a hard look and put another log on the fire. So he didn't want to talk about it. He seemed to be more comfortable the less talking they did. Maybe that's why he didn't go to mass. Someone might expect him to put three words together.

Careful to keep the resentment from her voice, she said, "I thought we might talk to people. I might find my friends."

When Jean Paul said nothing, she added, "Some people do that, you know. Talk to each other."

He leant an elbow on the mantle and rubbed his eyes. "All right. We'll go to Fort Louis tomorrow."

Catherine managed to keep the glee out of her face. Jean Paul didn't want any glee in his life, of that she was sure.

Twice during the rest of the day, Catherine took time to peek into the bird's nest. The four little babies were covered in soft fuzz now, and their eyes and necks didn't look so stark. She swore she could see them growing if she stood there long enough. Since he was in one of his sullen moods, she did not invite Jean Paul to watch them with her this time. Instead she chose to enjoy being honorary auntie to four precious baby birds all by herself.

As always, the day passed with a different chore to accomplish every time she turned around. Ashes had to be scraped from the grate, the big pot had to be scoured, and on and on. Sleep came easily when she put her head on the pillow.

Late that night, Catherine turned over and in her near-wakefulness, she became aware Jean Paul was not in the bed. The fire had been stoked and there he sat with a quill pen and a bottle of ink, writing in his book. She'd peeked into it that first day and remembered the peculiar line she read before she heard him coming in. *Wine the color of rage, water thick with guilt.*

She'd been so overwhelmed these last weeks she had forgotten her husband wrote poetry. She watched his dark head bent over the book, intent on the blank page he filled. She really didn't know him, did she? She'd lost her former life, all her expectations if not her dreams; what had Jean Paul lost? What thoughts pressed on him so that he had to express them in poetry? She would bet there were no poems of joy in his book, no light-hearted idylls.

Had there been happier days when Jean Paul wrote silly love poems like the ones the swains of Versailles had written to her? Odes to her lips, to her ankles, even one to the shape of her ears. How she'd laughed to herself at such frivolous wooing.

She didn't know a Jean Paul like that. But he didn't know her as she had been either. What if he'd heard her singing, perhaps the aria from Handel's *Almira*? Would he have been struck down with love? It amused her to imagine her humorless, grim husband smitten by Eros.

If he knew she watched him as he composed, he would slam the book shut and scowl at her. She should leave him in peace. He must sometimes feel she had invaded his life, as solitary as he'd been, as closed-off as he was.

Besides she could read what he wrote tomorrow or the next day when she was sure he'd not come in. She shouldn't though. It would be disrespectful and intrusive. Maybe she wouldn't. No, she definitely wouldn't.

She closed her eyes and fell back to sleep to the sound of the quill scratching across the page.

~~~

Jean Paul certainly had seen women take longer to make themselves presentable, but considering there was no looking glass, no maid, no change of clothes involved, Catherine's ten minute toilette amused him.

First she unbraided her hair and combed it as best she could. It was too long for her to manage strokes from her scalp to the end of the hair, so it had to be done in stages.

He could have hurried her along by helping. He had always enjoyed brushing out a lover's hair, feeling its weight in his hands. His wife's hair was dark blonde, heavy, and beautiful. He imagined running his fingers through its length, burying his face in its mass. But she was not his lover. He turned away.

Once she'd re-braided her hair, she straightened the skirts of the same sad blue dress she'd worn every day.

"Why do you never wear the other dress in your basket? Are you saving it for a soiree or a visit from the Dauphin?"

She gave him a wry look and pulled the dress out of the basket. She shook it out -- a brown cotton affair -- and held it up in front of her.

"I see." Most of Catherine's body was visible behind the little gown -- it would certainly not accept the width of her shoulders or even the girth of her waist. Not that his wife was a large woman. The dress was tiny.

"If, or I hope when, I see my friend Agnes, I will give it to her."

"Why do you have such a dress? Were none of you fitted for these clothes?"

Catherine turned her face away from him. Why the mystery? It seemed a simple question.

"Is this some deep secret you can't reveal, the true reason King Louis provided you with a dress fitted for a doll?"

She let out a puff of air. "The dress was not meant for me. Nor the basket. A girl, Marguerite, died on board the *New Hope*. I inherited the basket, and the gown."

Why did all the girls but Catherine have a basket? She didn't volunteer the information, so he wouldn't ask. He didn't need to know, did he?

Whatever the cause, a woman who arrived in an expensive satin gown had one garment to her name. He marveled she had not complained. The dress, even made of strong silk, could not last much longer. He would have to find a way to clothe her, though certainly not in the manner she was apparently accustomed to. Once the indigo crop paid some cash, he could buy what she needed.

She did at least have two pairs of stockings, full of holes as they were. His own were more hole than cotton. He should buy some yarn, if she knew how to use it. He certainly didn't.

"Can you knit?"

"Crochet," she said with a smile. For a woman who'd traveled from prison to the back of a wilderness, Catherine smiled a lot.

"Maman and I used to crochet shawls and baby clothes to take to the -- Well, we spent many an evening with our needlework before the fire."

"What were you going to say? You took clothes to the peasants?"

She busied herself with her shoes and didn't answer him.

"Who are you, Catherine?" He heard the accusation in his voice, but by God she was his wife.

She lifted her chin and gave him a cold look. "I am your wife. Catherine Dupre."

He huffed a laugh. "Very well. You were born three months ago at Ft. Louis, is that it?"

"As apparently were you, monsieur."

He stared at her, wondering. "They called you a murderer."

She straightened her back and looked him straight in the eye. "Well, if they say so, it must be true."

"You came aboard the *New Hope*. With the girls taken from the Salpêtrière prison."

"I did."

"It is not a pleasure resort."

"So I understand."

He had never seen that guarded look in her eyes, never seen her bristle at him. If he were fair, he'd let it go, leave her alone. "Why were you with them?"

"Why is a musketeer clearing land in the wilderness, Monsieur Dupre?"

He narrowed his eyes at her standing there with her nose in the air. She preferred to keep her mysterious past to herself? Very well. It made no difference to him.

He strapped on his sword and picked up his musket. "Come, Débile."

When he held out his hand to help her into the dugout, Catherine ignored him. So she was angry with him. Why should he care? Why should he care what had happened to her in France? That was half a world away, another lifetime.

With her determinedly looking at the trees, sky, water, anywhere but at him, he could study her as she had studied him that first day in the dugout.

Already she didn't look so hollow-cheeked, nor so pale. She could use a good scrub, as could he, but there would be no hot leisurely baths for either of them. Imagine how bright her hair would shine if it were fresh and clean.

She still wouldn't look at him. With her face closed to him, he realized how much he counted on her smiles. Not that he deserved them, but she'd been free with them, even if she were only talking to Suzette or Débile. And now she was angry with him. His own fault.

At the fort, he pulled the dugout up far enough that Catherine could step ashore on dry ground and offered his hand to steady her. She pretended not to see his gesture and got out on the other side of the boat. Jean Paul rolled his shoulders, tense under her cold displeasure. But why should he be? What difference did it make if she were unhappy with him?

She strode toward the women across the square, her step lively and determined. As she joined her friends from the *New Hope*, he saw they enveloped her with open arms.

# Chapter Thirteen

*Marie Claude*
*Reunion*

On Sunday morning, Marie Claude was surprised and very glad when her husband announced they would go to mass. She supposed he would like a chance to wear his brown velvet coat with the brass buttons, the fawn breeches, and the cream-colored hosiery. He was still ugly, in Marie Claude's opinion. Of course she was still ugly, too. She had washed her dress, however, and was as neat and tidy as she could make herself.

When they pulled into the landing at Fort Louis, there were dozens of people on the grounds. She found her friends clustered in a knot of pine trees outside the chapel and strode toward them to be welcomed with open arms and smiling faces.

She let out a long sigh. She'd missed them.

The women were talking about their husbands, a natural topic of interest. "Agnes has the handsomest of them all," Gabrielle declared. "What do you think, Agnes?"

They all looked across the yard to where Monsieur Villiers leaned against a post, talking to other men. He was tall and lean -- everyone here was lean, working as hard as they all had to. His black hair curled around his shoulders, his brows and lashes were dark and thick, and he sported a narrow black moustache above his lip. Marie Claude was glad she hadn't been claimed by a man like that. She could never be comfortable with anyone that beautiful. With a plain man such as Monsieur Joubert, she could at least forget about her own looks.

"I suppose he is handsome," Agnes said with a shy smile and a lingering look at her husband. That was nice, to see that Agnes liked her man.

"I suppose mine is the ugliest man in the colony," Marie Claude said. "Not that it matters since I'm as plain as curdled cream." She ought not to have said it. Nobody cared what she looked like, and she ought to have gotten over the disappointment of being the plainest girl in the village long ago.

Catherine shook her arm a little. "You always say things like that. Your complexion is smooth and rosy, and you have lovely hair."

Marie Claude was struck by the thought. "I guess I do at that," she said on a laugh.

Then here came Bridget sashaying across the yard toward them, that annoying little half-smile on her face. Bridget was always quick to remind her she was plain if Marie Claude ever forgot it for more than half a minute.

Nobody reached for Bridget to welcome her. Marie Claude figured she had insulted all of them at one time or another.

"Such a touching scene," Bridget said, "all of you huddled together like so many puppies."

They all stared at her bedecked in a velvet cloak over a muslin gown. Not so many days ago, she had been as ragged as they were.

"Where did she come by them clothes?" Gabrielle whispered.

"A devil always gets what she wants," Anne Louise muttered.

Bridget eyed them in their rough clothes and then smirked as she focused on Catherine's new cloak.

"Turned him up sweet did you?" she said. "Always knew what you were underneath your fancy airs."

Marie Claude plucked a long stalk of grass and put it in her mouth. "Catherine wasn't no whore like you and me, Bridget. Looks like you the one sweetened up a man to get you them pretty clothes."

Bridget's chin came up. "I don't suppose a man with fifteen slaves and forty acres planted in indigo needs sweetening up to dress his wife."

Marie Claude considered that. She supposed Bridget was pretty enough to get the richest man in the territory, if that's what he was. She wondered if Bridget's husband would like her once he got to know her better.

"Who knows how to make a broom? The dirt on my floor is almost to my knees," Catherine said.

Marie Claude agreed it was time to change the subject. They had better things to think about than Bridget.

Renée knew all about broom straw and how to bind a bundle together. Gabrielle knew how to make baskets -- next time she'd bring rushes and show them.

"Let's decide now who'll do what and when so we can be prepared when it's our turn to teach something." That was little Agnes. Marie Claude would hardly have known it was the same girl, talking out like she cared about something. It had seemed a near thing, getting her across the ocean alive. Marie Claude supposed Agnes had Catherine to thank for that. She'd been the one to keep talking to her and touching her face and her hands even when Agnes seemed to be a dead woman on the inside.

And now here she was getting them organized. Marie Claude glanced across the way at Agnes's pretty husband. Maybe he was a good man to have waked her up to the world.

"I know how to raise chickens," Agnes said.

"I'm going to try making candles," Selina said. "My husband killed a bear so we have plenty of tallow. If I get it right, I'll tell you how to do it."

"You can make soap out of tallow," Annette said.

"Can you?" Catherine said. "I have to admit, I don't know how to do a thing."

"You can read," Renée said, a little shy. "Someday, I'm going to want my children to learn how to read."

"I shall be most happy to teach them, and I shall be grateful for anything you can teach me."

Bridget sneered. "Your fine education no good to you out here, is it, miss high and mighty?"

"No, it isn't." Catherine looked her right in the eye when she said it. Marie Claude was proud of her.

"You know how to do anything but lay on your back, Bridget?" Gabrielle said.

Bridget let out a snort. "That's skill enough to keep me out of the fields." She held out her hands for their inspection. "No calluses, no split nails for me, ladies."

"Anyone else?" Agnes said, ignoring Bridget.

Selina blushed, as she always did if she were noticed. "I know all about cattails. Free food, my papa always said. We made flour out of them, used them to roof the chicken house, ate the roots. Don't never need to be hungry if you got cattails."

Marie Claude felt their excitement. "My husband says it rains all the time here," she said. "I can show you how to drain your gardens."

"We will all be as wise as the oldest farmer in Provence!" Agnes said.

Marie Claude was sure she'd never seen Agnes smile before, and here she was, her face shining with enthusiasm.

"I'm sure I've no interest in being a farmer," Bridget said and flounced off as if there were anywhere else to be.

The other women let her go as if she hadn't spoken, but Marie Claude watched her. That girl was going to have trouble, someday. Everyone did. And Bridget in all her spite would have not a single friend to turn to.

"We can meet here every Sunday!" Selina said. "After mass, we can make ourselves a kind of school."

This is what Marie Claude wanted, all of them staying close, helping each other.

"I don't know if my monsieur will allow it," Renée said.

"My husband, he likes to sleep in on Sundays," Annette said.

"Then we will make it worth their while. Bring a picnic," Gabrielle said. "Maybe organize games for them."

"You mean like competitions? Who can shoot the best?"

"That's it. Some of them even fence, don't they?"

~~~

Catherine couldn't stop smiling being among these women. She had missed them, Rachel's snippy tongue, Renée's sweetness, Anne Louise's pithy comments. And her two best friends, Marie Claude, full of good sense and steady as oaks, and little Agnes, so wounded and vulnerable.

They actually had plenty to talk about, everyone discovering some new way to make life easier, or delighting in birds and flowers no one had ever seen before. When she thought about it, she couldn't remember a single conversation with Antoinette, her oldest friend in Paris, that held any substance or any real delight. The same old observations of this gentleman's coat or that lady's regrettable choice of colors. Hardly out of the school room, and already their lives were narrowed to fashion and etiquette and gossip. Catherine would have remained within that narrowness the rest of her days, never learning another thing or accomplishing a single task.

Had she truly been happy, her focus on status and appearance and entertainment? Had she not had an unacknowledged dissatisfaction underneath all the gaiety?

Catherine had to say no. She had not been bored. She'd had her music and her books, but, basically, she had been absorbed in her preoccupations with beauty and fashion. She would like to think with maturity she might have built a less superficial life for herself, one that did not dwell on just how much lace is enough and how high her powdered hair should soar above her head.

Mature or not, she had been hustled by fate to consider more practical matters. What a comeuppance that she, who'd been admired for her taste and wardrobe, had now worn the same ruined gown for months. It had been one of her favorites, and she had worn it with satisfied vanity the night Cousin Hugo had abducted her. One could laugh at God's little joke.

But no one here laughed at her or raised an eyebrow at her shabbiness, except for Bridget, but she didn't care about Bridget. She breathed in contentment listening to the genuine excitement her new friends shared. No snide remarks, no catty observations, just women sharing themselves.

Catherine spied Jean Paul across the way, talking with two other men. She narrowed her eyes at him. So her husband could hold a conversation if he wanted to. Just not with her. Not unless he was prying and poking.

How dare he! He had practically accused her of being a criminal. Maybe *he* was a criminal.

When the priest came out of the chapel and rang the bell, calling them to mass, Catherine fell into step with Agnes. "How are you, *mon amie*? Your husband is good to you?"

Agnes turned her face up and Catherine was so very pleased to see a smile. "He is good to me." Agnes squeezed her arm. "And I am doing as you said. I am present, all the time now. What about you?"

What could Catherine say? Her feelings for Jean Paul ranged from gratitude to attraction to resentment, depending on the time of day and how recently Jean Paul had snubbed her.

"My husband is a decent man, Agnes."

Inside the chapel, the women sat together. Some of the men found places. Jean Paul did not come in.

~~~

Once Jean Paul saw Catherine safely with her friends, he joined Chevalier and Laroux standing in a patch of sunshine for the warmth. Chevalier was a short, stocky man with a snub nose and a head of unruly curls. Laurent Laroux, his opposite, had the kind of looks that made women swoon, if there were any within a thousand miles given to swooning.

The three of them were all dressed as if they were threatened with imminent attack, muskets at hand, swords in their belts. He doubted Chevalier knew much about sword play, he seemed to be forever banging his sheathed blade into something, but a gentleman was not seen in company without one. His friends seemed to be gentlemen, but in truth, the three of them knew little about each other. That was not cause for remark in this world -- many of the men in this God-forsaken place had left behind a past they did not care to relate.

But the three of them had formed a bond -- first Jean Paul and Laroux on board ship during the long passage across the sea, then Jean Paul and Chevalier because he was Laroux's good friend.

Jean Paul greeted both of them with genuine warmth, but he kept a little piece of himself back. No doubt they did the same.

"You sown your indigo yet?" Chevalier asked him.

"Just have. Been chopping down trees," he said.

"Time well spent," Laroux said. "Last year I sowed a small plot and found the indigo growing in the shade did not thrive."

"Did either of you take a bride home from the *New Hope*?" Chevalier asked.

Jean Paul tilted his head toward the women gathered together. Catherine's blonde head was clearly visible among the shorter women. "The tall one. My wife." An unexpected feeling of pride surprised him as he pointed her out.

Laroux shook his head. "Not me."

"Not to worry, my friend," Chevalier said. "Another ship carrying young women is expected in early summer. Good girls, this time, from convents." Chevalier nodded toward the women chattering to each other. "Not that I think there is anything wrong with a girl who's had a hard life. That little short dumpling is mine."

As Chevalier gazed fondly at his new wife, Jean Paul followed Laroux's gaze to where the Biloxi Indians were congregated. His attention was on Mato's sister, Catherine's friend Fleur. Any man who had ever yearned for a woman would recognize what was in Laroux's eyes. But that woman, she was not for a French settler. She had her own people, and with a babe in her arms, she must have a husband. Jean Paul glanced at Laroux again and then turned aside so Laroux would not realize what his unguarded expression had revealed.

"Meanwhile," Chevalier went on, unaware of Laroux's focus, "a ship of provisions has arrived. The store is filled with flour, only a dozen weevils to the pound. Cotton and wool cloth, shoes. Cost the world, but a man must have shoes."

Father Bouchard rang his bell and people began to move into the chapel. "Are you coming in?" Chevalier said.

Jean Paul shook his head and watched Catherine enter the church. When she was out of sight, he walked over to the Biloxi, Débile at his heels.

"*Bonjour*, Akecheta."

"*Bonjour*, Monsieur Dupre."

Débile ambled up to Akecheta, plopped down and put his big head in his lap. The Biloxi chief rubbed his ears absently.

Jean Paul shook his head in disgust. "A man's own dog . . ."

"He comes to the village, this one. A shameless beggar," Akecheta said with a smile. "Always after a scrap of food or a belly scratch."

As they whiled away the duration of the mass with talk of felling trees, trapping otters, and hunting deer, Jean Paul's eyes continually returned to the chapel door where Catherine would emerge once mass was over. A knot ached between his shoulder blades. Even if he were not interested in his wife, it was still uncomfortable to know she was cross with him.

Why had he prodded her? She didn't quiz him about his former life.

When people began emerging from the chapel, Jean Paul excused himself and strode across the yard to collect his wife. He needed to know if she were still angry with him, though what could he do about it if she were?

Catherine's back was to him as she said good-bye to her friends. That knot of tension in his back tightened as he approached.

"*Au revoir*," she called over her shoulder and nearly walked into him.

Her smile faltered when her eyes lit on him and Jean Paul felt his stomach twist.

She stared at him a moment as if she were reading him. He swallowed, and he scowled at her, but she stepped close, put her hand on his crossed arms, and said, "Will you take me home now?"

His lungs filled with air. He placed her hand on his arm as if he were a courtier and escorted her to the dugout, that painful ache between his shoulder blades forgotten.

# Chapter Fourteen

*Agnes*
*An Unwelcome Guest*

Agnes's first quarrel with her husband came on a lovely evening. Agnes liked to star gaze, and sometimes she wanted to see if the will-o-the-wisps were hovering over the pond. The dark was wonderfully peaceful, frogs singing to the owls, fireflies flirting in the night. Even the occasional grunt from an alligator, as long as it sounded far away, added an exotic note to the evening chorus.

She wrapped her shawl around her shoulders and opened the door.

"No more of these night time expeditions, *ma petite*. You are not to leave the cabin after dark."

"Why ever not?"

Valery sighed. "Do you not know these woods are full of animals? Wolves, for instance."

Agnes frowned. "I have heard no howling."

"And pumas. Do you know that alligators sometimes come onto the land?"

"They do not."

"Yes, they do."

"Valery, I like the dark. I want to see the stars. And the moon. Sometimes the clouds drift like gauze across her face, sometimes they loom like dark mountains."

"Nevertheless, you will not."

"Valery -- "

"I will remind you, madame, you have promised, before God, to obey your husband."

This was not like Valery to dictate to her. She held his eyes, thinking. "Valery, are you afraid of the dark?"

He scowled at her. "I am not. But you should be. You are no bigger than a kitten."

No bigger than a kitten? Ridiculous. He really was a lovely man, rather sweet, in fact. But she meant to go outside as she pleased.

"Valery, I mean to obey you. As I promised. Nearly always. But I wish to say goodbye to the day before I come to bed. I won't be out long."

She stayed in the open night only long enough to draw a few deep breaths and note the clouds scudding across a quarter moon. Another week, she hoped for a night so clear the Milky Way would shine like diamonds tossed into the sky.

Valery would be angry with her. She had pledged to obey her husband. Perhaps she had made a mistake.

But her sweet Valery sat before the fire with a piece of wood he was carving with exquisite skill into some creature, a bear, she thought, and he gave her a mocking glower when she came in.

"So, madame, you have not been eaten by a creature of fangs and claws."

She heard no real anger in his voice. She smiled. "Not this time. Perhaps another night you will be proven right."

Valery shook his head and sighed. "I see the kind of woman I have married. A rebellious, shrewish, ungovernable woman."

Agnes stepped behind him and wrapped her arms around his neck. "You will not find me rebellious, shrewish, nor ungovernable, monsieur. At least not very often."

"But you will go out into the night and star gaze while red-eyed creatures stalk you in the dark."

She nuzzled his neck. "All I need do is scream and my valiant husband will come to my rescue."

"Your valiant husband, eh?"

Her teeth teased at his ear lobe. "The most valiant husband in all of Louisiana."

Valery set his knife and wood away and pulled her into his lap. "Agnes, you will not go into the woods." With that voice, she would not argue.

"I won't."

"Very well, then. I will allow these nightly forays to say *au revoir* to the day. But you will stay very close to the cabin so that I will hear the puma pounce on you and eat you up." He goosed her in the ribs to make her laugh, and then he kissed her. "To bed, my shrewish wife."

The next day the sun beat down on the earth. Winter really was behind them. On the other side of the bayou a pink dogwood bloomed, providing perfect camouflage for her favorite spoon-billed birds. Agnes tended her chickens, worked in her garden, and continued to discover what could be done with an opossum in her cook pot.

That evening, as Valery continued carving his pine-wood bear, Agnes kissed the top of his head and stepped out into the night. She decided to walk down to the pond to see if her fairy friends had come to visit, and there they were, not merely two or three glowing lights this time, but nine of them! Valery must see this. She strode back to the cabin and stuck her head in the door. "Valery, I want to show you something."

"Have you seen a great bear with red eyes and bloody teeth?"

She grinned at him. "Something better. Come with me."

They walked through the starlit night toward the marshy pond. "You must approach them quietly or they will disappear," she whispered.

Perhaps thirty feet away, green globes floated above the grassy water.

Agnes's steps slowed. She hung back, dread coiling in her belly. She shouldn't have brought him out here. He was going to laugh and tell her these beautiful beings were merely swamp gas bubbled up from the muck beneath the shallow water. He was going to ruin this miracle that brought her such joy.

"Ah," Valery said, tugging at her hand to come on. "I have not seen these lights since I was a boy."

Agnes peered at his face and could swear her heart skipped a beat. He was smiling, staring at her beautiful friends.

He kept her hand in his and together they watched, silent and still, as the swamp fairies hovered, gently shifting up or down, right or left.

"When I was a boy, my mother used to introduce each ball of light as if they were fairy royalty."

"Oh, my mother entertained French royalty, King Charles and Queen Madeline."

Valery shook his head. "No, in our pond, we did not meet King Charles. There were Oberon and Titania, Eglantina, Eolande, Mayblossom. Frog."

"A fairy named Frog?"

"Most certainly. This particular fairy threw his voice into the bullfrog among the rushes, so of course we named him Frog."

"And who do you suppose these lovely fairies are?"

"Oh, I recognize them. There is King Oberon and next to him Queen Titania. They have come all the way from France to pay us a call. And with them are, yes, my old friends Eolande, Frog, Mayblossom."

"Then those must be Eglantina, Breena, and Donella."

"You are undoubtedly right. They must love us very much to have come such a long way to visit."

Valery draped his arm over her shoulder, and Agnes leaned into him, her fine husband who saw swamp fairies instead of swamp gas.

The last little corner of her heart opened to him. What happiness, standing here with her husband, held close to his side, the beautiful will-o-the-wisps blessing them with their presence. *Everything will be fine*, that's what she'd so fervently prayed that first day when she got in the dugout with the stranger she had just married. And her prayer had been granted. Everything was fine. More than fine.

They watched until the mosquitoes found them and commenced to feast on them. With a slap at the back of his neck, Valery grabbed her hand and said "Come on!"

With a last glimpse of her swampy friends, Agnes ran to the cabin, laughing as Valery tried to run and slap mosquitoes at the same time.

In the morning, Agnes woke eager to begin the day. First she would finish hoeing the weeds from around the indigo plants. They were maybe eighteen inches high already, and if Valery was correct, he would make a nice purse of cash from selling them to be processed into dye.

After the hoeing, Agnes meant to try her hand fishing off the banks of the bayou. How hard could it be? Valery had a bamboo pole, line, sinker, and hook. All she needed to do was dig for worms. There was a time that handling a wiggling purple worm would have horrified her, but she was resolved to do it.

Valery grabbed her arm when she tried to climb over him to get out of the bed. "Come here," he murmured in his sleepy voice.

The first weeks together, her husband had engaged her in a few quick powerful thrusts before he let her rise. These days, he took his time and made sweet, leisurely love to her. Which he proceeded to do this morning, followed by a lazy cuddle.

"This is the morning you mean to catch us a mighty fish for dinner? You want me to dig you some worms for bait?"

How very tempting to let him handle the slimy things. But she could not be the bookish city girl here. On a sigh, she said, "I will have to do it."

"My brave girl," he said and nuzzled her neck.

After breakfast, Agnes hoed her weeds, dug her worms, marched to the bayou, baited her hook, and waited. Boring work, this fishing. Why did men like it so much? She looked over her shoulder at Valery toiling on the far side of the clearing. Perhaps if she wielded a heavy axe all day, she would appreciate the respite.

At a sudden tug on her line, Agnes shrieked and jerked the line up. Valery came running. "Careful," he called. "Let him hook himself before you haul him out."

She raised the pole to display a ten inch trout, its scales shining in the sunlight as it struggled to get free.

"Ah, you have done it!"

"Beginner's luck," she said.

He showed her how to hold the fish in a firm grip as she removed the hook. "Let me get the bucket for you. He will stay fresh if you let him swim in a little water until it's time for the cook fire."

She fished another hour, eagerly anticipating another bite at any moment, but her beginner's luck had deserted her. She dumped her remaining worms in the mud and carried her trout to the cabin where Valery was sharpening his knife.

"My knife is very sharp, *mon chou*. I will clean the fish for you this time."

"I am pleased to let you do so," she said and set the bucket at his feet.

"Will you watch?"

Agnes sighed. "I suppose I must."

"Well," Valery began. "First you must kill it, so. Then you remove the scales."

Cleaning and gutting a fish was as gruesome as she had expected. But she did love fish, especially poached in a little white wine with mushrooms. Of course, they had no wine and no mushrooms. She would do what she could with her perfectly filleted trout.

Valery pronounced her poached fish *magnifique*. Agnes was so pleased that as she passed behind him to clear away the plates, she let her fingers drift across his back.

He reached for her fingers and drew her into his lap. "So you are now a fisherwoman," he teased.

"*C'est moi, une pêcheuse extraordinaire.*"

What would she have thought of Valery Villiers had she met him in Paris on Germaine Street? He didn't seem a man who would frequent book stores. Perhaps she would have met him at a musical evening, but no -- the clothes stored in his chest put him in a class above hers.

"I suppose," she said, settling herself in his lap, "back in Paris you adorned your hats with extravagant ostrich plumes."

"You surmise I cut a dashing figure in Paris, eh? You are right. A white plume on my hat, my cape lined with blue satin." She gave him a quiet moment as he remembered his former glory.

"You were a nobleman then?"

That brought his attention back with a grin. "Very distantly, but indeed, I most certainly am a noble man."

"Then you would have disdained a bookseller's daughter."

He pursed his lips, thoughtful with a glint in his eye, a smile on his lips. "Is she a beautiful bookseller's daughter?"

She laughed. "Let us assume she is acceptable."

"Then of course, a bookseller's daughter, especially if she is well-dowered. A wealthy wife is always welcome to a second son of a second son."

As a mere merchant's daughter, Agnes would not have had a dowry, nor was she beautiful. Well, what did it matter? Fate had decreed Valery would wed a dowerless, bookseller's daughter, and had furthermore decreed she would marry a penniless man who knew the names of the fairies in his pond.

She toyed with the strings at the neck of his linen shirt. "What were you when you lived in Paris, Valery?"

"Ah. You are asking questions. Well, perhaps it is not so much to tell you that I was a member of the King's Guard."

She raised her brows. "You were a musketeer?"

"You may well be impressed, *ma petite*. I was a musketeer of the king's own household. He did not stir from the palace without me, you may be sure."

She was impressed, actually. There were no finer soldiers in all the world, and the musketeers possessed a cachet, a mystique, that no other elite group could match.

"Then why are you here, Valery?"

His face took on a pinched look. "Let us say I dueled with the wrong man." He gently moved her from his lap and went outside.

Agnes supposed everyone here had a painful past, why else come to such a difficult life? Valery did not inquire about her secrets, she would not pry into his.

The next morning Valery was his usual cheerful, affectionate self. He kept her abed with lovemaking well past cockcrow. She hated to leave his arms except that the chickens were fussing to be let out.

The coop Valery had built for the chickens was a pleasure for her hens, she was sure of it. They clucked and churred gently when she cautiously lifted them to check for eggs.

"Augustina," she murmured. "Two eggs? What a fine hen you are. Babette, you lazy thing, not a single one. Maybe tomorrow, hmm?"

"You're talking to those chickens again," Valery said.

She smiled. "Would you like to say hello to Augustina? She is a very friendly sort of hen."

He snorted a laugh. "I'll leave the chicken conversations to you." He picked up his axe. This clearing of land was a never-ending task.

"Valery?"

He looked at her over his shoulder. "Hm?"

"Every day I hear someone else chopping wood, that way I think. Do you know who it is? How far away they are?"

"*Bien sur*. That is Leopold Joubert. He has a place half a mile downstream."

"Did he take a woman from the *New Hope*?"

Valery nodded. "The big one, chosen right after you."

"Marie Claude!"

He started off to his work, but she fell into step with him, two steps to his one. "Are you friends with this Monsieur Joubert?"

He shrugged. "I know him."

"Perhaps we could visit them."

He shrugged again, maddening man.

"Does that mean yes?"

He gave her a grin and another shrug.

"Valery."

"Perhaps. Not today though. A very stubborn hickory tree awaits. So far, he resists every stroke of my mighty axe."

"Do you know all the homesteads on the bayou? You know who lives where?"

"Hm," he said without commitment.

"It would be wonderful to know where all my friends have settled." A brilliant idea struck her. "I could make a map where everyone is."

"Agnes," he said. "I have work to do."

"I know, but you have to rest some time. Oh! Why don't you teach me to row the dugout and I can go by myself?"

He shook his head. "You, who cling to me in the night when you dream of alligators in the bayou? This clinging is very pleasant, *ma petite*, but you are very foolish if you go off without me. You comprehend why this must be so."

She remembered the first alligator she saw sunning itself on the bank, its evil eyes tracking them as they passed. "Still, if it is not so far to my friend Marie Claude . . . "

"You are so lonely here with me?" The dear man. For all his teasing, Agnes heard a vulnerable note in his voice. Her husband, who had seemed so full of himself in their first days together, was a more complicated man than she had understood. He had come to need her, she realized.

"You are good to me, Valery." But he still didn't know her. Didn't even know she could read and write.

"But?"

She smiled, peering at him from under her lashes, perhaps the first flirtatious look she'd ever attempted. "But you are not Marie Claude."

He laughed, as she hoped he would. "One day, then."

Happy, Agnes returned to her chickens. She was keeping an eye on Augustina who showed signs of becoming broody. Perhaps, with warmer weather and a fine coop to keep their nests safe from marauding foxes and raccoons, her feathery friends could think about raising some chicks. She looked at the rooster. "You will do your best, eh, Lucan?"

When she heard the sound of a paddle bumping against the side of a dugout canoe, she held her hand over her brow to see who was on the bayou.

At the landing, she called a cheery "*Bonjour*!"

A well-dressed man greeted her with a big smile as he came ashore. He might have just come from a stroll through the Tuileries in his velvet jacket and folded-brim hat, though his jacket and breeches were in sad need of brushing.

"Madame," he said and swept his hat from his head to entertain her with a deep bow. "I am looking for my friend Valery Villiers. Perhaps you know him?"

Agnes beamed at him. "I am Madame Villiers." She turned to her husband coming with the axe over his shoulder. "Look, Valery. You have a friend come to call on you."

"Nolet!"

The visitor held a hand out to Valery. "Villiers, my old friend."

The men engaged in friendly slaps to the shoulder, and then Nolet said, "I find you a married man, Villiers?"

"Ah. My wife, Madame Villiers. Agnes, Robert Nolet."

Agnes felt quite tall. *My wife* sounded very fine. She smiled and curtsied, then caught a narrow-eyed look from Monsieur Nolet. He quickly replaced that moment's piercing gaze with a charming smile.

"A pleasure to meet you, madame."

"What are you doing in this land of storms, serpents, and struggle?" Valery asked.

"Money, of course. I hope to make some."

"Of course, you must stay with us. We are not *un grand hôtel*, but we can keep the rain off."

"*Bien*. A moment," he said, and retrieved a squirming pink and white piglet from the dugout. "I had hoped this little fellow would be my contribution to the cook pot."

"Oh, no!" Agnes hugged the piglet protectively. "He is not for the pot. I will raise him to be a great boar and find a female for his company." She grinned at Valery. "Soon we will have a yard full of little pink piglets, *n'cest pas*?"

Valery stroked a finger down the piglet's snout and smiled. "I suppose you, your hens, and this little pig will have fine conversations of a morning."

"Yes, indeed."

Monsieur Nolet bowed. "I am pleased the piglet makes you happy, madame."

"He does, monsieur."

Nolet reached into the dugout again and held a jug aloft. "It's a rough brew, my friend, but perhaps you will welcome a glass."

Valery grinned. "I will happily bend an elbow with you."

The two men ambled off in conversation, leaving Agnes with her adorable piglet. Her grand-mère had made pets of the piglets on the dairy farm. After they were weaned, they followed her around, hoping for the bits of carrot she kept in her pocket just for them.

"You shall be called Fulbert, after your cousin in Anjou," she said, holding the piglet up to look into her eyes. "What a fine fellow you are. You must not tell Augustina I said so, but chickens are sadly lacking in expression. You and I shall have many interesting conversations."

She fed Fulbert a corncob and left him to forage in the yard, then entered the cabin thinking about what she had to offer for supper. At home, she would have slipped across the street to the *boulangerie* for fresh bread, served ox tail in brown sauce with green beans and baby squash, then laid out a board of lovely ripe brie to be finished off with a pear compote. *Hélas*, no ox tail, no pear compote.

Valery cocked his chin toward her to come to him. "We'll have a chicken for supper, my dear."

"My business should take only a few days," Nolet continued. "Then I will hire a boat to take me to New Orleans. I hear it is growing quickly..."

Agnes did not want to kill any of her chickens. She needed them to breed so that eventually she would have an egg business. She could feed their guest bacon and beans from the general store. Under Monsieur Nolet's voice, she whispered, "But, Valer -- "

"A chicken, *mon chou*," Valery whispered back. To Nolet, he said, "I understand there are several hundred people in New Orleans already. I believe to get there, one does not travel from the great river's mouth?"

"So I understand. The boats travel along the coast and then into the lakes to wend their way to the strip of land separating the lake from New Orleans. I hear the surrounding area is mostly marsh, perhaps not the healthiest spot to build . . ."

As Monsieur Nolet talked, Agnes felt his eyes on her. She flushed and went outside to choose which of her precious hens to sacrifice.

Hands on hips, she walked around the yard, looking over her brood. Never Augustina. Of course not Lucan the rooster. There was Evangeline, so pretty with her black and green feathers. No, not Evangeline. There, scratching in the dirt, was Adelaid whom Agnes thought might be an old hen. She had yet to lay an egg in all these months. Very well, if she must sacrifice one of her lovely hens, it would have to be poor Adelaid.

She caught Adelaid up and cradled her in her arms, crooning to calm her. She swallowed back tears. She had never killed a chicken before herself, but she'd seen grand-père chop a head off with his axe. The memory of a headless chicken running across the yard made her want to gag.

"You are distressed, Madame Villiers."

Agnes whirled around to see Monsieur Nolet watching her from the doorway. He stepped into the yard.

"My sister, she was the same. She made pets of all the chickens, the lambs, the pigs until she would have had us sit down to a table of nothing but turnips and bread. Shall I do this for you?"

He ran the back of his fingers down Adelaid's neck, and then allowed those same fingers to drift across Agnes's breast.

Agnes jerked back.

"I have remembered where I have seen you, madame."

Did he mean in the bookstore? No, not with the way he looked her over -- he meant the brothel. The sunny day suddenly felt cold and gray. The old shame and misery washed over her, wiping out all the happiness she had begun to find here with Valery.

She shook her head, her stomach roiling. "No, monsieur. You don't know me."

"Oh, yes. Quite a memorable little piece, to lie beneath a man, no more animate than a stiff mattress. I don't believe you even blinked. So Madame De Bree kicked you out, is that it?"

Cold gripped her hands and feet. She struggled not to reel.

"Do you play the dead fish when Villiers lies with you, *ma petite*? My friend, he was reputed among the ladies to be a most satisfactory lover. Perhaps he persuades you to participate in the act, to show a little enthusiasm?"

"Leave me alone," she whispered.

He gently took Adelaid from her, both of his hands brushing freely against her breasts.

"Perhaps I will discover what it is like to take a tiny little thing like you now that you have come alive, eh?"

Without warning, he gripped Adelaid's neck, performed a quick swing and jerk, and handed her back to Agnes. "At your service, madame," he said with a mock bow.

Clutching poor Adelaid, Agnes ran from him, finding refuge behind the cabin. Trembling, she sank to the ground and, leaning over Adelaid's still-warm body, wept bitter tears. Of all the thousands upon thousands of men in the world, how could one of *them* have found her?

Valery knew she'd been a whore. From the age of ten, isn't that what he'd assumed? Perhaps he would not even be surprised when this Monsieur Nolet told him he had once lain with his wife.

She folded in on herself, her heart squeezing itself into a hot, heavy ball. What if Valery didn't even care that his friend had once lain with her?

Valery found her there, hunched over Adelaid's still body.

"Agnes?" He knelt down in front of her. "You're as white as chalk. It was so hard to kill your chicken?"

What if she told him herself, before Nolet did? Would it make a difference? Would he despise her to actually know one of the men who had taken her? Or worse, maybe he would even allow this man Nolet to have her again. She nearly retched at the thought.

Valery took the chicken from her and helped her to her feet. "Come now. I thought you said you raised chickens in your back yard? Can it be so hard? Can you not do your plucking and get the bird ready for our dinner? Of course you can."

He handed the chicken back to her, gave her a kindly pat on the shoulder, and left her to it.

Once she'd plucked and prepared the chicken, she fed the men, not able to eat a bite herself, and retreated outside where Fulbert was digging for grubs. She gave a low whistle and the piglet trotted to her where she sat on the stoop.

Petting him and crooning to him comforted her. Fulbert did not see a spoiled piece of humanity when he looked at her.

Valery stepped out and gently touched her hair. "Our guest will be staying a few days," he said.

She looked at him. "We won't eat Fulbert?"

"Fulbert, is it? It is hard, I agree, to name a creature and then invite him to dinner as a nice, crispy roast."

Nolet came out and Valery told him, "My good wife fears for her piglet, Robert."

Her face burned with humiliation, but she didn't back down. "He should be kept for breeding," she insisted.

"What a tender heart you have, madame," Nolet said. He bestowed a kindly smile as if he had no carnal interest in her. Valery had no idea the danger Agnes felt from this man.

When dark came, Valery and his friend stayed up talking by the light of the fire and Agnes went to bed. They'd been merry comrades in Paris at one time. Women, wine, song, and sword play. Much of the conversation began with "Do you remember," to be followed by embellishments and laughter.

Valery reverted to boasting as the night wore on. Why did he need to boast? He had been a musketeer, a position of great esteem in her eyes, but perhaps he did not feel so sure of that himself. Nolet encouraged him, even flattered him. What did this man want that he should so shamelessly build up Valery's pride? And why was her husband so ill-at-ease?

Lulled by their voices, Agnes fell asleep, but she woke when her husband came to bed. Nolet was stretched out on the floor on his bedroll.

She closed her eyes tight and prayed Valery would not touch her with this man in the cabin. She thought she would have to disappear if he did that.

Valery left his breeches on and climbed into bed beside her. She rolled away from him, her face to the wall. Surely that would be enough to show him she did not wish to be touched. She felt his hand lightly stroke her arm. "Good night, *ma petite,*" he whispered.

# Chapter Fifteen

*Catherine and Jean Paul*
*Soapberries*

Catherine added a pinch of salt to the pot of corn meal mush bubbling over the fire. While it cooked, Catherine chopped up the last tattered winter cabbage they would eat tonight, stewed with whatever creature had wandered into Jean Paul's snare. She was sick of cabbage, sick of the sweet potatoes that were beginning to sprout in their bin. And now began the age-old scarcity in the spring time when the winter stores were eaten or spoiled and the new crops were not yet in. They would not go hungry, though. The woods were full of game, the bayou full of fish, and the guava trees still carried luscious yellow fruit.

Not to mention the ever-present corn meal. She ladled the mush into a gourd bowl and set it in front of Jean Paul. With great restraint, she did not mention how a dab of butter and a dollop of sweet cream would improve it.

Jean Paul blew on the steaming bowl. "I need to go to the store this Sunday. I don't suppose you want to go with me."

Catherine snapped her head up. "You just try and go without me."

His mouth quirked in a small smile. "That's what I thought."

They had been to mass every Sunday the last few weeks. Catherine took those forays into civilization as a sort of apology for the day Jean Paul had interrogated her as if she were a criminal. She had certainly resented his inquisition at the time, and had planned to be annoyed with him until he should apologize, which meant forever, but when he'd met her after mass, there had been misery in his face. He had been scowling, of course, but there was the giveaway of his throat moving in a dry swallow, and the hint of vulnerability in his eyes. She wasn't so proud as to insist on a verbal apology; she accepted the one she saw instead of heard.

"What do you want to buy?" she asked him.

He stared at her, his gaze dropping to her pitiful blue dress. "I do have some silver, Catherine, but just barely enough to see us through until the indigo brings in some money. I can't buy you a new gown. Not yet."

It was true she dreaded putting the thing on every morning. How long had it been since Hugo tossed her on board the *New Hope*? It must be late April. Nearly six months. Hard to believe when once she had changed her dress several times a day.

But here she was, healthy and strong. This sad old gown didn't hurt anything but her pride, and she had mostly lost all of that. She did want, she needed, a new dress, but she didn't dwell on it. Besides, who was there to impress here on the bayou?

She smiled at Jean Paul. "You bought me the cloak that got me through the winter."

He nodded curtly, which didn't surprise her. Being gracious enough to accept a little gratitude was probably beyond him. But he had bought her that warm cloak.

"So what will we buy?"

"Seeds."

"You know what kind? You know how to plant a garden?"

"I know enough."

"And how did a musketeer learn to farm?"

He smiled, only a little, but it was there. "I was not born a musketeer, a sword in one hand, a musket in the other. I grew up on a farm."

He had never mentioned his family. He'd never mentioned anything about his past.

"So you know how to grow crops even in Louisiana? Is it much the same as home?"

"Not entirely. But the old men, the first Frenchmen, they learned from the Indians. They talk, I listen."

"Where are these first Frenchmen?" she asked. "I haven't seen anyone over thirty or forty since I've been here."

"They're mostly dead, or managed to get back to France. In fact . . . " He looked at her with a glint of mischief in his eyes. "In fact, the first women who came over staged a rebellion, demanding to be sent home."

The women who came over on the *New Hope* had nothing to go home to. "Did it work? Did they send them home?"

"Somebody asked the Indians to teach the women how to cook with what they had so that they didn't eat corn meal mush the live long day."

"I like corn meal mush. Well, I like it well enough."

He actually gave her a little smile. Three smiles in one morning!

"Good thing. Anyway, the settlers who came later were better prepared. They brought garden seeds, for instance, and a notion of how to get them to grow."

"When do we plant those?"

Jean Paul nodded toward the field. Grass was sprouting up in the ground she'd already cleared.

Catherine groaned. "I'll have to hoe those weeds out all over again, I suppose."

She glanced at Jean Paul, hoping for just an inkling of sympathy, but his face had no expression. Which was, she thought, a kind of expression. Well, so be it.

"When do you think you'll have it ready?"

"I think I can get it weeded in two days. I *will* get it weeded in two days." At least the little indigo plants were out-growing the weeds in their quarter of the garden.

With renewed enthusiasm, Catherine attacked the grasses growing where beans and squash should go. Could they possibly have carrot seeds at the store? And would Father Xavier stand there scowling at the people going in to shop on the Sabbath? She had little sympathy for him. It was not as if the settlers could drop into shop just any day. It would take her and Jean Paul most of the day to paddle down the bayou, cross the sound, go to mass, shop, visit with friends, and then paddle home again. A day well spent, but meanwhile, the weeds would be peeking up through her newly hoed ground while she wasn't looking.

Catherine sang quietly, counting her blessings as she worked. Her hands were nicely callused so that she didn't have to think about blisters any more. Her muscles had accustomed themselves to all kinds of labor. And she had had an actual conversation with her husband this morning.

Jean Paul had even asked her opinion about when they would plant! How often had that happened in her marriage? In fact, she wasn't sure anyone in her life had asked her opinion about anything weightier than the exact color of a swatch of silk.

Jean Paul passed by on his way to the bayou. "Where are you going?" she called.

"Saw some otters up the bayou the other day. Going to see if I can get one."

What Catherine wanted to say was *be careful*, but she thought she was less likely to earn a blank look if she said *good luck*, so that's what she said. He told Débile to stay and pushed off in the dugout.

Catherine resumed her attack on the weeds until mid-day when she put her hoe aside to rest and eat a bite. Débile lazed in the shade with Suzette and the piglets, taking it easy in the heat. Good idea, if you were a dog or a pig, but Catherine aimed to finish her hoeing. She stretched her arms over head and got back to work.

When Débile alerted her that Jean Paul was home, she strolled down to the landing to watch him paddle the last yards. "Did you get one?"

He grinned at her. "I got two."

She clapped her hands and backed up so he could pull the dugout ashore.

When he stepped out of the boat, she wanted to hug him. She was proud of him, the mighty hunter, and she had missed him. Instead, she merely said, "Well done!"

He hauled the dead otters out of the dugout and held them up. "Worth a dress, don't you think? Once I cure them?"

She bit her lip. He'd done this for her.

"You aren't going to cry, are you?" he said with a scowl and a warning note in his voice.

She pressed the back of her hand to her nose. "No, certainly not."

~~~

The next day was Saturday and by mid-day, Catherine had the entire garden hoed and ready for planting. She surveyed the turned earth arranged in rows and furrows and experienced an altogether new sensation. Accomplishment. She, with her own two hands, had prepared this soil to nurture the plants that would feed them through the next months.

If her friends in Paris could see her with rough hands, fingernails caked with dirt, sunburned, and very pleased with herself, they would be amazed, and completely baffled.

When had Catherine or her friends ever accomplished anything? She had learned to play the piano forte and learned to speak German, but those did nothing to feed anyone, and, truthfully, it wasn't as if she had actually mastered the piano, or German either. Yes, she had planned a glamorous soiree that was deemed a great success, but other hands had polished the floor, arranged the furniture, lit the candles. *This* she had done all by herself. Imagine, working people must experience this sort of gratification all the time. She had never guessed the peasants on Grandfather's estate led such fulfilling lives.

Catherine set her hoe against the side of the cabin and walked over to where Jean Paul was tacking his otter hides to a frame. They lay flat so the sun could help the salt draw out the moisture on the fleshy side of the hide.

"I used all the salt," he said. "We'll have to get some more tomorrow."

"I've finished, Jean Paul." She felt like a school girl showing her governess the perfect row of letters she'd written.

He straightened up and looked over her garden ready for planting. His dark eyes were impossible to read. Was he proud of her or not?

Very soberly, very quietly, Jean Paul said, "Well done."

Catherine drew in a big breath and grinned, yes, just like a child proud of her lesson book.

"We should take the afternoon off," she said impulsively.

"And do what?"

Well, they couldn't enjoy themselves in the music room, or go riding across the hills, or attend a cotillion. "We could visit our friends in the village."

He hesitated. "The Biloxi, you mean?"

"The chief said we'd be welcome, when you carried the boy home that day. We do need to be good neighbors."

Jean Paul ran his fingers through his hair. "All right."

"Just let me gather some nuts to take."

As Catherine and Jean Paul entered the village, Akecheta and two of the uncles greeted them. Or rather they greeted Jean Paul. The men did no more than glance at Catherine, they being men and so very much more important than she. With her nose in the air, she strolled past them to find Fleur for a friendly chat.

She followed the voices of the women to the stream where several were washing each other's hair. Shampoo? Where did they come by that?

Three little naked children splashed and shrieked with glee. Their mothers allowed this? When Catherine was a child, her nurses would never have let her get wet from head to toe. They swore it would lead to a fatal chill. But what fun the children were having.

Fleur poured water from a gourd to rinse the hair of one of her friends. Another woman wrung the water from her long black tresses.

"*Bonjour*," Fleur called to her.

The women put their clothes back on and moved into the open spaces of the village where the sun could dry their hair. Catherine admired the heavy straight tresses, gleaming blue-black in the sunshine. Her maid used to wash her hair with lilac soap and just a touch of vinegar to make the blonde highlights shine. Then she'd rinsed it with lilac water and she'd smelled like springtime.

"You wash your hair often?" Catherine asked, fingering her own lank, dirty hair. More than cream or butter or oil lamps, she missed soap.

Fleur shrugged. "It's spring time."

"And you buy soap at the general store?"

"Buy soap? Why would I buy soap?" At Catherine's evident confusion, she added, "You don't know how to make soap?"

"I have no idea how to make soap." It was humbling to be so ignorant of the things everyone here seemed to know. She nearly excused herself thinking how Fleur knew nothing about René Descartes, or about dancing at a grand ball, or . . . But these were hollow comparisons. Who cared if you knew the great philosophers or the latest operas if you needed to work to feed yourself, if you needed to make your own soap.

"Come. I'll show you." Fleur led her to a small tree where they picked golden fruits with wrinkled skin. "Take these, boil them in water. Let it sit a while to cool, and you have soap."

Catherine wrapped the fruit in a large leaf, eager to wash her own hair. "I brought your favorite nuts," she said, hoping they were as welcome to Fleur as the soap was to her.

Fleur's little boy slept in her lap, and two friends joined them to share the nuts. This time, after so many days of wielding a hoe, Catherine's hands surely were hardened enough to crack the nuts as Fleur did.

No, they were not. The women tittered at her, but she didn't take offense. Maybe by the end of the summer -- how absurdly proud she would feel when her once smooth, white hands would be strong enough to crack nuts.

On the way home, Catherine followed Jean Paul down the narrow path, chattering all the way. Now she could make him a gourd of shaving soap, could keep their clothes clean, and best of all, they could truly bathe with something besides water. She could heat water, just enough, and they could take turns -- She blushed as an image arose of the two of them standing naked in front of a pot of warm water, washing each other with bare hands, skin to skin.

She hushed the rest of the way back to the cabin.

As soon as they were home, she put the pot on to boil. There was plenty of day light yet for her hair to dry. She made the shampoo as Fleur instructed and let the concoction cool.

Out in the yard, she stripped down to her shift. Who was there to see except Jean Paul and he was not interested in what she looked like. She wet her hair and poured a gourd full of the soapberry mixture over her head. It felt wonderful, working the warm suds through her hair. The smell was not objectionable, but next time she would squeeze some of those little orange fruits into the soap, the ones that smelled a little like oranges, a little like lemons.

When she was ready to rinse, she reached blindly for the gourd. Not there. She patted around in the grass, eyes closed, frustrated and puzzled. Then a splash of water over her head told her where her gourd had gone.

He poured gourd after gourd of rinse water over her head, Catherine very aware that her rear was sticking up in the air. Finally she spluttered, "That's enough."

She sat back and wiped her eyes, expecting the deluge to be over, when another full measure of water splashed right across her chest.

She looked down. Her breasts might as well have been bare with her wet shift stuck to her like that. He had done that deliberately.

She narrowed her eyes at him. Was he playing with her? But there was no playfulness in his face. His eyes were on her breasts, then on her mouth. Desire was new to Catherine, but she felt it in full force, as strong as when he'd kissed her, and he was only looking at her. But with such a hungry, yearning look. She rose, wanting him to kiss her, to touch her.

She took a step toward him, her eyes locked on his.

Abruptly, he turned from her and strode away.

Her whole body tingled with disappointment and confusion. He had kissed her, he had held her. She didn't understand.

That night, she lay awake a long time, hurt and angry. She knew he didn't sleep, either, his body tense in the bed beside her.

# Chapter Sixteen

*Catherine and Jean Paul*
*Calico*

The bell for mass rang as Jean Paul pulled the dugout onto dry land.

"We'll have to hurry if we don't want to stand in the back," Catherine said.

When he didn't follow her, she turned around. "You aren't coming."

It was not a question, he noticed. He simply shook his head.

She hesitated, nodded, and headed for the chapel.

Farther along the landing, Jean Paul spotted Laroux in discussion with a settler he didn't know. The two shook hands and the stranger strode off toward the fort.

"*Bonjour*," Jean Paul said. "You've sold another dugout?"

"I have. This one, you see, has a sharper prow for cutting through lily pads and grasses in shallow water. And along here," he said, bending to show Jean Paul, "I've added a sort of bladed shape to the front of the keel."

Jean Paul admired Laroux's skill. The dugout Jean Paul had made for himself was crude and shallow, the chip marks from his crude carving giving the whole thing a ramshackle look. He might try another one someday. He ought to study one of Laroux's first so he didn't end up carving out another boat that still looked like a cypress log.

"More settlers coming, I hear," Jean Paul said. "If you show off your handsome boats, you'll have no trouble attracting one of the convent girls when they arrive."

Laroux shook his head. "I'm not looking for a wife. I'm going home as soon as I have a stake."

Men did not ask personal questions, of course, but Jean Paul's expression was a clear invitation to explain.

Laroux grimaced. "I mean to buy back the family estate. My father, poor fellow. He was confused the last years of his life, and a con man talked him into gambling the entire farm, house, lands, everything."

Jean Paul eyed him. Every musketeer was a swordsman of great skill, and Laroux had also been a musketeer. "You did not solve the problem with your sword?"

Laroux's smile was genuinely amused. "Running the fellow through would have been satisfying, I admit. But since the blackguard was the local magistrate, and had arranged the scam so that it had every appearance of being legal, I would have ended up an avenged man in chains. No. I will buy it back. Gold will be convincing, I believe, and I will not have to kill the man."

So Laroux would not seek a wife here in Louisiana. A wife would tie him to this land, to this life. There might be children. He might never be able to reclaim his inheritance. Which meant that Laroux must live a lonely life, just as Jean Paul had before Catherine came to him.

Jean Paul remembered the naked yearning on Laroux's face when he'd stared at Catherine's friend Fleur across the open ground. Even a dream, a goal, like Laroux's didn't keep a man from wanting.

~~~

Catherine paid little attention to Father Xavier as he droned his way through the mass. She was more interested in seeing the women from the *New Hope* sitting with their husbands, amazed at what she could deduce just from looking at their backs. Ahead of her, Rachel sat close to a narrow-shouldered man with curling brown hair, not a sliver of light between them. Catherine felt a quick pang that she and Jean Paul would never sit close like that. On the same bench, Selina sat very straight next to the thick-necked man who'd married her, a full six inches between them. The stiffness of Selina's posture suggested she was angry, not simply indifferent. Maybe angry was better. Maybe anything was better than indifference.

She lived with Jean Paul, ate with him, worked with him, even slept beside him. But she was lonely. He had been friendlier the last few weeks, but there might never be any warmth, any true companionship, between them, and she had to prepare herself for that. With that ache in her heart, she closed her eyes, in need of the comfort the priest offered.

After mass, the women fetched their picnic baskets where they'd left them in the dugouts so the ants wouldn't get into them.

Catherine spread a cloth on the ground next to Marie Claude's and Agnes's blankets. The three of them laid their provisions out together as they had the last several Sundays and called their husbands to come eat.

Jean Paul and Valery Villiers had become friendly since their wives brought them together. Marie Claude's husband remained aloof and rather surly. While the other five chatted over the cold meat and corn cakes, Joubert scarfed his food down and left them to their picnic.

"Where is your husband going?" Catherine asked.

Marie Claude nodded to the well-dressed man standing at the fort's gate. "That's Monsieur Nolet. He wants to do business with Joubert." She shrugged. "After that, I imagine he'll throw dice with some of the soldiers."

"What is it, Agnes?" She'd gone pale when she saw the stranger Joubert spoke with. "Do you know him?"

"He is staying with us, in fact." Catherine wasn't fooled at the bright smile Agnes pasted on her face. "A friend of Valery's from the old days."

"You don't like him?"

"Oh, of course I do. Monsieur Nolet is most charming," Agnes said, and changed the subject.

"I am sure it can be done," Valery was saying. "As soon as I find out how, from the Indians or perhaps another Frenchman, I shall experiment. Corn liquor, I've heard it called."

"And I've heard that stuff will burn a hole in your gut," Jean Paul said.

Valery stroked his moustache and smiled. "So you will not be joining me in a glass?"

Jean Paul grinned. "I didn't say that."

After luncheon, if so grand a word could be applied to such simple fare, the men and women separated. "What will you do?" Catherine asked Jean Paul.

"Watch the men shoot. Chevalier is arranging a competition."

"Will you shoot?"

He shrugged and shook his head.

"You're not a good shot?" she teased.

He smirked but didn't say anything.

"You are a good shot," she guessed.

"Hm hmm," he said with a slight nod, and gave her a quick grin.

"You could win? You don't want to?"

He trained his eyes on the row of gourds Chevalier arranged along a log. "I don't need to win."

That was interesting, this glimpse into Jean Paul's confidence. While his attention was on the men preparing to shoot, she studied this man she lived with but didn't know. His hair, tied back with a leather string, was almost as straight and dark as his friend Mato's. His skin was bronzed from working in the sun, and he was fresh-shaved this morning. He had used the soap she saved for him in his own little shaving gourd, and his jaw was smooth and firm. If she had seen him across some salon at Versailles, she would have thought he was aloof, even forbidding. She would have matched his cool demeanor with her own haughty air, and she would have secretly yearned for Grandfather to present him to her.

"What are the ladies doing today?"

"Ah, I will teach them how to make shampoo! And Rachel has promised to show us how to weave straw hats. If you ask very nicely, I will make one for you first, monsieur."

The look he gave her could have melted cheese. What did he mean by it? He was forever throwing her off balance, cool one day, almost friendly the next, and occasionally, he seared her with a look that turned her whole body hot. She swallowed hard. "Yes, very well. The first hat is yours."

Flushed, she turned on her heel and joined the other women.

Later in the afternoon, Jean Paul came for her. "Let's go get our seeds."

It took a moment for Catherine's eyes to adjust to the dim interior of the store, and then she made out a group of settlers crowded around the display of little paper sacks.

The seed packets were labeled pumpkin, onion, green beans, cucumbers, peas, peppers, squash, carrots, and of course corn.

One little packet of all the dozens and dozens remaining was labeled *spinach*. Catherine reached for it, her mouth watering. "Oh, Jean Paul, please can we grow spinach? And carrots?"

"We can try."

At home, they had pieces of potatoes with the eyes sprouting to plant, so they needn't buy those or corn either. Seeds were dear, and Jean Paul settled on onion, pumpkin, squash, beans, spinach, and carrots. "Peppers?" Catherine wheedled.

He gave her a scowl, but she knew he didn't mean it. He added a bag of salt and packet of pepper seeds to his order.

"Nothing else?" he said, just a hint of sarcasm in his voice. "Truffles, perhaps? Bon bons?"

She gave him a sunny smile, hoping to amuse him, or irritate him. Either one would be satisfying. "Peppers will be sufficient, my lord."

On the way out of the store, Catherine paused at the table laden with bolts of woolens and cottons printed with gay patterns. Jean Paul stopped. "Which do you like the best?"

"Yellow," she said. She ran her hand over cream cotton printed with yellow flowers. "I love yellow."

Jean Paul plucked the bolt off the table with one hand and carried it back to the proprietor. He and Peppard conferred quietly, their heads together. Peppard took the yellow cotton and set it underneath his counter.

Jean Paul took Catherine's elbow and guided her through the shoppers to the outdoors. "He'll hold it for us two weeks. I'll bring the otter skins in, and the yellow cloth is yours."

Catherine threw her arms around his neck and kissed him right on the mouth, heedless of the people around them. That he would go to so much trouble for her. He did care for her, no matter how much he scowled.

"Catherine." He gently removed her arms from around his neck, his face bright red. He glanced around, but Catherine didn't care that some were snickering, some disapproving.

She blinked to keep the tears from falling. "Thank you, Jean Paul."

"All right," he growled, and took her home.

# Chapter Seventeen

*Marie Claude*
*First Strike*

In the afternoon, the man Marie Claude had seen talking to her husband pulled his dugout ashore. She walked down to the bayou to greet him.

"*Bienvenue*, monsieur."

"Madame."

The man removed his modest hat and greeted her with a nod of his head. Marie Claude answered with a warm smile. She couldn't think when a man had shown her such courtesy. The farmers and the miller in her village had only worn caps, and they didn't see any need to take them off just because a female came into view.

The visitor raised his hand in greeting as Joubert strode from the field to shake his hand.

"Nolet," Joubert said.

"I've come to make you an offer."

Marie Claude was disappointed when the two walked off without another word to her. She'd hoped for a little conversation with a new acquaintance, but never mind. She had work to do.

She attacked the weeds in her vegetable garden while Joubert showed this Monsieur Nolet their stand of indigo. They actually were *her* indigo plants since she was the one who had planted and nurtured them. They were growing well, pretty plants with sweet little leaves either side of the stem.

She swung her hoe over her shoulder and walked down the row so she could hear them. The visitor was gesturing at the indigo and then holding his hand out level and turning it side to side as if to say, maybe this, maybe that.

Shameless in her eavesdropping, Marie Claude wielded her hoe not ten feet from the men, but they ignored her. She'd thought they would.

"These vats your men are making, they're too small for the kind of production I'll need. Can't really do business with you at that scale."

"You promised -- " Joubert accused.

Nolet held his hand up. "I did not promise. I merely pointed out an opportunity. To make the most of this opportunity, you will need to invest in industrial vats. Large ones. I can supply these, for a fee, of course."

"You're nothing but a damn vat salesman. I took you for a broker."

"You produce enough dye, I will be your broker. I have the king's patent in this part of the territory, and you won't get a better price for your indigo cake than through me. But I must deal in volume."

Marie Claude's husband jutted his chin out so that he looked like a stubborn billy goat.

"Come, Monsieur Joubert. All these settlers bringing you their indigo to process? You stand to make a fortune."

"And where am I supposed to get that kind of cash to buy vats?"

Nolet spread his hands. "You're an enterprising man, Joubert. That's why I approached you in the first place. I'm sure we can come to terms."

After Monsieur Nolet left, Joubert stood on the shoreline, his arms crossed, and stared at the water. Marie Claude doubted he even noticed the great gray bird flying low down the bayou.

In the evening, Marie Claude watched him as she served his dinner, the anger coming off him like stink.

Well, she couldn't help him. She certainly had no money to buy vats. Was he as poor as he seemed? He had not declared to Monsieur Nolet that it was an impossibility to buy these vats. Perhaps he had diamonds hidden in his chest. She smiled at the absurdity.

"What are you smiling at?" he snarled.

She was very tempted to say *not much*, but that would only make him angrier. He behaved like a spoiled child, so maybe she should simply treat him like one. She turned her back on him as if he were a dreadful little boy having a tantrum.

He stood up so suddenly he knocked his chair over. Marie Claude whirled around on instinct and caught Joubert's wrist before he could pound his fist onto her back. That he would hit her in the back -- he was a gutter rat, no more than that. She squeezed his wrist and pushed steadily, forcing him back and down.

"Let go, you whoring bitch!"

"You ever hit me, monsieur, I will kill you in your sleep." She tossed his arm in his face and turned her back on him. Her ears attuned to his breathing, to his movement, she took hold of the iron ladle. If he moved to attack her, she was ready.

He chose wisely. He stomped out of the cabin, leaving his dinner unfinished. Good. In the beginning, she had not been sure but what it would be the right thing to submit to a husband, and she certainly didn't want to murder anyone. But when she felt him come at her from behind, she had decided, all at once, that she would tolerate no violence from Leopold Joubert even if he was her husband.

She finished her supper and cleaned up. For a while she sat on the stoop watching the sun go down. Across the field, Thomas and his friends were singing in low, sweet voices. A mournful song, tonight, that made her heart ache for home. Did her family, her mother, her father, her brother and sisters, did they think of her? She wished she were in her father's cottage, right now, braiding Evangeline's hair and coaxing Annique to go to sleep.

The four slaves were a long way from home, too. She wondered if Thomas had a family he ached for?

Full dark, the clouds covering the stars, Marie Claude prepared for bed. She put on her plain nightgown that only reached the top of her calves. The loose nightgowns in the small casket each girl was issued were all of a size, and of course hers was too short. She combed out her hair and rebraided it. Catherine was right. She did have nice hair, the color of ripe wheat, and now she was clean and healthy again, it had a shine to it. Well, wasn't she silly, indulging in vanity, a woman like her.

Joubert had not come back yet. Where could he be on such a dark night? This was not Paris where there was always a brazier lit or a torch being carried down a street or a lantern over someone's door. Too dark to be hunting possum out there, and his musket sat in the corner. Fishing? She'd never seen him fish before. He left the fishing to Remy and Pierre and expected half of what they caught. Besides, there was no moon and everyone knew the fish didn't bite on moonless nights.

He'd had a bad day, and all his anger was directed at her. She'd threatened to kill him, but it was more likely he was thinking about killing her. No one would call him to account for it out here. All he'd have to say is *poor Marie Claude, got bit by a cottonmouth moccasin,* or *swallowed by a gator,* or *eat up by a fever.*

She fetched the kitchen knife and slipped it in her sleeve before she climbed into the bed. Just in case.

# Chapter Eighteen

*Agnes*
*Her Champion*

Mid-morning, their guest Monsieur Nolet shoved off in his dugout to go about his day's business. Until the evening, at least, Agnes was free from the man's sly looks. She was not free, however, from the gnawing fear that Nolet would take her, and Valery would not care. Her fingers trembled as she took a cup of water to her husband, the piglet Fulbert following along behind her.

With a determined breath, Agnes tamped down her fear. She need only live in this moment, and this moment offered many pleasures. Agnes loved her chickens, and Fulbert was a joy. She swore he listened when she talked to him, and he was pleased to keep her company, which Augustina did not deign to do.

In the field, Valery labored over a stubborn clump of roots, the muscles of his back straining against his thin cotton shirt.

"*Ah, mon petit chou*, you are too good to me," he said as he accepted the cup of water.

Her husband was free with his endearments, which she supposed meant that they had little meaning to him. She enjoyed them just the same. "You work hard, monsieur. I am pleased to bring you a cup of cool water."

He leaned against a tree trunk in the shade and drank, taking his time, resting.

"Valery," she said after a moment. "I do not like your friend."

He gave her a sharp glance.

"I don't think you like him either."

He shrugged, tossed back the rest of the water. "It does not matter whether I like him or not. He is here." He handed her the cup.

"What does he want, Valery?"

"He wants to sell vats. He wants to make money." He gave a disgusted look at the tangle of thick roots he was struggling with. "I'm going to have to burn that stump out."

She nodded, her mind on whether to tell Valery that his friend meant to take her. "That would save your poor back."

He gave her a crooked smile. "Too bad I didn't think of that in the first place."

"Shall I bring you some kindling?"

He gave her shoulder a quick squeeze. "What an excellent woman you are."

She headed for the cabin to gather kindling and the tinder box, aglow with his compliment, but that warmth lasted only a moment before her doubts reasserted themselves. Evidently Monsieur Nolet had not told Valery he had once lain atop her in a brothel. But he still could.

She could not stop the trembling in her hands and knees. Could any man accept knowing that his own friend had taken his wife? Valery knew she'd been a whore, but a man's pride could twist his thinking.

Valery might take a disgust of her. He might return to the way he'd treated her their first days together, as if she were merely a convenient vessel to satisfy his needs. A painful tightness in her chest made it hard to breathe. If he withheld the friendship and the warmth they'd built between them, if he once again saw only a whore when he looked at her, her heart would break.

She stopped right in the middle of the cabin as if her limbs suddenly locked. What if Valery didn't care? What if he let his friend take her again and laughed about sharing a whore? A rising cold iced her spine and stole her breath. If Valery cared so little for her, she could never allow herself to feel again.

Fulbert snuffled his way into the cabin and leaned into her skirts. Her breath returned in a shaky gulp. She knelt to her piglet and scratched behind his ears. "You are a very naughty pig to come into the cabin. You know you should not." She sat on the floor and hugged her little friend to her breast until he squirmed to be let loose.

She laughed, she actually laughed, to see him scamper off her lap to sniff around the floor after crumbs. What a fool she was, to borrow pain and sorrow. It was her own dread of feeling worthless, as she had in Paris, that had her thinking the worst of her husband. He did not deserve it. He had shown her every kindness. He had just told her she was an excellent woman. He would not betray her.

Determined to believe in him, Agnes fetched the kindling and warmed at the kiss Valerie planted on her cheek as a thank you.

Taking a break from her chores, she sat on the stoop with her knife and a length of wood. She'd peeled a short, split log from the woodpile and was using it to create her map of the *New Hope* women. She regretted there was no lovely parchment or black ink to be had, but her kitchen knife marked the soft pine well enough. She began with a straight line for the winding bayou. With Valery's help, she had placed their farm just so along that line and marked it with a starburst. Now that she knew Marie Claude lived just downstream, she nicked the wood, then carved M.C. next to it.

It was not such a big piece of wood. She could carry it with her next time she went to the fort. Some of the women would know where their farms were. Eventually, she would get it all worked out. Someday, maybe the store would have paper to sell, and she could make copies of her map.

Valery came in from the field and rested his axe against the side of the cabin. He looked at her for a moment, a gleam in his eye, and she knew what that meant. He had not bedded her since Nolet arrived, for which she was very grateful, all of them piled into the one room at night.

He touched her hair. "Come, *mon chou*."

She followed him inside, took off her clothes, and lay down for him.

It had been weeks since memories of those nights in the brothel had swamped her as she lay under her husband. Weeks since she had lain like a dead woman while he used her body. Yet, in spite of her resolve to put her doubt and fear away, Nolet's threat sucked out all the confidence, all the pleasure she had learned with Valery, and she felt again the shame and the rage and the helplessness of those months she had been in the brothel.

But this was her husband, who loved her. Didn't he? Could he kiss her so tenderly and then allow Nolet to touch her, to take her? Her throat tightened as she tried to hold back her tears.

"Agnes?" Her husband looked at her, a question in his beautiful brown eyes. If this -- these loving moments -- was an illusion, if he could share her, then her love for Valery would shrivel and die.

"*Mon chou*?" His big thumbs traced her jaw. "I have been too hasty, eh? Let me love you a while, until you're ready for me, sweet Agnes."

These kisses, tender and slow, how could they not be from his heart? Her fingers tangled in his lovely hair, her body warmed to him. She shut away the anxiety Nolet had infected her with and allowed herself to feel, to respond, to love.

~~~

The next morning, Agnes fed Valery and his guest eggs and salt back for breakfast. Nolet put himself out to be charming, including Agnes in his conversation, amusing her with tales of life back in the glittering capital city. She did not remind him that she was quite familiar with Paris.

After breakfast, Fulbert accompanied Agnes to the chicken coop. The piglet was always interested in the chickens, and in the egg Agnes occasionally fed him.

"*Bonjour*, Augustina. Ah, pretty Capucine, at last you have laid an egg? What a fine hen you are. And you, Babette?"

Agnes turned and found Monsieur Nolet watching her from the cabin door, one arm braced on the jamb. He stepped into the yard and lazily walked toward her.

"*Jolie fille*," he said softly and touched her cheek. "Pretty as the dawn, *ma belle*."

His soft tones and pretty words made her stomach churn. She darted past him, toward the safety of the cabin. If that man took her -- she couldn't bear it.

Her mouth was so dry she couldn't swallow. This is how she had felt every time Madame De Bree had sent a man to her room, shame and revulsion searing her throat and shoving her into that dark place in her mind where she could hide, where she could be safe.

Agnes curled her fingers into fists. No. She had promised herself. Whatever happened, she would not hide away inside her head. She would not retreat like that ever again.

Determined to be strong, she went about her usual tasks. Meat had to be dried into jerky, the floor had to be swept. She worked, and she kept an eye on Nolet.

In the afternoon, the two men laid their pistols on the table to clean them. They meant to have a competition later, shooting at gourds to refine their skills. While they oiled and polished, they engaged in their endless reminiscences. One might have thought they were the best of friends, but Agnes suspected that was not so.

Agnes went outside to see to her new cabbages at the far end of the garden. Marie Claude thought the cabbages grew best in cool weather and that it would soon be too hot for them, but Agnes lovingly picked worms off the leaves and whispered to them that they should grow strong and round.

A shadow fell across her own, and she knew. She jumped to her feet, her fingers ready to claw and tear.

He looked at her, one leg cocked, a smirk on his face. "It pleases you, *ma petite*, to scowl at me?" He took a step closer. "It does not diminish your allure, my dear, I assure you." He reached a finger out and traced a line between her breasts.

Agnes reared back, but Nolet grabbed her and yanked her to him as if she were no more than a rag doll.

"No more of this foolishness, madame," he said, and mashed his lips to hers.

When she bit down on his lip, he twisted her around so her back pressed into him, his hand clamped over her mouth. She kicked at his shins, but he laughed and dragged her toward the woods.

She heard the schish sound of a blade being drawn, and then a voice as cold as the steel in the sword.

"Let her go," Valery said.

Nolet snorted. "She's a whore, don't you know that? I had her myself at Madame De Bree's. Remember Madame De Bree's house? I'm sure you were there a time or two." The man's hand squeezed her breast. "Tiny little thing like this with perfect little titties, you think I'd forget your Mademoiselle Agnes?"

Valery assumed the *en garde* position, his blade just out of Nolet's reach. "I said let her go."

The two men stared at each other while Agnes watched her husband. There was no flicker of indecision in his face, only calm certainty.

On a laugh, Nolet shoved her aside and moved to draw his sword, but Valery flourished his own blade under his nose.

"Remove your hand from your hilt, Monsieur, or I will take that hand."

"Oh come now," Nolet said. "All this fuss over a woman? A whore, at that. Let's have a drink and be finished with such foolishness."

Valery had not taken his eyes off Nolet nor removed the threat of his sword pointed at the man's nose.

"You will apologize."

Nolet grinned. "I am sorry, *mon ami*, that your wife is a whore."

Too fast for her eye to follow, Valery's sword snipped off the tip of Nolet's nose. The man screamed. Blood gushed from his wound, drenching his chin, his shirt.

"Agnes, you will return to the cabin, *si'l te plaît*."

"But Nolet still has his sword -- "

The smile on Valery's face spoke of blood and power. "Did you think it a mere idle boast, *mon bien-aimé,* when I told you I was the best swordsman in all of France? You may fetch Monsieur Nolet's belongings, *mon chou,* and bring them to his canoe."

Valery herded the man before his sword, Nolet blubbering and bleeding.

Her hands trembling, her heart thrumming, Agnes rushed to the cabin to gather up Nolet's belongings. Valery had rescued her, he had saved her. Even if it were just for his own pride, she was part of that pride.

Agnes met them at the dugout. Valery gestured toward the sword on Nolet's hip. "You will remove your sword and lay it on the ground."

"By God, Villiers!" Nolet still held his nose, the blood flowing through his fingers. "You can't take my sword."

"As it happens, I can. I will, however, not. You may have it when you are in the dugout and leaving my home."

"What is this?" Nolet complained. "All this over a whore, Villiers?"

Valery's face darkened and Nolet held his hands out in a gesture of peace.

"Valery, the best of friends do not fall out over a woman, *mon ami.*"

"She is not simply a woman, you see. She is my wife."

"You owe me. Back in Paris -- "

"Yes," Valery interrupted. "I owed you, and so you have had my hospitality, for old times' sake. Now you will leave."

"After all I did for you -- "

"Yes, you did me a kindness when you did yourself an even greater one, ingratiating yourself in a powerful man's esteem. Very clever, very self-serving. I owe you nothing more."

Valery nodded to Agnes for her to put Nolet's bed roll and pistol in the boat. She backed away while Nolet climbed in, Valery's sword at his back.

Valery shoved the boat off with his boot, making Nolet stumble. The man seated himself as the boat moved into the stream. "Damn you, toss me my sword."

Valery heaved the sword at him, deliberately making Nolet lunge for it. It clattered on the floor of the boat and Nolet's face twisted in a ghastly, bloody grimace. "Damn you to hell, Villiers."

Agnes stood with Valery watching Nolet paddle down the stream with furious strokes, "Will he be back?" she asked.

"Not to worry, *mon bien-aimé*. He is a man of much talk. Besides, have I not told you I am the best shot, the best swordsman -- am I not the best man? Let him come."

Agnes looked at her husband's handsome profile. He had called her his *bien-aimé*, his beloved. He had protected her.

"You do not mind? That I was at Madame DeBree's? You did not wish for a virgin bride?"

He looked down at her, his dark eyes serious. "I knew you had been a whore. What does it matter at which brothel, eh?" He touched the tip of her nose. "As for a virgin bride, she's only a virgin the one time, is it not so? It is a loss I can bear, *mon chou*."

Sunshine returned to the world, and Agnes's whole body hummed with joy. She was herself again, not the woman Nolet remembered, a ragged whore of no worth to anyone. She was worth something to Valery Villiers.

He stood with his arms crossed, looking stern. "You were witness to a violence, madame. I must apologize."

She saw the flicker of uncertainty in his eye. He wondered if she were shocked he had drawn blood, if she were displeased with him?

She stepped into him and made him uncross his arms and embrace her.

"Will you tell me about your debt to Monsieur Nolet?"

He let out a breath. "If you wish." He rested his chin on the top of her head. "I killed a man in a duel. An important man whose wife had shared her favors with me. The gentleman's even more important brother put a price on my head. Nolet helped me escape. And here I am, in the wilderness." He tipped her chin up and kissed her briefly. "With a very sweet wife."

"The woman was your lover?"

"Of course, a willing accomplice in our little affair. But she had not bargained for a dead husband because of it. Fool of a man, not shrugging it off as most husbands do."

Agnes shook her head, glad there were few women here to tempt him. "You were a Lothario, I think."

He smiled and pressed his thumb against her bottom lip. "With so many beautiful, willing women, does it surprise you, *mon chou*?"

She bit his thumb. "No, *mon cher*, it does not."

He touched his forehead to hers. "But now I am a married man. You understand?"

Agnes clasped his face in her hands and kissed him, her foolish, gallant husband.

"And I am a married woman whose husband -- in truth, Valery, you were *magnifique*."

She pressed her breasts against his chest.

He grinned at her. "Ah, now you see what a great man you have married, you want to express your admiration, eh?"

"I do."

"Well, I do not mind," he said and let her lead him back to the cabin.

---

Valery lay in the bed in the middle of the day with Agnes snuggled up against him. It had been a personal insult, of course, that Nolet would approach his wife, but as he turned it over in his mind, he realized he had been incensed for her sake as well as his own.

Certainly he knew Agnes had been a whore. But she was not a whore now. She lived a respectable life, and she did not deserve to be manhandled by a barbarian like Nolet. Some men simply did not deserve to have a woman.

As for himself, all his life Valery had been a man who loved women. He'd pursued his first girl at the age of fourteen and been rewarded with bliss by a rosy cheeked dairy maid. He could not remember every face he'd loved, but his regard for each of them had been sincere. He never bedded a woman who, however plain other men might find her, had not enchanted him. His pleasure was all the greater for ensuring that his lovely lady enjoyed his attentions as much as he enjoyed hers. He was, in fact, a very great lover. That was not merely his own estimation -- he was not so foolish -- but any number of enamored ladies had told him so.

That had not meant his regard was lasting, of course. He'd never contemplated binding himself to one woman, making love to the same pair of breasts, nuzzling the same set of ears year after year. Were not the first days of a new romance the most exciting, the most memorable?

With Agnes, a stranger, a whore, he had not expected romance, hadn't expected that rush of romantic ardor that had typified his liaisons until now. But he'd had nothing against whores.

The day he chose Agnes, he had arrived after the first girls were already claimed, and the remaining choices on the platform were a bedraggled lot indeed. None of them boasted the glamour of a Parisian sophisticate, none of them had a gleam of humor in her eye. He'd sighed. Perhaps he would endure a lonely bed until the next ship arrived. Rumor was that good girls taken from convents and orphanages were on their way.

Valery had pursed his lips, considering. A girl from a convent was not likely to be pleased with him, nor he with her. Such guilt they felt over simple human pleasures. An orphan, perhaps, would be a grateful girl. Though he preferred ardent participation, there was something to be said for gratitude

Anyway, he had reasoned, those girls might be months away from this lonely outpost on the edge of the Louisiana territory, and the thought of returning home, alone, had filled him with dread. What he wanted, what he needed, was a female. She didn't have to be charming or alluring. Amenable would be adequate.

Three women had stood on the platform. One was an Amazon, probably taller than he was. She surely would outweigh him once she regained her strength after crossing the ocean. A woman bigger than himself did not appeal. One was rather beautiful, tall and slender, but her eyes gleamed with, what? Distress? No, he did not care to deal with a woman's sorrows or anxieties.

That left the little brunette. A tiny little thing, but well proportioned. She had seemed quite calm standing on the platform with all those men eyeing her. A peaceful kind of woman. A woman who would have few expectations.

"I'll take the little one," he'd heard himself say. And it was done.

Once he got her home, he was eager to have her. A whore would not anticipate wooing, of course. She would not look for romance or real love-making any more than he did, but he would be gentle with her, and kind. Whore that she was, she was a woman and deserved to be treated well.

The first beddings had been hardly more satisfactory than what he could do for himself. She was not stiff, not uncooperative. She was simply . . . not there.

He had not known how to behave with her. He couldn't understand a woman who never smiled, who didn't warm to his touch. He felt gauche bedding her, her body as unresponsive as her eyes. And so he had prattled like a fool, telling her -- hoping to convince her? -- what a fine fellow she had married. As if she would thaw if she only knew her husband was the best swordsman, the best shot, the best lover in all of France.

Valery did not know exactly when that changed. He supposed there had been no defining moment, but gradually she seemed to waken. Gradually she became Agnes, not some stranger who happened to sleep beside him at night.

Agnes, who talked to her chickens. Who gazed at stars and communed with glowing balls of swamp gas. And who had, one glorious morning, discovered the pleasure his body could give her. He'd been shaken how much her first orgasm had moved him. He had been remiss assuming she, as a whore, would never do more than acquiesce to his sexual needs.

But Agnes did more than acquiesce, once she'd found her own pleasure. She was in truth his lover. And his wife. He would protect her all their days together.

# Chapter Nineteen

*Marie Claude*
*A Friend*

Marie Claude's husband absented himself a lot these days. Maybe he was raising money to buy big steel vats for the indigo, or maybe he spent his time down at the music hall drinking ale and winking at all the girls. Marie Claude snorted. The nearest music hall was probably two thousand miles away. More likely someone in the area had set up a still and Joubert was imbibing in hard spirits.

Today he was home though he was still abed, snoring loudly, undisturbed by Marie Claude's bustling about. She left her husband's noon-day meal on the table and took most of the corn cakes outside with her. Let him eat alone, he liked his own company so much. She was tired of his ugly face sneering at her across the table, of his nasty petty remarks. She was too ugly, was she? Yet he took her body every night. He certainly was not doing that for her pleasure, was he?

The four black men made room for her on their log. She passed around the plate of corn cakes, they gave her a rabbit leg. She didn't have much to say to them, or they to her, but they talked among themselves.

The youngest one, Pierre, left a sweetheart back in Martinique. Someday, he swore, he would go back and get her, they would strike out on their own, maybe join the maroons on one of the islands.

"How you going to get back to Martinique?" Simon asked. "You gonna fly?"

"Leave him alone, Simon," Thomas said without bothering to look at him. She'd noticed they all did pretty much whatever Thomas said.

"Where is Martinique?" she asked.

Remy was the one today who couldn't seem to clear his chest. He'd been coughing all morning. She'd brew another batch of ginger tea this afternoon.

"Long way, madame. Need a big boat, very big, to cross so much ocean," Simon told her.

And Pierre would need to be free, wouldn't he?

When she went back to her work and they to theirs, she thought about Pierre, so sore of heart. What would it be like to love someone, to think about them even though they were far away?

She was sorry for him, and just a little envious too that he knew what it was to love. And to be loved. Well, she had loved her mother and father, her brother, her sisters.

She touched her belly and had to smile. It looked like she might have a baby to love before Christmas. She would love that child, boy or girl, she didn't care. Probably Monsieur would try to make a son into someone as mean as himself. Well, she wouldn't let him.

She hoped it was true, that she'd have a little person to love. She'd never had anyone all to herself, someone who would love her back. She rubbed her rounding tummy and imagined a tiny foot pressing against her belly.

She laughed to herself. With a father who looked like her husband and a mother like herself, her child would not be beautiful. All the more reason to love it.

She went back to the grease she was rendering over low heat. Joubert had had the luck to kill a black bear with his musket, and she expected she'd have a pot full of bear lard out of it. Pierre was in charge of cutting strips of meat to dry on a rack for jerky. Joubert himself worked on the hide. Yesterday they'd all eaten their fill of bear steaks and by tonight, she'd have oil for a liquid candle.

Next time she had lunch with the slaves, Remy handed her a piece of honeycomb. Surprised and pleased, she bit into the waxy sweetness and closed her eyes. Heaven. "Where did this come from, Remy?"

"Follow the path a while till you come to a zig and then a zag. Go on a bit more, there you find a big tall tree. The hive was there, about so high." He licked his fingers.

"You ever put honey on a bee sting?" Marie Claude asked. "That's what my brother did when he went honey-hunting." She dabbed a bit of honey on Remy's arm and rubbed it into the red welt. "See if that don't help."

Remy looked at the sticky spot, then at Marie Claude. They were all looking at her, in fact. Should she not have touched Remy?

"Anyway, that hive not there no more," Remy said. "I had to knock it down to get the honey."

"I didn't know there was a path," Marie Claude said. "Where does it go?"

Thomas sucked the honey off his thumb. "It's a long path, goes along behind the trees, behind these farms up and down the bayou. There's another one the other side of the bayou."

She could take the path and find out who was in the next farmstead. She could hear their rooster of a morning, could hear the axe at work. Clearing trees, seemed like that was the main work of the whole bayou. Maybe they had eggs to trade for. That was something she really missed, eggs.

"I show you where it is if you want," Thomas said, not looking at her.

She hadn't felt like smiling in such a long time. "Let's go. Right now."

She stood up and waited. Thomas seemed to need thinking time. "What Monsieur Joubert say about it?"

Her husband was still in the cabin snoring. "He doesn't say anything about it, that's what."

Simon shook his head. "They's wild animals hereabout. You ought to stay home."

"I got a knife. Come on, Thomas."

They took a faint path from the farmstead through pines and brush to the better defined trail the Indians used. She was full of questions. Did the Indians use it often? Where were they going? Did they have a village nearby? Did Thomas know other slaves to visit?

It was wonderful, finding this track. She could set off anytime, whether Monsieur was willing for her to use the dugout or not. She could use her own two feet and be free for an hour or a day, whenever she felt like it. That's why Thomas came back here, to feel free for a little while.

Marie Claude followed Thomas for ten minutes when she heard a woman's voice through the trees.

"Over there," Thomas said. "A farm. They have not made a trail from their cabin to meet the path."

Undeterred, Marie Claude pushed her way through the palmettos and brush until she came into the clearing. She paused, taking it in. The rude cabin, the cleared land, the small garden – and standing at the chicken coop, her friend Agnes.

Marie Claude strode into the yard, calling out, "Agnes!"

Agnes's mouth opened in astonishment and then she ran for her. Marie Claude had learned long ago that hugging a small person made her feel like an awkward galumph, and no telling what Agnes would think being mashed into her big chest. She held her hands out instead and Agnes grasped them.

"Marie Claude! How did you get here? My husband knew that was your place downstream -- and you're here! Come in, come in."

Marie Claude turned to introduce Agnes to her friend Thomas, but he had gone back into the trees. Well, if he felt shy, that was all right. She could find her way home.

They sat on the stoop of the cabin and talked and talked as Agnes's little pig snuffled around them looking for something tasty. Marie Claude did not mention her husband was a disagreeable man, but it seemed Agnes's husband pleased her very well. When Monsieur Villiers saw Agnes had company, he set aside the turtle shell he was scouring and sauntered over.

Agnes stood to introduce them, grabbing hold of Marie Claude's hand. "Valery, this is my friend Marie Claude. She is married to Monsieur Leopold Joubert. Just one farmstead down, as you said. Isn't that wonderful?"

Agnes's husband pantomimed taking an imaginary hat off with a flourish and bowing deeply to her, one leg bent, the other straight and pointed. As if she were a grand lady, she, Marie Claude. She felt heat rise up from her neck.

"Madame," he said. "You are most welcome."

"Oh, Valery. The best news. There's a path through the woods. I won't need you to paddle me downstream to go visit."

Monsieur Villiers frowned. "Yes, there is a path, but you are not to go into the woods alone. Ever, *ma petite*."

"But, Valery, it is not so very far. We can hear Monsieur Joubert's axe from here, remember?"

He shook his head emphatically. "Never. You will remember you have promised this."

He held her eyes until Agnes sighed. "Yes, I did promise. I won't go in the woods."

"But I can come to you," Marie Claude said.

"Madame, you are a capable woman, I have no doubt. But you must not come alone into the woods either. The forest is dangerous, you understand."

"But I have not come alone. Thomas, my husband's slave, brought me. He can do it again, whenever I ask."

"Very well, madame. I am sure *ma femme* will be pleased for your company." He dipped his head in farewell and returned to his work.

Agnes drew her down to the stoop again. "You have slaves? From Africa? Are they not fearsome?"

"They are just people, Agnes, like you and me."

Eventually, Marie Claude had to go back. "My husband doesn't know I've come. I should go."

"First, let me give you some eggs. My chickens are laying very well now that I see to their feed and make sure they feel safe at night. Isn't that so, Augustina?"

Agnes handed her four eggs.

"Not so many, Agnes. They are very dear, these eggs."

Agnes shrugged. "We have all the eggs we can eat. Take them, please."

Marie Claude made her way through the shadowy woods to the main path and found Thomas sleeping against a tree, his arms draped over his knees, his hat over his eyes. What a kind friend, to wait for her.

She touched his bare foot with her booted toe. "Thomas?"

He jerked awake.

"You didn't have to wait. I know the way back."

He rubbed his hands over his face, waking up. "A woman," he said on a yawn, "don't go into the woods alone."

She looked down the path, trying to hide how absurdly pleased she was. Agnes's husband was careful of her safety, and she, Marie Claude, had a friend just as careful.

# Chapter Twenty

### *Marie Claude*
### *Mourning*

Today was the day. The vats were ready, the plants were blooming. It was time to harvest the indigo, turn it into chunks of blue dye, and become rich.

Such pretty blooms, it seemed a shame to cut down the whole plant, but that's what they did, Marie Claude and the four slaves, Joubert supervising by strutting up and down the rows advising them how to cut the branches just so many inches above the ground. As if telling them once were not enough.

"No, don't cut any more," Joubert said when they had decimated the first row. "They have to be fresh cut when we start the process."

Thomas and Remy exchanged glances. Marie Claude figured they knew that, but it was their way to pretend not to think or know or care when the master was around.

Still early enough the sun was barely two fingers' width above the tree tops, the men packed the first vat, the largest one, with the indigo plants and carried bucket after bucket of water to fill the vat to the rim. They'd made something that looked like giant butter churners out of cypress and the four slaves took turns standing on stumps and pounding the churners into the soaked indigo.

Marie Claude went about her own chores the rest of the day while Joubert hovered, conducting the rhythmic pounding as if it were a marching tune. Every half hour, he had the two working slaves rest and the other two take up the endless pounding.

Marie Claude provided an extra hardy meal for everyone, though Joubert certainly hadn't earned it. The men ate quickly, then lay down for the remainder of their rest period. Hard work, she could see that.

By evening, the mess had begun to ferment. The water turned blue, thickened, and bubbled. Lord, she had never smelled anything so foul. She pitied Thomas and the others having to stand over that vat, continually pounding and stirring. All that effort stirred up the coughs the four of them had not been able to shake since wintertime.

Before dark, Joubert chose Pierre to wade into the vat and remove the plug at the bottom of one side. The nasty water drained down a sluice into the next vat. Thomas and Remy moved their tree stumps to either end of that vat and churned the thick blue liquid.

Joubert set several torches in the ground and the work continued on into the night. Marie Claude fed the four slaves frequently, and finally went to bed for a few hours' sleep.

When she woke, it was still dark. She prepared a big meal and took it out to the men who were now transferring the sludge at the bottom of the second vat into the third vat.

"Where's Pierre?" she asked.

Joubert spat on the ground. "Worthless piece of shit. Coughs like his lungs are coming out so he can go lie down."

"He's sick?"

"Hmmph," her husband answered.

Marie Claude brewed ginger tea and sweetened it with honey to take to Pierre. She had never been inside the slaves' hut before. It was crowded but tidy. The men had made bedsteads a few inches off the ground so when it rained they'd stay dry. Their mattresses looked like hers, moss-stuffed and thin. There were pegs on the wall on which they'd hung a single spare shirt and a leather pouch.

"Pierre?" He didn't seem to hear her. His face was gray and his breathing ragged.

She knelt beside him. "Pierre, sit up so you can drink this."

He didn't even open his eyes. She pressed her hand on his forehead. He was burning up.

Marie Claude marched back to the house for a bucket, filled it from the bayou, and carried it back to the hut. She mopped Pierre's body with a wet rag over and over. He looked at her but she didn't think he knew who she was.

The cough periodically shook him so she had to keep him from falling off the bed. She could hear the men outside coughing and spitting out phlegm. All of them, though not of course Joubert.

Thomas came in for a few minutes to check on Pierre. She gave him some of the ginger tea to soothe his throat.

"Thank you, madame," he rasped.

Marie Claude sat on the ground, still wiping Pierre's chest with the wet cloth. "This coughing, it's not from a winter cold you can't shake off, is it?"

Thomas shook his head, but he wouldn't look at her.

"It's the indigo fumes, isn't it? You four made indigo back in Martinique and got sick then."

She saw the slightest nod. So this is what it meant to be a slave. To have to do what made you sick because some white man said you had to.

"Pierre will get better now winter is over," she said.

Thomas looked at her, his face a mask. That's the face he showed Joubert, but he hadn't been like that with her, not since the first days.

"Won't he?" she said.

Thomas rested his gaze on Pierre for a long while. Then he stood up and went back to work.

When Marie Claude left Pierre sleeping fitfully in order to fix a mid-morning meal, she found Joubert staring at the muck in the third vat. She guessed he was seeing how rich he was going to be, imagining every bit of that blue goop turned into gold livres.

Marie Claude spent the day nursing Pierre. She got the fever down enough that he wakened and knew who she was.

"Madame," he whispered. She didn't think she had ever seen a smile as sweet as the one he gave her.

"You don't talk now. You just rest. When Thomas comes in to sit with you, I'll make you some broth and some more tea. We'll have you up and singing in no time."

Pierre shook his head. Did that mean he thought he wasn't going to get better? And still, he smiled. She sat on the ground close to him so that she could take his hand.

"I used to sing, back home, with my mother and sisters," she said.

"Did you sing about God?" Pierre's voice was weak and thready.

"Sometimes. Sometimes we sang about sweethearts and soldiers, and sometimes about being too drunk to get home."

"Sing to me about sweethearts."

Marie Claude was not self-conscious about her singing. Her body might be ungainly, but if for nothing else, people had praised her alto voice. *Mon ami me délaisse,* she began. Oh, she thought as she sang the familiar lyrics, maybe she should not have chosen a sad song of a woman whose beloved had left her. But Pierre was smiling. He didn't mind.

Thomas leaned in the doorway, listening as she sang every lyric and finished with *vive la rose et le lilas.* He stepped inside and touched the top of her head with his fingertips. Marie Claude blushed. That couldn't be proper, a man touching her hair. But he couldn't mean anything by it.

"*Mon ami*, how do you fare?" he asked Pierre.

Pierre's dark brown eyes held Thomas's. They seemed to understand one another, and Marie Claude feared what that communication meant. But Pierre had her to take care of him now. She would get him well.

"I'll stay, madame, if you wish to tend to other tasks."

"If his fever comes back, cool him with the wet cloth, and holler for me. I'll come."

On her way to the cabin, Marie Claude passed by Remy and Simon scraping a thin layer of sludge from the bottom of the third vat. Joubert had cloth bags ready for them to fill. Already one was hanging from a branch in the shade, dripping water. So this second day of processing the indigo was easier than the first. She supposed Joubert would soon have his chunks of blue gold.

Marie Claude, however, did not intend for her friends to lose their health making a mean man rich. Joubert would have to breathe the noxious fumes himself if he wanted indigo.

She could hear Pierre's cough from across the yard. She took a deep breath and held it, waiting for him to gasp in enough air himself. She'd never heard such a cough. She pressed her own chest, as if she could help poor Pierre's lungs draw in air.

The spasm passed. He was quiet.

Marie Claude fixed a meal for everyone and took a gourd of broth for Pierre.

Thomas sat where she had, on the ground beside the bed. His voice was low and soothing, a steady stream of soft words in their strange French. Martinique French. It was a prayer, she understood. Pierre's eyes were closed, but she knew he was awake because his hand gripped Thomas's as if he would never let go.

Marie Claude stepped out again, the gourd trembling in her hands. She mustn't cry in front of Pierre, and she couldn't not cry. Pierre was dying. Thomas believed it. Pierre believed it. And Thomas's own cough interrupted his prayers.

She must make her husband understand. He had never grown indigo before this year. He didn't know what it did to the lungs.

Still holding the gourd she marched to where Joubert was fingering the hanging bags of blue sludge. Remy and Simon sat in the shade, their labor over for the moment.

"Monsieur," she said quietly, "I must speak with you."

"You must, must you?"

"The coughing – your men have coughed ever since I came here, and long before that, I think. It is the fumes from the indigo that has damaged their lungs, monsieur."

Joubert held his hand under a bag, letting the slow drip accumulate in his palm.

Did he not hear her? "Monsieur, the indigo makes them very sick. We must find another way."

"Another way to what?" Joubert said, his attention on the water tinged with blue.

"Another way to process the indigo. Another way for you to make money."

When he still didn't answer, she said, "Those vats Monsieur Nolet wants you to buy. Maybe they come with lids that would keep the fumes from rising up. Maybe the men wouldn't have to breathe that bad air."

Joubert dropped his hand and gave her his attention at last. "This is how it is done, madame. All over the world." He ambled off as if they had been discussing what kind of chicken feed was best.

Behind her Simon coughed deeply and spat out the nasty stuff.

"I'll bring you some tea, soon as I get this broth into Pierre." He and Remy both stared at her. She wanted to snap at them, What? Have I grown another head?

She heard Pierre coughing again and took her broth to him.

In the afternoon, he seemed better. Marie Claude stayed as Simon, Remy, and Thomas sat with him, telling stories, reminding each other of how it was on Martinique: cool breezes, the smell of the ocean, their families and friends around them.

Marie Claude could smell the salt air and hear the singing in those evenings the men described. They were more homesick than she had ever been.

Pierre only listened, his eyes luminous and his face smooth, as if he had no cares, no fears.

"Tell me about Giselle," Pierre whispered.

Remy dredged up a laugh. "Ah, Giselle. The most beautiful girl on the island. When she walks by, butterflies follow her and birds alight on her shoulder to sing just for her. Is that the Giselle you mean?"

Pierre's smile was wide. "That's the one."

"I was there," Simon said, "when the lightning struck you, you know. We were both sixteen, and Giselle was, what, fourteen? She walked by, a basket on her head, her mother walking three steps ahead of her. And she looked at us from the sides of her eyes, watched us as she passed by."

"She was not looking at you, Simon," Pierre rasped. "You only wished she would."

"Too true. At that moment, I knew I had no chance with her. She was yours."

"And I was hers."

"I think, just now," Thomas said, "Giselle is bathing in the pool back in the woods. You know the one. She leaves her skirt on the rocks and dives into the water, her hair flowing behind her."

"We swam there together," Pierre said.

Thomas nodded. "You dive in after her. Giselle tries to swim away from you, laughing at you, but you catch her. You pull her into your arms."

Marie Claude could see the two of them, naked, wet. Thomas caught her eye and she looked away.

"We have madame present, Pierre, so I will not describe to you what the cool water does to Giselle's breasts. You remember well enough, is that not so?"

Pierre grinned. "I remember."

Heat rose up Marie Claude's face. "It's time for me to cook supper. I'll bring it down here for all of you."

"Thank you, madame." Thomas touched her hand, with one finger only, but she felt its heat all the way up her arm.

He shouldn't touch her, not when it made her feel this way. And she shouldn't feel this way.

Marie Claude stumbled once as she crossed the broad yard. She hadn't had enough sleep. None of them had. And she was afraid. Pierre reminded her of her grandpa just before he died. He had been cantankerous for weeks. Nothing and no one could please him. And then he let all that irritation go. The lines on his face seemed to smooth out. Before, he had cursed them when they shifted him in the bed to change his linen, but now he smiled and said thank you. The last day of his life he had been serene. Like Pierre.

She pressed the back of her hand against her nose. It wouldn't do to be crying when she talked to monsieur again.

She entered the cabin where he sat with his knife and whet stone. "Get supper on the table," he said without looking at her.

"I will. But first we must come to an understanding. Your slaves will not die from making indigo for you. You will have to find another way."

His hand stopped, the knife mid-stroke across the stone. He looked up at her, his eyes narrow and mean.

"Pierre is dying, monsieur."

Joubert shrugged and continued the stroke. "There are plenty of slaves in the world."

"Monsieur Joubert, I want to be sure that you know this. This making of the dye. Those foul smelling fumes. They make the men sick. So sick it kills them."

His attention remained on sharpening the knife. "This is known to everyone."

"Then we will not do it. We will not make Thomas and Simon and Remy sicker."

He tested the edge of the blade with his thumb. "And what about your little pet Pierre?"

Marie Claude could hardly force the words out. "This may be his last day."

"He wasn't worth much. Always coughing. His arms like matchsticks."

The man was a monster. Marie Claude slapped her hands on the table and leaned toward him.

"There will be no more indigo made on this place."

Joubert set the whet stone aside. She noticed he kept the knife in his hand, but she was not afraid of him. He might try to hurt her, but she could break his arm if she had to.

"You shut your mouth, woman. You have no say in what I do with my slaves. You have no say about anything."

Marie Claude drew herself up, her spine stiff. "I do. I say there will be no indigo made here. Ever."

Joubert's fist shot out and punched her right in the chin. She flew back, hitting her head against the bedpost as she fell.

He strode toward her. He was going to kick her if she didn't get up. She couldn't let him hurt the baby growing inside her. She scrambled to her feet and caught his fist before it could punch into her gut, but he jerked it free and socked her in the eye, the blow so hard she feared she would black out. Then what would he do to her? She struggled to stay on her feet, to think as she took another blow to the face.

Where was the knife? Still in his left hand. She grabbed for that wrist with both hands and shoved him back, step by step, until his hips bumped into the table. She held on to his knife hand and punched him in the face with her other hand.

He growled like a wild beast and yanked his wrist from her grip. With a feral gleam in his eye, he crouched, the knife held ready to rip her open.

She risked her arm to block his knife and rushed him. His blade sliced her forearm, but she kept coming and fisted him right in the throat. He fell to the floor, gasping for air, and she twisted the knife from his hand.

"I'll kill you for this," he panted.

"I'll kill you first. Get out of this cabin while you still can."

He laughed and it raised every hair on her body. She kicked him, hard, as near to his groin as she could get. It was close enough. He howled and clutched his parts.

"When I get back," she said, surprised at how steady her voice was, "if you're here, I will beat you again."

She went out into the dusk. Swelling already closed her left eye and blood sheeted from her arm. She got a bucket of water from the bayou and took it to the big stump next to the woodpile to wash her face and arm. How was it that she felt so calm? Wouldn't a person be shaken by such violence? But she wasn't. She felt simply, prepared. There would be a next time, she was sure of that.

The gash in her right forearm needed attention. And she was right handed. She crossed the yard in the growing dark to the hut where the four men sat talking. She stood just outside the door and said, "Thomas."

He got to his feet and saw the blood dripping off her arm. In one quick step, he was at her side. He took hold of her good arm and walked her toward the cabin.

"Where is monsieur?" he asked.

Marie Claude nodded toward the bayou. Joubert's form was shadowy in the twilight, but clear enough. "There. He's leaving."

In the cabin, Thomas lit the lantern. She tore a strip of cloth off the bottom of her night dress and fetched the pot of unguent she kept for scrapes and bruises.

"We got to put stitches in this," Thomas said.

Of course. She didn't know why she was so fuzzy headed.

She handed him her needle and a spool of thread, and then gazed at the far wall as Thomas worked the needle in and out of her flesh. At home, she and Mama couldn't stomach stitching up wounds, so her father had always done it. With her own arm opened up like this, she simply concentrated on not whimpering like a baby as Thomas pinched the skin together for sewing.

He daubed on the unguent and wrapped the clean bandaging around her arm. Blood still seeped through. She would have to tear another strip off her nightgown. It would hardly come to her knees. That seemed important somehow. Dizzy, she put her hand to her eyes.

"Put your head between your knees," Thomas told her and pressed her head gently down. "It's just loss of blood."

"I'll be all right in a minute."

When her head cleared, Thomas gave her a ladle of water. "This was about Pierre?"

"Yes. About all of you. About the indigo."

They were very quiet, the two of them. She heard the nightjars outside, looking for moths to break the day's fast.

"When he comes back . . ." Thomas said.

"When he comes back, I will be ready for him. I have his knife, and I have my kitchen knife."

"He has a sword."

"I'm stronger than he is. He knows it."

"But a sword does not require greater strength. You must hide the sword."

"Yes. All right."

"Madame." Thomas waited until Marie Claude looked at him. "Next time he hits you, you must scream. We will come, all of us."

She stared at her hands.

"You must. Promise this."

She shook her head. "I can take care of myself."

Thomas stood. "Next time, you will scream."

No, she wouldn't. If Joubert wanted to, he could kill a slave and answer to no one for it. He could kill her, too. But she wouldn't let him.

~~~

Marie Claude carried a candle, Thomas carried the pot of possum and rice down to the hut.

Remy and Simon shifted over to make room for them at Pierre's bedside, making a point that Marie Claude should join them. Pierre sipped at Marie's ginger tea as the rest of them ate.

The crickets chirped and occasionally another animal added to the chorus, an owl, a bullfrog. The men talked about Martinique, about the biggest fish they ever caught, about lazy summer nights, weary from a hard day's work yet awed by the beauty of a starlit sky. They talked about their mothers and the women they'd loved.

Pierre had another bout of coughing, this time so severe that blood came up from his lungs. Such bright blood, so red, so hot to the touch. Marie Claude cleaned him up and he lay back exhausted. Remy began to hum, one of the favorites she had heard them sing many times. Thomas and Simon joined in and sang soft sweet songs. Sometimes Pierre doubled over with the force of coughing spasms. Marie Claude wiped his face and chest and held his hand while his friends sang. There might have been no other place in the world, merely this circle warmed by candle light, by friends loving one of their own.

Late in the evening, Pierre whispered, "Simon."

"I'm here."

Marie Claude moved so that Simon could sit closest and grip Pierre's hand.

"You'll take care of Giselle."

Simon bit his lip and managed to answer. "Of course I will. Until you come home to her."

"All right." Pierre closed his eyes. Marie Claude watched to see if his chest still rose. His breath grated through his throat. He merely slept.

They all needed sleep. Marie Claude didn't blame him as Simon leaned against the edge of the bed, Pierre's hand clasped in his, and nodded off. Remy too needed to touch Pierre and wrapped his fingers around Pierre's thin ankle as he fell asleep.

Marie Claude bowed her head over her bent knees and listened to Thomas hum. At some slight noise, she raised her head and stared at Pierre in the candle light.

He was so very still. That had been his last painful breath she heard. Pierre had left his wracked body behind.

Thomas pressed his fingers against his eyes. Simon roused, and then Remy at the sudden quiet.

Simon buried his face in his hands and abruptly fled the hut. Remy still held on to Pierre's ankle and softly wept.

Marie Claude felt wet tears flowing across her cheeks, but she was calm. And Thomas was calm. He passed his palm over Pierre's eyes, closing them, and then sat back, his arms around his knees.

As sunlight crept into the hut, Marie Claude stirred. Her back and legs were stiff, her arm ached, her face ached, but she had something to do. She stepped out into the early morning, noticed the sky turning from gray to lightest blue. Noticed a mockingbird singing in the trees. A fine morning for a burial.

She chose the axe Joubert always used. At the largest vat, she raised her arms and brought that axe down with all her strength. The blade bit into the cypress again and again until she had cut it enough it would be useless as a vat. She started on the second vat, but Thomas touched her shoulder.

"You make your arm bleed. It is enough, this one vat."

"No," she said. "It's not enough."

She hacked into each of the other vats, anger and grief spilling out of her chest in noisy sobs. She paid no attention to them. She persevered until her axe had rendered vats number two and three as useless as the first.

Thomas had stood by, his arms across his chest. He took the axe from her hand. "Now," he said. "I will rebandage your arm and you will rest until we have made Pierre's grave."

The sun was high when they lowered Pierre's shrouded form into the earth. Thomas said a prayer and then they sang. Marie Claude added her voice to the songs she had heard before, and they sent Pierre on his way.

# Chapter Twenty-One

### *Agnes*
### *A Friend in Need*

"Valery?"

"Hmm?"

Agnes poured him another cup of the brew she was pretending was coffee. At their last Sunday gathering, Rachel claimed she had made a palatable brew by steeping ground hickory nuts in boiling water. Gabrielle said she'd heard you could use dandelion roots. Agnes had hickory nuts, gathered from beneath the tree where they fell after last season's fruition, and she had dandelions, so she tried brewing the two together.

"What do you think?"

"About what, *mon chou*?" His attention was on his plate of eggs.

"The coffee, Valery."

He looked in his nearly-empty pewter cup. "Ah. It is coffee, is it?"

"Put a little more honey in it."

He obliged her and took another sip. "Much improved."

Agnes gave him a hopeful smile. "Would you like another cup?"

Valery considered for a moment. "Would you like me to have another cup?"

Agnes laughed. "You are the dearest man. The point, Valery, is whether you are happy to drink this concoction or would you prefer a cup of spring water?"

Valery, she could see, intended to be careful. "Do you yourself, Madame Villiers, enjoy this coffee?"

She pursed her lips. "Not so very much."

"I will be delighted to drink what you have brewed, *ma chérie*, but perhaps we will welcome your next effort in the winter time when we shiver and yearn for something hot."

She kissed him on the cheek. "Agreed."

As she finished her breakfast, Agnes said, "Valery, I've been thinking."

Valery smoothed his moustache. "Married men have told me those are the three most dangerous words out of a woman's mouth."

"Oh, you. All I want is for you to walk me down the path to Marie Claude's. You can come back for me in a while."

Dramatically, Valery put a hand to his heart. "You would trust me with the care of Augustina and Babette and all the rest of your feathered friends? I am honored."

"You will not eat them while I am gone?"

"Well." He patted his tummy. "I am quite well fed. I perhaps can refrain from eating your friends before you return."

"I, and all my friends, are most grateful. So you will take me?"

"Of course." He raised his cup with a gleam in his eye. "Let me finish my coffee."

After Agnes gathered the remainder of the morning's eggs, Valery strapped on his sword. Any bears or pumas would be sorry indeed to offend her husband. The path was leafy and cool. The trees that had been covered with red buds were now leafed out, but other flowers brightened the forest. A tree with glossy thick leaves bore huge, fragrant, creamy white blooms.

"It would be nice to take one of these flowers to Marie Claude," Agnes said, raising her brows at Valery. "But, alas, I am too short to reach the lowest bloom."

"A dilemma, I agree. If someone were to reach up and pluck such a bloom for you, how might he be rewarded?"

"Oh, I am quite sure that such a person would be well-pleased with his reward."

"In that case." Valery broke off one of the flowers and presented it to her with a gallant bow. "Madame, *pour toi*."

"What an amazing fragrance."

"I cannot disagree, but there is the matter of a reward, madame."

With great fanfare, Agnes set her egg basket down, placed the blossom on top, and loosened her shoulders. She stepped as close as one body can get to another, reached her arms around Valery's neck, and kissed him. Senseless, she hoped.

When he came up for a breath, he murmured in her ear. "We are not so very far from our own little bed, sweet Agnes. We could perhaps delay your visit by an hour or so?"

"I once read of these mythical beings called satyrs. Are you perhaps descended from these virile creatures, *mon coeur*?"

He pretended to think a moment. "It is entirely possible. This presents a difficulty for you?"

"Certainly not. Although I would prefer to postpone the relief of your distress by a few hours. That would be acceptable?"

With a great sigh, he kissed her nose and handed her the egg basket. "I will probably require extra soothing after such a disappointment, you realize."

"And you shall have it, *mon amour*."

At the edge of Marie Claude's cleared land, Agnes saw her friend across the fields. She waved and called out haloo, then turned to Valery.

"Will you come say hello?"

"I will visit a few minutes when I come to pick you up, shall I?"

She kissed him quickly on the cheek and took her egg basket from his hand.

Valery gave Marie Claude a friendly wave and headed back into the forest and the path to take him home.

Agnes noticed how quiet the place was as she crossed the field, Marie Claude waiting for her at the other side. She'd thought the slaves would be working and talking, but not even the birds had much to say at the moment.

The strains of a mournful song began. The slaves of Monsieur Joubert were not working, and they were sad? When she got closer to Marie Claude, Agnes saw the deeply bruised, swollen jaw, the blackened eye. She dropped the basket and grabbed her friend's arms. "Marie Claude, what has happened to you?"

Marie Claude shrugged. "I'm fine."

"You are not fine. Come sit down and tell me what this is all about."

They sat on the cabin's stoop and Agnes took one of Marie Claude's hands in hers.

"Don't fret, Agnes. I'm all right."

"You don't seem all right. And I don't just mean the bruises. What is wrong?"

"Pierre died last night. The youngest slave."

"How? What happened?"

"We poisoned him." Marie Claude pressed her free hand over her eyes. "It's the indigo. The fumes from making it into dye are poison, and these men have been breathing it for years."

"The other men?"

"They're sick, but maybe if they don't ever breathe it again they can get well. But Pierre, he was the sickest. And when he stood over those fumes again, it was too much for him."

Now Agnes understood the sorrowful song the men were singing, the heaviness in the air. Everyone was grieving.

"You were fond of Pierre, Marie Claude?"

"I'm fond of all of them. They're my friends."

"I'm sorry you've lost a friend." In a moment, Agnes added, "But Marie Claude, this doesn't explain your bruises. And your arm is bandaged."

Marie Claude told her about arguing with Joubert, about their fight.

"He didn't come back last night. I suppose he will turn up."

"You should come home with me. You shouldn't be here when he comes back."

"I can't leave. When he sees I have destroyed his precious vats, he'll be murderous. I can't let him take it out on the slaves. I'm the one who chopped them up."

"Then Valery and I will stay with you until Joubert finds the vats and gets past his first anger."

Marie Claude shook her head. "That won't do any good. I'd rather deal with him when he is in his rage. I have to prove to him that he cannot hurt me, ever again. Either that, or he will murder me in my sleep. No, you and Monsieur Villiers cannot do this for me. But I thank you."

They sat on the stoop, listening to the three remaining slaves sing their songs. Now and then, the women would talk a few minutes, but Agnes could see Marie Claude was too grieved to carry on a conversation. She simply sat with her and hoped her presence was a comfort.

When Valery returned for her, Marie Claude saw him striding across the field.

Marie Claude stood abruptly. "Don't tell him, Agnes." She stepped inside and closed the door.

Agnes met Valery mid field. "Marie Claude sends her apologies, but she is not well enough to greet you."

A furrow appeared between his brows. "She is ill? Many serious ailments befall the French in this climate."

Agnes didn't like lying to her husband, but Marie Claude had asked her not to tell. Still, if Marie Claude persisted in wanting the beating kept secret, Agnes would have to tell Valery anyway. They were neighbors and he would want to know that Marie Claude was hurt. But for now, she just said, "It's a female complaint."

# Chapter Twenty-Two

*Marie Claude*
*Defense*

With Pierre in the ground, Marie Claude washed herself and tidied her hair. At the moment, she didn't have the heart, or the strength, to fight Joubert when he came back. He might very well kill her, and if this were to be her last day on earth, she wanted to be presentable when she met her Lord.

The gash in her arm ached, her whole face throbbed, but she could ignore that kind of pain. What she couldn't get her mind off was Pierre's gray face, his unseeing eyes. His sweetheart didn't even know he was gone.

Nothing to do now but wait for Joubert to come back and discover all his vats had been destroyed. She was glad Agnes had gone home. She didn't want Agnes hurt, and she didn't want her to see what was going to happen, for it was sure to be violent.

Marie Claude slid the knife under her pillow and lay down, her weary bones sinking into the mattress.

She blinked and held her breath. The baby moved. Just then. Her baby had quickened in her womb. She pressed her hands to her belly and felt a rolling sensation, as if her tiny one were turning over. A sobbing laugh shook her and tears bathed her grinning face. Her baby. Her beloved child was awake inside her body.

Joy eased her grief for Pierre, her fear and anger with Joubert. Sleep eased the pain of her bruises and her wounded arm.

When she woke in the afternoon, peace seemed to reign over her little farmstead. Birds were singing, the only other sound a soft breeze sifting through the trees. Thomas and the others had to be exhausted just as she was. She hoped they were asleep.

Marie Claude lay her hands over her belly. The little one was sleeping, too. Whatever she had to do, her husband would not harm this baby

Her husband. Certainly there were many other bad husbands in the world, some of them maybe worse than hers, but the word ought to mean something besides the man who gets to sleep with you and knock you around. It ought to mean somebody like her father and her brother. They were husbands, responsible men who took care of their wives and children. Who didn't beat them or insult them. She would not call Joubert husband anymore.

Whatever she called him, he would be coming after her. She hoped he came after her and not Thomas or Remy or Simon. She didn't want him punishing them for what she'd done. She would tell them to go off in the woods for the day where they'd be safe.

She heaved herself off the bed and paused. The birds had gone silent.

With startling speed, Joubert was in the cabin and on her.

"You did it, you cow." He backhanded her on her sore jaw and she gasped at the pain. He switched from open hand blows to fists, driving her back against the wall. "Those vats were worth six of you, you bitch."

The knife was on the bed, hidden in the blanket, but she couldn't reach it.

She fought back as she could, but he kept coming at her. A memory of that other time, in Paris, flashed in her mind. That man who'd beat her so bad had come at her like this, mindless and relentless. That time she had ended up in the Salpêtrière, but this time -- she had a child to protect.

She lunged onto the bed to find the knife, but Joubert jerked her back by the hair, pounding his fist into her back, between her shoulder blades, down low at her kidneys. She could hardly breathe with her head pulled back so far, with the pain from every new injury.

She fumbled in the blankets. There, her fingers touched the blade. Before she could grab hold of it, Joubert dragged her to the floor.

She saw the boot coming at her belly and twisted to take the kick in her back. She blacked out, but for only a moment, for Joubert had not paused. Here came his boot again, aimed at her middle. If he kicked the baby --

Propelled by fear and rage, Marie Claude screamed and caught the boot and wrenched Joubert's leg so that he fell backwards. She fumbled for the knife. Joubert was on her again, his fists pummeling one after the other, again and again. Marie Claude hardly knew where he hit her, but she had strength enough left to grab that knife, to draw her arm back, and to drive the blade straight down.

Blood spurted all over, stunning in its heat, in the reach of its arc.

Joubert went down. Marie Claude collapsed on top of him, the weakening arch of hot blood drenching her hair and face. She fainted.

Marie Claude thought she was dreaming when gentle arms lifted her off Joubert's body. When she was small, her papa had carried her like this, tenderly, as if she were precious to him.

"Madame." That was Thomas's voice. She opened her eyes. She hurt so bad, everywhere. She panted, trying to bear the pain. And then the pain doubled her over, her knees drawn up to her chest.

She felt the hot wet between her legs. "Thomas."

He put his hand on her forehead. "Don't try to get up."

"The baby, Thomas. Don't let me lose the baby."

"Oh my sweet Jesus."

She saw Thomas reach for her skirt, and then she blacked out.

# Chapter Twenty-Three

*Valery*
*No Loose Ends*

Valery paused in his labors over the deer hide he was scraping to watch Agnes step delicately over a row of seedlings in the garden. She moved like a little fairy, his wife. Any day now he expected her to tell him the names of all the frogs in the pond.

"Valery, I need to talk to you."

"Very well." He tossed his scraper aside and guided her into the shade with an arm around her waist. He loved touching her, even if only to escort her six feet.

"This morning."

"Yes?"

"I didn't tell you. Marie Claude has been beaten. She went into the house when you came for me so you wouldn't see the bruises."

Valery's lovely face frowned, a line between his eyes. "Why didn't you tell me?"

Agnes took his hand by way of apology. "She didn't want me to. But we have to do something, Valery."

Her Valery heaved a heavy sigh. "It is a sad thing, *ma petite*, but the law allows a man to beat his wife."

"Valery!"

He shrugged and held his palms up. "What would you have me do?"

She paced away and then back to him. "Something!"

"Agnes, what can I do?"

"We could bring her here. She could stay with us."

"Very well. Your friend is most welcome to stay. But what happens when she goes home again?"

"You could talk to her husband. Tell him he must not beat her ever again."

"I could. Do you believe this will deter him?"

She was red in the face, his little Agnes, so angry, so indignant.

"You're good with your sword."

"Agnes, I do not draw my sword lightly. I do not snip off noses every day, and to tell you the truth, my darling, it is easier to kill a man than to simply wound him. And I am sick to death with skewering people with my blade."

"You've had to kill people?" She looked shocked. What did she think musketeers did, simply strut around looking glamorous?

"Not many. But I do not want yet another face to haunt me."

She kissed his hand. "I'm sorry, Valery."

He touched her face. "Thank you, my dove."

"Will you come with me? We can at least bring Marie Claude here until she is healed."

"Yes, we will do that. I must finish this scraping before it stiffens. Give me half an hour."

Before that time had passed, a black man appeared at the edge of the woods, one of Joubert's slaves, he assumed. Agnes was in the garden and Valery saw her start when she saw the man. Dressed in rough homespun, his skin the color of plums, he held up his hands to show her he meant no harm. Agnes listened to him only a moment and then came running to him.

"Valery, Marie Claude needs me. I must go."

"Hold on." He strode across the field to the black man. "Who are you?"

"Thomas, sir." The man had to cough, harshly, before he continued. "I am Monsieur Joubert's slave."

"What happened?"

The man hesitated, but he came out with it. "Madame Joubert is very bad." He looked at Agnes. "She needs a woman to be with her."

What did that mean? She had been raped? "Indians?"

"No, monsieur."

"Joubert then."

Thomas nodded.

"Where is he?"

"Gone, monsieur."

Agnes brushed past him and ran toward the cabin. "I have to go to her."

"You will go nowhere without me."

She kept striding toward the cabin, ignoring him.

Valery caught up to her. "Agnes. Calm down. I will take you, of course I will."

She turned abruptly, buried her face in his shirt, and burst into tears.

This he knew how to handle. He wrapped his arms around her and let her cry. When she settled, he kissed her forehead. "Gather what you need and we will go."

Valery decided to arm himself. Perhaps Joubert would return and still be in a combative mood.

When they arrived at Marie Claude's cabin, Agnes rushed inside. Valery stayed outside to talk to Thomas without his wife's hearing.

"Do you know where he is?"

The man who had been open-faced and straightforward suddenly looked like a man about to tell a lie.

"He is perhaps in the swamp."

"The swamp."

"We find it when we are out hunting. A mile back that way, it is swamp."

"Yes. I've seen it. Why is Joubert in the swamp?"

"He want to hunt a gator."

"I see." A man beats his wife and then decides to go on a gator hunt. Of course. "When did he leave?"

"Only a short while ago."

Valery held the black man's gaze another moment, wondering what the lie was, but Thomas did not falter.

Valery stepped into the cabin. Agnes was on the bare mattress with Marie Claude's head in her lap. Another slave sat on the floor next to the bed.

Dear God in heaven, Valery had never seen such bruising. The woman's jaw was blackened, her lip badly split, and one eye was swollen shut. By the way she held herself so carefully, she likely had broken ribs.

What the hell had happened? Why would a man do this to a woman?

Valery was finished with violence, but he didn't see how he could prevent another such beating without killing the man. And the man needed killing.

The floor was wet, and that wall. Thomas and the other man had cleaned up blood? Marie Claude's blood? Or Joubert's?

Valery looked at Agnes and understood it was very bad, what had happened here.

He glanced at the rafters to see what sort of herbs Marie Claude had drying. In a burlap bag, he found crushed willow bark. "Boil some water, make a tea, if you please," he said to the slave on the floor. As the young man rose, he bent double, coughing. Were they all suffering some ailment?

Marie Claude appeared to have gone to sleep. It was hard to tell with her face so swollen, but her shoulders seem to have relaxed.

"There was a baby, Valery," Agnes whispered.

He nodded. That explained the bare mattress, the spots of blood on the nightgown.

Valery went back into the sunshine and walked around the place. It was a neat, well-run farmstead. The garden was growing well, the cabin in good repair. Down at the landing, there was no dugout. Joubert would have taken that if he were hunting gators.

Valery wondered about the large vats on the far side of the garden and strolled closer. It would have taken a lot of work to carve the cypress into these containers. For processing indigo, he presumed. He had himself expected to sell his indigo to Joubert. And somebody had taken an axe to the vats. There would be no dye made here this season.

A rudimentary cabin, a shack, stood at the edge of the clearing. He peered in. Four beds. He had seen only two slaves. Further on, Valery came to a freshly-covered grave.

Joubert might be in that grave. He heaved out a sigh. He didn't think he wanted to know.

Thomas joined him and stood staring at the grave.

"Who is buried here?"

"My friend. Pierre."

Valery eyed Thomas. "How did he die?"

"His lungs. They could not work for him anymore."

"You and the other slave have coughs."

Thomas said nothing.

"And the vats are destroyed. Who did that?"

"Madame."

And so Joubert had beat her half to death. "Why? Why did she do it?"

"Because the indigo air killed Pierre."

And these two slaves had bad lungs, their coughs so deep it hurt to hear them. Yes. He thought he understood now.

Four beds, one man in the ground. One missing.

"It is dangerous to hunt gators alone," Valery said.

"I tell monsieur. We hunt gators on Martinique, never alone."

"So he took a slave with him?"

Thomas took his time about answering. Be careful, Valery thought.

"No. Monsieur went alone."

"But there is a man missing."

Thomas shook his head. "Not missing. Simon is fishing. For our supper."

"He took the dugout?"

"No. Monsieur took the dugout."

So, if Valery was right, Thomas had it all taken care of. Joubert was dead. The missing slave, this Simon, had taken the body to the swamp in the dugout.

"Monsieur was a good master?"

"Very good master."

Valery doubted that. "And madame?"

"Madame -- do not worry. We will take care of madame."

Valery nodded. He didn't know which of the souls on this place had killed Joubert, but everything was in hand. There was nothing he need do except help Agnes help Marie Claude.

# Chapter Twenty-Four

*Catherine and Jean Paul*
*Loss*

After breakfast, Catherine went out to visit her little sparrows. She stretched up from her perch on the log and found all four of the fledglings had flown away. She felt a little cast down, which was silly. She'd known this day was coming, but she was going to miss them. She looked and listened and finally heard the rather unlovely song of the sparrow, if that's what they were. Then her little ones were still in the area. She would see them again. It was sad, really, that she would miss them while they would not give her a single thought.

Well, she was being maudlin and this was to be a good day, a planting day. She went back to the cabin and carefully put all the seed packets in her basket. She and Jean Paul would work together this morning, just like real farmers, planting seeds for the next crop.

She walked with Jean Paul to the field, enjoying the birds still chattering about what a frightening night it had been, but, what joy, it was over now and the sun was shining. No doubt her little sparrows sang as loudly as the rest.

They walked past the indigo plants thriving in the sun. The seedlings were now six inches tall and promising to become fine bushes.

"I gather some plants need more sun than others?" she asked.

"Apparently."

So Jean Paul didn't know any more about that than she did. "Well, there is plenty of sun for all of them, don't you think?"

"That's the expectation, yes."

"Well. Carrots here?"

"Why not."

Jean Paul used her hoe to cut a shallow, narrow trench along the top of each built-up row.

Carefully, not wasting a single seed, Catherine placed the seeds in the little trench and gently covered them over.

"What's next?"

"Spinach?" he asked.

Oh this was fun. "The spinach seeds, they look like little pebbles," she said.

"You like spinach?"

"I hated spinach, but when I saw the seeds, I suddenly craved it. You like spinach?"

He wrinkled his nose. "I can eat it." He gestured to the next row. "Pumpkins next. They spread out, so we allow them lots of room."

"Hmm. Pumpkin custard with cinnamon and nutmeg. And whipped cream on top."

Jean Paul laughed. "You can make that, can you?"

"Oh, no, but I was sure an enterprising musketeer must have learned to make pumpkin custard at some time."

"Indeed. Part of every swordsman's training."

Catherine couldn't think when she'd been happier, working alongside Jean Paul, doing something useful and important.

After a cold meal of left over rabbit and corn cakes, Catherine announced she would make Jean Paul a hat. "You get the first one, which is of course a great honor. It also means your hat will have all my mistakes in it."

"Always a catch, isn't there?" he said, smiling.

He helped her cut palmetto fronds, for which she was grateful. Snakes liked to lie in wait under the shady fronds for an unsuspecting bug or toad to come in range, and when they saw a great galumphing woman approaching, they would dart away, scaring her half to death.

She chopped the leaves off the stalk with the hatchet, piled her materials in the shade, and set to work.

Jean Paul watched as she lay the first palmetto blades down, then wove new ones in and out of the first blades.

"You look like you know what you're doing."

Catherine sighed. "So far."

Jean Paul left her to her weaving to see to his own chores. He hadn't chopped a tree in days. What was the poor man to do with himself? She smiled as she saw him go to work. Going to learn how to make charcoal, he'd told her last night. "How hard can it be?" he'd said.

It took until supper time to finish her hat, her second hat, really. She had had to start over when the first effort collapsed in a disorderly, flat pile. She plopped it on her head and stepped out into the sunshine. Well, it worked. No sun on her face or in her eyes. She couldn't stop smiling. She'd made a hat!

She found Jean Paul sitting in the dugout, the nose still on land, he in the stern lazing with a cane pole in his hand and his feet dangling in the cool water. "Catch anything?"

"Yep. Fish for dinner."

Catherine peered into the dugout where two nice-sized bass lay in the bottom. So far, Jean Paul had done all the fish cleaning. She hoped that was a law written in stone. Women do not scale or clean fish.

She stepped into the dugout and carefully made her way to where Jean Paul sat. "*Voila*," she said, standing behind him, and placed the hat on his head.

He adjusted it a bit and turned his head side to side. It slid all over his head.

"Oh dear," she said. "Too big."

"Better than too small. It'll do."

Jean Paul twisted around so he could see her. "Thank you."

His eyes were warm and brown, and oh so solemn. Catherine wanted to touch him, just to graze his jaw with her fingertips. When he was like this, warm, approachable -- she could fall in love with him when he was like this.

The trouble was, she couldn't trust that he would remain warm and approachable. So far, every time she let herself believe they were becoming close, he had turned cold again.

"You're welcome," she said, hoping this time he wouldn't withdraw. He turned back to his fishing. Not really a withdrawal, was it? Just not an exuberant oh thank you thank you with a smacking big kiss for emphasis. She sighed and went to whittle a few palmetto stalks to spit the fish on.

They ate a companionable supper, Débile between them under the table. When her shoes were off, Catherine had taken to resting them on the hound's back. He seemed to like it.

She tried to start a conversation, looking for things they would have in common. Had he enjoyed strolling through the Tuileries? It seemed that musketeers did not stroll. Had he seen the great carnival held outside Paris, with jugglers and pantomimes and sword eaters? He had, but he had nothing to say about it. Jean Paul was not rude, but neither was he talkative. There never was a broodier man in all of France. Or Louisiana either.

After supper, Catherine cleaned up while Jean Paul went out, as he usually did at dusk. Catherine supposed he was saying goodnight to Suzette and the piglets. They were his best friends, after all. She tamped down her irritation. Jealousy, not irritation, if she were honest with herself. Jean Paul talked to Suzette more than he did to his own wife.

"Sou-eee," she heard him call. So the pigs hadn't yet come back from the day's foraging, but they would come running when they heard him call. Catherine hadn't known that about pigs, that they would come to a sou-eee like dogs did to a whistle.

Well, she wasn't waiting for Jean Paul to finish his tête-a-tête with Suzette. She climbed into bed and found she couldn't fall asleep. When he finally came in and climbed into bed beside her, she relaxed and drifted off.

"Sou-eee," woke her. The sun shone directly in her face, confusing her. It was morning, and he was still calling Suzette and the piglets?

When he came into the cabin, Catherine was fixing breakfast. He stamped his feet to get the mud off. She eyed her floor. She was going to make a broom after breakfast if she didn't get anything else done.

"Suzette has gone off looking for acorns again?" she asked. She would not be snippy over a pig.

"I suppose. Not like her to keep the piglets out all night with pumas in the woods."

"They'll turn up. Now that I think of it, where is the piglets' father?" She squeezed one of the little sour oranges into their cups of water. It wasn't chocolate, but it brightened up the water.

"I salted some of the meat."

She grimaced. She'd come to think of Suzette and the little ones as individuals, not as bacon. "But why did you not keep him for breeding?"

"Louis tangled with a bear and lost the fight. No way to save him."

"Oh." She paused. "We have bears here?"

"Boars, bears, puma, gators, snakes, wolves."

She frowned. "I think you left out bears last time."

"Nevertheless, madame -- there are bears, and one of them tore into Louis."

"Poor Louis. He must have been so frightened."

She thought Jean Paul, the man of no expressions, looked a little distressed. "I'll help you call Suzette to come home so we don't have to worry about her."

They went outside and hollered into the woods, "Sou-eee!"

~~~

Instead of Suzette, Débile came rushing out of the woods and commenced barking and dancing around Jean Paul. He tried to calm him down, but Débile backed out of reach, barking, running towards the woods and back. A tickle of unease ran up Jean Paul's spine.

"What is it?" Catherine said.

"I don't know. Go to the cabin."

When he saw Catherine was going to do as he asked for once, he said, "All right, boy. Show me."

Deep into the woods, Débile's bark changed pitch. Dread slowed Jean Paul's steps as he moved into a small clearing, and there was Suzette with her throat cut, the flies buzzing over the bloody ground, over the gaping wounds. She had been butchered, the great hams taken away.

He fell to his knees. Suzette. He pressed his palm against her belly and held his breath until he got himself under control. He could not have kept his sanity out here if it hadn't been for Débile and Suzette. She'd looked at him from those intelligent eyes when he talked to her, had snuffled in his hand or rubbed her great bulk against his thigh.

Débile licked his face and at last lay down beside him in quiet companionship.

When he could think again, he stared at the wound in her throat and on her flank. Neither a wildcat nor a bear had done that.

"Sou-eee," he called, hoping the piglets would come running. He listened, but he knew they wouldn't come. They were dead or gone.

His mind snapped into awareness -- Catherine, alone in the cabin. "Débile, home!" He ran, branches slapping his face, Débile dashing ahead to show him the way. He sprinted across the field and tore into the cabin.

"What is it? What's happened?"

His heart pounding, he grabbed her up and pressed her face into his chest. As his pulse slowed, he became aware of woman, warm and pliant in his arms. He closed his eyes and rubbed his nose against the side of her neck, inhaling the scent of sweat and woman. If anything had happened to her . . .

"Tell me," she said, her voice muffled by his chest.

With an exhale, he stepped back. "Someone killed Suzette."

"Someone? Not an animal? A big cat?"

"No. Someone with a knife."

She looked at him, her busy brain thinking. "Indians?"

"I don't know." Not Akecheta's people. He hoped to God not them. "Catherine, if you leave this cabin, you're not to be out of my sight. Promise me."

"I promise."

"I'm going to bury Suzette. You keep the knife. Débile, stay." The dog was more protection than that knife in her small hands.

~~~

Catherine felt very sorry for Jean Paul. He was badly shaken, losing Suzette. Every morning and evening she'd seen him at the wallow talking to his pigs and petting them. They'd been his friends those months he and Débile had lived here alone. Well, Jean Paul had a wife now. He didn't have to bury a friend alone.

She carried a cup of water into the woods, following Débile. "Find him," was all she needed to say, and the hound led her to Jean Paul.

Before she saw, she smelled the sow's corpse and pressed the back of her hand to her nose. Flies buzzed all over poor Suzette.

Jean Paul greeted her with a scowl. "What the hell do you think you're doing wandering around out here? I told you to stay in the cabin."

She felt very small, and very unwelcome, but she was not a child to be scolded. "I thought you needed company," she said, meeting his glare with her own.

"You made a promise!" He jammed the shovel into the soil and put his hands on his hips, stared at the sky, and shook his head. "Christ," he muttered. "You get lost out here, I might never find you. Do you realize that?"

"I've been in woods before."

"Did the woods you knew have bears? Poisonous snakes? Quicksand? Was the foliage so thick you couldn't see more than ten feet ahead?"

"What's quicksand?"

"Jesus, Joseph, and Mary."

She stiffened. "I am not accustomed to such blasphemy, monsieur."

He strode to her and seized her shoulders. "You'll hear more of it you keep acting like an imbecile. You could die out here! And maybe not from pumas." He gave her a hard shake. "Does it mean nothing to you, that somebody slit Suzette's throat? That they could do the same to you?"

His eyes were wild. He wasn't just furious. He was frightened. She wanted to cup his cheek, to soothe him, but she did not dare. She offered him the cup of water, half spilled.

He looked at the cup, looked at her, and seemed to deflate.

"You drink it." He picked up his shovel and dug into the dark earth.

Catherine set the cup down for Débile who lapped into it with enthusiasm.

She had seen pigs slaughtered, sheep, too, on her grandfather's estate. But it had seemed somehow normal, the usual course of things in providing meat for the family. But Jean Paul's pig was his friend.

Her husband dug into the earth, tossing the dirt into a pile with controlled, angry exactitude. She didn't dare speak to him.

He wiped his face with his forearm and put the shovel aside. Grabbing hold of Suzette's bloodied tail, he tried to drag her big body over into the grave, the muscles in his thighs, shoulders, and back straining.

Catherine took hold of the front two legs, her skirts dragging across the horrid wound in the throat, and tugged. Between the two of them, the body fell into the hole.

Débile sat solemnly at her side as Jean Paul tossed dirt into the grave. He was calm now, taking his time. When he finished, he rested the shovel on his shoulder. "Home, Débile. You," he said to Catherine, "you walk in front of me."

Once they emerged into the cleared land around the cabin, Jean Paul said, "Get in the cabin. Stay there." She watched him head for the bayou, to wash, she supposed. Another day she would insist on hearing a *please* when he wanted her to do something.

When he returned, she was subdued, he was silent. She sat on the edge of the bed with her hands in her lap.

Jean Paul, still damp from his swim, put on his clean shirt. He retrieved his sword from under the bed and pulled it from its scabbard. Again and again, he drew the whet stone down its sleek line. The blade gleamed like silver, but that beauty was spoiled by the grating, nerve-zinging sound of metal on stone.

"Do you think Akecheta's people did this?" Catherine asked.

"I'm going to find out."

"If you go to the village armed for combat, it will not be a welcomed visit."

"If thieves have come into the area, I will be ready."

He fetched his long gun from under the bed and gave it a thorough cleaning.

"Will you eat before you go?"

"We'll eat later. And you're coming with me. If there are hostile Indians in the neighborhood . . . Not out of my sight, remember?"

He untied his knife belt. "Come here."

If there had been a tender note in his voice, she would have gladly stepped closer, but he was as cold and distant as ever. Wary, Catherine took two steps toward him.

He tied the leather knife belt around her waist and adjusted the blade in its sheath. Then he strapped the sword around his waist, slung the powder horn over one shoulder and hefted the musket to the other.

Catherine followed him to the path, wondering about the piglets. They might have got away, might be hiding in the woods. "We could call for the little pigs."

Jean Paul just shook his head. "They're gone."

# Chapter Twenty-Five

*Catherine and Jean Paul
Renegades*

Jean Paul glanced over his shoulder to be sure Catherine was following close behind. Whoever killed Suzette should be long gone, but what if they weren't?

He stepped onto the path leading directly to the village, and a boy popped up out of the brush, an arrow cocked in his bow. Jean Paul didn't move. It was Cheta, one of Mato's brothers.

The boy looked at him, then at Catherine, and lowered the bow.

Jean Paul approached him. "What's happened?"

"Raiders."

"So it was strangers," Catherine whispered behind him. "I didn't believe it could be these people."

Jean Paul nodded and continued up the path, Débile at his side. When he stepped into the clearing, the usual bustle, the usual hum of voices was absent. The women and children were all inside the huts while armed men stood in groups of two and three, their gazes on the wooded perimeter.

Akecheta strode across the ground toward him, his lips set in a grim line.

"What have they taken?" Jean Paul said. The tribe kept only chickens -- and then he knew. He should have said *who* have they taken?

"My granddaughter."

"When?"

Akecheta shook his head. "Before daylight, that's all we know."

The chief looked at Catherine. "Fleur is in her hut."

Jean Paul touched her hand as she passed by him. Why had he done that? She was perfectly safe for the moment.

"Come," Akecheta said. "I am old. I need to sit down."

They settled in the shade, and Akecheta's wife brought them gourds of sweet water. Jean Paul knew there was no hurrying him. He waited until the old man was ready to tell him.

"We think Ita went out in the night to make water. No one heard anything, so they were swift."

Jean Paul didn't know Ita, whether she was a child or a woman. He looked around for Mato. "Who has gone after them?"

"Her uncles, her brothers. They will find her."

"And the soldiers from Fort Louis?"

"I have sent word to your Colonel Blaise. They will come or they will not."

Jean Paul nodded. The colonel could alert the other settlers, but Jean Paul did not know whether French soldiers would pursue the abductors of an Indian woman. If it had been a French woman . . .

"These men who took your granddaughter," Jean Paul said. "Do you know them?"

"I know of them. A small band of misfits and outcasts. Twelve or fifteen, we think. They come through the southern tribes every few years." Akecheta took a big breath. "They will not get away this time."

"They have meat. They killed my sow."

"The big pig you talk to?"

Jean Paul blinked. He'd thought he was quite isolated on his little farm, and these people with their eyes and ears were all around him.

He and Catherine could stay here, add one more man to defend the village. "I have my sword, my musket -- "

Akecheta shook his head.

"I could -- "

Akecheta interrupted him. "The renegades are running for their lives. Go home, monsieur."

As Jean Paul stood, the old man added a caution. "They are gone, I believe. But be careful of your woman."

~~~

Catherine watched the woods as she followed Jean Paul toward home, looking for wild men. Would they look crazed? Would their faces be painted? It was Fleur's cousin Ita the raiders took, and her only fifteen years old. Fleur's eyes had been swollen from crying. Catherine didn't think she had much hope of seeing Ita again.

Once they were in their own clearing, Catherine felt more at ease. It had been a long time since breakfast. "I'll get us something to eat."

"Catherine." She stopped at the command in his voice.

"What is it?"

He stood at the corner of the cabin, looking at the ground. With a jerk, he raised his head and scanned the clearing and into the darkness of the woods.

"They were here." He pointed, showing her footprints leading from behind the cabin to the doorway. Taking her arm, he backed her up against the log wall. "Stay here."

Her heart pounded as he withdrew his sword and crept around the corner to the doorway. In a moment, he called, "You can come in."

The bedding was tossed on the floor, their clothes strewn about, and the bag of seed potatoes was split open. Their cornmeal and salt were gone.

"Oh! Did they take my cloak?" Frantic, she looked around and found it fallen behind the bed. "Thank heavens. They were foolish not to take it. It's the best cloak . . ." She crushed it to her. She loved this cloak. Jean Paul had given it to her.

"I'm not sure people on the move think about the future. Right now, they don't need a cloak." He stepped to the doorway and looked to the sunny patch where he had stretched the otter skins to dry. "They got my skins." He looked over his shoulder at her. "I'll get more."

Catherine bent to pick up the potatoes. "I guess this means they're not on the run after all."

"Some of them aren't."

"They won't come back. They've already taken Suzette, and stolen what they wanted from in here."

"They know a woman lives here, Catherine."

A shiver of fear ran up her backbone. She took in Jean Paul's set jaw, the determined gaze. He would keep her safe.

"You're going to stay in my sight every minute."

"Yes. All right."

"And if . . . in case -- you're going to learn how to use my knife."

He meant if they killed him first. That was not going to happen. She knew it wasn't. He was too smart, too strong.

"I have the kitchen knife."

"Not big enough. You'll use mine."

He led her to the open unplowed ground beside the cabin. "How fast can you get the knife out of its sheath?"

She darted her hand for the knife, drew it out of its sheath, and brandished it at him, grinning.

"This is not a game, Catherine. Do it again."

She was even faster that time.

"Too slow."

"No, it wasn't."

"God, your head is hard as a rock." He went to the woodpile, chopped a strip off a log so he had a decent stick, and came back to her.

"Come at me."

She lunged. He knocked the knife out of her hand.

"Swipe, don't jab. Do it again."

This time she made a large arc with her arm. Jean Paul stepped into the arc and poked her in the chest with his stick.

After an hour working on her knife play, she was bruised, resentful, and sobered. "Enough," she called.

"It's not enough." He made her work another half hour until she was exhausted. Then he rated her progress. "Good. Now maybe you'll stay alive an extra two minutes."

# Chapter Twenty-Six

*Catherine and Jean Paul
Love at Last*

If the renegade Indians didn't make Catherine uneasy, Jean Paul certainly did. He could not relax. He kept his musket within a step's reach and wore his sword at his waist. Today he was curing moss, smoking out the chiggers, to make them a new mattress. Quiet work, tending the smoky fire, so he could at the same time listen to the forest, to the birds, to the wind, constantly scanning the perimeter of their clearing. Even Débile felt his master's tension and remained alert instead of dozing in the shade.

Wherever the marauders were, they weren't here. If someone were coming, Jean Paul had told her, the birds would grow silent while they assessed the danger. This morning, the birds were in full song.

Jean Paul's heavy sheathed knife clunked against Catherine's thigh as she made her first attempt at grinding corn into meal. She wanted to try it because it would be cheaper than buying the meal, so Jean Paul had made her a shallow wooden trough and a hardwood grinder. The work made her fingers sore and her back ache as she knelt before the trough and put all her strength into crushing the hard kernels, but she kept at it. That, of all that she had learned, was probably the most important. To just keep at it, no matter how much she would rather lay abed and eat chocolate coated strawberries. Ha. What a thought. No chocolate, no strawberries.

"Take a break," he said. "We'll practice your knife play."

With no enthusiasm whatsoever, Catherine assumed the stance.

"Look where your thumb is."

She corrected her grip, and, trying to catch him by surprise, she lunged for him. He grabbed her forward arm and jerked her past him so that she fell on her face in the dirt.

"I keep telling you not to lunge. Try it again."

"I believe that's your favorite word."

"What?"

"Again." She made the word drip with scorn.

Jean Paul laughed. "Again."

She blew the wisps of hair out of her face and faced him with bent knees, the knife poised to swipe or parry. He came for her with his stick of wood. Catherine executed a perfect defensive maneuver.

"Well done!"

Catherine drew a big breath. She had pleased him. She might burst into song.

But, quick as a finger snap, that lovely warm look he gave her was gone, and the lovely, warm Jean Paul hid himself again. She should not feel any surprise at this abrupt reversal. That was what he did, wasn't it? Make her glow, and then kick her in the teeth. Well, all right, she was being dramatic, but that is how it felt to have your feelings hurt time after time.

"See if you can do it again." Before she was quite ready, he came at her. She did her best and figured the worst that would have happened to her in a real attack was a defensive wound on her forearm. At least, that's where Jean Paul's stick scraped her.

"You're improving."

"So now I might stay alive two and a half minutes?" She was still angry at that two-minute remark.

"Maybe even three. That'll do for now. I need to tend that fire."

She returned to her grinding trough, but Jean Paul's indifference seemed to suck all the strength from her arms as she worked.

She glanced at him as he smoked the moss. He wore the palmetto hat she'd made for him. He wore it all day every day, in fact. And it didn't even fit. And he'd laughed, like she'd meant him to, when she'd snarled *again* at him. Why was she thinking about hurt feelings?

Because they hurt, she told herself, just as cross as if she were saying the words out loud.

Catherine straightened up to ease the ache in her lower back. If she weren't careful, they'd knot up and then she'd be in for it. Sometimes simple walking helped. She wandered down to the bayou thinking she might see another of those pink birds with the funny beaks.

She stood on the bank, her hands kneading her aching muscles when Débile came loping up, his tongue hanging out, his tail wagging. She turned to give him a good scratch behind the ears. "You're a friendly fellow, aren't you? You don't turn to stone if I so much as smile at you."

What was wrong with Jean Paul Dupre, anyway? To be on guard against her every moment, as if she were some sort of danger to him. It wasn't normal. All those scowls and blank looks, it was a form of cruelty, was it not?

She heard his footsteps behind her and turned, ever hopeful that he had come to take a breath, to be friendly. But at the look in his eyes, she stepped back, nearly tumbling off the two foot bank.

He loathed her. That's what she read in his face. He despised her. He wished she were dead.

He grabbed her arms. "So. You've come down here alone. A wild Indian steps out of the woods, just there, grabs you and slits your throat. Or maybe he would prefer to take you off somewhere and play with you a while before he kills you. If we're lucky, he will leave your body somewhere close enough I can find you."

The threat he described was less frightening than the cold, hard look in his eyes. He crowded her, the two foot drop behind her, his chest two inches from her nose.

He gave her a shake. "Do I have to tie a rope around your waist to keep you near? Are you so stupid?"

The woman was impossible. She had a head made of hickory. She didn't listen. She didn't think. What did she expect, an estate full of footmen and hired guards would protect her?

*And* she was hopeless with the knife. Any man could disarm her in ten seconds, and she goes wandering off where he can't see her. He ought to do it, tie a rope around her waist. She would be mad as hornets. She'd resent him, even more than she did now.

So let her be mad. Better mad than dead.

"Stupid? I'm stupid?" Catherine shoved him with both hands. "Get out of my way."

She strode up the path to the cabin, her whole body hot with fury. She was finished with him. He would never hurt her feelings again, not ever. She didn't need him anymore than he needed her. She could build a wall just as high as the one he hid behind.

"Catherine!"

"What do you care if I'm dead?" she threw over her shoulder. "Leave me alone."

He was striding right behind her. "What do I care? It's my job to keep you safe."

Catherine stepped into the cabin, Débile on her heels. She whirled around to face Jean Paul as he came after her.

"What is wrong with you?" he demanded.

Débile looked from Catherine to Jean Paul and slunk out of the cabin.

"What is wrong with me? I'll tell you what is wrong with me. I've been an idiot, but I'm through with you. I'm through with hoping you'll be kind to me, that you'll talk to me. That you'll throw a smile my way every few days."

She stepped close enough to jab a finger in his chest. "Do you know how many times you've laughed in all these weeks? Three times. Three. What is wrong with *you*?"

He stood there, like a dumb post, like he couldn't even hear her. She tilted her chin up and glared at him. "You won't tell me anything about yourself. You won't even look me in the eye unless you forget yourself for half a minute."

And still he stood mute, his eyes unreadable.

Catherine threw her hands in the air. "Why did you bring me here, Jean Paul?" She heard her voice rising, but she didn't care. "Why don't you want me -- do you have a better offer?" She could gag on the bitterness rising in her throat. "What have I done to deserve this ice wall you erect between us?"

He simply stared at her. She might as well rail at a tree stump.

The last thread of hope for a good life together unraveled. Catherine's shoulders slumped. Her lungs deflated. She didn't understand him. She would love him if he'd let her. What was so wrong with her that he wouldn't let her?

"Why won't you love me?" She pressed her fingers to her lips, trying to hold the grief in. "Why won't you touch me?"

~~~

His wife looked at him with her splotchy face, her eyes filled with hurt. He had done that to her.

He stepped toward her, to touch her, to tell her he was sorry, but she backed away as if she thought he would hit her. He would never ever do that. "Catherine," he said.

The look in her eye, questioning him, afraid of him -- it broke his heart.

He raised his hand to her cheek. "Catherine." Her breath shuddered in, watching him, wary and on guard.

He touched his lips to hers and for a moment he thought she softened --

She tore away from him. "You kiss me and then you'll go right back to being cruel and cold." She wiped her hand across her mouth. "Don't you ever kiss me again."

She turned from him and stood with rigid back and fisted hands.

He couldn't blame her. Why should she trust him when he had pushed her away time after time?

What an ass he'd been. Punishing her. Punishing himself. Why had he done that? Because Belinda had betrayed him, he believed all women were false, that there were no good women in the world? Was he such a fool?

"Catherine. Please. Look at me."

She turned and studied him from her reddened eyes, her chin up and her lips firmed.

"I do want you," he said. "I do."

Without taking her eyes from his, she shook her head.

"I'm sorry I didn't -- " He lost the ability to speak for a moment. He reached to touch her again. "I never meant . . . will you let me . . . "

Catherine backed away, her eyes cold.

He dropped his hand. That was it then. He had ruined everything.

He left the cabin and ended up at the bayou where the water flowed along, the lazy stream indifferent to the pain he felt or the pain he'd caused.

Just there, he had spread his fingers under Catherine while she learned to trust the water would hold her up. She'd trusted him, too. He could have loved her then. She would have let him. But what if he had let himself love her, and she hurt him as

Belinda had? That's what he'd feared, though he had told himself any number of lies besides that small truth. He'd been a coward.

It all came down to trust. He had not trusted her, and now he'd lost any hope that she would trust him.

The problem was, he had loved Belinda. There had been other women, of course, but he only ever loved this one woman. It had never occurred to him not to trust her, and Belinda, his beloved, had taken his heart in her traitorous hands and torn it apart.

And he had behaved as if he were the only man in the world to have been betrayed. As if he had so little spine, so little heart, that he could not recover.

Jean Paul's face heated with shame. Every time Catherine had shown him a little tenderness, he had run from her into the safety of his coward's prison.

When Jean Paul had arrived two winters ago, he'd thought the living would be easy. No snow, no ice. Then came summertime with the biting insects, the relentless sun, the suffocating humidity. He'd grown desperate for home, for the breeze blowing off the Seine, the relief of ale cooled in the well, drunk with good white bread – and friends. And he'd become shaky inside himself.

He still did not understand what had happened to him, but he had begun talking to his pigs, to himself sometimes. Even when he had traded a deer skin for Débile, the great quietness was not defeated. A trembling emptiness had sometimes come upon him, as if the aloneness would swallow him whole. That's what he'd felt, like he was about to disappear, the morning he'd made a mindless rush to get himself a companion. Catherine.

She had saved him. He had not felt that yawning white emptiness since she came here, yet he'd let himself be blinded by Belinda's treachery so that he could not see Catherine herself -- he saw only female and danger, and so he'd guarded himself, trying not to see her or to let her see him.

Catherine was the one with the courage, insisting there be more between them than hard work and poor food.

He'd never thought himself a coward. As a musketeer, he'd been bold, resourceful, even acclaimed. But that was a different kind of courage, a bodily courage. His cowardice had been of the heart. Was his heart so tender, then, or feeble, or frail that he had allowed one hateful woman to break him?

Yes, he had been brutally injured, but he had kept picking at those wounds, never allowing them to close. Had his persistent torment simply become a habit? Was he so fainthearted?

Jean Paul breathed in deeply. And again. He straightened his back. He was a better man than this. He *would be* a better man than this, for his own self-respect, and for Catherine.

He walked slowly back to the cabin, still afraid. Her forgiveness would not be easily won. Why should it be?

What if she never forgave him?

He stepped into the cabin. Catherine sat at the table, her hands in her lap, her head bent. She looked at him without expectation, as if she were resigned to a cold life. A lonely life.

He sat down across the table from her and drew in a breath. "First of all, I am Jean Paul Desjardins." She narrowed her eyes at him, but she didn't speak.

"And I killed someone."

Catherine set her hands on the table. "Tell me. You owe me that, at least."

"Yes." He took a deep breath to steady himself. "I was part of the escort for Marie Angelique, one of the old king's granddaughters. Not one of the princesses, but his blood nonetheless."

"I've met her," Catherine said.

"You've met her?"

"Once. At a garden party. Never mind that. What happened?"

"My friends, Cordier, Foucault, Remarque -- we were excellent marksmen, superior swordsmen, and so we were chosen to routinely escort Marie Angelique between Versailles and the small country estate where she lived. She was very young, fourteen, I think." He rubbed his hand over his mouth. "I used to tease her to make her blush, to make her laugh.

"The regent had just given her a collection of rubies to be her dowry -- her grandfather Louis had always intended them for her. Some of them she wore in a necklace that day, and foolishly, she told us there were more in a pouch, so proud her Grandfather had given them to her, so trusting, as if we were all her big brothers.

"When we passed into the forest, Remarque yanked Marie Angelique out of the carriage and ripped the rubies from her throat. 'Where is the pouch, my lady?' He asked it as if he were asking her for a cup of tea.

"I went for my pistol. Foucault bashed me over the head and pushed me off my horse. I found my feet, my head reeling, and pointed my pistol at Remarque. 'Let her go,' I said.

"He reached for his pistol. I fired."

Jean Paul held his breath, his hand over his eyes. "I killed her, Catherine. I killed Marie Angelique."

Catherine's hands covered his fist on the table top. "It was an accident, Jean Paul."

Jean Paul rubbed his hands over his eyes. "I see her face over and over, the surprise when the bullet caught her, the question in her eyes when she realized it was I who had shot her. I grabbed her as she fell. There was a bubble of blood at the corner of her mouth, just here," he said, and touched his own mouth, "but I told her she would be all right, that I would not leave her."

He struggled to get his breath under control. "Once she was dead, Remarque jerked her out of my arms and plundered the pockets of her skirt to find the rest of the jewels.

"Foucault drew his pistol on me. 'What do you think?' he said to Cordier. 'A quick bullet to the head?'

"Cordier -- my best friend -- he said, 'Go ahead.'

"I leapt at Foucault, and the shot went over my shoulder. I ran for my horse and fled."

"Thank God," Catherine said.

"It took two days, hiding, riding by night, to get to Belinda." He glanced at Catherine. "She was the great love of my life, I thought. I sent word to her to meet me at her grandfather's house. No one would look for me there. I could catch my breath, come up with a plan. But mostly, I had to see her.

"During the night, I woke to find Belinda gone from the bed. There were voices murmuring from downstairs, a man's voice and a woman's. I pulled on my boots, shrugged into my coat, and slipped onto the dark landing to peer down at the hall below.

"And there was Cordier, my Belinda in his arms, his hands pressing her bottom against his cock. And her grinning up at him, her arms around his neck.

"I must have made some sound, for Belinda looked up and saw me standing there. The look on her face, guilt, triumph, but not sorrow. Not regret. She had given me away for a handful of rubies. She had told Cordier where I was, knowing he meant to kill me."

Jean Paul couldn't sit there anymore. He got up, walked to the door and told Catherine the rest with his back to her.

"I fled to the balcony outside the bedroom. Foucault and Remarque were waiting below, their pistols primed, but I took to the roofs. I made it to the coast and caught the first ship out of Le Havre. And here I am."

He spread his hands on the table. "So you see, you have married a murderer."

Jean Paul couldn't tell what she was thinking. Her sea-green eyes simply stared at him, giving nothing away.

Very slowly, she shook her head. "It's only murder if you meant to harm Marie Angelique. And you didn't."

How badly he'd needed someone to forgive him. With a deep breath, he said, "Then you believe me."

"Yes. Do you believe what they said about me? That I'm a murderer?"

He could smile at her now. "Are you?"

At last there was a light behind her eyes again. "What do you think?"

"I think you are not."

Catherine rose and rounded the table. She put a hand on his shoulder. "From now on, Jean Paul, you will please to remember I am not Belinda. You won't shut me out anymore. Promise me."

His breath shuddered. "I promise."

She leant over and pressed her lips beside his mouth. Her kiss felt like mercy. It felt like deliverance.

Catherine felt the tremor in his hands as he pulled her into his lap. She thought she understood now. He had been frightened that she would hurt him as Belinda had. So he had hurt her, pushing her away over and over. Could she trust him not to hurt her again? Could she believe in this embrace, so tight it felt as if he would never let her go?

He touched his forehead to hers and traced her lip with his thumb, so gently it felt like love.

And if she wouldn't trust him not to hurt her again? If she drew away from him? What kind of life would they have together? Maybe, if she dared to risk her heart, maybe they'd have a chance. Maybe they could love each other.

His kiss, tender and warm and slow, spoke to her of yearning. Did he need her?

His kiss said *Have faith in me. Please. Love me.*

With his hand in her hair, his mouth was hot, but gentle. There was no room in a kiss like this for distrust.

Catherine relaxed her body against his. *Trust me, Jean Paul, and I will trust you.*

As he kissed his way up her neck, tiny shocks pulsed through her blood, warming her from her heart down into her womb.

She stirred to the sensuality in his hands as he unbraided her plait and wove his fingers into her hair. She felt his hardness press against her thigh and marveled at the heat penetrating her skirt. She opened her mouth under his, asking for more.

Jean Paul thrilled to her growing insistence. Her mouth turned greedy and in his own lonely desperation, he made his kisses hotter and more urgent. His hand cupped her breast -- how long he'd wanted to touch her here, to caress and squeeze and kiss.

His face in her hair, he breathed her name. "Catherine?"

"Yes."

Hesitantly, carefully, keeping his desire in check -- for his need for her was neither gentle nor patient -- he undressed her, caressed and stroked. He kissed her eyes, her cheeks, her jaw. He wanted to see her, all of her. He stepped back to gaze on her beautiful body and when he raised his eyes to her face, she was calm, her eyes clear and trusting.

"Now you," she said, and untied the shirt strings at his neck.

Jean Paul feared she would be frightened to see his arousal. He heard her inhale, but she stepped close to him, put both her hands on his chest, and kissed him.

It was overwhelming, the feel of her smooth skin under his hard hands, the stroking of her long fingers down his ribs. He held the back of her head so that he could plunder her mouth, take all she had to give him standing in his embrace.

When he didn't think he could wait any longer, he lay her on her back and spread her legs with his knee.

"All right?" He didn't know how much experience Catherine had with men, if she understood what was going to happen between them.

Catherine saw his hesitation, his worry. She held her arms up for him, wanting him, needing him. When he entered her, she gasped and her eyes flew open. He stopped and kissed her softly, waiting as she adjusted to the feel of him inside her.

He searched her eyes, a line between his brows. She moved under him, signaling she was ready, and he smiled and kissed her with tender sweetness.

Slowly, he moved into her, setting the rhythm. She began to move with him, her hands stroking his back.

When his breath came too short, he broke the gentle surging and moved his mouth to her breast. Catherine's own breath caught. His whiskers scraped the tender flesh, and she arched her back. "Jean Paul?" she whispered.

Catherine was filled with wonder. This was what she had yearned for, the feel of Jean Paul's body on top of her, inside her. She rocked with him, glorying in the weight of his body on hers.

His rhythm quickened. She dug her fingers into the muscles of his back. She felt enveloped, claimed by his crushing kiss as his body plunged into hers. Catherine had never felt -- any of this -- the heat, the urgency, the frantic need for more and more.

She was swept along in a furious tide, reaching reaching reaching for a far away shore. Then all at once, she was tossed into a roiling maelstrom, helpless, exhilarated, drowning in the feel of him, of his hips pummeling hers, of her own body pushing back. She cried out, and he released all the power he had been holding back until just this moment, carrying her with him through the turmoil, through the tumultuous waves and vehement heat.

Catherine clutched him to her, her body still shuddering, sheltered in his arms, safe, together on a sun-warmed shore.

Jean Paul buried his nose in the crook of her neck. "Catherine," he sighed. This had to be truth between them. A connection, unbreakable, now and forever. She was his, and by all that was holy, he was hers.

He rolled off her and pulled her close as she fell into sleep. The cabin was silent, but from outside he heard the wind in the trees and the squawk of a crow. He didn't deserve her forgiveness, he really didn't. But, blessed Mary, she had given it.

As his fingers played with her hair, she opened her eyes. "Don't shut me out again, Jean Paul," she whispered.

He traced her jaw and shook his head. "No, I won't."

They spent lazy moments touching, learning each other. He hoped she could see it in his eyes -- he would not hurt her again.

He linked his fingers with hers. "You were a virgin."

Catherine laughed. "You're worried about that now? I'm your wife, Jean Paul."

He shifted his weight, one arm draped over her belly, his other arm propping up his head so he could look into her eyes. "I never meant to hurt you."

She touched his cheek. "I wanted this."

"That's not what I mean. I -- "

She grabbed his face and kissed him, hard. When she let him go, he cupped her cheek with his rough hand. "This is not the life you were meant to live. I can't give you jewels or carriages. I can't --"

She pressed her fingers to his lips. "I know that. And that life, with jewels and carriages? Apparently that is not the life I was meant to lead. I'm here, with you. I'm meant to be here, Jean Paul, in this cabin, in this bed, with you."

His kiss was so tender, Catherine's throat tightened and tears flooded her eyes. "Love me, Jean Paul."

When they had once more plumbed the depths of their need for one another, Jean Paul pulled her into his arms, her back to him.

"Jean Paul Desjardins," she said on a sigh. "I'm Madame Desjardins."

He kissed the spot behind her ear. "No, you married Jean Paul Dupre. That's what's on the register."

"I'm perfectly happy to be Madame Dupre."

# Chapter Twenty-Seven

*Catherine and Jean Paul
Bliss*

Catherine woke the next morning with Jean Paul's arm flung across her hip. She stared at him in the early light while his face was relaxed. The line between his eyes was eased, his dark lashes were fanned across the tender skin under his eyes.

Men tried so hard to be tough, to not feel. The good ones, though, like Jean Paul, did feel. Sometimes they felt so much they had to hide it even from themselves. Everyone knew it was a man's world and that women suffered many difficulties just because they were women; however, it seemed to Catherine, it was not easy to be a man either.

Jean Paul's great secret had weighed him down and nearly strangled him, but maybe he could be easier inside himself now. A sore heart shared was a heart that could heal.

She wouldn't wake him, but she wanted to smooth the hair back from his forehead, to touch the curve of his bottom lip. How she loved touching him, being touched by him. Yesterday, after the terrible storm of her anger, after the intense joy of making love, they'd been peaceful. Even after they had finally risen from the bed, there had been a quiet harmony between them. And touching. Whenever she passed by, he trailed his fingers down her arm. When she set his supper in front of him, she leaned her hand on his shoulder.

They were going to be all right together. No doubt they would have days when they would not be in such harmony, but surely from now on they would have an abiding union, a deep affinity, between them. She wouldn't call it love, not on his part anyway. Maybe, someday, he would love her as she did him.

Her gaze roamed over his bare shoulders, the swelling of muscle in his upper arm, the smoothness of his skin. When she returned to his face, he was watching her. Catherine smiled at him, but he didn't smile back.

"What is it?" she said.

He cradled her face in his hand. "You have forgiven me. Truly?"

She could tell him she loved him, but she did not believe he was ready to know that. She turned her mouth into his palm and kissed it. "I want to be happy with you, Jean Paul. No regrets, no resentments."

"You humble me, Madame Dupre."

She laughed. "A man once told me I haunted him, but no one has ever said I humbled him."

"I suppose he was a fancy fellow with lace at his cuffs and a beauty patch on his cheek."

"Oh, indeed. No one without a beauty patch and at least as much lace as I wore myself dared approach me."

He was so sober. She supposed that was who he was, a sober man, even when he was happy. She thought he was happy this morning, his eyes on her, his hand cupping her cheek.

Jean Paul sighed. "You need a new dress. But there will be no lace and no silk."

"I will be more grateful than I can say simply to never put that poor bedraggled blue dress on again, however plain and coarse its replacement." She kissed him lightly on the mouth.

"You kiss a man in the morning, you know what happens."

She grinned at him. "I have no idea. Perhaps you would show me."

Now he smiled. Moving on top of her, he smoothed the hair off her face.

When they lay sated in each other's arms, Catherine dozed off. Jean Paul held her, smelled the salty, smoky scent of her skin, and choked down the emotion that swelled up. A fool like he was didn't deserve a second chance with a woman like Catherine, but oh God how grateful he was to have it.

Waking up, she took in a big breath and stretched. "I have to get up," she said.

"You sure?"

She goosed him. "I have to pee."

"Wait. Let me look around first."

He slipped his pants on and untied the leather door. "Come, Débile."

Catherine waited while Jean Paul checked for signs there had been intruders around the farmstead. She thought the marauding Indians must be miles from here by now with Mato and the other Biloxi pursing them. She closed her eyes for a moment to pray that Ita still lived.

Jean Paul stuck his head in the door. "It's all right." He waited outside for her to go to the privy in her nightdress. Never out of his sight, that's what he'd said when they learned of the raiders, and he had not relaxed that rule.

Back in the cabin, Catherine took the tattered blue dress off its hook. She had to grit her teeth to put the ragged thing on every morning. She'd washed it several times, but it still was a horror. What she wouldn't give for even a scullery maid's serviceable gray frock.

"I'll get more otters today," Jean Paul said, eyeing her dress. "As soon as they're cured, we'll take the skins in and get that bolt of cloth put aside for you. Purple and orange, wasn't it?"

She smiled. "With big pink flowers."

"That's the one."

When breakfast was ready, Jean Paul seated himself at the table, and Catherine presented him with a plank of meat and a cold potato. "Squirrel à la Louisiane, compliments of the chef."

"I believe I'll have truffles with that, my love."

"Of course, and a nice hot croissant."

Jean Paul wrapped an arm around her hips and drew her close. "You miss your life, Catherine."

She considered how she felt about the day ahead of her. The chores were endless, and every task had to be accomplished with their own two hands. It would be very nice to say to a maid, *sweep the floor, trim the candle wicks*, to direct the gardener to tend the indigo, the cook to serve *blanquette de veau* with a nice Bordeaux. But alas, no maid, no gardener, no cook.

If Catherine were not making a garden or weaving hats or grinding corn, what else might she be doing? Going to yet another round of boring teas? Yet another ball? Well, she would be pleased to go to another ball, but she did not regret all the flummery of her old life. Let Cousin Hugo spend his time worrying about matching his pantaloons to the exact shade of the embroidery on his velvet coat.

Ah. Cousin Hugo. At odd moments, she still wanted to stake him out for the wolves, but in truth, she didn't think of him much. All the hatred, resentment, and anger seemed to belong to another woman. All she needed was this man.

Catherine pushed the hair off Jean Paul's forehead. "Not as much as you might think, my love. And you?"

He shook his head. "I don't want that life anymore."

She kissed the tender skin next to his eye. "Then we'll make do with squirrel à la Louisiane and boiled potatoes."

In the late afternoon, Catherine settled herself in the shade with a pile of slender reeds. She meant to create a basket and then fill it with the sweet ripe mulberries she had found in a clearing in the woods. Rachel had promised all of them they could learn to do it as well as she, but Catherine was not yet convinced. She would try anyway, and truly, what difference would it make if her baskets were a little lopsided?

Voices traveled up the bayou. Who could that be? They seldom saw even a solitary dugout passing by their landing. Four big rowboats, not dugouts, came round the bend, the first boat filled with armed men, their muskets held straight up like so many flagpoles. Catherine pressed a hand to her stomach. This couldn't be good, not after those men took Ita.

The second boat carried seven women rowed by two men. Gabrielle and Annette and Selina waved. The third boat had no passengers, only the soldiers at the oars. And the last boat bore only soldiers and settlers.

Jean Paul stood beside her, tense and still, as the boats stopped. Jean Paul's friend Laurent Laroux stepped out of the first boat. "*Bonjour*," he said.

"Laroux."

Laroux glanced at Catherine. "Bad news, I'm afraid."

"Tell me."

"Renegade Indians have burnt out a farmstead further up the bayou. The colonel is mustering a militia, and the women are going to the fort until we get this settled."

Catherine didn't want Jean Paul going off to fight wild Indians and coming home with an arrow in his chest. "Do you have to go? Let's just stay here, Jean Paul," she whispered.

He frowned at her. "A musketeer is a soldier, Catherine. Of course I have to go."

"Madame," a soldier from the women's boat called to her. "Collect what you need. We need to move on."

"I'll get my musket and pistols," Jean Paul said. He had her by the hand and took her with him.

Inside the cabin, he gathered powder, shot, two pistols, and his musket. His sword he wore all the time since the first news of the marauders.

They stood before the bed where they had loved each other only this morning. "You'll be careful," Catherine said.

He stepped to her and ran his thumb along her jaw. He kissed her, just the merest brush of his lips across hers. Then he kissed her forehead. "Let's go."

At the boat, Jean Paul squeezed her hand and helped her settle in the last bit of space. Her boat turned in the bayou to head back to the fort while the other carried on to pick up other women.

Catherine watched Jean Paul as long as she could. Just before her boat followed the turn of the bayou, he raised his hand to her. She clutched that goodbye to her heart to hold until she could see him again.

# Chapter Twenty-Eight

*Valery*
*As Long as Agnes is Safe*

Valery was antsy. Agnes would not leave Marie Claude and he would not leave Agnes, so they had spent the night here at the Joubert cabin. He was accustomed to laboring about his own farm from morning to night, but there was little for him to do here. This morning he had carved a large spoon for the cook pot and then spent a half hour sharpening his knife. He pulled a few weeds in the garden. Finally he took himself down to the bayou and fished from the banks.

The third slave had come back to the farmstead just before dark last night. Valery was not surprised that he had not a single fish to show for his hours away. Nor would he be surprised when in a few days the men "found" Joubert's dugout. A boat like that was too valuable to leave in the swamp for the gators.

Marie Claude's slaves seemed devoted to her. They fetched water for Agnes to bathe her, they cooked for everyone, and they hovered near the cabin, eager to provide whatever was needed. No one seemed to be waiting for Joubert to return. Their lack of tension only firmed his suspicions of where the master was. In a swamp, what was left of him.

He watched the bob on his fishing line, the tedium occasionally broken when a nice bass caught hold of his hook. It would be his contribution to the day, to spit the fish and roast them over the fire.

A boat full of men came up the winding bayou and pulled in where he sat fishing. He knew Jean Paul Dupre, Laurent Laroux, a couple of others. He eyed the muskets and pistols and swords and tensed.

"Villiers," Laroux called and stepped ashore. "Those marauding Indians have struck again."

"Marauding Indians? I didn't know -- "

"They took an Indian girl from the Biloxi village two days ago. Last night they burned the Granger place, killed Granger. His boy got away, but -- " Laroux looked him in the eye -- "they took Madame Granger."

Granger's wife. That was Agnes's friend Rachel.

"Colonel Blaise and his soldiers wait for us upriver."

Valery shook his head. "I cannot leave my wife and Madame Joubert."

"Valery," Laroux said.

Valery smirked at the use of his first name. Yes, they were well acquainted, but it was obviously a prelude to persuading him to do what he would not. "Laurent," Valery said in return.

Laroux matched his smirk, but he sobered quickly. "The colonel does not issue invitations, my friend. We are commanded to join the soldiers in pursuit of the raiders."

Valery suspected Laroux thought he was a coward. He was not a coward, never had been, and he didn't need to prove it. He would not let pride dissuade him from what he had to do, and that was to protect Agnes.

"The colonel has his duty. I have mine. I will not leave my wife in danger."

Jean Paul Dupre stepped out of the boat. "The women are being taken to the fort, Valery. My wife is already on her way and a second boat is right behind us to pick up the remaining women."

"I see." If Agnes and Marie Claude were kept safe, then of course Valery would have to help. "A moment. I will speak to my wife."

Inside the cabin, Agnes sat beside Marie Claude's bed. The poor woman was still in pain.

"Agnes, I must leave. There are marauding Indians in the neighborhood, and the colonel has called for a militia. You and Marie Claude will follow the other women to the fort."

"Marie Claude is too sick to be moved, Valery. We will stay here."

He shook his head.

Agnes lowered her voice. "You don't understand. She has lost so much blood and she has not yet entirely stopped bleeding. If she's moved, if she starts bleeding again, Valery . . . "

"You cannot stay here, either of you. It isn't safe. We will take every care to get her gently to the boat." He regretted Marie Claude would have to endure the passage down the bayou to the fort. If he could, he would hide Agnes, and Marie Claude, too, somewhere safe, in the treetops, behind the clouds, but a cabin was not a fortress, and the woods had their own perils. They must go to the fort.

"Valery -- "

"No."

He turned to Marie Claude as he buckled his holsters across his chest. "I regret, madame, that you must leave your sick bed, but you see it is necessary."

Agnes took his arm and turned him aside to whisper. "Remember also, husband, the very visible marks of a severe beating all over Marie Claude's face. When people know her husband is gone, they will have reason to think she killed him."

Valery drew in a breath and thought a moment. "Thomas's story, the gator hunt, it will be good enough. In spite of Marie Claude's bruises, no one can say Joubert didn't get himself lost out in the swamp after he beat her."

Agnes gripped his forearm. He held her eyes with his own. "My dearest," he said, "they have taken Madame Granger."

Her mouth fell open and she seemed to stop breathing. "Rachel." She pressed her fingers to her lips. "Valery, they'll -- "

"Yes, they will. Get your things together. When I see the women's boat arrive, I'll come help Marie Claude down to the landing."

When Thomas stepped into the cabin, Agnes exchanged a glance with him. "Thomas can help me with Marie Claude," she said. "You go on."

"Very well." He touched her chin with a gentle finger and then gathered up his weapons.

"I -- Valery, you will -- "

"Not to worry, *mon chou*." He gave her a quick kiss. "I will return unharmed."

At the landing, one of the soldiers asked him, "Where is your wife, monsieur?"

Valery scowled at the man. "She will come when it is time."

"It's time now." The soldier pointed down the bayou at a boat coming their way. Valery could see there were already two women in it.

"The colonel is waiting for us. Come aboard, monsieur."

Valery looked back toward the cabin. Thomas stood in the doorway and raised a hand to him. Very well, he would go on.

~~~

"Is he gone?" Agnes said.

Thomas nodded.

"Agnes," Marie Claude said, "get on the boat. You don't need to stay here. I have Thomas."

"I am not leaving you, Marie Claude."

Marie Claude shook her head. "Your husband thinks you are going to the fort, and I don't need you. Go, Agnes."

Agnes wasn't just being stubborn. Marie Claude had not yet quit bleeding from the miscarriage, and she could not be moved. Aside from her injuries, Marie Claude's heart was broken at losing the baby. She needed another woman by her side.

"Hello, the house!" The soldiers were here to take them away.

"Thomas, don't let them come up here," Agnes said. "You know what to say."

He nodded and closed the door behind him.

In only a few minutes, Thomas returned.

"What did you tell them?" Agnes asked.

"Just what you said, madame. That the two of you had taken the earlier boat and were already gone away."

"And they believed you?"

"They seemed to. They left."

Agnes wiped her hands on her skirt. They were alone, she and Marie Claude, Thomas, Simon and Remy. The Indians were far from here by now and would keep running with the colonel and all the settlers in pursuit. They would be fine.

Thomas took Monsieur Joubert's pistols off the shelf and sat down at the table to clean and load them. "You will have the two pistols," he said and looked at Marie Claude. "You can shoot?"

"Point, pull the trigger," she said.

He smiled. "Yes, madame."

"Even I can do that," Agnes said. "You stay in the bed, Marie Claude."

"No more fires today. Better there is no smoke rising here until the renegades are caught."

He loaded the pistols and lay them on the table. "We will be in the woods, keeping watch. You will be safe, I swear it."

When Thomas was gone, Marie Claude tried to sit up. "Agnes, if anything happens to you -- "

"You heard Thomas. We are safe."

" -- I'll go straight to hell and your husband will clang the gates after me."

Agnes laughed. "We'll be fine. Why don't you try to sleep?"

While Marie Claude slept, Agnes lifted the pistols to feel their weight, to squint one eye and aim out the window. As Marie Claude said, point and pull the trigger. And maybe kill somebody. She set the pistols down, her fingers trembling. Even a wicked renegade had a soul. But if a wild man rushed into this cabin, a tomahawk raised to kill her and Marie Claude -- she would pull both triggers.

# Chapter Twenty-Nine

*Valery*
*The Hunt*

Valery counted eight soldiers and eight men from the farmsteads. Jean Paul and Laroux had been musketeers like him, but he expected the others would make indifferent soldiers. Their allies, however, Mato and three other Biloxi Indians, would be excellent shots with their bows and arrows.

A mile upstream from Marie Claude's homestead, Colonel Blaise had set up a quick camp. The blackened ruin still smoldered, filling the air with the scent of pine smoke. Hiram Granger's mounded grave stood twenty yards from the ruins.

The colonel nodded toward the grave. "He lived a while after we found him. He knew his boy was safe before he died."

Then he also knew his wife had been abducted.

The colonel glanced at the fading light, the sun already below the tree line. "First light," Colonel Blaise said, "we'll be on the hunt."

They found places to bed down and wait for the dawn.

Only a sliver of light along the horizon shed any light when they arose. Just north of Granger's place, the main path split into three and the footprints told them that the renegades had split up. The colonel divided his men and sent them down each fork to track the killers.

In Valery's group, Mato with his superior tracking skills took the lead with him, Jean Paul, and Laroux following north, the bayou a few hundred yards to the side. Sweat rolled down Valery's back even so early in the morning, and he panted in the humid air of the thick woods. The birds hushed at their passage, and the only sounds were their own footsteps.

Valery could not get his mind off Agnes. He wished he had waited to see her in the boat, safely on her way to the fort. But of course she was safe. There were soldiers in that boat, and the raiders would be heading north, not south. Still, he didn't like it. When this was over, Agnes could complain all she wanted, but he wasn't going to let her out of his sight.

When Mato held his hand up and crouched low, they stilled and listened. The faintest sound of voices filtered through the trees.

The sun was not yet above the tree tops, yet it was a reckless, foolish band who would linger over breakfast when they must know they would be pursued.

Mato whispered the bobwhite call of the quail to indicate how he would signal them, then eased into the brush to circle around and flank the raiders. Laroux moved in the other direction. Valery and Jean Paul waited, giving the others time to get in position.

Valery fought the sickness in his stomach. It wasn't fear. He had learned this about himself after his first battles. It was dread. What did it do to a man's soul to kill another human being? He had already killed men in the years he protected the king against assassins and conspirators. Though the priest promised he was forgiven because he had sinned in service to God's anointed king, Valery was not certain the priest knew what God thought.

*Bob bob white* traveled through the trees. Jean Paul sprinted ahead of him, Valery close behind, both of them unsheathing their blades and letting out a battle shriek meant to confuse the enemies' senses.

A raider drew his arm back to throw his knife, but Valery skewered him before the Indian let it fly.

In a blur, Valery saw Laroux leap from the forest, his sword singing in an arc as a renegade dodged and slashed with his own blade. Another raider twisted and fell with Mato's arrow buried in his chest. Jean Paul stood over a man on the ground.

And it was over. Valery blinked. Had it been even half a minute? He looked around. Laroux lay on the ground, blood pumping from a wound in his chest, an Indian fallen across his body. And lying on her side, there was the woman, Rachel Granger. Jean Paul knelt over Laroux. Valery strode to Rachel and cut through her bindings. "All is well, *ma chère*," he murmured. "Take my hand, that's right." She was bruised, she no doubt had been raped, but she was alert and not otherwise injured.

Valery wrapped his arm around Rachel's waist to hold her steady and thoughtlessly turned the two of them toward the scene of carnage. Four Indians lay dead, their young bodies splayed on the ground, their blood scenting the air. They were young and too thin. One of them had sores around his mouth. Their lives had not been easy, or healthful. So helpless, they seemed, like sleeping children.

A fly, the first of many to come, lit on the pool of blood spreading from the nearest body. Valery swallowed down nausea and raised his eyes to the tree tops. He did not like the sight of blood.

This was a secret Valery had managed to keep all the years he was a musketeer. If his fellow soldiers had known, he would have suffered from a thousand pranks designed to trigger his neurotic fear. He swallowed down the bile and spoke some nonsense to distract Rachel, and himself.

"We've got to get Laroux some help," Jean Paul called. "I can't get the blood to stop flowing."

Mato nudged Jean Paul aside and pressed on the deep wound in Laroux's upper chest.

Laroux cried out in pain.

"You're pressing too hard," Jean Paul said.

"I am not pressing too hard," Mato answered him.

Mato was right, for the bleeding slowed enough that Laroux could be moved.

"Let's get him back, find a needle and thread."

"What about the bodies?" Valery said. Surely they would not leave them here for the ants and the animals. They were bad men, but they were men.

"I'll bring the soldiers back here to bury them," Jean Paul said. "Let's get Laroux to a bed."

Mato and Jean Paul half carried Laroux while Valery helped Rachel follow the path back to the burned cabin. When they arrived, none of the other soldier groups had returned and the home site was quiet.

Rachel Granger lurched out from under Valery's arm and stumbled to her husband's grave. Sobbing, she pressed her fingers into the soil.

"A hard place for a woman to live alone," Jean Paul said.

"They will send her back, if that's what she wants," Valery answered.

Laroux fainted and fell to the ground, his face clammy white. His shoulder began to bleed again and Mato pressed the heel of his hand into the wound till the flow was stanched.

"He lives alone?" Mato asked.

"He does," Jean Paul answered.

"My people know how to heal a wound like this," Mato said.

"You'll take him then?"

Mato nodded. "He fought bravely."

With Jean Paul's help, he lifted Laroux to carry him to the dugout. Mato pushed off down the bayou to take Laroux to the village where the women could care for him.

The sun had passed its ascent by the time the other groups returned. Ita, the Indian girl, was with them, dirty and bruised, but alive. Valery helped Rachel rise to take the girl into her arms. A more manly man would not have had tears in his eyes, Valery supposed, but he had to turn away until he had swallowed down his relief.

The renegades were either dead or on the run, Colonel Blaise reported. He expected what few had escaped would head west and hide themselves in the lakes and marshes.

Then it was done. Valery breathed in deeply and loosened his shoulders. All over. He squinted at the sun. Plenty of time for him to take the main path downstream to spend the night in his own bed and wait for Agnes to return tomorrow.

He shook hands with Colonel Blaise and Jean Paul, and headed for the woods to take the path homeward.

"Colonel!" A soldier's shout from the bayou stopped Valery. A boat pulled into the landing and a soldier shouted as he ran toward the colonel. Something about the women.

Valery walked back to see what the news was.

"They did a head count of the women at the fort," Jean Paul told him. "They have two fewer women than they expected."

"If Indians got them -- " Colonel Blaise was saying.

"Who's missing? Do they know?" someone said.

With a sudden certainty, Valery knew. His spine turned to ice. The air froze in his lungs. Agnes and Marie Claude had not got on the boat.

He sprinted for the forest and the path. Mindless, he hardly knew his boots pounded the ground, that his arms took the lashings of leaves and branches.

A vague image of Agnes arguing with him, of that time when she had disobeyed him -- going out into the dark -- and just yesterday, of her telling him she couldn't let anyone see Marie Claude. He'd trusted her, and she had disobeyed him, again.

Those Indians who escaped could be creeping up on the Joubert cabin even now.

He pushed harder, his chest bellowing great breaths of heavy air, his heart pumping ice through his veins.

He didn't let himself think, he just ran, minute after minute of desperate running.

Nearly there. Nearly there. And then shouts.

Heart thundering, he rushed into the clearing. From the corner of his eye, Valery vaguely understood that Thomas stood over a bloody Indian as the other slaves felled two more with machetes.

Wild with fear, Valery sprinted for the cabin and burst through the door.

A pistol flared and roared. The whiz of a ball passed his ear.

Agnes's mouth gaped as she dropped the pistol.

Valery fell to his knees, Agnes's scream echoing in his ears.

Her frantic hands were all over him, looking for a wound.

Valery began to laugh. He rolled to his side and couldn't stop the deep-belly guffaws. Lord, Lord. He bent double, lost in great gulping laughter.

Agnes grabbed him by the shoulders and shook him. "What is the matter with you?" She was furious, and that was funny too.

Agnes, his little Agnes, threw herself on top of him, grabbed his head, and kissed him so hard his teeth cut into his lip.

# Chapter Thirty

*Laroux*
*Brown-Eyed Angel*

Laroux felt like a rag doll as Mato and Dupre laid him down in the Indian's dugout. His wound hurt hardly at all. He'd always heard that was a sure sign of a very bad injury.

He seemed to be far above the scene, watching Mato paddle the two of them downstream. Blood loss, he supposed. That was his last thought.

He wakened when Mato heaved him out of the dugout. Two more men appeared to help carry him into the village.

"The bleeding has started again."

"We're almost there."

Time jumped from moment to moment with blessed blackness in between. The next he knew, someone was cutting his shirt away.

"*Sainte Vierge*," someone muttered.

"What is his name?"

"Laurent Laroux."

An angel's face hovered above his. Not like any of the golden-haired angels in the chapel at home. This angel had eyes as brown as fine tobacco, hair black as coal. She smelled of smoke and honeysuckle.

No rosy cheeks, just smooth brown skin. "His eyes are open, but I don't think he sees," she murmured to a shadow behind her.

"Better clean the wound, Fleur, while he's barely conscious."

"Ahh!" He thought that was himself who cried out. Strange how he couldn't tell for sure.

Next time he woke it was night and he was in a hut. A dying fire lit a young Indian woman sleeping nearby with her baby. The same woman he had seen at the fort, the one whose beauty had struck him to his very core. He stared at her, the thick dark hair fallen over one shoulder, eyelashes sooty against her smooth cheek. He raised his hand to touch her face, but of course he had no business touching her. He dropped his hand.

Why would the Biloxi have put him in the hut of a young woman? Her husband could not like it. Unless Laroux was dying. No man would be jealous of a dying man.

He fingered the bandage on his chest. Three inches above his heart, this wound. Perhaps he was not dying, then. He was out of practice to have let an untrained boy get past his defenses. He was lucky to be alive.

In the morning, Mato came to tell him who had lived and who had died the day of the ambush. "Twelve renegades dead, two captured."

"And the girl, Ita? And Madame Granger?"

"They suffered what women suffer when bad men take them. They will be changed or they will not. They are alive."

Laroux thought about what it must mean to a woman to have been used as the renegades had doubtless used Rachel and Ita. He shook his head. He couldn't imagine it. All he could do was care.

"My sister says you are a good patient."

"She is your sister? Where is her husband?"

Mato stared at him. Laroux understood he should not have asked. He was here only because of these people's kindness, not so he could steal away some man's woman.

"Her husband is dead," Mato finally said and left Laroux to watch the day slide by.

When Laroux woke again, he was alone in the hut. Sunlight streamed in the open doorway. Somewhere children screamed in laughter. Women's voices hummed nearby. The hut smelled of smoke though the fire had died out.

Tentatively, Laroux drew in a deep breath. The knife had missed his lung. Missed his heart. The low feeling he had suffered for months – gone. Near-death did wonders for a man's spirits.

He tried to rise and fell back. He raised his arm to wipe his face and felt as if he lifted a keg of nails. He wouldn't be walking out of here on his own today. Where was Dupre?

In the late afternoon, he woke to the pain of a thousand bees stinging him all at once. The woman had peeled the bandage off to examine his wound. He clenched his jaw and managed not to scream like a little girl, keeping his eyes on the angel.

"What is your name?" he asked her.

Her attention was on his chest, gliding her fingertips all around it. "In your language, I am called Fleur."

"Flower. A beautiful flower. "

She spared him a glance with no expression whatsoever. Angels didn't like flattery?

She daubed a paste on the wound and rewrapped it.

"Water?" he asked.

She propped him up and held a gourd to his lips. He drank, half of it dribbling down his neck onto his bare chest. His head rested on her breast. He wanted to stay there, to feel her softness and smell her scent.

By nightfall, fever had him in its grip. He heard groaning in the hut and wondered who it was. The water gourd was pressed to his lips again and again. The small fire of the night before now blazed like an inferno, like a bit of hell had risen to occupy the little hut. He held a hand out to stop the heat engulfing him. It seemed to work, he thought as he fell back into blackness.

~~~

Fleur dipped a cloth into a gourd of water and cooled the Frenchman, wiping his face, his chest, his arms. He was not a brawny man as her husband had been. His limbs were slender and his body lean, his wrists small enough that a man of her tribe could wrap his fingers all the way around them. He was a pretty man, but not a weak man. His arms were cut with muscle, his belly flat and taut. Too flat, too thin. He did not eat enough.

His fever would likely kill him this night, though she would do what she could to keep him alive. With the wet cloth she cooled his face. His thick dark eyebrows had no arch to them at all but stretched in straight lines over his eyes. His face had been shaved, but a heavy growth of beard had begun in the days he'd been here. She ran her fingers across the rough whiskers. The first time she had seen a beard on a Frenchman, she had been amazed, and a little revolted, but she thought this man's beard might be very fine to look at, to touch.

She dampened his hair and pushed it off his face. Fleur had never touched hair like this, thick and dark, but fine, too, and curling around her fingers.

The Frenchman was restless in his fevered sleep, muttering, murmuring, and thrashing. She drew the cooling cloth down his arm, soft black hair growing on his forearm and on the back of his hand. If he were not a man who worked hard, this hand would almost look like a woman's with long delicate fingers.

She wiped the column of his browned throat and onto the whiter skin of his chest. Hair grew here, too, over his breast, and then in a dark line down his belly. Gently she stroked the cloth over his chest and followed that dark invitation below his navel and toward his manhood. As she wiped the skin above the waistline of his pants, he swelled beneath the fabric.

How she missed the weight of her husband on top of her when he loved her. She missed the feel of him entering her body, moving in her, with her, over her.

The Frenchman would be cooler if she opened his trousers. Lightly, she traced the shape of him through the trousers, imagined the weight and thickness of his erection. He stirred, and she flinched. What she did was not respectful. It was not proper.

She moved her wet cloth back to his chest, then lifted the hair and bathed the back of his neck. When his erection subsided, she would get Mato to remove his trousers.

~~~

"Is he better this morning?" This time the angel was blonde.

"No. No better." Two angels then.

The fire died down. Shivers wracked his body so hard he heard his teeth clicking together. Someone lay behind him and arms encircled him.

Again the fire roasted him. Dreams and visions occupied his mind. People from his home village outside Paris. Maman. Yves. King Louis. A girl with blonde curls. "Adelaide?" someone whispered. The ship rocked. They were in a storm, tossed about on towering waves. Nausea rose and he retched.

Wet cloths wiped his body. Blessed relief.

Laroux woke to pressure on his chest, to fingers patting his cheek. A baby sat on top of him, staring into his eyes and fingering his nose.

"Mahkee, no." The child's mother lifted him off and put him in her lap. Her cool hand felt of Laroux's forehead. When she smiled at him, he thought for a moment she really was an angel.

"You are going to live, monsieur."

"Am I?"

"You are perhaps a very stubborn man."

"And I was blessed with you for a nurse."

She laughed. Fleur. That was her name.

"Thank you, Fleur."

"Catherine comes to help, too. You will have some broth," she told him and took the baby away with her.

At dusk, he lay in the hut, exhausted. The baby crawled over him and tried to touch his eyes.

"It is because they are blue," Fleur said.

Laroux took the baby's fingers and pretended to bite them. The child pulled away, giggling, then shoved his fingers back in Laroux's mouth.

"Enough, Mahkee." Fleur pulled her boy into her lap, shucked off her tunic, and gave the baby her breast.

Laroux could not take another breath. His entire body stiffened. She was beautiful, her skin golden in the fire light, a heathen Madonna and child. She rocked gently and crooned, Mahkee's little hand reaching up to touch her cheek.

Laroux turned to the wall to hide his arousal. Tomorrow, he must return to his own home. He couldn't stay here another night.

# Chapter Thirty-One

*Val and Agnes
Regrets and Solace*

Valery sat on the stoop letting the early morning sun bathe his face. When had he not risen eagerly and begun his work with a lively step? He still felt slow and dull.

He had been terrified those moments running for Agnes. It had taken the sap out of him, but a man recovers from fear once it is past. What knocked him down and kept him down was that he had killed a man, and he had wanted never to kill anyone ever again. He supposed the renegade -- thief, kidnapper, rapist -- needed killing, but he wished it had not been he who'd had to do it.

Agnes too had been very quiet since the day of the killings. When he'd quit laughing like an idiot, had saved himself from the humiliation of crying like a baby instead, Agnes had followed him outside where the three dead Indians lay. A machete does terrible damage to a body, and Agnes had seen before he turned her back into the house.

She was not used to such violence, but in her subdued mood, she had not neglected him. If anything, she had been hovering and fussing over him. She was worried about him, he supposed. She was a good woman. Too good for him.

Valery looked at her flitting around the chicken coop, talking to her hens. What god had taken pity on him and sent Agnes to him? Look at her, a perfect little Venus now she had filled out. Her step was light, her face made for smiling. She amused him. She enchanted him, this woman who saw fairies in balls of swamp gas.

He had not expected to love or be loved out here in the wilderness. Attraction, a mild affection – that's all he'd hoped for. But Agnes had become essential to him. Maybe someday she would love him, too.

He breathed deeply, letting the sun soothe his soul. He supposed he should get to work. This farm would not create itself. He heaved himself to his feet.

"Look, Valery," Agnes said. She showed him her basket filled to the top with eggs. "It's time to take some to the fort on market day. What shall we buy with our coins?"

"Hmm. A bottle of wine?" When Agnes shook her head, he said, "No?"

He chucked her under the chin. "Typical woman. You ask, but you have already decided. Why do women do that?"

"It is common knowledge that a wife must consult her husband in all things. This will keep him happy and secure in the knowledge that he is the superior being."

"But I *am* the superior being, am I not?"

"Oh, indeed. I am merely acknowledging that fact."

"As long as we both understand, then, what are we going to spend your egg money on?"

She stepped into him and wrapped her arms loosely around his waist. "Nails. We need to build another pen. We will have fuzzy yellow chicks any day now. They need space to grow in, space where Monsieur Fox and Madame Coon cannot get to them."

Valery rested his head on her crown of dark braids. "You will build this new coop yourself?"

She nuzzled his shirt front. "The superior being always builds the chicken coops."

He surprised himself with a laugh. He hugged her close and she began to hum and sway.

"Dance with me, Valery."

Dance with her? His heart felt like a chunk of wood and she thought he could dance, here, in the dirt, not a violin or a horn within five hundred miles.

She didn't give up though. Humming still, she stepped away, took his hand, and held it high. As she stepped through the arc of their arms, he could only follow.

In the small steps of a minuet, they paced and turned, Agnes quite expertly providing a stately tune.

She was utterly charming, his bride. He whirled her into a rapid spin, grinning at her happy face.

They stopped in a close embrace, just standing in the sun, her face tucked against his chest, his chin resting on her head.

"You're a good man, Valery. I know you didn't want to kill that Indian, but you did what you had to. And Rachel, and Ita -- they're safe again." She drew her head back to look at him. "I am so very proud of you."

He pressed her face against him. His throat closed and his chest heaved once. Oh, God, he wasn't going to blubber, was he? He was a musketeer, for God's sake.

He got his breath under control and kissed the top of her head where the sun had warmed her brown hair.

"I do not deserve you, *mon chou*."

"Of course you do not, but you have me just the same."

# Chapter Thirty-Two

*Catherine and Jean Paul*
*No More Secrets*

Jean Paul checked the new otter skins he had salted. The pelts the renegade Indians took had been thicker furred. This pair of otters had already thinned their coats for the warmer weather, but they were plush enough to trade for a bolt of cloth. He really had been in a fog to have let Catherine wear that hideous blue dress so long.

A great heron flew overhead looking for a pond full of fish to hunt in. Only a few weeks ago, Jean Paul would have let that long streak of blue pass over without noticing, he'd been so tightly wound, guarding himself. The renegade Indians had been less threatening to him than his own fears. How had he let himself be such a fool? Now, the marauders were gone, the walls he'd built around himself were gone, and life was sweeter than he'd ever known it.

"Débile," he called to his hound. "Come." He pushed off in his dugout, eager to collect his wife and bring her home. Catherine had spent the day with her friend Marie Claude. The woman was making a slow recovery. Jean Paul had seen it in wounded soldiers back home. Too much blood loss took longer to get over than the wound itself. Catherine, however, said the worst of her injuries was a broken heart over losing the baby. She and Agnes took turns keeping her company.

Under the shade of an ancient oak, Jean Paul found his wife sitting with Marie Claude and Valery and Agnes Villiers. Débile frisked over to greet Catherine, stretching his neck for her to scratch under his chin.

"Imagine trying to chop through this fellow, eh?" Valery said, gesturing toward the enormous trunk of the oak.

Jean Paul folded himself to sit on the ground next to Catherine. He gauged the tree must be six feet in diameter. "Beyond me and my axe."

"We are talking about what to do instead of planting indigo," Catherine said.

Since Marie Claude had told them of Pierre dying from the fumes rising from the indigo vats, Jean Paul had thought of little else. He needed a cash crop if he and Catherine were ever going to do more than subsist on their little farm.

"Valery and I will raise chickens and eggs and sell them at the market," Agnes said.

"Yes, we will, *mon chou*, but that will not be enough, I think."

Agnes turned to her friends. "Valery makes the most charming little animals out of wood."

Valery chucked Agnes under the chin. "Men struggling to make a living have no need of my charming little animals."

"I've been thinking about growing tobacco," Jean Paul said.

Valery pursed his lips, thinking. "Do you know how to cure tobacco?"

"No. But Akecheta does."

"I didn't see any tobacco seeds at the store," Catherine said.

"We won't need them. Akecheta has a tobacco plot he cultivated from wild plants. I'll either look for wild tobacco myself or trade for some of his seeds."

"And we're going to have a pig, aren't we, Jean Paul?" Catherine said.

"A pair of pigs, male and female. It takes one of each if you want more pigs." He nudged her shoulder with his own and grinned at her blush.

"What about you, Marie Claude? Do you have plans?"

"Thomas wants to raise pigs, too. And I'm going to be a dressmaker. And pants maker, and shirt maker."

"When you're well enough, Marie Claude," Catherine added.

"It's time we got you back to bed," Agnes said.

Marie Claude didn't argue. She was pale and leaned heavily on Jean Paul as he helped her to her feet.

As if he'd been waiting and watching for this moment, Thomas appeared and took Marie Claude's arm to walk her back to the cabin himself.

At home again, Jean Paul got to work on the woodpile. He couldn't think of a man back home in France who hadn't smoked whenever he had the chance. The men here in Louisiana would too if they could get tobacco.

If he made money on tobacco, he could buy more dresses for Catherine, giving Marie Claude work, and Marie Claude could buy her pigs. Maybe the man with the pigs would buy his tobacco. And someone else could make a living carving pipes. And so the colony would grow.

At home he had been aware of none of these intricacies of community. It was exciting, in a mild sort of way, to be part of this experiment in building the colony. Self-reliance was essential, but depending on other people, and being depended on -- that's what civilization meant. Someday there might be a city here. It could happen.

He set his axe aside and watched Catherine cross the yard with a gourd of water. "I thought you'd be thirsty."

He'd drunk his fill not long ago. This particular gourd he did not need, but he accepted it.

"What's that smile on your face mean?" Catherine backed up a step. "I don't think I like that smile." She backed up another step.

Jean Paul tossed the water on her chest and grinned when she shrieked.

"You depraved, degenerate, ogre!"

"You think so?"

"Yes, I think so. Who would do such a thing!" She plucked at the wet bodice clinging to her chest. His wife knew very well who would do such a thing. He had done it once before, but this time he meant to follow through.

"A man who wants to see what his wife is hiding under that hideous blue dress."

"I'll have you know this dress was made by Madame Celestine herself!"

"Then we had best take it off so that it doesn't get ripped."

"Why would it get ripped?" He would remember forever the look on her face when she understood his intent.

"Oh, no! It's not even dark." She backed away. "Jean Paul."

He advanced, she retreated.

"Jean Paul, do not rip this dress!"

"Then you had better take it off yourself."

Catherine turned and sprinted for the cabin. He followed at a leisurely pace. Let the anticipation build, he thought. Once he'd got her in bed, minus the pitiful dress, he took his time, little kisses, little strokes. Her eyes were luminous and green in the forest-tinted light from the window. He loved her with his eyes gazing into hers, with his hands, with his mouth.

She moved under him, too new to passion to understand she could make it last. "Patience," he murmured as he tasted her mouth.

Slowly he allowed her need to grow, to swell, to overtake and toss them both into a rich, wondrous, overwhelming pleasure.

Both of them drowsy with satisfaction, he spooned her back against his chest and lay skin to skin with her. He wouldn't be able to lie here long with her bare bottom pressed into him before he'd need to show her again how much he loved her.

He stilled. Loved her? Of course he did. He simply had not had time to think about it, but what else did it mean when his every waking hour was spent thinking about how to take care of her, how to make sure she didn't miss her old life too much. He wished he could offer her more than a calico dress and a couple of pigs.

Before dark, they went down to the stream and caught crawfish and frogs. Now the weather was hot, they often cooked over a fire pit beyond the woodpile. The water in the big pot was aboil by the time they got back. Jean Paul dumped his crawfish in the water and set about dressing frog legs for Catherine.

Over supper, they chatted aimlessly. "Maybe someday we will have a cow?" Catherine said.

"I don't see why not. Someday."

"We'd have cream. And butter. Imagine it. Not that I do not appreciate boiled frog legs."

"You know anything about cows?"

"Um. I do not. But Marie Claude will."

As the night creatures wakened, hooting, whirring, chirruping, Jean Paul sharpened his axe. Catherine mended a tear in his shirt by the light of a candle. A heart-deep contentment came over him. He had never felt such a heart-whole peace, such a quiet, sustained joy.

Catherine hummed as she sewed.

"Pachelbel?" he asked.

"You know it?"

"It was a favorite at St. Cecelia."

"The church on Rue de Montfort?"

"That's the one."

"I've been there! My governess married in that very church."

He set his axe down and held her gaze. "Catherine. It's time you told me who you are."

She laid her mending on the table. "Yes. Very well. I am Catherine de Villeroy, granddaughter of le comte de Villeroy."

Jean Paul nodded. He was not surprised she was of the aristocracy.

"And how did you come to be on board the *New Hope*?"

"Oh, it's a sorry story, Jean Paul."

"No sorrier than mine."

She smiled at him. "That is very true."

She told him about Hugo's treachery, his greed, and his complete dominance over her aging grandfather.

"So your grandfather could not save you."

"I don't know what Hugo told him, but there was no rescue, no."

Jean Paul stared at the way the light played over her features. "Your grandfather's heart is broken, losing you."

Catherine closed her eyes. "I expect so, yes."

If he had the funds to pay her passage home, would he do it? He'd have to, wouldn't he? If that's what she wanted. But he had no money, not enough for that. "You're grandfather would like to know you're all right." He reached for her hand. "*Are* you all right, Catherine?"

Her smile was full of sweetness. "I am."

"Another ship is due any day. If you wanted to send a letter back."

Then, maybe, her grandfather would send for her. He kept himself from gripping her hand too hard. She didn't belong here. She'd been meant for a grand life of luxury and pleasure. But if she left him, God, he couldn't bear it.

"No message, Jean Paul. Grandfather has surely made his peace with whatever he believes happened to me. Leave him be."

He nodded, swallowing his relief. "You are safer if Hugo doesn't know you have survived your ordeal. I imagine he expected you to perish. Many do."

"My death would make Hugo very happy." She laughed with genuine amusement. "But I have never wanted to make Hugo happy."

"Then it's decided."

He played with her fingers, guilt and relief all tangled up in his breast. "So my wife is an aristocrat."

"And my husband is a dashing musketeer."

"Was."

"Yes. Was. And now I am a farmer's wife."

"Maybe you'll come up in the world to once again be a pig farmer's wife."

"How splendid. Now, if you are still in a mood for confidences, husband, I think it is time you read me a poem."

His eyebrows arched. "A poem?"

"You can't imagine I don't know what is in that book you keep."

He pursed his lips. "Have you read them?"

"No. Such restraint – I impress even myself."

"Then I will reward you." He thumbed through the pages, looking for what he wanted. He cleared his throat and read.

*Come live with me and be my love,*
*And we will all the pleasures prove*
*That valleys, groves, hills, and fields,*
*Woods or steepy mountain yields.*

Catherine laughed out loud and recited the next verse.

*And we will sit upon the rocks,*
*Seeing the shepherds feed their flocks,*
*By shallow rivers to whose falls*
*Melodious birds sing madrigals.*

Jean Paul grinned. "So you know this one."

"I believe my governess had a secret hankering to be Christopher Marlowe's sweetheart."

Jean Paul set his book aside and took Catherine into his lap. "You remember how it ends? *And if these delights thy mind may move, Then live with me and be my love.*"

She kissed his cheek. "These delights do move my mind, Jean Paul. I will live with you and be your love."

He tightened his hold on Catherine and nuzzled her neck. The poets should write about how contentment could lighten the soul and fill all the hollow places in a man.

"I thought you wrote your own poems in that book," she said.

"I mostly do. But one day I remembered this one."

"What day?"

"The day Suzette and the piglets bowled you over."

"That day? But you laughed at me."

"I hadn't laughed in a long time, Catherine. And there you were, mud in your pretty hair, on your pretty face. I felt like singing, not just laughing."

"Maybe you'll sing for me one day."

"Definitely not. But I will write you your very own poem."

"Not about my ruby lips and eyes like celestial light, please. I've had a few of those already."

"No ruby lips. No celestial lights."

"And no eyes like limpid pools."

"I shall have to think deeply, I see."

"I believe in you, Jean Paul. Let's go to bed."

Catherine blew out the candle. Jean Paul banked the fire. In bed, they lay in each other's arms. "We're going to have a good life together, Jean Paul."

"If I can make you happy, Catherine -- "

"You do."

"I want to take make you happy, to keep you safe. I promise -- "

She touched his mouth with her finger. "Don't promise. There are no guarantees in life, Jean Paul. We both know that. But I believe it. We will make a good life together. "

Jean Paul squeezed his eyes shut and held her tight.

# Chapter Thirty-Three

*Marie Claude*
*Debt*

Marie Claude lay on the bed resting. So she was a widow now. Poor sod, her husband. Not a soul to mourn his death. Idly, she wondered if he had an old mother back in France who would want to know what had happened to him. Well, if that were so, Marie Claude could do nothing about it. She didn't know where, or if, such a woman existed, and she could not write to send her a message anyway. So – Leopold Joubert had left this earth, and no one wished it otherwise.

Oh, but her beloved child. Gone, without ever being cradled in her arms, without ever hearing his mother sing to him. Her little one would be mourned as long as she lived. Marie Claude pressed the heels of her hands against her eyes. No use crying any more.

She should get up, do some work. Lying abed never solved anything. But she was so weak she could hardly swing her legs off the bed. She'd rest a bit longer.

Hours later, Marie Claude woke to the smell of chicken stewing and Thomas sitting nearby.

"Madame Joubert," he said, helping her rise. "Your friend Madame Villiers sent a chicken. She says you are to drink the broth, every drop of it."

"I don't have to be Madame Joubert anymore, Thomas. I am Marie Claude. That is enough name for me."

"Madame Marie Claude . . ." he began.

"No, not madame. Marie Claude. That's all."

Thomas took her arm. "You want to go to the privy, I will help you."

"Just to get down the steps onto solid ground. I can go the rest of the way by myself."

On the way back to the cabin, she heard Remy and Simon singing across the clearing. And inside the cabin, Thomas waited for her. Marie Claude had no husband, but she had these three friends. And a farm with plenty of water and sunshine. God had decided to be good to her.

In the afternoon, voices on the bayou announced visitors. They sounded as if they had stopped at her own landing.

She rose from the bed very carefully and shuffled her way across the floor so as not to jar her aching head. She leaned out and saw six, no eight, men poling a barge into shore.

That Monsieur Nolet, the vat salesman, was back. As he strode up to talk to her, she saw his eyes narrow. If he was noticing the yellowing bruises on her face, he didn't say so. "Madame, I have come to conclude my business with Monsieur Joubert."

What on earth had happened to the man? The end of his nose was a deep red wound, the scab flaking off. He'd lost the tip of his nose. How did a body lose the tip of his nose?

She raised her hand to shield her eyes from the sun light. "You are too late, monsieur. My husband is dead."

Nolet stood there as if he were stupid. Was it so hard to comprehend? People died every day.

Nolet looked over his shoulder where the men had hauled the first vat onto dry land. He turned back to Marie Claude.

"What are you doing with those vats?" she asked.

"This was sudden," he said, talking over her. "What happened to him?"

Marie Claude couldn't remember what they had decided to say. Her head throbbed and the light was too bright. Was it supposed to have been snake bite, or a fever?

Thomas had quietly come up behind Nolet. She looked at him, confused.

"My master likely got caught by a gator, monsieur. He went hunting in the swamp by himself."

"Damned fool, then. Regardless, we had a contract for these three vats." He checked to see the men were continuing to unload them. "I shall expect payment, madame."

She pressed her fingers against her forehead. "Take them away. You can't have a contract with a dead man."

"Oh indeed I can. My contract is now with his estate." He looked around the farmstead. "There is value in cleared land along the bayou. And I see you have this black fellow here. Slaves are as good as cash, Madame Joubert."

Marie Claude straightened. "No! Take your vats back with you. I don't want them." *Could* he take her friends from her? Her head pounded. She couldn't think.

"I have no wish to remove you from your home if you will only adhere to the contract." His tone was so very reasonable, as if he were pointing out to a child the most obvious explanation for why he should eat his turnips. "You will need these vats to process the quantities of indigo I require. You will make a profit as well, madam, I assure you."

Could the man not hear her? She fisted her hands. "No and no and no. I will not turn your indigo into dye. Take your vats and go, monsieur. You are not welcome here."

She could see his jaw tighten, but he couldn't hurt her any more than Joubert had. Let him be mad.

Nolet's men had the third vat unloaded now. She felt dizzy, standing up so long, but she would not sit down, not in front of this man. He would think that made it easier for him to bully her if she looked sick. But whether she was sick or not, he couldn't make her use those vats, or pay for them. If he wouldn't take them away, they could just sit there and rust.

Thomas stepped forward, but he kept his head respectfully bowed. "We three slaves, monsieur. We can help your men load the vats back on the barge."

"Madame Joubert," Nolet snapped, "if you allow your slaves to speak without being spoken to, I must advise you to take a firmer hand with them." Nolet straightened his hat and attempted what Marie Claude assumed was meant to be a kindly tone. "You are grieving for your husband, I have no doubt. I will return when you are in a better frame of mind to discuss the terms of our contract."

Marie Claude wished she were the one who had snipped off the tip of his nose. If she were not so weak, she would step out into the yard and shove the man, maybe even sock him in the gut. "There is no contract," she declared once again.

Nolet pretended not to hear her and left with his crew, the three vats still on her property. They would be in the way every time they wanted to take the dugout onto the bayou. Well, as soon as her head quit aching, she would cut a new landing.

~~~

Marie Claude went through Joubert's trunk and found a handful of écu and Louis d'or. Too little to interest Monsieur Nolet, but enough for a few necessities. Thomas and the others were in sad need of clothing.

Thomas stepped into the cabin with a bucket full of crawfish for supper. "Look," she said. "Joubert had a little money. Ours now."

"Yours," he said.

"Same thing. I wish it were more. I wish it were enough to buy your freedom."

"Buy ourselves from you, Marie Claude?" He smiled at her. "With your money?"

She flushed. "Now I feel like a stupid head."

"Not stupid, no, but you do not understand. We cannot travel to our home as free men in this black skin."

"You can't go home, even if you're free?"

He shook his head. "We would be taken up again on the way or as soon as we got there. A free black man in Martinique? It will not happen."

Marie Claude stared at the few coins she had, useless even if they had made up a fortune. "I guess I own you, like it or not. Is that what you're saying?"

"Yes, madame."

She put her hands on her hips. "I say you are to call me Marie Claude. And I say you are not my slaves. I don't want any slaves. What I want are men to help work this farm, to make it the best farm on the bayou." She looked directly in to his black eyes, almost afraid to tell him what she really wanted. "I want to make it a home for all of us."

Thomas's Adam's apple bobbed in his throat. He stared at her with his deep dark eyes, and Marie Claude couldn't tell what he was thinking. Did he think she was a fool?

"Marie Claude, we will make this farm for you."

She shook her head. "No. I want you to make it *with* me."

He licked his full lips. "Remy, Simon and I will gladly make a farm with you."

# Chapter Thirty-Four

*Marie Claude*
*And Still no Peace*

Every time Mare Claude looked at those big vats on her landing, she wanted to kick them. Monsieur Nolet would be back any day wanting money. She was almost certain her husband had not entered into a contract with this man, not even orally. She had watched the two of them. There had been no handshake, no smile when they parted company. Nolet was bluffing. Wasn't he?

So much was a blur to her. Her head had still not cleared from the beating. Maybe she had misunderstood; maybe there really had been an agreement between Joubert and Nolet. And if there had been -- could Nolet take Thomas and Simon and Remy away from her?

With a sick feeling in her belly, Marie Claude realized Thomas and the others were more helpless than she was. Most people didn't even know slaves were people. If Nolet took them, he'd sell them to somebody who would use them to make indigo, and that would kill them.

It was up to her, ignorant as she was, to protect them.

She put a pot of beans on to boil and added fat back and an onion the last hour. When the corn pone was brown and crispy, she called the men in to supper.

Since she'd been well enough to cook, Marie Claude had insisted Thomas, Simon, and Remy eat with her in the cabin. No point in cooking two suppers when she could fix enough for all of them. At first, the men had been uncomfortable eating at the table with her, but they got used to it. They talked about the garden and made plans to clear more land, to build a second dugout, to use Monsieur Joubert's musket to hunt. They even joked and teased. Just like a family.

Thomas glanced at Simon and then looked at Marie Claude, all the fun gone out of his face. "Marie Claude. We will not eat in the cabin after tonight."

She blinked at him, and then she felt the heat rise up her neck. "Why not? I told you, I won't have slaves."

"It is improper, Marie Claude, and if someone were to stop by and see us all together like this, it would cause trouble for you."

She stiffened her spine. "I don't see how. And I don't care anyway."

"You are a woman alone. You will remarry. And Frenchmen will not approve of our . . . friendship."

Marie Claude shoved back from the table. "What makes you think I would ever want another husband after Leopold Joubert?" She stomped out of the cabin, hurt and angry and frustrated. How could they think she would ever marry again? Or that she would need to? She could work this farm as well as any man, even if she didn't have three friends to help her.

Thomas found her down at the bayou staring at the water. He stood next to her, his posture mirroring hers with his arms across his chest. He let out a deep breath. "We do not mean to make you unhappy, Marie Claude."

She wouldn't look at him. "You act like you don't care if Nolet takes you away from here."

"We care."

"But you don't want to -- " She swallowed hard. "But you don't want to be friends."

"We are your friends, always, Marie Claude. Do not doubt this."

"Then why -- "

Thomas held his hand up. "You know why. You are a white woman. We are your slaves. There can be no appearance of more than that. You cannot risk it. Not in a colony full of white men looking for white wives, especially wives with property."

"I told you. I don't want a husband."

"You might change your mind. Not all men beat their wives."

"I don't need a husband."

Thomas looked her right in the face. "You are a woman who should have children, Marie Claude. You cannot tell me you don't want to be a mother."

When he'd left her alone, she sank to her knees right there on the bank of the bayou. She closed her eyes, reminding herself that only a few days ago, she had declared herself blessed by God. She still had the farm. She still had three friends to help work it. Nevertheless, blue loneliness filled her chest.

~~~

Marie Claude tied one of the Louis d'or in a strip of cloth and pinned it inside her bodice. This one coin would be more than enough to buy cloth for all of them and have plenty left over.

She took Simon with her to paddle the boat and to give him a little variety in his days. Simon had become moody and discontent since Pierre died. Sometimes he stood at the edge of the bayou and simply stared into the slow moving water, like she did when she was upset. She didn't know who he might have left behind when he came here, but he clearly wished he were somewhere else. Now she understood though that even if he were free, Simon would never make it home without white men enslaving him all over again. Maybe a day away from the farmstead would cheer him.

He wandered off to explore the area around the fort, as lonesome a figure as she had ever seen. He missed Pierre. They all did. And she supposed Simon needed a woman. She shook her head. She couldn't help him with that. Women were scarce in these parts and she didn't know if there was a black woman in the whole colony.

Her first task was to report Joubert's death. It wouldn't do for it to seem she was hiding it.

With the help of a young soldier, she found the right office and knocked on the door. A harried looking man with ink on his fingers invited her in.

"Yes?" he said. An abrupt young fellow.

"I want to report my husband's death."

"Oh. Yes. That is important." He gestured toward the second chair in the room and resumed his seat behind the desk. With a fresh sheet of paper squared off in front of him and his quill held at the ready, he said, "Now, madame. Your name."

Marie Claude wiped her sweaty palms on her skirt and made a quick prayer to Mother Mary to forgive her for the lies she was about to tell. She took the clerk through all the particulars.

"Alligator, eh? The whole colony is invested with the loathsome things. Snakes even worse. I can't wait to get home where there is only one snake for every thousand trees in a wood."

"There are a lot of snakes, yes. I have noticed," Marie Claude said. "But there are a lot of very pretty birds, too, and red and yellow flowers growing in the trees."

"If you say so. And you can prove you are Madame Joubert?"

"My name is in the church record, monsieur. I came aboard the *New Hope*."

The clerk gave her a speculative look. She knew what he was thinking. A prostitute before she got here, and with no husband, that's what she would be again. And, that look said, he might have the use of her soon.

No, he would not. She had her own farm and three friends to help her work it.

"Is that all?" she said and stood up.

"For now, madame."

The door opened behind her and Colonel Blaise stepped in. She had seen him only from a distance but recognized his authoritative air. She stared at his unusual eyes, pale blue with a dark ring around the iris.

Colonel Blaise nodded to her politely.

"Sir, this woman has come to report the death of her husband."

"I'm sorry to hear of your loss, madame. Who was your husband?"

"Leopold Joubert."

The colonel nodded to show he knew Joubert. "How did he die?"

It had been hard enough to lie to the young clerk, but this man looked at her like he could see every thought in her head. Could he see she had murdered her husband? Was there a black shadow hovering over her head? She hid her nervous hands and told him the story again.

"A terrible death. I am sorry you are grieved, madame. And no body to bury?" He eyed the faint hint of yellow bruising on her face.

"It would be a comfort to have buried him on the farm." Her voice sounded high and false in her own ears, but she swallowed hard and carried on. "I could have visited his grave whenever I missed him." Oh, an excellent lie. The devil would be proud of her.

"If you find, Madame Joubert, that you are in difficulty, you will let me know. I will not have a widow in distress in my province."

She stared at him. Would a man in his position, the most powerful man in many miles, in fact, really concern himself with her welfare? Did he realize she had been a whore?

The colonel's gaze remained respectful. "Perhaps it would be wise if I sent Lieutenant Gage to inventory the property and possessions your husband left you. They are, of course, yours now, but as a woman alone, you may prefer to return the property to the crown and find another life. There are provisions for women such as yourself to be returned to France. Or perhaps you would look for another man to wed."

He didn't seem to be able to help himself. He scanned her big body from crown to toe and then lingered on her plain face, evaluating her likely future. Marie Claude thought the colonel deemed remarriage an unlikely eventuality. She agreed with him.

"I will not be in distress, Colonel. I have three slaves on the property. We work well together." She had nearly described them as friends instead of slaves, but she assumed the colonel would disdain that possibility.

His hands behind his back, Colonel Blaise nodded. "You should do well enough if you grow indigo like everyone else."

"No, Colonel. I will not grow indigo." She eyed him for a moment. It would cost her nothing to try him. "Do you know this Monsieur Nolet?"

"I know he intends to broker the indigo made in the colony."

"He delivered three very large vats to my property after my husband's death and claimed he had a contract with Joubert and I must pay him for them. There is no money to pay, Colonel, but also there is no such contract."

"You are sure there is no contract, Madame Joubert? A man does not tell his wife his business dealings."

The devil would snicker at how easily she took to lying. "They had had a falling out, the two of them, and my husband cursed this man Nolet and swore he would never do business with him. I believe he is a shyster trying to take advantage of a helpless widow."

The colonel's mouth drew up on one side. "I don't see a helpless woman, madame. I will make enquiries for you, but if Monsieur Nolet shows me a signed contract, I will have to honor it."

Marie Claude left the colonel anxious and angry. What was to prevent Nolet from making a false contract? Forgery, they called it. Who would know what Joubert's signature really looked like? She was a woman, and Nolet was a man. How could she expect to win if he presented a paper with signatures? Even if she didn't have money, she had three slaves.

Calm down, she told herself. Nothing bad had happened yet. Colonel Blaise was not a stupid man. He would know if Nolet lied.

The colonel didn't seem to know she herself had lied, however. She'd never felt so anxious in her life, not even when she was waiting for Joubert to come and discover she had destroyed his precious vats.

What could she do but pretend everything was well? She took Simon into the general store with her. The place smelled of wax and turpentine and very old apples. She looked for the apples, suddenly hungry for them, bruised or not. She could stew them with a little honey and it would be like tasting home.

She added the least shrunken ones to her basket and picked up a bag of salt.

From the bolts of cloth piled on a plank table, Simon chose an unbleached calico printed with red flowers to be made into shirts and unbleached canvas for pants. Marie Claude chose a plain white cotton to make a nightgown for herself. Even though she was alone in the cabin now, it embarrassed her that her gown hardly covered her knees. Once the merchant totaled her costs, she paid him from Joubert's coin.

Monsieur Nolet came into the store, saw her overflowing basket, and scowled. He took off his hat and did the pretty manners, but his eyes were narrowed on her.

Simon came to stand at her elbow. That was kind, but Marie Claude didn't want Simon drawing attention to himself. Nolet was a bully, and if he saw a way to use Simon against her, he would.

"Madame Joubert," Nolet said. "You are not impoverished after all, I see."

The end of his nose was still raw. He would have a nasty scar right in the middle of his face. Marie Claude felt mean enough to be glad of it. "I'm poverished enough to buy cloth and apples. What made you think I wasn't?"

"Oh, I think you know. You have convinced Colonel Blaise there is no contract, but I have presented to him a perfectly legitimate, signed agreement between your husband and myself. Your dear colonel then suggested you be allowed to renege."

She looked him right in the eye. "I don't know what *renege* means, but there was no contract. And you will remove your vats from my property."

"Your property," he said. "What did you do to make that property yours, madame, but lie on your back?"

Marie Claude ignored the insult and held his gaze. Monsieur Nolet stared at her with as hateful a glare as she had ever seen, as if he were worse than Joubert. She doubted it.

"The fact is, monsieur, even if there were a contract, I cannot pay for the vats. Therefore, you will want to reclaim them. Before the month is out," she said as she passed him, "so that I do not have to speak to the colonel again."

Marie Claude's knees knocked as she walked out of the store and down to the dugout. This Nolet would not let her get away with this. He would persuade the colonel that it was his duty to enforce the law, to honor a legal, signed contract. And then he would take Thomas and Remy and Simon.

# Chapter Thirty-Five

*Catherine and Jean Paul*
*Skins for Cloth*

Catherine woke with her nose pressed into Jean Paul's bare back. With the merest touch of her tongue, she tasted his skin. A little salt. A little bayou d'eau, and all Jean Paul.

Catherine felt filled with -- not contentment, her life was too intense for such a pale word -- she was filled with joy. Wasn't the sky bluer these last days, the sun brighter?

Jean Paul's skin was quite brown, right down to his hips. If she shifted, the sheet would reveal where the untanned, sleek line of his flank began. She wouldn't waken him. She'd just rest her hand on his hip, right where the golden tan met the unexposed white skin.

A subtle change in his breathing alerted her he was awake. She eased her fingers over his hip, feathering touches across his belly.

When his hand caught hers, she giggled and he rolled over so he was half on top of her.

"You giggle, madame?"

She looked into his laughing eyes and bit her lip.

"A man might take offense at his wife giggling as she contemplates touching him just there. You were contemplating such a touch?"

She nodded her head, trying not to grin like an idiot.

"Perhaps this will be allowed, later." He kissed her neck and jaw, taking his time. Catherine didn't want any more time. She caught his mouth with her own and ran her hand across his ribs.

"So impatient, Madame Dupre?"

"I am," she said and pushed her hips against his.

"You wouldn't rather wait till after breakfast? Or maybe wait until tonight? Or next week?"

She goosed him and he laughed. With hot kisses and tender hands, Jean Paul made love to her. If Catherine had known just what she was missing those first months, she would have besieged him in this bed until he took her in his arms and loved her.

Such a marvel, she thought, this build up to heat and need, and then pleasure overcame thought. She grew frantic as he tortured her with tender kisses and slow hands. She pushed at him with her hips.

"It's not a race, my love."

She knew how to make it one. She gently scraped her fingernails down his belly to take his hard length in her hand -- and shattered Jean Paul's infuriating control. This is what she wanted -- the fevered plunges and surges of sensation, the soaring intensity, the searing heat -- until she flew apart and her lover carried her with him into glorious bliss.

When they lay quietly together in each other's arms, Catherine linked her fingers through his and brought the back of his hand to her mouth.

"I suppose I would get bored lying in this bed all day."

"I believe I could keep you entertained."

"Stories?" she grinned, as if that was what her naked husband had in mind. "That's the kind of entertainment you mean? By all means, tell me one."

"There once was a lazy girl -- "

She stopped his mouth with a big sloppy kiss and got up to start the day.

"Such a rude girl."

"Today's the day, is it not? Let's get dressed."

After breakfast, Catherine checked the silent bird's nest as she did every morning, waiting to see if her enterprising sparrows would lay another clutch of eggs. With a big smile, she called Jean Paul.

He tied the last cord around his bundle of cured skins and came to see.

"Look," she said. "Four little eggs."

"And this makes you happy?"

"Very. And you? Are you not pleased we'll have four more baby birds chirping morning and night?"

"Ecstatic. This time we should name them, don't you think?"

She would never have guessed her husband had this whimsical side. "After kings or queens? Or heroes? What about flowers? We could have a Rose, an Iris, a Peony -- "

"Some of those birds are going to be male. They would perish if they knew they were named after flowers."

And so they dickered while Catherine packed a lunch and they headed down the bayou.

By the time they arrived at Fort Louis, mass had already begun, and they slipped into the back of the rude chapel for the remainder of the service. Father Xavier ended by urging his flock to refrain from commerce on this holy day, but Catherine had heard this before and knew none of the settlers would heed him. They traveled too far on Sunday mornings to lose the chance to trade goods in the store or out on the grounds.

She chose not to feel guilty when Jean Paul took her to the store immediately after mass. He had caught those otters and cured the hides just for her. She couldn't be more pleased if he had presented her with a diamond bracelet.

Jean Paul unrolled his otter skins on the store counter and Peppard, the storekeeper, ran his fingers through the fur. Turning the skins over, he examined their suppleness and smoothness. "Well cured."

Peppard leaned down and retrieved the bolt of yellow cloth he had held back for Catherine. "Glad to trade you for the cloth. Or, let's see, I could give you a whetstone instead. Or twenty foot of good hemp rope. Three bags of salt?"

"Another time. Today, it's cloth."

Catherine squeezed her hands together and bit her lip, trying not to grin like a child at Christmas.

Jean Paul leaned in close and whispered in her ear. "You can thank me later." He waggled his eyebrows and she embarrassed herself with a girlish giggle. She, a married woman, giggling.

Peppard threw in a spool of thread and Catherine walked out of the store with her cloth of yellow flowers on a cream background. All that remained was for Marie Claude to cut out the pieces, for Catherine to sew the pieces together, and *voila*, a new dress.

Out on the grounds, Agnes waved a hand to call them over to picnic with them. Besides Agnes, Valery, and Marie Claude, Rachel and her stepson were settled under the oak.

The Granger boy looked thin. Rachel had dark circles under her eyes and she'd lost weight, too. Maybe Rachel had formed an attachment with her new husband just as she and Agnes had. Maybe grief kept her from eating and sleeping.

Catherine unloaded her misshapen basket of corn cakes, mulberries, and dried meat and passed Jean Paul a strip of jerky.

"You've brought your log map?" Catherine asked Agnes.

"Now it's finished, Selina and Annette are both going to copy it. But, listen, Rachel has news."

Rachel gripped her hands together in her lap. "I'm going back."

Catherine gaped at her. "You're going home?"

"The *New Hope* has returned. She's docked off Ship Island, gathering water and provisions. Henri and I will sail back to France on it."

No one said anything for a moment. It was a prodigious undertaking to cross the Atlantic once again. Spoiled food, seasickness, fever, rats -- Catherine didn't know if she could face two months of such misery again.

"My husband spoke to Colonel Blaise before he died. He said Henri's grandfather will take us in, and there's a little money. So we'll go to Bordeaux." Rachel wrapped her arm around her stepson and he leaned in to her. "We'll help Grand-père Granger milk his cows, won't we?"

Catherine reached over to squeeze Rachel's hand. "We'll miss you, you know."

"It'll be an easier life than here, a better life than Paris."

Valery sat with one knee up, his elbow draped over it. "I must know, Madame Granger. Have you ever milked a cow before?"

Rachel laughed at his gentle tease. "I have not, but Henri remembers how. He says he will teach me."

"From the Salpêtrière to the wilderness to a dairy farm in Bordeaux," Marie Claude said in her blunt way. "It will be nice to think of you with your cows. Cows can be good company, you know."

"Remember us when you have new calves," Agnes said. "I would like to think you have a Marie Claude, a Catherine, and an Agnes with you in your new home."

"Even if you must sleep in the barn?" Rachel laughed, and added, "I won't forget you, ever, even without naming cows after you."

Their picnic over, Jean Paul and Valery joined the men gathering to take part in the games set up for the afternoon. Catherine and her friends joined the other women from the bayou.

"The new girls are supposed to arrive today," Gabrielle told them. "Not from the Salpêtrière this time. From convents and orphanages."

"They'll still have to make a life in this godforsaken place," Antoinette said. "They'll get mosquito bit, sunburned, and overworked just like the rest of us."

"You having a hard time of it, Antoinette?" Agnes asked.

Antoinette looked embarrassed. "I guess it's better than the Salpêtrière. I complain too much, don't I?"

"You'll feel better when the weather cools off. In four or five months," Gabrielle said to make her laugh.

The women admired Catherine's calico and Gabrielle's straw hat. And here came Bridget. The group hushed as she approached them, her hand on one hip.

"What a self-satisfied little *salope*," someone muttered.

"Look. She's pregnant," Agnes whispered.

Marie Claude stood with her arms crossed. "Must have been pregnant when she left France to be that big."

"Must have."

"*Bonjour*," Bridget called out in an annoying sing-song.

"When is the baby due, Bridget?" Antoinette asked.

Bridget waved a vague hand in the air. "Later in the summer."

Then yes, Catherine thought, she was pregnant before she met her husband. Catherine looked carefully. There was a hint of an old, yellowed bruise under Bridget's eye.

"Your husband must be thrilled," Antoinette said.

"Of course. We'll have the first child born from the *New Hope*."

"First child, maybe," Selina said, "but not the only one."

As their friends congratulated Selina, Catherine caught Agnes's eye. Bridget probably didn't want a baby, but Marie Claude had wanted hers. Life didn't even pretend to be fair. She glanced at Marie Claude and saw no hint of feeling on her face, but she and Agnes had spent too many hours with her after the miscarriage not to know how she grieved.

"All those slaves your husband owns," Antoinette said to Bridget. "Any of them women?" Catherine was thinking the same thing. Hateful as she was, Bridget was going to need someone when her baby decided to be born.

Bridget's eyes darted to the side. "Oh, I'm sure I haven't noticed."

Even Bridget must have felt the unfriendly silence as the women eyed her velvet dress. Catherine knew from experience how hot velvet was in the summertime. No one's first choice for June.

"Well, lovely to have seen you all." Bridget waved her fingers at everyone. "Ta ta."

A couple of the women sniffed and turned their shoulders at Bridget's retreating form. Catherine didn't like her either, but there was something sad about her these days. Her superior act was looking rather brittle.

"You think her husband beats her?" she murmured to Marie Claude.

Marie Claude pursed her lips. "Who wouldn't?"

Catherine pulled her head back and let out a shocked laugh at Marie Claude's callousness.

Marie Claude shook her head. "I shouldn't have said that. It did look like an old bruise on her face, didn't it?"

Agnes leaned in. "I don't know what we can do about it, do you?"

"We can't do anything about it," Marie Claude said. "A wife is property, just like a slave is."

The three of them stood apart, letting the conversations go on around them.

"It was just luck, wasn't it, that decided which man we'd belong to," Agnes said. She turned a brilliant smile on her two friends. "You know what my husband said when I teased him about the new women coming to Fort Louis? He said, 'None of those women know how to fix my eggs.'"

Catherine smiled. As compliments went, it could be worse. At least it wasn't about ruby lips and limpid eyes. And it had made Agnes radiant.

Across the grounds, the men were setting up an arena for fencing, another for wrestling, another for target practice. Jean Paul stood with Valery and Laroux watching those who had the knack and the will to organize these things.

"Should you be standing up?" Valery asked Laroux. "You're still pale faced."

Laroux answered with a scowl. "I'm fine."

Jean Paul changed the subject. "You going to fence, Villiers?"

Valery raised an eyebrow. "Are we expecting a horde of enemies descending upon us?"

"Probably not."

"Well then, I will not flash my very handsome sword about and arouse the envy of other men."

"Very good of you. What about you, Laroux?" Jean Paul could have bit his tongue. Laroux, for all his pretense of being "fine," had no business wielding a sword this soon. Laroux, however, paid the question no mind. His attention was on the Biloxi Indians setting out their blankets under the pine trees. Or on one of the Biloxi.

"You should go say hello," Jean Paul said.

"Maybe take her something from the general store," Valery added.

"Like what?"

"Anything. A candle. A needle."

"Her brother won't mind?"

"Surely in any culture it is customary to show gratitude when someone has nursed you back to health."

Laroux wiped a hand over his mouth. He nodded to himself. And he marched across the grounds to say hello to Fleur.

"He forgot to get the needle. Or the candle."

"She won't care," Jean Paul said.

Jean Paul and Valery watched the first pair of fencers assume their positions, swords crossed.

"Do you miss the old life, being a musketeer?" Jean Paul asked him.

"I do not. And you?"

"I do not."

"Born to be farmers, are we?"

"It would seem so."

# Chapter Thirty-Six

*Marie Claude*
*Poison*

"*Puis-je avoir votre attention, s'il vous plaît?*" Monsieur Nolet called. "Gather round, gentlemen. It's indigo time!"

Nolet climbed onto the very same platform on which Marie Claude had stood with Catherine and Agnes the day of the choosings. She'd been afraid no one at all would take her, and then Leopold Joubert had called out, "I'll take the ugly one." Not Marie Claude's worst day, she considered. That day came later.

Nolet introduced himself as the king's appointed agent. "I am here to facilitate your efforts, everything from planting and tending the indigo, to harvesting, to delivery to the processing vats." It seemed nearly every man in the colony had planted indigo, and for the next half hour Marie Claude listened as Nolet answered their questions.

She stood in the back with the Dupres and the Villiers. Even from here she could see Nolet's bright red wound where he'd lost the tip of his nose.

Her friends had agreed they would not plant indigo, but for Marie Claude, who had lost her friend Pierre to *l'or bleu*, the discussion raised bitter gall.

She waited for Nolet to mention how making indigo dye sickened the men, but he clearly did not plan to reveal this to the planters. What if she told them herself? Nolet would be furious. She had not heard from him in this last week, and she had begun to hope he would find another buyer for his vats and would leave her alone. If she spoke out, however, he could wave that false contract under the colonel's nose and insist on payment. He could take the farm. He could take her friends.

Marie Claude pressed her fingers against her mouth, sick with fear. She couldn't bear it if Thomas and Remy and Simon were taken away from her.

Yet if the settlers planted more and more indigo, more and more slaves would sicken and die. She had to speak up, for Pierre, and for all the men who would be breathing in those poisonous fumes.

Her hands twitched in her skirts. Her heart pounded. Summoning all her strength, she made herself march to the front of the assembly and climb the three steps onto the platform.

"Remove yourself at once," Nolet said. "Get off of this platform."

Marie Claude's voice carried over Nolet's protests. "It's poison," she said.

Men put their heads together, murmuring.

"The fumes from making the plants into dye are poison."

Nolet tried to take her arm, to shove her toward the steps, but she shrugged him off.

"The vats require someone to stand over them and stir the mess for hours and hours. Whoever does that will sicken. His lungs will weaken. He will eventually die of it."

"Tommyrot," someone called out.

"Of course it's tommyrot," Nolet shouted. "This woman has a grudge against me. She'll say anything. Just ask Colonel Blaise." He gestured toward the colonel standing to the side, his arms crossed.

Marie Claude lifted her chin and stared at the colonel. He gave her the merest nod.

"I had four slaves breathing in the fumes from those vats. One of them died. The other three cough, all the time. Indigo kills people."

Nolet took hold of her with both hands and pushed her, toward the back edge of the platform. Out of the corner of her eye, she saw Colonel Blaise take a step forward, saw Catherine and Agnes's husbands rise from the ground where they sat. She didn't need their help. She grabbed one of Nolet's hands and bent it back at the wrist, further and further until he fell to his knees.

With a nudge of her foot, she toppled him over. Enraged, Nolet scrambled to his feet and took a swing at her. She grabbed his fist with her own and punched him in the jaw. He went down, stunned and still.

Marie Claude stepped over his unconscious body. "Making indigo kills people. I will not make indigo on my farm. Now you know what it does, you have to decide if you are the kind of person who would kill people just to make money."

She left the platform as the settlers buzzed among themselves. She was right to tell them. If they hadn't known before that making indigo raised poisonous fumes, they did now.

And now she would lose everything.

Marie Claude returned to her friends on wooden legs, feeling Nolet's vengeful gaze charring the flesh on her back.

Catherine and Agnes both reached for her and drew her into the shelter of a large oak tree.

"What a brave woman you are," Agnes said. "I am so proud of you."

Marie Claude's lips felt numb. "I may have lost . . . " She had to start over. "I may have lost my friends."

"Your friends?" Catherine said. "Of course you have not. We will be your friends no matter what, you must know that."

Marie Claude shook her head.

"I think she means Thomas and the other slaves," Agnes said. "You saw, when you were there. Those three men are devoted to her, and it was for their sakes that Marie Claude chopped up her husband's vats."

"But why should she lose them?"

Agnes nodded her head toward Colonel Blaise huddled in conversation with Monsieur Nolet. "Nolet says she must pay him for those indigo vats. If the colonel allows it, he will take the slaves in payment since Marie Claude doesn't have the cash."

"But that's outrageous."

"Tell that to the colonel."

"I certainly will." Catherine started for Colonel Blaise, but Agnes held her back.

"He's coming. Wait and see what he says."

Marie Claude gripped Agnes's small hand and took comfort from Catherine's grip on her arm. Maybe with her two friends beside her, she would not collapse when the colonel told her he had to let Nolet ruin her.

Colonel Blaise honored her with a bow. "Madame, you are a courageous woman."

Marie Claude's other friends, Valery and Jean Paul stood with her. She was as ready as she would ever be to face ruination.

"You have infuriated Monsieur Nolet, of course. He has a document, you understand, to back up his claim to your property."

Marie Claude's knees gave way and she would have fallen except that Valery grabbed her and held on. "Don't," Marie Claude breathed. "Don't let him take -- "

"No, of course not. A piece of paper may lie as readily as a man's mouth. Not every Frenchman has your scruples nor your care for your slaves. I believe a Monsieur Ouellette will buy Nolet's vats, and you will retain your properties."

A great gulping sob wrenched through Marie Claude's chest and Agnes's husband took her in his arms. When she got hold of herself, Valery patted her back and walked her toward the landing where Thomas waited for her.

All her strength was drained from her. Thomas helped her into the dugout, and Valery pushed the boat into the water. Of all the horrid moments of her life, these last minutes had been the most terrifying, but she had stood up for her black friends, and her French friends had stood for her.

"It's over, Thomas. You're safe, and you and me, Remy and Simon, we can be a family now."

# Chapter Thirty-Seven

*Catherine and Jean Paul*
*New Arrivals*

Catherine gathered up her picnic basket, her mind on Marie Claude. All the troubadours sang of bold knights and courageous *héros* while the women in their songs were merely beautiful and passive as they waited for their true loves to rescue them. Someone should write a song about Marie Claude, as brave a *héro* as the great Roland.

Jean Paul took the basket from her hand to carry back to the dugout when a commotion at the landing caught everyone's attention. Sailors pulled several rowboats ashore and then helped young women disembark.

"The new girls," Agnes said at her side. "New wives."

Every conversation stopped as everyone, men and women, gawked at the young women. Catherine remembered how exposed she had felt when she'd been stared at, but even so, she could hardly look away as the girls bunched up together, wary and fearful.

"They look better than we did when we got here," Catherine said.

"I heard they've been in a camp for two weeks, resting and eating and cleaning up," Selina said.

"Why didn't we get that?"

Selina gave Catherine a look. "These girls did not come from the Salpêtrière."

"I heard they're from convents and orphanages," Rachel said. "Huguenots, some of them."

They stared silently, wondering which of the girls were Protestant heretics.

"I'm surprised the king allowed them to come on the same ship with good Catholics," Gabrielle said.

"They're women, that's why." Catherine didn't imagine these men starved for women would much care what their religion was.

"Ladies, *Bienvenue*." Colonel Blaise's voice carried across the yard. "Your quarters are ready if you'll follow the sergeant."

"They'll have *quarters*? We had two nights in tents before we were sent off with strangers."

"Again, Gabrielle," Selina said, "these women did not come from the streets and prisons of Paris. They're *good* women."

The girls straggled in rough parade between the settlers on both sides of the path. Tall ones, short ones, blonde, red-headed, brunette. Some faces were closed, no expression to give away what they thought or felt. Other girls looked around with wide eyes, taking in all the strangeness of a hot, humid, flat terrain.

Two or three rough colonists made rude comments to their friends about this one's bosom or that one's face, but for the most part, the men were silent, their faces intent as they gazed at the young women parading past them.

Bringing up the tail end of the procession, two nuns walked arm in arm. One was a bit stooped, the other young and straight of back. So these young women had arrived under the protection of the Catholic Church.

"No auction for them?" Gabrielle said indignantly.

"It's going to be the opposite of the way we had it," Selina said. "They are to choose their own husbands from among the planters instead of being handed out like so many cows or goats."

"Don't be bitter, Selina. You do all right with the husband who picked you."

"Oh! They're calling me." Rachel looked panicked for a moment.

Catherine gathered Rachel in her arms and held on for a moment. "Be well, Rachel, you and your son."

Rachel hugged all these friends who had come over with her on the *New Hope*, one after the other, took her step-son's hand, and marched down to the landing where the sailors handed her into the boat.

Catherine and Agnes followed to wave her on her way.

"The *New Hope*," Agnes said. "A way home for Rachel. A ship of deliverance for me."

"I suppose it rescued me, too, and I didn't even know I needed rescuing."

"From luxury and ease?" Agnes said and poked her playfully.

"From boredom, from superficiality, from frivolity. You have no idea how tedious luxury can be."

"No need to fear such tedium here."

Catherine laughed. "No. I am saved."

~~~

Jean Paul's eyes were on his alluring wife as she approached in her old blue dress, her hips swaying, her lips smiling. When she drew close, he opened his arm and brought her to his side. He leant close and whispered, "Are you happy, Madame Dupre?"

There was that dazzling smile, the one that had so frightened him the first weeks they'd been together, that had threatened to pull down all the barriers he hid behind. Now her radiance filled him with joy. He gave her a quick kiss to make her blush.

Catherine raised her lips to Jean Paul's ear. "I feel sorry for all these new girls."

"Why is that?"

"I already married the prize."

Jean Paul felt his chest fill up. This beautiful woman, with the big smile and the sea-green eyes. His.

"You ready to go?"

"A splendid idea," she said. "I'd like to show you how grateful I am that you carried me off from that auction."

"I carried you off?"

"That's the way I remember it. And that's the way I'm going to tell it to our grandchildren."

"Maybe we do need to leave. This very interesting dispute may turn into a mad, thrilling argument, and we'll need to be someplace flat and horizontal to reconcile our differences."

"I know just the place. Let's go home, my love."

# ABOUT THE AUTHOR

Gretchen Craig's lush, sweeping tales deliver edgy, compelling characters who test the boundaries of integrity, strength, and love. Told with sensitivity, the novels realistically portray the raw suffering of people in times of great upheaval. Having lived in diverse climates and terrains, Gretchen infuses her novels with a strong sense of place. The best-selling *PLANTATION SERIES* brings to the reader the smell of Louisiana's bayous and of New Orleans' gumbo, but most of all, these novels show the full scope of human suffering and triumph. Visit Gretchen's Amazon Author Page at
www.amazon.com/author/gretchencraig

Made in the USA
Middletown, DE
27 July 2024